A LONDON SEASON

A LONDON SEASON

by

Anthea Bell

St. Martin's Press
New York

Library of Congress Cataloging in Publication Data

Bell, Anthea.
  A London season.

  I. Title.
PR6052.E432L6 1984   823'.914   83-21133
ISBN 0-312-49547-1

First published in Great Britain in 1983 by Souvenir Press Ltd

First U.S. Edition

10 9 8 7 6 5 4 3 2

1

"Well, what is it *this* time?" demanded Miss Grafton, putting her head in its Dunstable straw bonnet trimmed with cerulean blue out of the carriage window, the better to view her surroundings. These evidently did not find favour with her, appearing as they did to consist of limitless expanses of farm land, both arable and pasture, broken here and there by the meagre lines of recently planted enclosure hedges. The country road along which the post-chaise had been travelling looked as if it, too, might go on indefinitely. It was deeply rutted in places, its puddles faintly reflecting the light of the springtime sun which had just come through the clouds. The sun also shone down on tender green leaves breaking out of bud, on primroses and a drift of pale blue dog-violets by the roadside, and on a flock of sheep accompanied by their frisking lambs which Miss Grafton, in a happier frame of mind, would have declared to be sweetly pretty.

On this early spring afternoon of 1826, however, she was intent upon finding fault. "Why have we stopped here, in the middle of nowhere?" she inquired imperiously of her cousin and guardian, Sir Edmund Grafton, who had got down from his seat beside her and gone to the horses' heads, to confer with the postilion and his man, John Digby. The carriage in which Miss Grafton sat had been lent to Sir Edmund by his brother-in-law: no ramshackle, yellow-painted hired chaise, but a very handsome private conveyance, most comfortably sprung, with Lord Yoxford's coat of arms discreetly traced upon the doors. However, it too incurred her censure. "Of all the *slow, fusty* ways to travel! One might just as well go by the stage!" she

7

exclaimed, with the lofty ignorance of a young lady who had never in her life set foot in so plebeian a vehicle. "At this rate we shall never be in Cheltenham at all!"

An impartial observer might have said that Miss Grafton was in a fit of the sulks. But then, few observers remained impartial once they had set eyes on the charming oval of her face, with its flawless roses-and-cream complexion surrounded by tumbling, dusky curls. Her large blue eyes, just the colour of her bonnet strings, were now clouded with annoyance and her lower lip was thrust out, but such is the injustice of nature that, as her mentors at the Miss Maddens' Select Seminary for the Daughters of Gentlemen in Bath had frequently had occasion to remark, what in another girl would be wilful temper could appear, in Persephone Grafton, merely a pretty petulance.

Miss Mary Madden, the younger of the two proprietresses of the Seminary, had felt mingled emotions of relief and regret at the departure of her pupil, attired in the most elegant travelling costume to be procured in Bath at very short notice. It had been Miss Mary's task to see Persephone provided with a new gown and mantle when the sisters were informed, only a few days earlier, that Sir Edmund Grafton, having succeeded to his elderly relative's baronetcy and estates, was returning to England. His present intention, it appeared, was to settle permanently in his native land, after eleven years spent in various Continental embassies and legations on behalf of the Diplomtic Service, which he had joined as a young man directly after Waterloo. Moreover, Sir Edmund wrote, he would be arriving within the next few days to bear his ward off to his sister in London, and to her first Season.

Of course, said Miss Selina Madden to her sister, Lady Yoxford would see to the acquisition of a wardrobe suitable for a young lady making her début. Not that Sir Edmund said as much, but a gentleman could not be expected to put his mind to such things! Meanwhile, however, she would like to think that Persephone did them credit upon her arrival in the capital. There could be no question of Sir Edmund's querying the expense of the new garments when added to their discreetly presented account – all the fees so promptly paid over the years, such generous allowance made for Extras!

And so Miss Mary had betaken herself to Madame Louise's exclusive establishment in Milsom Street, escorting a strangely rebellious Persephone.

"But do you know, Selina, once we were there, she was really most biddable!" she confided wonderingly to her elder sister, as they took tea together in their private parlour on the day when Miss Grafton had left their care. She was to put up with her guardian at his Bath hotel for a night, before they set off early next morning to post back to London, with a detour to Cheltenham where Sir Edmund had business.

"You mean," said the more forthright Miss Madden, drily, "that she had at last passed from a towering rage into the sullens! And I only wish I knew the reason for either," she added, more to herself than her sister

"Well, I do believe that when Madame Louise showed her how prettily the blue challis for the mantle would hang, and how becomingly suitable was the sprigged muslin, though not at all *missish*, her spirits were a little raised," said Miss Mary hopefully.

"If so, they rapidly fell again, judging by this afternoon's scene!"

"I, for one, was very thankful to Madame Louise!" insisted Miss Mary. "For I own that I was in the greatest dread of Persephone's insisting on – on purple gauze and spangles!" she added, conjuring up the most horrifically unsuitable vision of which her inward eye could conceive. "And I am not perfectly sure, Selina, that I should have been able to overbear her."

Miss Madden, who knew very well that her sister, while held in affection by all the pupils, had not the remotest chance of ever being able to overbear anyone, regarded her with amused indulgence. "No, no, Mary: I told you that

9

you might be easy in your mind, don't you recollect? For one thing, if Madame Louise did not know what she was about in matters of fashion – *and* in her ability to deal with young girls' wayward fancies – she would be in no position to charge such prices as she does. For another, Peresphone herself may be trusted in *that* respect. Her taste in dress, at least, is impeccable!"

Even the kind-hearted Miss Mary could not miss the implications of what was left unsaid. "Oh, you are too hard on the child, sister!" she protested mildly. "She can be so taking in her manner when she chooses, though I will confess that this afternoon – well, *that* is all over and done with, and I am sure that by now she is perfectly reconciled to going to London, the dear girl! I am persuaded she will conduct herself just as she ought, and – and go on very well in Society, and most likely make a truly brilliant marriage!"

"With that fortune, it would be strange indeed if she did not," agreed Miss Madden.

"Impulsive she may be," Miss Mary persisted, "but with those excellent precepts which you have been at such pains to instil into her –"

"Few of which, I fear, have taken root," sighed Miss Madden. "Ah, well, I did my best, Mary. I did my best." She set down her teacup, visibly brightening as she let her mind dwell on the very handsome sum of money, well in excess of the fees outstanding, represented by the banker's draft which had been conveyed to her by Sir Edmund himself. He had transacted the business in the most tactfully considerate manner, thought Miss Madden, speaking words of appreciation which suggested that he considered herself and Mary in the light of friends who had done him a favour, rather than persons involved in any sordidly commercial bargain. "And Sir Edmund was good enough to say," she reminded her sister with satisfaction, "that he was sure she must regard us as *family*, from the circumstance of her being so often obliged to spend her holidays here."

"Oh yes!" said Miss Mary, eyes misting over. "*And* that

though it was certainly time for her to leave us and mingle with Society – which is very true, as I am sure you have said yourself a hundred times, sister – he felt it was her great fondness for us that accounted for – for her behaviour today!"

"Her *extraordinary* behaviour!" snapped Miss Madden.

Both sisters fell momentarily silent, recollecting the unedifying scene, similar to many they had endured over the last few days, since the arrival of Sir Edmund's letter. Once again, and in front of her guardian this time, Persephone had inexplicably stormed and raged and wept, sobbing that she *wouldn't* go to London, they couldn't *make* her, it wasn't kind or right or fair!

But somehow or other, Sir Edmund had contrived to stop her in full flow, pointing out in a few quiet words the distress she was causing to both ladies. Eventually, she had taken a tear-stained but calm and even affectionate farewell of them, reserving her smouldering glances of fury for her guardian himself.

"Well, it *is* very true that she should be out by now," pronounced Miss Madden. "Indeed, she ought to have been out for a full year. I may say, however, that Persephone has only herself to blame for that! Had it not been for that unfortunate business at Lord Yoxford's two years ago, when she was but sixteen, I dare say Lady Yoxford would have brought her out last spring."

"Yes, yes," Miss Mary hastened to agree. "You are very right!"

"You may well say so! As it was, one can hardly blame Lady Yoxford for declaring herself too frail in health to undertake the responsibility."

"It was not dear Persephone's fault, precisely!" Miss Mary ventured timidly to suggest. "The child could not help it if her young cousins' tutor developed a – a *tendre* for her."

"*Tendre*? He fell head over ears in love with her," said Miss Madden roundly, "and you need not try to tell me that she could not have nipped that in the bud! No girl of

11

principle should or would allow a young man to proceed to the very point of an elopement! It was only by the greatest good fortune that Lord Yoxford discovered what was afoot in time to prevent their actually setting out for the Border!" Miss Madden shuddered at the memory. "And all Persephone could say, when I endeavoured to bring her to a sense of the gravity of her conduct, was that she thought it would have been good fun! *Good fun!*" she repeated, in tones of retrospective incredulity.

"She *was* only sixteen, and I dare say, being so innocent, had little real idea of what the married state entails," suggested Miss Mary, whose own ideas on the subject were somewhat hazy.

"No idea whatsoever, I hope and trust! The fact remains that the Yoxford boys' tutor was neither the first nor the last person to become most improperly infatuated with Persephone!"

"Very true," said Miss Mary sadly, then, with an unexpected flash of shrewdness, "however, I don't know that *she* has been infatuated with any of *them*, has she, sister? I mean, to suppose something would be good fun is not precisely an infatuation – or so I believe! And while it was wrong of them to let her know of their sentiments, perhaps they could not help it. Of course," she continued, striving to look on the bright side, "she can pick and choose, what with that and her fortune!"

"What with *what* and her fortune?" inquired Miss Madden austerely.

"Oh, the – the decided partiality that the gentlemen feel for her!" said the flustered Miss Mary, lamely.

Her sister Selina permitted herself a ladylike snort. "Humph! You could not," she commented, allowing her mind to range with fastidious distaste over Persephone's various conquests, "have described the gardener's boy as a gentleman, and he, as I recollect, was the first. Well, *he* soon got his marching orders!" she remembered with satisfaction. "Next it was the young man in the lending library, was it not? And just as we thought the child had at last acquired a taste for improving literature! Then there was Henrietta Bury's papa's footman . . ."

"I do recall that he *was* a handsome young man," Miss Mary unwisely put in.

"Handsome!" Miss Madden's snort was less ladylike this time. "If *he* had no business even to look at her, *she* had still less to encourage him! And as for the fact that when Persephone spent Easter with Augusta Dereham's family, Augusta's brother chanced to be just down from Oxford – well, nothing could have been more unfortunate, though to be sure the Derehams very well knew how improper it was in him to be making up to the child before she was even out, and they soon put a stop to that! I forget now whether Mr Jones the music master was before or after young Dereham . . ."

She fell to musing, and Miss Mary seized her chance to put in a good word for her former pupil.

"You must own, Selina, that Persephone's performance on the pianoforte did improve quite remarkably when Mr Jones was taking such a great interest in her talent. What's more," she added, with the air of one faintly surprised to find herself in possession of an indubitable point, "even though you could not, of course, employ him to instruct our girls in music any longer – and Mr Ford, good man, must be forty-five years of age if he is a day, besides having all those children, so we are safe enough with *him* – where was I? Oh, yes – well, at any event, Persephone's music has *continued* to improve to a remarkable degree, and Mr Ford is full of praise of her gifts. You cannot deny that she is talented, Selina, indeed you cannot!"

"I don't," responded her sister, but in a gloomy tone, as though the circumstance afforded her little satisfaction.

Miss Mary seemed to read her sister's unspoken thoughts and to sympathize, for she too fell silent for a while, before rallying to Miss Grafton's defence again. "And there has not been anybody at all since poor young – I mean that

13

misguided young Mr Jones," she finished triumphantly. "Has there?"

"Apparently not," said Miss Madden thoughtfully, "and that, you know, has me in a puzzle!"

"It can only mean that Persephone is learning conduct, sister!"

"For why, when surely she has been afforded no opportunity for any indiscretion," continued Miss Madden, pursuing her own train of thought, "why should she have been so reluctant to leave Bath? One would have fancied her only too happy at the prospect of going to London for the Season. *Any* young lady would be, let alone one with her prospects!"

"I dare say she is afraid of the Yoxfords. I am sure Lady Yoxford must have given her a dreadful scold two years ago, after that unfortunate business."

"Persephone is afraid of very little," said Miss Madden, with a certain grudging respect, "and certainly not of Lady Yoxford! Whom, between you and me, Mary, I consider very poor-spirited not to have taken charge of her before this."

"Oh, but as you said yourself, Selina, her health precluded it!"

"Fiddlestick!" declared Selina, performing an abrupt volte-face on the subject of Lady Yoxford's health. Her private opinion of that good-natured but indolent lady was not high. "I fancy that even now, Lady Yoxford has undertaken to bring Persephone out only because Sir Edmund recalled her to a sense of her plain duty! However, he tells me that he intends to engage some suitable lady to act as chaperon and take part of the burden from his sister's shoulders. It is certainly true that Lady Yoxford is not in the way of taking a girl about during the Season, since all her family but the youngest child are boys. Well, if he can find a lady equal to the task –"

"Oh, and a music master," put in Miss Mary, "for she would not be at all happy without her music, dear child! I

14

do trust Sir Edmund will also engage a music master."

"Preferably of advanced years and unprepossessing appearance," said her sister drily. "Yes, well, I dare say nothing very dreadful may happen after all. On the other hand," she added, after a moment's sober reflection, "on the other hand, there is The Voice!"

Evidently even the partisan Miss Mary could not counter this mysterious but significant utterance, for she was able only to nod, saying faintly, "Dear me, yes, there is The Voice!"

And both ladies remained silent for a moment, shaking their heads. Then Miss Madden said, bracingly, "Well, my dear Mary, no one can say we have not done our duty! All that about Persephone's *regarding us as family*, you know, was mere flummery – though very prettily said upon Sir Edmund's part, I grant you! But I will confess to you, Mary, that I entertain a fondness for the child."

"I knew it!" cried Miss Mary, radiant.

"And I well know that she is a favourite with *you*," said Miss Madden indulgently. "Yes, all things considered, I am confident that with the precepts of the Seminary behind her, and in the good hands of Sir Edmund and the Yoxfords, Persephone will soon become less wild!"

2

Lady Yoxford could not have been said to share Miss
Madden's confidence. When her brother, calling on
her the day after his arrival in London from Berlin,
first broached the subject of Persephone, she was a good
deal put out. "It won't answer, Edmund!" she said, as
firmly as her spirit allowed – which was not so very firmly,
for hers was a pliant, easy-going nature. "*Indeed* it will not
answer!"

"But my dear Bella, there's nothing else for it! I'll make
sure the child is as little of a charge on you as possible. Good
God, my dear," added Sir Edmund, a little impatiently,
"surely I explained everything in my letter! Didn't you read
it?"

"Yes, I dare say," admitted Lady Yoxford, vaguely.
"Only I may not have perfectly understood . . . do you
really mean her to *reside* here?"

"Well, she can't stay with me, can she?" pointed out her
widower brother. "Uncle John's old tenants wish to
continue leasing the Grafton town house, and I'm more than
happy for them to remain there. *I* don't want to be saddled
with its upkeep, as well as that barracks of a place in
Westmorland. I'd prefer to let that too, or even try if the
entail can't be broken and sell it," he added thoughtfully.
"Well, that's all for future consideration. Myself, I don't
wish to live anywhere but Waterleys when I'm in the
country."

Isabella Yoxford could sympathize. Like her brother, she
felt a strong affection for their childhood home of Waterleys
Hall, a pleasant Queen Anne mansion of modest size on the
small but thriving Hertfordshire estate inherited by Sir

16

Edmund from their late father. "And that will be very agreeable for us, since now we shall see more of you!" she said comfortably. "I can quite see that to reside in Westmorland would be most inconvenient, when you are for ever needed at the Foreign Office."

"Yes," said Sir Edmund, returning to the matter under discussion, "but the thing is that when I'm in town, my old set of rooms will do for me quite as well as they've done these last few years, whenever I was home from the Continent. And I can hardly accommodate a young female in what is decidedly a bachelor establishment!"

Lady Yoxford was forced to admit the truth of this. "Oh dear, if only —" she began, and then caught herself up. She had been about to say, "If only Catherine had been alive," but she knew better than to risk opening old wounds by the mention of her brother's wife to his face. In answer to his look of inquiry, therefore, she amended her sentence, and finished, "If only Jack had not been so foolishly reckless! And it's my belief," she added, "that Sophia, far from exercising that restraining influence upon him that Uncle John had hoped for, positively encouraged him! Indeed, I would almost say it served her right to be with him in the carriage that day, except that of course it would be very dreadful to *wish* anyone dead in such a shocking accident, especially when one was sincerely fond of that person, but still, you can see where Persephone gets her wildness! Not to mention her fanciful nature — for was ever a poor baby burdened with such a ridiculous name?"

"That was a sad day for us all — more particularly Persephone, despite her being too young to know anything about it," said Sir Edmund quietly, remembering his dazzling cousin Jack: Jack, so uncritically admired, and so tragically dead in a carriage accident along with his young wife, fifteen years ago.

In point of fact, the admiration between the cousins had been mutual. With no brothers or sisters of his own, Jack Grafton, heir to one of the premier baronetcies in the

17

country, had spent much of his childhood at Waterleys. He and Edmund had attended Harrow together, and he had passed many a school holiday with Edmund and Isabella in Hertfordshire, rather than make the long journey up to the Lake District. Sir Edmund allowed himself a moment's nostalgic remembrance of those carefree days. And now, he thought, his and Isabella's parents were gone, Jack too, and last of all old Sir John himself. But surely the saddest loss because the most untimely, had been that of Jack, whose daring, quicksilver nature had fascinated Edmund, and who in turn had known how to value his cousin's agility of mind and clever knack of getting the pair of them out of scrapes into which he, Jack, had led the way.

Almost with his last breath, as he lay dying by the roadside near his shattered carriage, dragged out of reach of the horses' threshing hooves, he had said faintly – though loud enough to be heard by the men who had run in vain to his aid – that he knew Edmund would look after the child. Edmund Grafton would not have needed this commendation from his friend and cousin to ensure that he kept a benevolent eye on little Persephone, but since his diplomatic activities kept him out of England so much, the relationship was necessarily an impersonal one. Indeed, Persephone Grafton was on his conscience, for he knew that her grandfather was too old and ailing to take much interest in the child whose mere existence reminded him painfully of his dead son. It was easy enough for Edmund to take care of the business matters relating to her upbringing from a distance, but he felt he should have done more. As it was, inevitably most of her childhood had been spent at school, with occasional visits to the Yoxfords in Upper Brook Street – although there had been none of those for the past two years. However, as Sir Edmund patiently explained to his sister yet again, the responsibility for Persephone's welfare had always lain morally if not in law with Jack's cousins, and now the legal guardianship of the Grafton heiress had passed to him, along with the baronetcy and the entailed Westmorland estates.

"That's all very well, but I am sure I did what I could to amuse her when she visited us last," said Lady Yoxford, apprehensively, "and you know what came of *that*!"

Her spirits visibly quailed as she recalled what she, like the Miss Maddens, thought of as the Unfortunate Business of the over-susceptible tutor. Since Isabella Yoxford's spirits quailed easily, she did not stop to reflect that the circumstance was unlikely to recur, but her brother, swiftly calculating her family's ages in his head, pointed that fact out to her.

"Well, you've no tutor in the house now, have you? I know Charley's at Cambridge, and surely Harry is away at Eton by this time! And didn't you say, in a letter, that you had no plans to engage another tutor for Edward, but would send him to share lessons with the Barleigh boys? How old *is* Edward now – ten?"

"Yes, and what with him and the twins, and little Maria on my hands too . . . " Isabella's voice died away, and she sighed plaintively. "You do not know what it is to be a Mother, Edmund!"

Calling to mind the small army of staff, headed by the stalwart, familiar figures of Nurse Barker and Miss Merriwether the governess, who so efficiently ran the Yoxford nursery and schoolroom, Sir Edmund was unimpressed by his sister's pathetic appeal, nor did he attempt to deny the obvious. "No, I don't!" said he, smiling. "Almost a shame! For when I see how well motherhood becomes *you*, I appreciate its advantages! I conclude it has a positively rejuvenating effect – I swear you look a year younger than when I last set eyes on you, Bella, and that was over a twelvemonth ago!"

Lady Yoxford did indeed present a pretty picture, elegantly disposed upon a sofa and clad in a gown of blush-pink barège ornamented with rouleaux of a deeper rose hue around the hem, its sleeves fashionably puffed and wide at the shoulder. Her prettily rounded chin nestled becomingly into a falling tucker. At thirty-seven, just two years older than her brother, she could boast of a complexion whose delicacy was hardly faded, while the shining deep gold of her hair was undimmed: the grey and white of her drawing room in Yoxford House set off her rose and gold beauty to perfection. Hers was an amiable character, and only the prospect of being required to stir herself to unusual activity on someone else's behalf could fret her for long. So she was easily enough cajoled by her brother's compliments into momentarily forgetting the tiresome matter of Persephone's impending arrival, and broke into a trill of laughter.

"Flattery will not serve you, Edmund!" she said, with mock severity.

"I'm not flattering!" he protested. "You look charmingly, my dear."

"So she does!" exclaimed a cheerful voice, as Lady Yoxford's husband entered the room. "Ay, so she does! Well, how d'you do, Edmund?"

"Very well, George," said Sir Edmund, turning to shake hands warmly with the Viscount, a sturdy, easy-going man whom he held in great affection. "And how do *you* go on? No need to tell me how Isabella is ! I can see that for myself, as I have been telling her."

"And pretty well for you I know your voice!" said his lordship, chuckling. "Hallo, said I to myself, coming in through the hall – by Jove, who's this fellow making up to my wife, and in my own house too? Imagine my surprise on finding it was you! We hardly expected you these two days yet. Made good speed, eh?"

"Yes, a remarkably easy passage to Dover," said Sir Edmund. "And how's the family?"

"Tolerably well, tolerably well!" said the proud father, smiling, as he turned to glance at the pictorial record of his offspring. "You know, you're right, Edmund: Isabella don't look a day older than when *that* was painted!"

The picture above the mantelpiece was a group painted by

Mr Charles Leslie two years earlier, representing the Viscount and Viscountess, their elder sons, the Honourable Charles and the Honourable Henry Hargrave, then young Edward and the twins Thomas and James seated at their parents' feet, while the baby Maria, pet of the whole family and then just one year old, was clasped in her mother's arms. Parted from his wife during the latter period of the French wars (in which, like his brother-in-law Edmund, he had served with some distinction), George Hargrave had succeeded to his father's title at about the same time as the Corsican Ogre was finally defeated. His absence from England with the Army accounted for the gap in age between his second and third sons, but on coming home for good, Lord Yoxford had been very ready to make up for lost time, and the longed-for daughter, after so many boys, had at last crowned his and Isabella's efforts.

He now said cheerfully, "So we're to have another addition to the family, eh? I collect young Persephone is coming!"

Thus recalled to her sense of grievance, Lady Yoxford said plaintively, "Yes, and what am I to *do* with her, Edmund?"

"Oh, take her into Society, show her how to go on," said her brother, rather vaguely. "Put her in the way of making a good match, I suppose – Lord, Bella, *I* don't know what it is one does with a girl in her first Season!"

"Nor do I, having sons only except for Maria, who is just three!" Isabella pointed out. "And when I merely *think* of that tutor of Harry's – Edmund, I can only say I shudder!"

"Poor young fellow – child's looks turned his head!" said Lord Yoxford indulgently. "Can't blame him, Bella! She bade fair to be a beauty even at sixteen, and I dare swear she's a stunner now! And she'll have learnt some sense too – eh, Edmund?"

"So I imagine, though I confess I hardly know – I had no time to visit Bath when I was last in England. But I must go down there for her as soon as I may. Persephone's eighteen years of age – it's high time she left that school of hers. Now, don't fret, Bella! What I propose to do is engage some respectable lady of birth and breeding to chaperon her about town. All *you* need to do is present the child, take her about a few times – and if you give a ball for her, I'll make sure all is arranged without the least need for you to bestir yourself. I promise Persephone won't be a charge on you!"

"Oh, very well!" said Lady Yoxford, partly mollified. "If you are sure you can find a suitable chaperon . . . for my health, as you know, is not strong! But I suppose we do owe it to poor Jack, and perhaps it will be only for the one Season."

"Can't be any longer!" her husband confidently predicted. "Not with young Persephone's face, as I remember it, and the Grafton fortune! By the by, Edmund, I trust the old gentleman left *you* enough to keep the estate up? It's the very devil of a thing to be burdened with a great entailed place like that if there's not the money to run it properly!"

"No, all's well there," Sir Edmund assured his brother-in-law. "And Sir John's isn't the only inheritance to have come my way recently, you know," he added, almost ruefully. "There's Cousin Sophronia's property too. I fancy I had better break my journey at Cheltenham when I fetch Persephone."

"Oh, ay – Isabella mentioned that. Old Lady Emberley – on your mother's side, eh?"

Sir Edmund nodded. "Yes, though a distant enough connection in all conscience! She lived at Cheltenham, very retired, and why she should take it into her head to leave me her property, which is considerable, I can't imagine, except that she had very little family apart from Bella and myself."

"And she didn't approve of *me*, not at all!" said Isabella, a sudden twinkle in her eyes. "Do you remember how she came to stay at Waterleys, Edmund, and made me read sermons aloud to her?"

"*Tried* to make you read sermons aloud to her!" amended her brother, with an answering smile.

"And scolded poor Mama for allowing me to have my hair in curl papers at night! And brought her own tea caddy with her, saying that she never went away without it – Mama was a good deal put out by that. Oh yes, and you and Jack found that family of baby toads and smuggled them into the caddy! Cousin Sophronia never did find out how they got there, did she? But she never came to stay again, either!"

"I'm not surprised," said Sir Edmund. "Jack and I must have been a pair of little toads ourselves! By rights she should have made you her heir, Bella, not me – I'm sure the toads would have been rated a far worse crime than curl papers, if she had but found us out."

"No, no, even if she *had* found you out, since then you have become worthy and respectable and a credit to the family!" laughed Isabella, throwing up her hands as if to ward off the playful cuff her brother pretended to aim at her, quite in their old childhood style. "While anyone can see that I am as frivolous as ever – though not, of course, of a strong constitution," she hastily recollected, lest all this merriment should make her seem too robust.

"Best wife and mother in the world," said Lord Yoxford, fondly. "Can't have her wearing herself to a thread over young Persephone, y'know, Edmund!"

"She won't. Trust Bella for that!" said Sir Edmund, unfeelingly. "But to return to Cousin Sophronia, she certainly did seem set upon leaving her property within the family – which reminds me, George," he added a little diffidently, "that should you find your brood becoming more of an expense than you'd bargained for, you must remember that their fond uncle has no dependants of his own, and is now far wealthier than he has any need to be!"

"Thank you, Edmund, but don't think of such a thing!" said Yoxford cheerfully, for indeed, his revenues were such that he could afford to keep his large family in luxury as well as comfort, and he did not in the least begrudge Sir Edmund the unexpected windfall of Lady Emberley's legacy. "I'm only glad that the Emberley money *has* come to you – old ladies have been known to get strange fancies, and leave things oddly."

"As a matter of fact, she did leave things oddly," said Sir Edmund, with a slight frown. "That's one reason why I must visit Cheltenham: to look into the matter for myself. But now, it's high time I paid my respects to that brood of yours!"

And rising from his armchair with loose-limbed grace, he directed his steps towards the schoolroom and nursery, to be received there with boisterous delight by Edward, the eight-year-old twins, and little Maria, for all of whom he had remembered to bring home presents from abroad, not forgetting a length of richly plum-coloured Lyons silk for Miss Merriwether, and some caps prettily trimmed with Brussels lace for Nurse Barker.

Unaware either of the relief occasioned by her departure in the bosom of Miss Madden (and, to a lesser degree, that of Miss Mary), or of the apprehensions still rendering Lady Yoxford uneasy at the prospect of her arrival, Miss Persephone Grafton continued to fume and fret while her guardian conferred with the post-boy and John Digby. The latter, who had been travelling up behind the chaise in the dickey, had got down when his master did; he was knowledgeable about horses, and had been with Sir Edmund for years, frequently combining the functions of valet and groom, since Sir Edmund disliked having many servants around him, except when protocol and etiquette demanded it. All three men now stood talking judiciously, examining the horses and the state of the road and glancing up at the sky, while Persephone waited with growing impatience to hear the result of their cogitations.

At length Sir Edmund returned to her and swung himself up into the chaise, apparently unaware of the discontent plainly visible on her pretty face, so that she was obliged to repeat her imperious question as the vehicle moved on. "Well, and what *was* the matter?"

"Nothing of very great consequence," said Sir Edmund, with the attractive smile that had melted many a female heart, although it totally failed to charm or mollify his present companion. "But after the offside horse stumbled in that pothole, the post-boy fears he may go lame unless he's carefully nursed along. And what with the shoe that was cast when we were half-way on the second stage from Bath, and the condition of these country roads after the rain, I'm afraid we are already behind the time when I thought to arrive in Cheltenham. John reckons we shall be the best part of another hour on the road. I have to call on a lady in Cheltenham – Miss Radley is her name – and I fear I shan't have time to take you first to the Plough, where we are to spend the night, so you must come with me. But I trust my business with Miss Radley won't take long."

Persephone sniffed slightly and said, morosely, "What does it signify, in any case? What do you care for *my* comfort or convenience? Why *should* I go with you to visit Miss Radley?" she continued, rather pleased to find a grievance upon which to seize. "Who *is* this Miss Radley?"

Experienced diplomat as he was, Sir Edmund sighed inwardly. In the changeable weather of this time of year, a journey of any distance was always likely to be interrupted by various delays and minor accidents to carriage or horses, and Miss Grafton bore very ill with such setbacks. Sir Edmund was beginning to find his ward's company excessively trying, and was at a loss to account for her determined dislike of him. Her attitude all day, and indeed the previous evening as well, had veered between moody sulks and fits of outright temper, interspersed with accusations of harsh tyranny on his part. Like Miss Madden, he could not imagine why Persephone seemed so set against going to London. He realised he knew little about young ladies, but surely it was the dream of any schoolroom miss to shine in Society? And shine Miss Grafton undoubtedly would, if he were any judge of the matter!

"Miss Elinor Radley," said Sir Edmund, "is a lady who

25

until recently was companion to my late cousin, Sophronia, Lady Emberley. Lady Emberley, who lived in Cheltenham, was close on eighty when she died, and I fancy that Miss Radley is of fairly advanced age herself, so you see, it wouldn't do for me to visit her later in the day than the usual hours for a social call. Old ladies dislike having their settled habits disturbed, and she would think it very uncivil of me to visit her late."

"But you came to Bath to take me to London!" objected Persephone. "Why should you concern yourself with *her*?"

Resisting the impulse to tell her that is was none of her business, Sir Edmund patiently explained, "Because in her will, Lady Emberley made me her heir and forgot to make any provision for Miss Radley. I had thought as much from my correspondence with her man of business, a Mr Stanfield, and when I called briefly upon him on my way down to Bath he confirmed it. That's a state of affairs which must be remedied at once, and I asked Mr Stanfield to let Miss Radley know I would call upon her today and hoped she would receive me. So I must go there directly we reach the town."

There was a pause, during which Persephone was evidently following her own train of thought, for she then observed gloomily, "It doesn't seem fair."

"What doesn't seem fair?" inquired her guardian.

"Everybody leaving *you* their fortunes!" She shot him a hostile glance. "I mean, you inherited Grandpapa's baronetcy, did you not? *And* his estate! It's not right, when I was his granddaughter and you are only a nephew!"

"My dear child, you're under a misapprehension!" said Sir Edmund, relieved to have discovered, as he thought, the cause of her ill humour. "Surely Miss Madden explained that your grandfather very properly left the bulk of his fortune to you?"

Persephone responded with a sulky nod.

"So you may set your mind at rest upon *that* count!" Sir Edmund continued. "He could not help leaving the estate to

26

me, you see, because it is entailed. I assure you, I'd as lief *not* have it, but as his closest male relative I had no choice in the matter. Everything else, however, is yours, and that makes you a very rich young woman." He wondered whether to add a little homily on the wisdom of being wary of fortune-hunters, but decided he was not yet on good enough terms with his ward to risk it. Better leave that to Isabella, at some more propitious moment.

"But not a baronet, though." Miss Grafton was sticking to her guns.

"Well, no – should you wish to be *Sir Persephone?*" inquired Sir Edmund, gently teasing.

For the first time he saw a faint glimmer of amusement in her eyes. "Don't be ridiculous! Though I shouldn't mind being *Lady* Persephone. That would sound pretty!"

"Alas," said Sir Edmund gravely, "you should have thought of that before your birth, and aimed at the family of a duke or earl for your own, not a mere baronet!" He was pleased to hear this mild pleasantry draw the ghost of a chuckle from her, and continued, lightly, "Of course – not that one would advocate this as grounds for matrimony! – should you find yourself with a titled husband some day, you would be able to call yourself Lady So-and-so: whatever his name may be."

At this, however, the brief sunny gleam in her eyes instantly vanished, and she said crossly, "Who cares for that? Such Stuff!"

While Sir Edmund agreed, he was a little surprised to hear this opinion expressed by a young lady of only eighteen who showed no other conspicuous signs of maturity. However, he said encouragingly, "Well, that's very laudable and level-headed of you!" Perhaps, after all, this was the time for the homily? "I may as well say now, Persephone, that you are likely to have a great many young men at your feet, eligible and otherwise, and –"

"Well, I don't want them!" snapped Persephone. Then a cautiously wheedling note entered her voice, and her pretty

27

brow wrinkled as she said thoughtfully, "I suppose I *cannot* have control of my fortune until I am one-and twenty?"

"No," said Sir Edmund firmly.

"Really not?"

"Really not."

"Oh, it's too bad!" she exclaimed pettishly.

"Why – do you think I mean to play the part of wicked uncle, and keep you without a proper allowance?" he asked, still gently quizzing her in an effort to draw her out of the dismals. "Come, Persephone, surely you don't suppose that you will want for anything suitable to a young lady of birth and fortune making her début in London!"

"London!" uttered Persephone, in tones of the deepest distaste.

"My dear," said Sir Edmund gently, "I wish you will tell me why you are so set against going to London?"

She evaded the direct question, and resorted to counter-attack. "You don't know *anything*!" she cried, fiercely. "You don't know anything about it at all!"

"No," Sir Edmund agreed, "and I can't help wishing I did. Won't you tell me? We are your own family, you know. I won't eat you! Nor will your Cousin Isabella –"

"Her! She doesn't even like me!" interrupted Persephone.

"Oh, but indeed she does!" Sir Edmund assured her. Here, perhaps, lay the real root of the trouble: Isabella, who, in the heat of the moment, had no doubt expressed herself pretty forcibly at the time of the Unfortunate Business. Knowing his sister's real good nature, he felt that Persephone was labouring under a misapprehension, and was only sorry that the matter had rankled so long. "I fancy she may once have given you a scold, my dear, but that's all in the past, and she is most sincerely attached to you. You know that she doesn't enjoy very stout health, or she would have brought you out last year – but now we mean to engage some suitable lady to help her take you about to all the routs and parties. And I promise you we won't accept anyone for

28

that post unless you yourself like her," he added shrewdly.

His carefully judged words, however failed of their effect. "Some old cat, of course!" commented Persephone, flinging herself back less than elegantly against the squabs of the post-chaise. "But it is all of a piece! Thinking you can – can cajole me with routs and parties! Overbearing my wishes, just because I'm not of age! Tearing me from all closest to my heart!" she continued, warming to her theme. "Wrenching me from those I hold most dear!"

This was a little too much for Sir Edmund, who could not help mildly protesting, "Really, Persephone, you cannot have wished to remain at the Miss Maddens' seminary all your life! Of course you hold the good ladies in affection, and I'm glad of that, but – "

"Oh, *them*!" Persephone dismissed the Miss Maddens. "They were old cats too! At least – " as her conscience momentarily smote her – "at least, Miss Madden was. Miss Mary was more of a nice, soft old *pussy-cat*! But I didn't mean them. I have *friends* in Bath!"

Sir Edmund hoped she would expand upon this theme, even if it meant he had to listen to a string of confidences about her girlish friendships at school, but she appeared to recollect herself suddenly, and in answer to his look of inquiry merely tightened her lips, adding, bitterly, "*True* friends!"

And she would say no more until, nearly half an hour later, as the chaise at last approached the spa town of Cheltenham, she roused herself to take up the conversation apparently just where she had left it off, remarking in the same discontented tones, "And now you are bent on dragging me with you to call on some other frowsty old cat! It's too bad of you, it is indeed, and I think you are the greatest beast in Nature!"

29

3

Disposed as he still was to regard Jack's daughter as a child rather than a young woman, Sir Edmund found this decidedly infantile burst of temper comical and even touching, but their arrival in Royal Crescent spared him the task of composing a reply of sufficient gravity. The chaise was soon drawing up outside the elegant, narrow façade of the house that had been occupied by Sophronia, Lady Emberley, until her recent demise full of years and – if the truth were told – full of ill will towards the greater part of her fellow men. This event had occurred over three months before, and there were no obvious signs of mourning left about the house. Sir Edmund, who intended to have the place put up for sale, gave it only a cursory glance before directing John Digby and the postilion to find their way to the Plough, and then, with Persephone, mounting the short flight of steps to the front door.

A quick look at his ward's face confirmed his impression that discontent and a sense of grievance were still seething within her. He thought, ruefully, that while he might be an old hand at dealing with the wilier politicians of Europe around the conference table, he had not the same happy knack with a wilful girl of eighteen. However, he knew better than to utter anything so sure to achieve the opposite of its intended effect as a sharp reproof, and said only, in a low voice, "I know you'll make yourself agreeable to Miss Radley, Persephone. Old ladies are so easily flustered and distressed, are they not?"

Persephone cast him a suspicious glance, but had not time to reply, for the door was being opened by an elderly butler. His wrinkled face was wreathed in smiles, but to judge by his failure to respond to Sir Edmund's civil greeting, he must have been stone deaf: he said not a word, but continued to smile with the utmost amiability.

A moment later, however, a neat, capable-looking woman in late middle age appeared in the hallway behind him. Straightening her apron and bobbing a curtsey, she launched into a speech of welcome, proving as voluble as the butler was silent. "And you must please to forgive us, sir, being all at sixes and sevens as we are!" she concluded, as Sir Edmund handed his hat and gloves to the old man. "For Miss Radley's been that busy, sorting out my lady's things – you see, sir, my lady never could abide to throw anything away, and if you'll pardon me for saying so, oh, but she *could* be such a twitty old lady when crossed! Well, so it has all fallen on Miss Radley's shoulders, and when she told us we might expect to see you today, why, Joshua here, who is my husband, sir, and Howell is our name, Joshua says to me it's his place to open the door. But *I* says to *him* – for you must know, sir, hard of hearing as he is, I *can* make him understand me – how will you ever hear the doorbell, Joshua, says I? Why, Mary, says he, *you* must listen for it and give me a bit of a nudge, and then I can open the door to Sir Edmund, as is only right, says he, and *you* can take him in to see Miss Radley! So that is what we did, sir," said Mrs Howell, unnecessarily. "And now, if you and the young lady will just step this way?"

Evidently satisfied that he had played his due part in the proceedings, Howell had disappeared half-way through his wife's speech. She was now ushering Sir Edmund and his ward through the hall, and into a drawing room which lay at the back of the house.

With memories of his draconian Cousin Sophronia in his mind, Sir Edmund hardly expected to receive so immediately pleasant an impression as he did on entering this apartment. The hall itself had seemed cluttered with graceless furniture, just the kind of thing he would have imagined

31

the old lady to possess, and certainly the drawing room contained a number of similar pieces: large, dark and heavy, some of them covered by dustsheets. These, however, had all been pushed to one end of the room, which was not particularly tidy, and indeed appeared to be in a kind of transitional state, as though it were being progressively dismantled. But it had large windows, through which the late afternoon sun streamed in, and a bright little island of comfort and warmth had been created beside one of these, at the other end of the room from the crowded furniture. Here, a fire of fruitwood logs burned clear and fragrant in the grate, some elegant chairs were disposed on a handsome Persian rug, and there was a sizeable desk in the bay of the window itself, standing in a pool of sunlight. This desk was covered with neat stacks of paper, and a young lady sat at it writing.

Sir Edmund was looking about him for his late cousin's companion, described to him by Mr Stanfield as *a very respectable spinster lady*. Miss Radley, he knew, was a distant connection of Lady Emberley's on the other side of her family from himself, and that was all the information he had about her. He now saw that the girl at the desk had risen, putting down her pen, and was coming to meet him.

"Sir Edmund Grafton?" she said, in a pleasantly modulated voice. "How do you do? I am Elinor Radley. I think Mr Stanfield has mentioned to you that I was Lady Emberley's companion for the last seven years."

Rapidly readjusting his ideas, Sir Edmund said, "I am very glad to meet you, Miss Radley; let me introduce my ward, Miss Persephone Grafton."

At a second glance, he saw that the lady was less young than he had at first supposed, being perhaps about five or six and twenty, and with a quietly assured manner that was not that of a girl. She was no dazzling beauty like Persephone, but nevertheless there was something very taking about the warm smile which extended to her fine grey eyes, her shining chestnut hair arranged in neat bands, and her slim figure in its sober dove-grey gown trimmed with black crape ribbon.

For her part, Miss Radley, who had felt a very natural curiosity about Lady Emberley's heir, was looking appraisingly at Sir Edmund. She liked what she saw: a tall, well-knit and athletic frame, clad in white doeskin panta-loons and a riding coat of blue superfine; a lean, strong-jawed face with what she suspected were deceptively lazy blue eyes, and a humorous set to the mouth. The first grey, she saw, showed in Sir Edmund's dark hair. From his easy manner, no one would have guessed how different he found Miss Radley from the elderly spinster of his imaginings, had not Persephone given him away by uttering a delighted trill of laughter (the first he had yet heard from her) and exclaiming, "Why, you're not an old cat after all!"

"Well, I *hope* not," said the other girl, gravely, "but one can never tell when old cattishness may overtake one, to be sure! I am so pleased to make your acquaintance, Miss Grafton."

"You see," confided Persephone, whose sulks seemed magically to have evaporated, as if unable to withstand the pleasant warmth of this room, "*he* was persuaded you were as old as the hills, and I have been most *sternly* adjured, I promise you, not to do or say anything *at all*, because old ladies are so easily flustered! Oh, how comical!"

"And how mortifying to me!" said Sir Edmund, smiling. He could not but be thankful for the improvement in Persephone's temper which Miss Radley had instantly, and apparently without the smallest effort, brought about, but he added ruefully, "Will you leave me with no credit at all, Persephone? But for you I might have extracted myself from my misapprehension without anyone's being the wiser! I see, Miss Radley, that I must confess I *was* expecting an elderly lady, someone of my late cousin's own generation – though I really don't know why. I dare say Persephone will now inform you that I have dragged her here against her will to visit you, because old ladies are sticklers for keeping correct hours!"

"No, I won't, though you *did* say so," Persephone promptly replied. "Because I think I am glad now that I came, and you did not take me to the Plough directly. So there!" she finished, challengingly.

"Good gracious, you mean you have only this moment arrived in Cheltenham? My dear Miss Grafton, you must be quite worn out!" exclaimed Miss Radley, with ready sympathy. "Do pray sit down – and you too, sir. I'm sure you would be glad of some refreshment after your journey."

She indicated the chairs by the fireside, pressed a bell near the desk, and when Mrs Howell appeared requested some Madeira for Sir Edmund. "And is there any of your excellent lemonade left, Mrs Howell? Good – then please bring a glass of it for Miss Grafton."

"Thank you, Miss Radley, you are very kind. I must apologize," said Sir Edmund, "for my late arrival; we were delayed on the road."

"Well, I'm sorry for the inconvenience to *you*." Elinor Radley had seated herself at the desk again. "But I own that, for my part, I was quite glad to have the time to finish putting Lady Emberley's effects in order for you. The papers in the desk here were the very last of it – you may say that I ought to have completed the task days or even weeks ago, but – "

"I should most certainly say nothing of the sort!" protested Sir Edmund. "It must have been a thankless task indeed! I collect there was a great deal to be done?"

"Well, there was," she confessed, "for Lady Emberley was – was so very much attached to the possessions of a lifetime, and so given to habits of economy, that she was quite distressed by the notion of disposing of anything whatsoever."

Was a miserly, acquisitive old jackdaw, thought Sir Edmund, adding his own unspoken gloss to this.

"Here, for instance," said Miss Radley, pointing to a bundle of papers, "is what I do believe must be every

34

receipted bill she received over the last twenty years. And this is her correspondence with Mr Stanfield, which of course she did quite right to keep, and *this* – " she indicated the biggest pile of all – "consists of letters from her family, all preserved for many years, as you can see."

"What an excessively boring time you must have had, sorting all that out! I fancy that a bonfire is the place for all but Mr Stanfield's papers!"

Sir Edmund was mildly intrigued to see a faint flush rise to Miss Radley's cheeks, and wondered what he could have said to occasion it. But she answered only, "Do you really think so? I own, I am not in favour of going through life cumbered with old possessions and papers myself! But I don't believe," she said earnestly, "that I have given or thrown away anything of interest or value. Whenever we were in the least doubt, Mrs Howell and I have been consulting one another. Ah, here *is* Mrs Howell!" And the Madeira and lemonade were brought in.

"How delicious this is! Thank you!" said Persephone, sipping from her glass, and beaming at the gratified housekeeper. Once again, Sir Edmund was astonished by the change in her. Let the child but continue in *this* frame of mind, he told himself, and she will be back in Bella's good graces directly – and if I know Bella's kind heart, they will deal extremely well together! He drank some of his own Madeira, and turned back to Miss Radley once the house-keeper was out of earshot.

"One of the matters which brings me to Cheltenham concerns the Howells: I believe they have been butler and housekeeper here for a very long time?"

"Oh yes!" said Elinor Radley at once. "Yes, and I know, for Mr Stanfield has told me, that *you* know how things are left – "

"Or rather, *not* left."

"Yes, that's precisely it!" she said with evident relief. "I felt – at least, I hoped that you would understand! They are such a worthy couple, you know, and have been with Lady

35

Emberley for ever, and though the work has been rather beyond Howell lately, and his deafness certainly hampers him, Lady Emberley kept him on, saying we should do very well with only Mrs Howell to run the house. Though I am afraid she has been sadly overworked, poor soul. But I'm sure it was good of Lady Emberley not to dispense with Howell's services when he could not really carry out a butler's duties any more."

"What you mean," said Sir Edmund drily, "is that she slave-drove the pair of them! And probably yourself too. From all I recollect of my Cousin Sophronia, I don't think that in general benevolence dictated her actions, do you?"

His eyes met hers with a hint of challenge, and in a moment she said, with an engaging little chuckle, "Dear me, you've hit the nail on the head! Yes, she knew a younger butler would require a higher wage – but it wouldn't have done for me to *say* so to you, would it?"

"Oh, you can say what you like about my Cousin Sophronia!" he returned. "I have the liveliest – and most uncomfortable – memories of her. And you have been her companion for – did you really say seven years? I can't imagine how you endured it, but that is none of my business. The Howells are my business, however, and I take it you know as well as I do that no provision at all has been made for them. And don't try telling me that was an oversight on my cousin's part, for I shan't believe you!"

"Then I won't – since I see I can't hope to humbug you, Sir Edmund!" said she, demurely, laughter dancing in her eyes.

"I'll ask Mr Stanfield to put something in hand directly: a codicil which he had previously overlooked, don't you think?"

"Oh yes!" she exclaimed, with warm approval. "A most thoughtful way of doing the thing – though rather unfair to *you*, Sir Edmund, since they won't know it is your own generosity. But of course she ought to have left them something, and I can't tell you what a load you have taken

36

off my mind! I – I was persuaded that you *would* do something of the sort, but naturally I could not be quite sure until I met you. How happy they will be!"

She favoured Sir Edmund with a delightful smile, and he, smiling back, had the impression that the warmth in the room proceeded from the young woman at the desk quite as much as from the little fruitwood fire in the hearth. However, he was frowning slightly as he said, "Well, that's settled! But now we come to another if related matter . . . is there a place, I wonder, where Persephone could amuse herself while we discuss it in private?" He glanced at his ward. Miss Grafton, bored with the conversation of her elders, had finished her lemonade and risen from her chair, and was now wandering among the furniture at the far end of the room, lifting a dust-sheet now and then to see what lay beneath.

"Yes, of course." Elinor Radley rose too. "Miss Grafton, all this business talk must be tiresome for you, but there are books in the little room next door, and also a pianoforte, if you care for music, and would like – "

"Oh *yes!*" interrupted Persephone, suddenly radiant. Reaching the door towards which Miss Radley was moving ahead of her hostess, she flung it open. "A pianoforte – oh, famous! I was thinking that I might find one over there, you know, but when I looked there was only an old bureau and a table. Oh, pray let me play it! You see, I have not been able to do any practising for *two whole days* now!"

Her tone made it clear that she considered this a major deprivation. She was already lifting the lid of the instrument, and picking out a scale.

"I'm afraid it may be out of tune, for I have not played much recently," Miss Radley apologised.

"It *is* a little out of tune, but never mind, I think it will serve," said Persephone absently – though with what, to Sir Edmund, was an entirely unexpected note of maturity and assurance in her voice, "Well, this is of all things great! I never thought to have a chance to practise on my way to

37

London! There, now you may talk all the business you want, and don't mind me! Yes, this is a very tolerable instrument, and I shall be happy to remain as long as you like," she graciously informed her guardian. "I may look through the music in your piano stool, may I not, Miss Radley? Good! I shall do very well in here," she finished cheerfully, shutting the door of the little book-room behind her. Presently, rippling cascades of arpeggios proclaimed the truth of her assertion.

"Music has charms!" said Sir Edmund, a good deal startled. "Do you perform miracles every day of the week, Miss Radley?"

"Miracles?"

"You should have travelled with young Persephone from Bath – or rather, you should *not*, for I wouldn't wish that experience on anyone else! She was given over entirely to a furious fit of the sulks. You've certainly coaxed her out of that, and how you contrived to do it I don't know, although I suspect that, as seven years of pandering to Cousin Sophronia's whims must have taught you how to deal with – er – a twitty old lady was, I think, Mrs Howell's wording – perhaps a twitty *young* lady is not so very different."

She gave a little choke of laughter, and said, "Well, I suppose I *have* had a little practice in – in the use of tact, but I can't think that necessary with your Persephone. The most charming child! Oh, do but listen!" For Persephone, in the next room, having run through her scales and arpeggios, had embarked upon a sonata by Clementi, which she was executing with great virtuosity. "I certainly never met a girl so willing, indeed positively anxious to sit down and practise! But plainly it's no hardship to her. How very well she plays!"

"So she does," said Sir Edmund, considerably surprised himself. "I'm not so well acquainted with her as I ought to be, having spent most of my time out of the country in recent years, and I own I had no notion of her talent. At least – one of her schoolmistresses did mention Persephone's *musical gifts*, but it struck me that the good lady was – how shall I put it? – oddly wary in her praise!"

"Yes, well, that's not to be wondered at," said Miss Radley thoughtfully. "You are taking her to London for the Season, I suppose? *Such* a gift, you see, might be a positive drawback! She is not only accomplished, but almost too accomplished – she plays so much better than most young ladies. I fancy that other girls – and their mamas – may not quite like to find themselves so easily outshone."

"True! But luckily she has a fortune to recommend her, as well as her looks, so I dare say the young *gentlemen* she meets won't object to her playing the piano well! Now, never mind Persephone for the moment." He looked into the clear flames again, the small frown between his brows deepening. "This is deucedly awkward, Miss Radley, but I take you for a woman of sense, and I fancy you may have some idea of my particular reason for calling on you. May I be blunt?"

"By all means, sir," said Elinor Radley composedly.

"We have satisfactorily dealt with the Howells, but there is still a far greater omission in my Cousin Sophronia's will, is there not? Plainly, you were better acquainted than I with the old dragon – indeed, I don't recollect setting eyes on her since my cousin Jack and I were boys, and filled her tea caddy with baby toads – "

"Did you indeed? How very shocking!" said Miss Radley, straight-faced, but with amusement in her eyes.

"Yes, wasn't it? We were in disgrace for days!"

"I wish you will tell me about it!"

He smiled and shook his head. "Well, I won't! Or not now. You are trying to distract me from my purpose, Miss Radley."

"*Touchée!*" She resigned herself. "I am afraid you are right."

"So – if I may finish what I was saying – you knew both the old lady and the excellent Mr Stanfield too well for me to be able to pretend to a *second* overlooked codicil! But I want to assure you that the deplorable omission of your own name from the will shall speedily be set right, and Mr Stanfield and I between us will see that an appropriate settlement is made on you."

"Oh dear! I was afraid you were going to say something of the sort," remarked Miss Radley. Conscious of all the awkwardness of the situation, she seemed a little breathless, but was otherwise in perfect command of herself. "To be blunt with *you*, Sir Edmund, the long and the short of it is that I could not – *would* not – accept of any such arrangement. It is not what Lady Emberley would have wished."

"Then she damned well should have done!" said Sir Edmund, forcefully. "Forgive my language, Miss Radley, but I never in my life heard of anything so shameful as her failure to mention you in that will of hers!"

"For all you know," suggested Elinor Radley, looking down at the desk and carefully picking her words, "she may have made me a handsome present before her death."

"Are you telling me that she did any such thing?" demanded Sir Edmund. "Look at me, please, and be honest with me, Miss Radley!"

Reluctantly raising her eyes to his, she gave a tiny shake of the head. "But you see," she said quickly, "matters are not at all as you had supposed. Were I the old lady you thought me, I'm sure I should be happy to accept your charity – please don't think me ungrateful. However, the thing is that I – I have had enough of charity in my life, and to tell you the truth, Sir Edmund"– here her firm little chin came up a trifle defiantly –"it has for so long been out of my power to refuse anything, that is a great luxury to do so! And I am *not* a frail old lady unable to earn my bread!"

"If I may ask without impertinence, how do you intend to do so?"

"Oh, as a governess, of course," she said at once. "It is a perfectly respectable calling, you know! I *was* a governess for a little while, before I came to live with Lady Emberley

40

when – when she offered me a home. And I'm not quite out of the way of teaching, because she let me take a few pupils here while she was resting in the afternoons, so I have been instructing small girls in the rudiments of education, and a little music – not that I could ever lay claim to Miss Grafton's proficiency!" Launching into the brilliant Rondo of the sonata, Persephone had reminded them of her presence in the next room. "That meant, you see, that I could earn my own pin money, and need not be a charge on Lady Emberley except for my keep."

Tight-fisted old harpy, thought Sir Edmund, apostrophizing his late relative again.

"And it was very agreeable to feel at least a little independent," she added, as if reading his thoughts.

This he had to allow. Remembering his puritanical, cross-grained old cousin, he could not help wondering what sort of life this attractive and intelligent young woman had led with her, nor contrasting it with the brilliant prospects of Persephone, blessed with a large fortune of her own, and with a dazzling Season and surely a fine marriage ahead of her. What puzzled him was why Miss Radley had not preferred even the dreary situation of a governess to such a life. He rather suspected the old lady of having exerted moral pressure by appealing to a young girl's sense of family duty, so as to provide herself with a useful and able companion at the minimum of expense. Choosing his words rather carefully, he said as much.

Miss Radley, however, gave a smile of wry amusement, and said, "No, no, sir, you are quite mistaken! The advantage was all on my side."

Sir Edmund did not believe it, but could hardly with propriety ask any more questions, and in any case their conversation now suffered another musical interruption. Reaching the end of the sonata, Persephone paused briefly, and then struck a resonant chord before raising her voice in song. And what song! thought both listeners, their minds momentarily diverted from all else.

"It is a scena and aria by Beethoven," said Miss Radley quietly. "She has found a piano arrangement I have of it – though I am afraid it is rather beyond *me*!"

"*Ah, perfido*!" Persephone's voice rang out pure, clear and loud: very loud. As her soaring soprano rose and fell to the accompaniment she was playing, the couple in the next room listened spellbound. Had Miss Madden been present, she would have recognized in the scene the realization of her worst forebodings. Miss Grafton had let loose the phenomenon known to Selina and Mary Madden as The Voice, and The Voice was in full cry.

"Good God!" said Sir Edmund softly, as Persephone drew to the close of the piece.

"Quite magnificent!" agreed Miss Radley. "And of course, quite out of place in a polite drawing room! No wonder her schoolmistress was wary! A few pretty, sentimental ballads are what a young lady should sing – performing them prettily too, if possible, but not in a voice of *that* quality! What a talent to possess, though! She plays very finely, but I think it is the singing voice which is the greater gift."

"I wonder," said Sir Edmund thoughtfully, "whether that is behind her extraordinary dislike of coming to London? You must know more about young girls than I do: can it be she fears she won't have as much time for music as she has been used to?"

Miss Radley considered this, and said she wouldn't have thought so. "For as to her style of singing, what is not quite the thing in London is not quite the thing in a Bath seminary either! Does she really dislike the notion of London so much?"

"She has been accusing me the whole way of the most monstrous tyranny in taking her there!" said Sir Edmund, and found himself describing to Miss Radley's sympathetic ear Persephone's puzzling behaviour on his first meeting with her in Bath, and on their subsequent journey to Cheltenham.

He made it entertaining enough in the telling to amuse his companion a good deal, but she bent her mind seriously to the matter, and when he had finished said, "Oh, well, that is plain enough! *Wrenched from those she holds most dear*, you said? *And torn from all closest to her heart*? The case is clear! Poor child, she is in love, no doubt with someone entirely unsuitable whom she has, perforce, left behind her in Bath."

"You think so? I own," said Sir Edmund, "that the notion did cross my mind, but I don't see how she could have formed such an attachment without the knowledge of her schoolmistresses. They did not seem at all remiss in supervising their charges, and I'm pretty confident they would not have concealed such a thing from me. However, it would certainly account for Persephone's attitude! Of course, she is pretty enough to turn heads wherever she goes, and indeed, there was some trouble with my young nephews' tutor a couple of years ago. Well, I can only hope that the pleasures of London will soon drive this hypothetical swain from her mind, for if not I shall never hear the end of it from my sister! You don't imagine, do you, that Persephone would do anything so rash as to run away from London?"

Miss Radley seemed to find this a difficult question to answer, but said at last, "It is hard to know just what an impressionable girl may do when – if she does not clearly see the right course to follow, but with Lady Yoxford's guidance, she cannot fail to know what *that* is ! And I am sure she will soon be very happy in London, and quite forget Bath."

"I trust so. Unfortunately, my sister is already a little apprehensive: her health is not strong, and we intend to engage a chaperon for Persephone," said Sir Edmund, without thinking too much of his words. A moment later, however, an idea occurred to him: an idea so blindingly obvious that he could only marvel at himself for not having thought of it half an hour before, or indeed the moment he

43

set eyes on Elinor Radley. "Miss Radley!" he began. "Or no, I shall presume upon our relationship, since we're cousins – "

"Are we? No, surely not."

"Yes," said Sir Edmund firmly. "Of course we are – you on one side of old Cousin Sophronia's family, I on the other. I shall therefore call you Cousin Elinor, if I may?"

She nodded, a faint blush staining her cheeks again.

"Well, Cousin Elinor, if you are really bent upon finding employment, our reprehensible old relative having failed in her plain duty to make provision for you – "

"No, *no*!" she interrupted him earnestly. "I really must set you right there! I would rather not go into detail, but the fact is, Lady Emberley thought she *had* made provision for me, only it was not – not in a way that I could like. Although I know she thought that ungrateful in me, as perhaps it was. However – "

"Yes, well, never mind that for now!" said Sir Edmund. "What I was about to say – "

But he got no chance to say it. There was a tap on the door, and a somewhat flustered Mrs Howell instantly entered the room, exclaiming, "Oh, I do beg your pardon, miss – beg pardon, I'm sure, Sir Edmund – only – dear me, Miss Radley, it's the Reverend!"

"Mr Spalding?" Elinor Radley's brows drew together. "Pray tell him that I am engaged upon business, Mrs Howell, and cannot receive him now!"

"Oh dear, how very vexatious!" exclaimed Miss Radley. "What *is* to be done? Oh, do forgive me, Sir Edmund; I was afraid of this visit, but just at the moment . . . oh, dear!" she repeated, rather helplessly.

Sir Edmund was a little amused to see Miss Radley's admirable calm ruffled for the first time, but said at once, "I'll go, shall I, Miss Radley, and leave you to your caller? Though I must first prise Persephone away from that instrument of yours!"

This task promised to be a difficult one. Although the

stormy drama of Beethoven's aria had been succeeded by a gentler selection of folk songs from the British Isles, arranged by the same composer, Persephone was carolling blithely away in a manner which did not at all suggest that she was ready to exchange the pianoforte for the comforts of the Plough Inn.

"No, pray don't go – that is, if you *would* be so kind as to remain?" asked Elinor, slightly pink and decidedly breathless. "The fact is, I should really be rather glad of company, sir!" She cast a distracted look at the door, which the housekeeper had left ajar. A hearty voice with a distinctly ecclesiastical resonance to it was to be heard in the hall, its owner assuring Mrs Howell that he would just hang up his hat, and then, why, he hoped he knew his way! "I – I am afraid that Mr Spalding, an excellent man, of course, who is curate of this parish – only I don't *wish* to – but Lady Emberley was so set on it, and whatever I say he *still* seems to think it is a settled thing, which I find excessively trying – dear me, I am explaining it all so badly!"

"Let me guess!" said Sir Edmund, considerably entertained. "The excellent clerical gentleman, curate of this parish, is the – what did you call it? – *provision* my deplorable old cousin saw fit to make for you? And he is now intent upon either making you an offer of marriage, or renewing one he has made before?"

"Yes, that's it in a nutshell," said Elinor, grateful for his quick perception. "Only he *can't* do so if you are present, sir, can he?" she added in an urgent whisper, as heavy footsteps approached.

"I hardly think so," said Sir Edmund, encouragingly.

In this opinion, however, he was to find himself mistaken.

4

It was plain from the outset that the tall and rather stout clergyman who now entered the drawing room, as good as brushing Mrs Howell aside, was not be be deterred from any purpose he had in mind by so trifling a detail as the presence of a third party who was, in addition, a total stranger to him. Composing herself with an effort, Miss Radley performed the introductions. Mr Spalding, advancing towards Sir Edmund with measured tread, shook his hand vigorously and at length. His ruddy, well-fleshed face wore a beaming smile, and with so much amiability in evidence, Sir Edmund was hard put to it to account for the instant dislike which he found he had taken to the clergyman. *Jacob was a smooth man*, he said to himself involuntarily, despite the fact that he had just learnt Mr Spalding's given name to be Samuel. Perhaps it was the smoothness of chin (freshly shaven for this visit?) and partial baldness of pate that suggested that patriarchal attribute. Sir Edmund judged Mr Spalding to be about his own age. His bearing was one of great assurance, not to say self-consequence.

"Delighted to make your acquaintance, Sir Edmund, delighted!" said he, effusively. "Well, well, and so you are the heir! Pray allow me to offer my congratulations!" Here his countenance suddenly assumed an expression of great gravity, as he added, "and of course my condolences upon Lady Emberley's death too, sir! So excellent, so God-fearing a woman, so truly thoughtful of others – so gratifyingly appreciative of our parochial work here in bringing spiritual comfort to the poor, as we may see even after her death!"

Sir Edmund suddenly recollected where he had met with the name of Samuel Spalding before. That gentleman must be referring to the solitary bequest made by Lady Emberley to anyone but himself as her designated heir: the sum of three thousand pounds left to the Reverend Mr Spalding, of the Church of St Mary. In fact, Lady Emberley had made no stipulation as to its use for bringing spiritual comfort to the poor, who in Sir Edmund's experience generally preferred the material variety. He interrupted Mr Spalding's encomiums to say civilly, but with no especial warmth, that he feared he himself had not met Lady Emberley for years, and though he supposed time might have mellowed her, he could not feel that her disposal of her estate did her much credit. "I myself," he remarked, "am not at all satisfied with the way things have been left, as I have been telling Miss Radley."

Far from taking this as implying any criticism of the bequest made to himself, Mr Spalding cried almost gleefully, "Aha! I take your meaning, Sir Edmund, indeed, I take your meaning! I apprehend – "

But here a loud trill upon the pianoforte interrupted him, and he glanced round, startled. "What in the world is that, Elinor?"

"Sir Edmund's ward, Miss Grafton, is practising on the instrument in the book-room," she told him.

"I see. I see. Well, well, very agreeable, I am sure! But to return, Sir Edmund, to the matter of which we were speaking. You are thinking, I dare say, that no provision was made for Miss Radley here. But, my dear sir, there is no need to concern yourself, none in the world! Provision *has* been made, Sir Edmund – *ample* provision, and not, I trust I may say, in worldly goods alone!" The prospect of dilating further upon Lady Emberley's benevolence seemed to exert a powerful effect upon the clergyman; his chest visibly expanded as he beamed again at his companions. "I surmise, sir, that with very proper modesty, and her customary delicacy of mind, Miss Radley has not thought it right to mention the matter to you. And to be sure, where betrothals are concerned, mum's the word at a time of mourning!"

He chuckled, evidently supposing himself to have uttered a witticism, and Sir Edmund, who was beginning to find him rather entertaining, noted with amusement that the expression on Miss Radley's face was closer to sheer outrage than *very proper modesty*.

"However, sir," continued the clergyman, "I collect that, although you and Elinor were related to Lady Emberley on different sides of her family, you, as the heir, may in some sort be regarded as the *head* of the family, so discussion of the matter is not altogether inappropriate. Indeed, it may be that I should apply to you for your approval!" This seemed to be another joke, for he chuckled again. "I trust, therefore, that I commit no solecism, sir, in informing you, in short, that Miss Radley is to become my wife!"

In short, Sir Edmund thought, was hardly an apt description for Mr Spalding's style of conversation, but after making this interesting announcement even he had to pause for breath, and perhaps for effect too. Miss Radley availed herself of the opportunity to say, mildly enough, "Never mind about applying to Sir Edmund! He is *not* related to me – and I do think, you know, you might rather have applied to *me* first!"

"You mean he hasn't?" asked Sir Edmund, diverted.

"Eh? What?" exclaimed the clergyman, momentarily – but only momentarily – taken aback. Next instant he had regained all his bland affability. "Ah, that is your modesty speaking, my dear Elinor, and very laudable too. But I am sure we need not stand on ceremony with Sir Edmund. After all, it is quite a settled thing!"

"Oh dear, I do wish you would disabuse yourself of that notion, Mr Spalding," said Elinor, vexed.

"Now, now, modesty is all very well, but there is no need to be *missish*!" remarked her suitor, a touch of impatience in his own voice. He addressed himself to Sir Edmund again. "While Lady Emberley was alive, of course, and in need of

48

her cousin's services and company, the case was quite different. Had the question arisen, I should have been the first to admit Lady Emberley's prior claims! But *now* – " here he turned to his intended bride again " – now there can be no obstacle in the way of our union!"

Elinor sighed. "Mr Spalding, need we discuss this now?" she said hopefully. "It can hardly interest Sir Edmund."

"On the contrary! *On* the contrary!" proclaimed Mr Spalding, who seemed to have a distinct predilection for saying things twice. No doubt, thought Sir Edmund unkindly, the habit served to swell his sermons to the requisite length. "I apprehend that Sir Edmund, very properly, is concerned for your future."

"Well, there is no need for *anyone* to be concerned for my future! It is entirely my own affair!" said Elinor, her indignation at last breaking through in a flash of temper. She composed herself again with an effort, and said, carefully, "Believe me, Mr Spalding, I am truly sorry if there has been a misunderstanding, but it was never of my making. It may be that Lady Emberley led you to suppose I should accept an offer of marriage from you after her death, but I do feel I should point out that though you may *think* you have made me such an offer, that is not the case!"

"Come, come, let's have no quibbling!" said her suitor, a little testily. "You must be aware that it was to dear Lady Emberley I spoke!"

"Yes, Mr Spalding." Elinor compressed her lips as she cast her mind back to the very disagreeable scene with Lady Emberley that had followed. "And *she* spoke to *me*, and I told her, you know, that should you be obliging enough to make me the offer she foresaw, I could only decline it, though with the deepest sense of – of the honour you did me, and with a true appreciation of your worth!"

"Just so, just so, and very right too while your benefactress was still alive! But, with her customary acuteness and foresight, it was of the future that Lady Emberley was thinking. Why, I *owe* it to her to unite my lot with yours!"

he exclaimed, rather unfortunately.

"Ye banks and braes of bonnie Doon . . . " warbled Persephone's remarkable soprano in the next room. It caught his attention once again, and once again Elinor seized her opportunity to speak.

"I do appreciate your feelings, Mr Spalding," said she, with what Sir Edmund thought commendable restraint. "But your mind may be quite easy now! You have done all that Lady Emberley could have expected of you. And if, as it seems, plain speaking is to be the order of the day – well, Sir Edmund, you see that *you* may be easy in your mind too, since your cousin had a very respectable future planned for me, and it's entirely my own fault if I felt I could not comply with her wishes!" The glint of humour was back in her eyes as she looked from one gentleman to the other. "Besides, you know, Mr Spalding, I shouldn't make a good wife for a clergyman. There are *many* who would suit you far better – think, for instance, of Miss Dunn." For a moment, Mr Spalding looked much struck by the suggestion. "I feel sure," she pursued, "that before long you will be very much relieved I have refused your obliging offer!"

The one he hasn't even made her yet, thought Sir Edmund, who was having some difficulty in preserving his own gravity, and found the task even harder when Mr Spalding rejoined, apparently with genuine indignation, "Not at all! I own, I have sometimes wondered if Miss Dunn . . . but no! Miss Dunn is all very well, all very well in her way, but I am persuaded that you too would make me an excellent wife, accustomed as you are to habits of thrift and economy, and full as you must ever be of a sense of obligation to those ready, in a spirit of true forgiveness, to overlook the past!"

"We will not say any more upon that head, if you please," said Miss Radley, her amusement entirely swept away again.

But Mr Spalding in full spate was not readily to be halted. "For now that there is inculcated in you, as I do sincerely

50

believe and trust, a salutary understanding of the inevitable consequences of deviation from the right way, I need have no apprehension as to your ever conducting yourself with the least impropriety, or other than as befits the wife of a man of the cloth! I have upon occasion, I freely admit, observed a certain frivolity in you, but once *that* is checked, I am persuaded you will enter into the state of matrimony in a truly fitting spirit. And consider," he said, as one producing a final and irrefutable argument, "that henceforth you will have at your side a husband, able to direct and advise you in all that you do. The benefits of *that*, to a woman, cannot, I believe, be over-estimated!" he concluded with great satisfaction.

Sir Edmund was here obliged to turn his head aside and devote his whole attention to a goldfinch perched on a bough just coming into leaf outside the window, lest his unseemly grin of amusement be seen by his companions.

There was little enough amusement in Miss Radley's own face as she said, rather wearily, "Well, I see it must be plain speaking indeed! Mr Spalding, pray believe that I mean it when I say I am *not* going to marry you. Ever!"

The bluntness of this actually shocked Mr Spalding into the use of monosyllables. He asked, baldly, "But then, what will you do?"

"Look about me for a post as a governess."

A distinct note of grievance, which the charitable (but not Sir Edmund) might have ascribed to disappointment at the dashing of his hopes, crept into Mr Spalding's voice as he inquired, "And who, pray, will employ you? You could hardly have expected to marry at all – and here you have a man of, I hope I may make bold to say, the highest respectability, prepared to make you his wife! What better prospect could you look to find? How, after what I am constrained to call your rash conduct of the past, can you hope to – "

"I wish you wouldn't feel constrained to call it anything at all!" said Elinor, with spirit. Sir Edmund silently applauded

51

her. "It *is* in the past, you know!"

"It is not, however, the kind of thing that can be forgotten!" pronounced the clergyman sternly. "Oh, dear me, dear me, no! A young woman's good name, once sullied – but enough of that!" he added rather hastily, seeing a dangerous flash in Miss Radley's eye. "Where, I ask, will you obtain a post? I shudder, I repeat I shudder to think what might become of you! I cannot, I must not, I will not permit it! My conscience would not allow of such a thing! Sir Edmund here will, I am persuaded, lend me his support in dissuading you from your ill-advised intention of attempting to obtain paid employment of a respectable nature, doomed to failure as such an attempt must be!"

"Then," said Elinor, her patience cracking, "I shall just have to attempt to find work which is *not* of a respectable nature, shan't I? And you will have all the satisfaction of being able to say it is exactly what you expected!"

She regretted this little outburst the moment the words were out of her mouth, but had not much time to rue her lack of self-control, since Sir Edmund, his sympathy growing in proportion to her evident distress, had decided it was time he took a hand in bringing this scene to an end.

"No, Mr Spalding," he remarked, "I'm afraid I can't in all conscience join you in wishing Miss Radley not to accept a position! I'm sure your concern for her welfare does you credit, but you will see that you may set your mind at rest when I tell you that, at the very moment when you called, I was doing my best to induce her to accompany me to London."

In the ensuing silence, Elinor gave a small gasp of shock and surprise, while Persephone supplied musical commentary in the form of a dazzling series of voice exercises.

"You, sir? Mr Spalding's naturally protuberant eyes appeared to be on the point of popping right out of his head. "*You*? Well! You amaze me. I must say you amaze me! Elinor, going to London with you?"

"Yes: to undertake the charge of my ward, Miss

52

Persephone Grafton, whom you can hear singing in there," said Sir Edmund frostily, not at all caring for the suggestion of a leer which he fancied he saw begin to creep over the other man's face. "From my point of view, it all falls out most fortunately. I urgently require a companion and chaperon for the child, since my sister Viscountess Yoxford, to whose house in Upper Brook Street I am taking her, is in delicate health. And here is Miss Radley, precisely the lady I would have wished to find for that position, about to seek a situation on her own account! Moreover," he said, rather enjoying himself as he tried to vie with the clergyman in unctuousness, "the fact of our being connected, however distantly, through Lady Emberley makes the arrangement quite particularly suitable for all parties concerned, doesn't it, Cousin Elinor?" he inquired, bending his very blue gaze on Miss Radley.

The expressions of amazement, amusement and relief rapidly chasing one another over her face as she appreciated the adroitness with which he was extricating her from her predicament were, he thought, a joy to behold. In a moment, voice quivering only very slightly, she responded demurely, "Y-yes, Sir Edmund. Thank you: it is all just as you say."

"You are going to *London?*" exclaimed Mr Spalding again, as his mind, not naturally quick, laboured to take in all the implications of what he had heard. "To Lady Yoxford's? To Upper Brook Street? As chaperon to Miss Grafton? But surely that would mean going into Society!"

"You doubt, sir, that my sister has the *entrée* to Society?" inquired Sir Edmund.

His assumption of an air of well-bred hauteur cast Mr Spalding into confusion. "No – no, Sir Edmund, to be sure! I mean yes! I mean, of course not – that is, I don't doubt it! Well, upon my word! But – but take, for example, Almack's!" He turned to Miss Radley as he uttered the name of this most exclusive of all social meeting places in the metropolis, as if producing an irrefutable argument. "Acceptance *there* . . . how will you contrive?"

53

"Without the least difficulty," Sir Edmund answered for her, still with the air of one patiently, but with boredom, elucidating the obvious. "I believe my sister Isabella is acquainted with most of the Lady Patronesses, probably all of them, and in any case, I have only to drop a word in Emily Cowper's ear myself. I am tolerably well acquainted with Lady Cowper through her brother Frederick, you understand," he added, addressing himself to Miss Radley. "I was for a while in the city of Munich, when Fred Lamb was British Minister there."

"W-were you indeed, sir?" breathed Elinor, fascinated as well as amused by the part Sir Edmund had chosen to play.

"But," put in Mr Spalding, almost querulously, "you can't go into Society, Elinor! What would people say? Can it be – I ask myself, can it be – that you have not revealed all to Sir Edmund? That you were proposing to perpetrate a deception – to enter Lady Yoxford's household under false pretences? I am amazed – I say again, I am amazed! I am disappointed in you! I ask myself – I repeat, I ask myself – can this thing be?"

Cast into the greatest confusion herself by these utterances, Elinor could not help glancing hopefully at Sir Edmund, who was proving such an unlooked-for tower of strength, and indeed he was already coming to her aid again.

"You repeat yourself a good deal too much, sir, if I may say so," he told Mr Spalding crisply. "If it is any of your business, which I take leave to doubt, let me assure you that I am entirely in Miss Radley's confidence. The matter to which you refer," he added haughtily, without any idea of what they were discussing, "is not of the smallest consequence. In agreeing to chaperon my ward, Miss Radley is doing me and my sister a very great favour. And now, sir, I am in some haste to complete my business in this town and make arrangements for our journey on to London."

Sir Edmund's manner made it very plain that he meant the clergyman rather than himself to take his leave, and Mr Spalding, mesmerized by that suddenly chilly blue stare, found that he could only open and shut his mouth once or twice, temporarily unable to utter a word. But at last, turning to look at Elinor with a certain new respect, he managed to say, "Well! Upon my word! This is an odd start – but then," he hastened to add, "one can never know, of course, just what is the thing in Society. Although – but no, I will say no more upon that head!"

"Good," interjected Sir Edmund, who was rapidly tiring of Mr Spalding and hoped he would say no more on any other head, either. But the rejected suitor, his powers of speech recovered, proceeded undeterred.

"If you are to be countenanced by Sir Edmund – by Lord and Lady Yoxford – by Lady Cowper . . . Well, my dear Elinor, I venture to believe that you will continue to bear in mind dear Lady Emberley's express wishes concerning our future union! Once your services are no longer required by Miss Grafton, I fancy you will wish to reconsider the advantages of a respectable marrige! Sir Edmund, should I find myself in London, I shall take the liberty of calling in Upper Brook Street – yes, indeed I shall!"

And with this, and another hearty and protracted shake of Sir Edmund's hand, he at last left the room.

Recovering from her stunned silence, Elinor said faintly, "W-well! Was ever anything so *mortifying*?" But the unsteadiness of her voice was mostly due to amusement, and resting her elbows on the desk and laying her head on her clasped hands, she gave way to peals of laughter.

"Or diverting!" said Sir Edmund, at long last able to give rein to his own mirth. When he could speak again for laughing, he inquired, "Good God, can my deplorable old Cousin Sophronia really have intended you to marry that – that ecclesiastical stockfish?"

"Oh, dear me, yes!" Elinor told him, wiping the tears of amusement from her eyes. "You see, she thought it just the way to provide for me, and to that end she left Mr Spalding some money – "

"Which I observe he has no scruples in accepting!"

"No, why should he? It was meant, I own, as a kind of – well, a dowry, and you must admit a generous one, but nobody actually said so. However, I could not like the notion – "

"I should think not!"

"I did try to be grateful. I even wondered, for a little while, whether it would do. Mr Spalding really is an estimable man, you know, and one ought to appreciate him at his true worth, only – only he appreciates it so well himself, that it somehow seems superfluous for a wife or anyone else to do so too. He *could* not believe that it was not merely out of consideration for Lady Emberley I refused to regard the engagement as a settled thing. And though you might not think it, I have *often* tried to convince him of that. Well! I can only say, Sir Edmund, that I am heartily grateful to you for coming to my rescue with that tall tale of yours. You did it quite beautifully."

"Tall tale?" said he. "I hope it will be no such thing, Cousin Elinor."

A flush again stained her cheeks as she stared blankly at him, quite bewildered.

"I see I am going too fast – too fast for you, that is, but your suitor led me, hopefully, to anticipate. May I in all seriousness beg you to consider the idea of coming to London to look after young Persephone? I *was* just going to put the suggestion to you, you know, when the good Mr Spalding insisted on interrupting us."

"W-were you?" said Elinor faintly, feeling as if the ground were not quite steady beneath her feet.

"Indeed I was. I *do* urgently require a lady to chaperon Persephone – and I warn you, it could be an arduous task. As I've discovered, she can be a very headstrong child, and it was thus with some trepidation that I was about to put my request."

Looking at Sir Edmund, Elinor could not believe that he had ever felt trepidation in his life. "But – but this is ridiculous!" she managed to say.

"Why? It is all just as I told Mr Spalding, Cousin Elinor – I have ulterior motives in claiming our relationship, you see. Who could possibly be better than a cousin to help my sister with the problems of Persephone's come-out? Problems like *that*," he added reflectively, as Persephone's voice soared up again, unleashed from all restraint, in a passionately felt lyric of what he fancied was very modern composition.

"Yes," Miss Radley soberly agreed. "Such a very marked talent – how wicked it would be to thwart it! And yet, I do see that it may make life more difficult for her."

"I knew you would. At least you're under no illusions! What's more, the child took to you at once, you can't deny that. So *will* you take her on ?"

"Oh, I should like it of all things!" Elinor could not help exclaiming. The dazzling prospect so incredibly opening out before her of escape from her life at Cheltenham – not into the servitude of a governess's lot, but to a London Season in the lively company of Miss Persephone Grafton – quite took her breath away. In a moment, however, she forced herself to say resolutely, "Only – only it won't answer, sir, truly it won't!" She took a deep breath, and continued, with some difficulty, "Didn't you hear what Mr Spalding was saying? About the impropriety of my applying for a governess's post?"

The visible effort it cost her to bring out these words was not lost on Sir Edmund. Naturally he had heard Mr Spalding's remarks, and had been first mildly intrigued and then, as the clergyman insisted on dwelling on what was plainly a painful subject, and he observed Miss Radley's distress, decidedly indignant on her behalf. He therefore said lightly, "Yes, and I never heard such stuff in my life. The fellow talks fustian, and is very ill-bred too. I do beg, Cousin Elinor, that you won't refine too much upon anything *he* may say!"

But she persisted. "Sir Edmund, surely I must tell you what it was he meant! I do think perhaps – perhaps he might be wrong, even though he is a clergyman, and it was not after all so *very* bad – "

"Of course not!" said Sir Edmund briskly, notwithstanding his total ignorance of the supposedly reprehensible matter under discussion.

"But you might not *wish* to employ me once . . . once . . . "

"I do wish it, if *employ* is the right word, considering the favour you would be doing to my sister and myself." Touched to see Miss Radley turn away to hide the tears that sprung to her eyes, he added, in a rallying tone, "Come, you don't mean to tell me that whatever shocking indiscretion you committed in the schoolroom – "

"Only just out of it!" she said almost inaudibly.

" – makes you unfit to take charge of Persephone, when my very strait-laced Cousin Sophronia considered you a proper companion for herself and a suitable wife for that fellow Spalding?"

"That's it, you see!" she said, grasping at this straw. "Lady Emberley *did* say that – that her giving me a home restored me to respectability. No," she added scrupulously, if with reluctance, "to a *measure* of respectability."

"Evidently she had a turn for fustian too. She was an old dragon when last *I* saw her, as well as clutch-fisted, and I can see she never changed to the day she died," observed Sir Edmund. Lady Emberley, he deduced, had for her own ends browbeaten a young girl into a sense of disproportionate guilt over some youthful folly: this was the interpretation he was most inclined to put on what he had heard. He would have liked to know more, if only to reassure Miss Radley, for his judgment of character was in general sound, and he could not believe that her conscience was really burdened by anything but the mildest of peccadilloes. However, he sensed that the subject was best left alone just now, and moreover, at this moment Persephone burst into the room.

She had apparently exhausted the music to be found in the piano stool, for she inquired, "Miss Radley, I suppose you have not got the music of Haydn's Canzonets, have you? I heard them sung not long ago, and have wanted to try them myself, but I couldn't obtain a copy in Bath."

"No, I'm afraid I haven't one here either," said Elinor, with an effort wrenching her mind away from the amazing vista of freedom before her. "But of course, you may easily obtain them in London."

"Good gracious, so I may!" It was obvious that this had not previously occurred to the single-minded Persephone. "Why, I may buy all the songs I want in London, mayn't I?"

"So long as you don't squander *all* your wealth upon them!" said her guardian gravely.

She now appeared to be feeling in perfect charity with him, for she said only, with a trill of laughter, "Don't be absurd! Oh, I see you are funning me."

"My dear Miss Grafton, how beautifully you sing," Elinor put in. "Forgive me, but I cannot help saying so. How much you must be looking forward to the Opera and all the concerts one may hear in London."

At this, Persephone brightened even further. "Of course, there *will* be concerts there, will there not? More than I could ever hear in Bath! Do you know, I never thought of that before! Why, I don't think I shall mind going to London so much after all!"

"Good," said Sir Edmund. "Then perhaps you'll add your voice to mine — and by the by, *I* had no notion either that you had so fine a singing voice – and help me to persuade Miss Radley, who is in fact our Cousin Elinor, or so she and I have agreed – to come to London and bear you company. You remember that I promised we should find someone who was agreeable to you."

"Oh yes!" cried Miss Grafton readily. "Oh, do say you will come! I should like it so much! You know, perhaps he is not so very bad," she said naively, contemplating her guardian, "for he *did* say I should not have an old cat as chaperon."

"And to my own discomfiture, we have already disco-

vered the evident fact that Cousin Elinor is no such thing,"
said Sir Edmund.

"I am so glad you are to come with us, Miss Radley," said
Persephone blithely. "For you will, won't you?"

"Yes – yes, if you really wish it." Overborne, Elinor
looked from one to the other.

"Then that is all settled," said Sir Edmund, with satisfaction. "It's fortunate that you seem to be fond of music
yourself, cousin! I dare say that once you are in London,
you will know how to provide for whatever Persephone
needs in that line."

"She will require a pianoforte," said Miss Radley.

"I shall require a pianoforte," remarked Persephone at
almost the same instant.

"Excellent!" said Sir Edmund, smiling. "I can see you
will go along famously together."

5

She had been swept off her feet: so much she acknowledged to heself. The sensation, while unusual, was far from disagreeable. Who could have supposed only two days ago, thought the bemused Elinor, retiring to bed in the charming room prepared for her in Upper Brook Street, that she would now be in London, welcomed into the Yoxford household quite as a member of the family?

During the last forty-eight hours, she had had very little leisure to reflect upon the extraordinary change in her fortunes. Such a whirlwind of activity as those two days had been! Sir Edmund had determined to spend a second night at the Plough in Cheltenham, to allow Miss Radley time to make her own preparations for travelling to London, while he took the opportunity of settling the outstanding business relating to his cousin's estate; he had therefore sent John Digby on ahead of the rest of the party, with a letter for the Viscount and Viscountess.

Elinor was relieved to know that this missive gave advance notice of her own arrival in London. Despite all Sir Edmund's assurances that she would be more than welcome at Yoxford House, and Persephone's disarmingly obvious liking for her company, she had quailed a little at the idea of appearing quite out of the blue. Not that she had much time to spare for misgivings, as she and Mrs Howell bustled about the house in Royal Crescent, completing the task of sorting its contents in preparation for the sale of the property. And *she* for one wouldn't be sorry to see the back of the place, Mrs Howell affirmed. "Many's the time Joshua and me would have given our notice, miss, but for the difficulty of finding another place for a couple at our age, and what's more, leaving you to my lady on your own! And where she would have found another respectable pair at the wages she paid us *I* don't know! But there, I won't speak ill of the dead, and to be sure, she did right by us in the end, miss, as I dare say Sir Edmund has told you, and we're to have our own little cottage and be very snug. And I'm as glad as I can be to see you off to London to enjoy yourself, miss. Time and again I've said to Joshua: this is no kind of life for a pretty young lady like Miss Radley, I've said."

"Oh, hush, Mrs Howell!" said Elinor, smiling. "I am not going to London to *enjoy* myself, you know, but to look after Miss Grafton."

"Ah, well, I dare say you'll have as many fine beaux as her," said Mrs Howell cheerfully, rising from her knees on the floor beside the linen cupboard, where she had been counting sheets. "Eh, just hark at her now!" For Persephone had not been at all averse to remaining in Cheltenham another day provided she might have the use of the Royal Crescent pianoforte, and she was now mid-way through a song by Mozart. Its liquid notes poured out from behind the book-room door. "I never in all my days knew a young lady so fond of playing the piano, never! And how *loud* miss does sing, to be sure! Still, she seems a nice young thing, and a very pleasant gentleman Sir Edmund is, too."

Elinor was very ready to agree whole-heartedly with this last proposition, but told herself sternly, as she carefully folded her own modest wardrobe and laid her gowns in tissue, that she had not been swept off her feet in *that* way! And would not be, either. It was one thing to acknowledge that she had taken an instant liking to a man who insisted, with such delicate tact, on the relationship between them, becoming her benefactor while making it seem that *she* was doing *him* the favour. That was a very natural way for her to feel in the circumstances! It would be quite another thing if she were to lose her head over him, just because he had a pleasing face and fine figure, combined with an engaging manner and a sense of humour that exactly chimed with her own. No, my dear girl, thought Elinor, firmly addressing herself, no, you learned your lesson a long time ago, or so I should hope! Not that Sir Edmund, of course, is in any way comparable to . .. but here she gave herself a little shake, and made haste to finish her packing, after which she went down to share with Persephone the light luncheon Mrs Howell had prepared.

Miss Grafton, partaking with relish of cold chicken in aspic jelly and a tart of leeks and cream, volunteered the information that singing always made her hungry. "But I must not sing much more today."

"No?"

"No, because at my age, it does not do to overstrain the voice," said Persephone, with an air of great wisdom. "If one *has* a voice, you understand, one must look after it: train it, and do one's voice exercises every day, of course, but not *force* it. Opera singers, you know, take the smaller parts in general when they first go on the stage."

"I see – but *you* are not going on the stage," said Elinor, with a smile.

"No," agreed Persephone, but with such lack of conviction in her tone that Elinor felt a stirring of alarm. Could the child be nurturing some fantastical ambition to become an opera singer? Elinor had been to the Opera herself during her single visit to London. Long ago as that was, she could not help feeling that Persephone's voice might well challenge comparison with that of many a professional performer. But Sir Edmund and the Yoxfords would hardly look kindly upon theatrical aspirations!

"The thing is," Persephone was continuing, helping herself to more leek tart, "that if I am careful of my voice, it should come to its best when I am a good deal older, perhaps about your age. Oh dear, I ought not to have said that!" she exclaimed, for once looking abashed. "I didn't *mean* to be uncivil, Elinor – I may call you Elinor, mayn't I? And you must call me Persephone."

"You may certainly call me Elinor: I wish you will! And

you were not a bit uncivil, for if I were *not* a good deal older than you, I should hardly make a suitable chaperon."

"No, I suppose not. But I did rather expect that whatever my own feelings, Cousin Edmund or Cousin Isabella would choose somebody *really* old, and *that* you are not, after all!"

"Thank you," said Elinor, gravely.

"And I must own," continued Persephone engagingly, "that when Cousin Edmund said you were to come with us, it made me think better of him directly, even if it *was* unkind in him to make me leave Bath without a chance to say goodbye to my friends"

"But, my dear, surely he would have let you take leave of them if you had but asked him!"

"Oh – oh, well, the thing is that my – that some of my particular friends are not in Bath just now," said Persephone, a little gruffly. Elinor observed that her colour was heightened. "They have gone on a walking tour in Wales, and – oh, and now how are they *ever* to know where I have gone?"

This came out as a little cry of despair, and went straight to Elinor's heart. "You can always write to them," she suggested.

"They don't reside in Bath," said Miss Grafton gloomily. She seemed about to fall into a downcast mood, but at that moment, most fortunately, Mrs Howell entered with her *chef d'oeuvre*, an ice pudding, at which Persephone exclaimed in delight. Her spirits much restored, she told Elinor, as she made inroads upon the pudding, "As I was going to say, you are not at all like a chaperon really, and I feel more as if we should be *sisters*, don't you? I am sure it must be a very comfortable thing to have a sister!"

Elinor, an only child herself, owned that she had often thought the same, and by the time it was established that both she and Persephone had lost their parents young, and had subsequently been brought up by rather elderly ladies, they were firm friends. Not so absorbed in her own affairs that she could not take a lively interest in those of someone

64

she liked, Miss Grafton soon elicited from Elinor the information that after the death of her widower father, a clergyman, when she was twelve years old, she had gone to live with her maiden aunts Jane and Matilda, and when she was eighteen she had spent a Season in London at the house of her eldest and only married aunt. "And did you like it in London?" inquired Persephone. "Did you receive a great many offers of marriage? Do tell me all about it!"

Elinor had some difficulty in complying with this request. She could not truthfully have said that her one London Season had been a great event in her life: her Aunt Elizabeth had felt that she did her duty in having the girl to stay at all, and since she and her lawyer husband did not move in very fashionable circles, she made no great effort to exert herself on her niece's behalf; the parties to which Elinor had gone had been few and rather dull. However, it was certainly no part of Sir Edmund's intentions for her to set Persephone against London. Equally certainly, the child's prospects there were brighter by far than hers had ever been.

"Well, yes, I liked London a good deal," she replied. "And I did receive one offer, but I'm afraid it was not very romantic! He was a widower of over forty, and rather stout, and I could not like him." She did not add that her Aunt Elizabeth had been so much disgusted by her refusal of this eligible *parti* (for the widower had been well-to-do) as to dispatch her straight back to Aunts Jane and Matilda in disgrace. "He meant well, and was kind, but I could not have spent the rest of my life with him."

"I should think not, indeed!" said Persephone sympathetically. "So after you did not marry the fat old widower, what did you do next? Has nothing of an *interesting* nature ever happened to you?"

"Oh, then I became governess to a family in Essex," Elinor said lightly, "and then it chanced that Lady Emberley needed a companion, and that is all there is to tell."

She was ruefully aware that she had skated over mention of the one event in her life which Persephone would have considered interesting, and felt a renewed stab of misgiving. Should she not have insisted on telling Sir Edmund the whole? He would have learned it from the aunts' letters if he had read his way through the family correspondence in that desk of the old lady's, but he had urged her to burn it all, and she had been glad to do so. Well, perhaps she had done wrong in allowing him to overbear her and persuade her to accompany Persephone to London, but at all events, she vowed to herself, now that she *had* been overborne, she would do her very utmost to justify the trust he so generously reposed in her.

Persephone spent much of their journey from Cheltenham the next day busily plying Miss Radley with more questions about London and the Season. Sir Edmund had solved the problem of accommodation in the post-chaise, which was not built to carry three persons inside, by declaring his intention of hiring a saddle horse to ride part of the way, and getting up behind in the dickey if this exercise palled, so that the two ladies were able to talk privately. Several times, when they stopped to change horses at the posting-houses along their way, Sir Edmund noted that his ward was now displaying the natural excitement and anticipation to be expected of a young lady on her way to the capital for her first Season, and was very well satisfied. She had plainly struck up an excellent understanding with Miss Radley, and he congratulated himself yet again on the good fortune which had led him to the house in Royal Cresent.

Indeed, it was not until Lord Yoxford's chaise drew near London that the animated conversation between Elinor and Persephone died away. Both, for different reasons, were feeling somewhat apprehensive as the moment of arrival actually approached. Persephone had uncomfortable memories of the tremendous scold Cousin Isabella had given her on their last encounter; Elinor could not but wonder whether Lady Yoxford would really be as pleased to

66

receive her as Sir Edmund thought. Still, the meeting must be faced.

In the event, Lady Yoxford was discovered reclining on her sofa in the Grey Saloon with an expression of acute apprehension on her own pretty countenance, and clutching a vinaigrette in one hand as if her life depended on it. Quickly realizing, however, that nothing to cause her faintness or severe palpitations was likely to occur in the immediate future, she very soon set down this article. Her imagination, refining upon the Unfortunate Business which sprang to her mind whenever she thought of her young cousin, had led her to forget that even at sixteen, Persephone had been able to behave very prettily if and when she chose. She chose to do so now, and consequently found Lady Yoxford not at all like the hysterically outraged figure of her own memories.

As for Elinor Radley, a very little conversation with her sufficed to show Isabella Yoxford that her brother had not been mistaken in informing her that he had found the very person to take charge of Persephone. Miss Radley's quiet elegance and air of good breeding were all that Lady Yoxford could have wished for, and like Persephone (and indeed Sir Edmund) she warmed instantly to the humour that gleamed now and then in her new cousin Elinor's eyes and smile.

"Oh, I am so glad that you have come to us!" exclaimed Isabella impulsively, very much like Persephone herself. "And I must own that Edmund has been as good as his word. For he promised me, you know, that as my health is not strong, he would find me someone to help with Persephone's come-out – and while I suppose it would be wrong of me to say it was *fortunate* for Cousin Sophronia to die just when she did, because it would be unfeeling to wish one's relative dead, still, I cannot help but think that since she was bound to die at some time, it was remarkably obliging of her to do so now, and make it possible for you to come here. In fact, I call it *providential*! And certainly not what Cousin Sophronia would have liked, for she never obliged anybody on purpose."

Elinor could not help smiling a little at this view of the workings of Providence, but she secretly agreed with her hostess's assessment of Sophronia Emberley's character. There could be little doubt that, given any choice in the matter, Lady Emberley would have died as she had lived, to disoblige her family. However, Elinor was spared the necessity of thinking of a suitable response to Isabella by the irruption into the saloon of the younger members of the family, shepherded by Miss Merriwether.

Elinor's own childhood in her father's country rectory had been a lonely one, and during her brief sojourn as governess at Royden Manor the little girls who were her charges had been kept strictly apart from the rest of their family, being produced in company only for half an hour after dinner, in their best frocks and on their best behaviour. It amazed her to find that, in this decidedly imposing house, Edward, the twins and little Maria were not only tolerated in the drawing room, but actually encouraged to romp and play there. Lord Yoxford and Sir Edmund even broke off their own conversation to swing Thomas and James up in the air, a performance which elicited shouts of glee from the little boys, and Isabella, quite forgetting to sustain a modishly languid air, showed an animated maternal interest in the storybook from which Edward was eager to read aloud to her.

Before long, the twins were engaged in a reasonably decorous game of hide-and-seek. Miss Radley (who suspected, correctly, that a much rowdier version was commonly played in the nursery) won their hearts by purposely failing to tell them apart. In point of fact it was not too difficult to do so, since although they were identical in feature, Thomas's face was a little thinner than his twin's and his figure not quite so chubby, but plainly it was a great object with the little boys to confuse strangers, and Elinor gratified them by pretending to be entirely at a loss when one or the other popped out from behind a curtain or sofa, demanding, "Thomas or James?" and uttering crows of mirth when she guessed wrong.

Miss Merriwether, reminding Persephone of the pretty tunes she had been used to play for the twins two years ago, wondered if she would give them the same treat now? Persephone was very willing to go to the pianoforte standing in one corner of the saloon and lift its lid, but it soon became apparent that Thomas and James had now joined their brother Edward in professing utter scorn for such juvenile things as nursery rhymes. Little Maria, however, was very happy to be taken on her cousin's lap and sung to, contributing her own mite to the performance by banging her plump fists upon the keyboard in a manner which Persephone tolerated with surprising good humour.

The little boys were all a good deal more interested in the contents of the box Elinor had brought with her. This item had come to light in the attic of the Royal Crescent house, and must have stood there for more years than Mrs Howell and Elinor liked to think. Inside it they had found a collection of curiosities: sea-shells, a delicately carved fan, some ostrich feathers and a blown ostrich egg, a miniature cabinet containing long-dead butterflies, a chunk of quartz showing amethyst gleams, an old and ornately pictured pack of playing cards, a kaleidoscope. It was hard to connect such intriguing frivolities with Lady Emberley: could she ever, Elinor wondered, really have been a child and played with those cards or that kaleidoscope? Presumably it was so, and her ingrained reluctance to dispose of any of her possessions had led her to keep the things hidden away in the attic all this time. It had immediately occurred to Elinor that the contents of the box were just what would have delighted her as a child, and she thought perhaps the younger members of the Yoxford family might like to rummage in such a treasure chest too.

She proved to have been right. Edward, fascinated, pulled out all the drawers of the little cabinet of butterflies one by one; Maria took possession of the lump of quartz and hefted it in one small hand, looking as if she would like to hurl it somewhere but could not quite decide where; and the twins, unable to choose between all these splendid things, scrambled for one treasure after another. Isabella, exclaiming at the pretty shells and the ostrich feathers as happily as any of her children, cried,"How clever of you, Cousin Elinor! And do you really mean to say that old Cousin Sophronia kept it in her attic for years and years? Quite forgotten, I suppose!" At the same time, she removed the gleaming stone from Maria, and had just forestalled the child's threatened howl of vexation by substituting a harmlessly soft but exotically coloured shot silk scarf, when her eldest son entered the room.

Sir Edmund had withdrawn again with his brother-in-law to one of the large bay windows overlooking the street, and resumed his conversation with him. "Yes, I fancy I shall have to go up to Westmorland in the near future, to see for myself how things stand there. Canning will give me leave of absence, and so – " But here he broke off to greet the newcomer. "Hallo, Charley! Down for the vacation? It's good to see you."

"Speak for yourself, Edmund," remarked Lord Yoxford, visibly blenching as he surveyed his heir. "Good God, Charley, what the devil is *that* you're wearing?"

As it happened, the Honourable Charles Hargrave was wearing quite a number of striking garments, whose high fashion served mainly to accentuate his youth, although he optimistically fancied they made him look quite the man about town. His blue pantaloons fitted very tightly and were ornamented with much braiding, while his coat, of a deeper shade of blue bordering on violet, boasted rolled lapels and a collar standing up extremely high behind, as well as gigot sleeves which bade fair to rival in width those of his mama's very fashionable gown. However, it was his fancy marcella waistcoat, composed of broad stripes of alternating crimson and salmon pink, which immediately

70

caught the eye, and it was to this item that his father more specifically referred. Lord Yoxford was a tolerant man, but as one whose own sartorial tastes had been much influenced in his younger days by the quiet elegance of that famous arbiter of fashion George Bryan Brummell, he could not but deplore the decline in popularity of the Beau's restrained style of dressing and the current tendency of today's young fops (his son included) to sport waistcoats of violent and often contrasting hues.

"It's a waistcoat, ain't it?" replied Charley defensively, flushing slightly. "Very latest thing – bang up to the echo, sir, I can tell you!" he assured his uncle, lest Sir Edmund, having been out of the country, should require information as to the current mode.

"Very fine indeed, Charley," said Sir Edmund, perfectly straightfaced. "Take no notice of your father; it *is* good to see you. I had forgotten that you'd be down from Cambridge this month."

Until Charley's arrival the previous day, the circumstance had slipped Isabella's mind too. Had it not done so, it would have figured high among her objections to receiving Persephone into her household. She entertained the liveliest fear that her eldest son, who had recently become very vulnerable to feminine charms, might fall an instant victim to Persephone's undeniable beauty. The thought caused her to get up off the floor, where she had been playing in the most animated manner with her younger children, and subside on her sofa again, murmuring, "Pray forgive me if I lie down for a moment, Cousin Elinor, for my health is *not* strong!"

She closed her eyes, but opened them again almost directly, glancing anxiously from susceptible young man to lovely young woman. However, her face quickly cleared when, after being introduced to Miss Radley and murmuring something civil, her son turned to his cousin and said only, "Let you loose from Bath, have they, young Persephone?" It was obvious that the passage of two years, though it had wrought considerable changes in Miss Grafton, left her still a child in Charley's eyes, to be regarded as just another member of his large family, since he added with kind condescension, "Tell you what – I'm taking these brats to Exeter "Change tomorrow, to see the lions and tigers." For Charley, notwithstanding the affectations of fashion, was a good brother to the younger boys. "You can come too, if you like."

But Persephone declined this treat, explaining that her very first errand in London must be to buy a pianoforte.

"A pianoforte?" protested Lady Yoxford. "Why, you may play this one, my dear!" She indicated the piano at which Persephone had been picking out nursery rhymes for little Maria.

"Yes, but not *all* the time; I should disturb you," said Persephone, and then rather spoiled the effect of her thoughtfulness by trying out the instrument again, and pronouncing, "Besides, I need one of better quality than either this or the schoolroom piano, and Cousin Edmund says *that* is one thing he will not grudge me!"

"I shan't grudge you anything in the nature of a reasonable request, I hope," said Sir Edmund mildly. "And this, my dear Bella, is a very reasonable request, as I think you'll agree when you have heard Persephone play and sing."

"Very likely," said Lady Yoxford, vaguely; she was not herself musical. "Well, of course she shall have a pianoforte, then – it can stand in the Yellow Parlour; yes, that would be the very place! But you will have a great many more purchases to make too, my dear: gowns, and hats, and – oh, all manner of things! So you will hardly be playing music *all the time*!" Persephone looked as if she might contradict this, but thought better of it as Isabella, her kind heart warming to the beautiful and unexpectedly pretty-behaved girl before her, and beginning to enjoy the prospect of bringing her out, went on, "There will be routs, you know, and balls and masquerades and assemblies! Breakfasts, and all sorts of evening parties! So we must lose no time in getting you a wardrobe. George, *we* should hold a ball for Persephone,

72

don't you think? Yes, I am persuaded we should! I shall not mind the exertion a bit, not now I have Cousin Elinor to help me. How delightful it will all be!"

6

How delightful indeed, thought Elinor, waking in London that first morning to see a dappling of spring sunshine on the prettily patterned bedroom wallpaper; to hear the voices of knife-grinder and seller of cresses in the alley down the side of the house, offering their services and touting their wares to the staff below stairs; to catch the occasional sound of horses' hooves ringing out in the clear morning air as a carriage drove down Upper Brook Street. In Persephone's place, she thought, she could have wished for nothing better in the world. If it came to that, she herself had very little left to wish for!

She was slightly disconcerted, however, when her charge joined her in the sunny breakfast parlour and remarked ingenuously that it was not so bad here after all. "At any rate," announced Miss Grafton, "I am determined to make the best of it, and one Season is not such a *very* long time!"

What, Miss Radley wondered, did Persephone suppose lay beyond that first Season? She could only conclude that the child's mind was still running on the unknown suitor who, she surmised, had been left behind in Bath – or no, not in Bath: on a walking tour in Wales! For Elinor had not for an instant been led astray by the use of the plural when Persephone spoke of her absent friends. *A walking tour in Wales*, and in changeable spring weather too, was hardly a diversion commonly undertaken by young ladies, or even by an entire family. If there were more than one friend in question, no doubt Persephone's swain was accompanied by some other young man.

Well, if her fancy were engaged, it was very natural that

74

she should regret the suitor from Bath for a while, but Elinor trusted that her thoughts would soon be given a new direction. Her guardian might hope that the prospect of parties and new gowns would serve that purpose, but for her own part, Elinor was tolerably sure that music was the best way to distract Persephone's mind. So she drank her tea, ate her bread and butter, and proposed that they go and put on their pelisses, to be ready for Sir Edmund whenever he arrived in Upper Brook Street to escort them in search of the very necessary pianoforte, as he had promised to do.

And really, thought Elinor some three weeks later, so much had happened in that space of time that the mind of the most lovelorn *ought* to have been distracted! The piano was duly procured. Sir Edmund, while willing and able to guide the ladies around town, was hardly required for any other purpose, since it transpired that Persephone herself was fully conversant with the names of the best emporiums to visit, and the makes and qualities of all the instruments they had to offer. Elinor wondered where she got her knowledge. It took her a long time to make her choice, and by the time she had tried almost every pianoforte in the establishment where her fancy finally came to rest, most of the staff of the place and quite a number of prospective customers had gathered round to listen to her. "Why, we are having quite a concert!" she exclaimed gaily, looking up and becoming aware of her audience for the first time. "Cousin Edmund, my mind is made up: I will take this one."

The handsome instrument she had chosen, made by the firm of Clementi, Collard and Collard, was delivered to Upper Brook Street that same day and installed in the Yellow Parlour, a pleasant apartment which was to be given over entirely to Persephone and Miss Radley as music room and private sitting room. She had followed up this purchase by the acquisition of a great deal of sheet music and several books of songs, lingering with greedy pleasure over the wealth of such material on offer, and eagerly scanning the bills posted up in the shop which advertised the forthcoming

75

attractions of various Concerts and Musical Recitals.

A music master was also quickly found. The Yoxfords gave a small dinner party a couple of days after Persephone's arrival in London – "Just the Barleighs and Mellises and the Derwents who are all very dear friends of mine," Isabella explained. Persephone did not look as if she thought the prospect of meeting these people was particularly enticing, but brightened a little when told that Miss Kitty Derwent, who would be with her parents, was very musical. And Miss Kitty, called upon to entertain the company after dinner, could certainly play prettily, although when Persephone duly took her place at the piano and began to execute a Haydn sonata, her performance was so very superior in every way that Elinor wondered, a little uneasily, how Kitty and her mother would like it.

But Kitty, a friendly soul, was open in her admiration, and exclaimed, "Oh, how beautiful! I only wish *I* could play like that – but then, one must practise for so many hours, and after a while that becomes such a bore, doesn't it?"

Persephone looked at the other girl with as much wonder as if she had been a freak on show at a fairground, but to Elinor's relief said only that she always liked to play. Elinor herself hastened to ask the name of Miss Derwent's music master. He was, it seemed, most particular in the pupils he would agree to take, but Mrs Derwent (graciously) had no doubt that once he had heard dear Miss Grafton, he would not demur at adding her to their number.

Such indeed was the case: the rather pernickety elderly musician, who unenthusiastically presented himself in Upper Brook Street to hear yet another well-born young woman show off her mediocre accomplishments, came away frankly astonished by his good fortune, and more than ready, in addition, to furnish Lady Yoxford with the name of an acquaintance of his who gave voice lessons. This acquaintance, an Italian of excitable disposition who had been a notable singer himself in his prime, was heard by Beale the butler muttering in his native tongue as he left the

Yellow Parlour after his second visit to Miss Grafton. Stopping short as he reached the front door, he appeared, though still speaking Italian, to be expecting some comment from the butler.

"I beg your pardon, sir?" inquired Beale.

"A thousand pities – I say, a thousand pities, *no?*" translated Signor Pascali, apparently addressing himself rather than Beale, after all. "Yes, a thousand pities! *Che voce!* With such a voice, to be born to rank! *É un disastro!*" And with this he hurried out, falling into indistinct but plainly ferocious Italian once again.

Alfred, the new footman, goggling after him, so far forgot himself as to ask, "What maggot 'ad 'e got in 'is 'ead, then, Mr Beale? Lor'! Was it Miss Grafton 'e meant?"

"Foreigners, as is well known, are apt to be Peculiar in their conduct," pronounced Beale austerely. "But that, young Alfred, is no reason for *you* to overstep the line and pass remarks about the Family!"

"No, Mr Beale," agreed Alfred, meekly accepting rebuke.

Persephone seemed very well pleased with both her musical mentors, so *that*, Elinor considered, was all very comfortably settled. She had been a little afraid at first that her charge might become mulish when required to tear herself from the piano to spend time in the choosing and fitting of new gowns, but luckily Persephone was not quite so single-minded as to despise pretty things. And no girl could have failed to be enchanted by the lavish display of gauzes, muslins, cambrics, silks and organdies and aerophanes laid before her. Mademoiselle Hortense, the dressmaker patronized by Lady Yoxford, was delighted by the prospect of dressing Miss Grafton, who, she saw at a glance, would do the greatest credit to her own skill in cutting and the industry of her busy seamstresses' fingers. Persephone and Elinor spent many a happy hour poring over fashion plates with Lady Yoxford and the dressmaker, choosing the patterns and fabrics for morning and evening gowns, carriage dresses, walking dresses, pelisses, reding-otes. Miss Downing of New Bond Street, to whose millinery establishment Isabella directed her cousins, was enthusiastic too: the higher-crowned hats and broader-brimmed bonnets now coming into the mode would set off Miss Grafton's delicately rosy cheeks and soft dark curls to perfection. And then there were visits to warehouses which seemed to both Elinor and Persephone a riot of colour and luxury, and where they purchased ribbons, laces and trimmings, gloves and handkerchiefs, stockings, tuckers, fichus, reticules and fans – there was apparently no end to the things a young lady of fashion and fortune needed in her first Season!

Without knowing just how it had come about, Elinor too found herself the possessor of a number of new garments. Her objections had been overborne when she protested that she must, *indeed* she must pay for them herself, out of what seemed to her the amazingly lavish sum upon which Sir Edmund had insisted as her salary. She fancied that his sister must share some of his talent for diplomacy, since without actually saying so, Isabella conveyed the general impression that it was a mere matter of course for Elinor to be provided with a new wardrobe, implying that Sir Edmund would find it tiresome if she mentioned the matter to him, and moreover that it would be quite improper for her to go about town in the outmoded dresses she had brought from Cheltenham.

There was a good deal of truth in this: she did need new gowns, and could not disgrace her cousins by wearing dowdy old-fashioned ones in the kind of circles where they moved. Though more than a little bewildered to find herself the owner of so much finery, she came to the sensible conclusion that there was nothing she could do but accept it with a good grace, and enjoy the wearing of it.

She had been quite surprised to learn that, in early April, the Season was not yet in full swing, since it seemed to her that she and Persephone had attended a staggering number of parties during their first two weeks in London. They had already crossed the sacred threshold of Almack's, that decorous but most exclusive club, to whose balls admission could be obtained only by vouchers from one of the Lady Patronesses. But as Sir Edmund had promised, there had been no difficulty here. Isabella Yoxford's cousins were sure of admission, and Emily Cowper herself, calling in Upper Brook Street, professed to be charmed by Sir Edmund's ward.

Once again, Elinor felt a little nervous when Lady Cowper asked if Persephone would not play something, saying she had heard from Sir Edmund of his young cousin's musical gifts. But Persephone's conduct was admirable. She executed a short piece on the instrument in the Grey Saloon beautifully but not showily, and accepted the visitor's praise with composure (if not with the blushing protests that some might have thought becoming in so young a girl). Lady Cowper only wished her own Minny could play the pianoforte half so well! She happily sponsored Persephone and her companion on their first visit to Almack's, where Miss Grafton wore a very pretty gown of white organdy with an overdress of pink gauze embroidered with knots and flowers, while Elinor could scarcely believe her own elegance in an evening dress of apple-green silk trimmed with velvet ribbons, its full sleeves stiffened with book-muslin. With an impish thrill of excitement, she allowed a quite wickedly improper thought to cross her mind: *If only Samuel Spalding could see me now*! Then she sternly put such notions from her mind. She was here only to take care of Persephone – though it was certainly gratifying to feel she looked so little like a chaperon that several gentlemen had asked her to dance. Of course she had refused them all, since chaperons did not dance, but all the same it was very pleasant! Her own private regret was that Sir Edmund was not present: he had gone up to Westmorland a few days after their arrival in London, and so did not make up one of the party. But of course, it was for just such reasons that *she*

79

had been engaged, and it would be ridiculous to repine at it!

She knew that she did fulfil a useful purpose, for it was very soon apparent that, as the Miss Maddens had foreseen, Persephone's beauty allied to her fortune had all the attractive powers of a magnet on the young gentlemen who came thronging round her. But it might have surprised the sisters to see that Persephone, who to their certain knowledge had already dabbled extensively in the game of breaking hearts, seemed indifferent to the members of her little court. Elinor thought that, while pleasant in her manner to them all, she favoured none above the rest: not even young Viscount Conington, heir to the wealthy Earl of Wintringham and a great catch on the Marriage Mart, who had quickly become most particular in his attentions. One of Persephone's charms was that, though she could not help being aware of her own looks and their devastating effect on susceptible young men, she seemed to set little store by them herself, although she did display what could be justified as a very proper pride in her musical talents. This, of course, served to attach her suitors further, especially those like Conington who were so eligible as to be generally pursued rather than pursuing.

Any alarm still lingering in Lady Yoxford's breast concerning her young cousin's behaviour in London was thus soon stilled; since that Unfortunate Business of the tutor, she thought, Persephone had learnt conduct. Plainly she no longer thought it *good fun* to break hearts. Elinor fancied that the energy she might, at sixteen, have put into that occupation now went into her music instead.

"I own myself very pleasantly surprised in Persephone," Isabella confided to Miss Radley. "I believe she will make a very good match! To own the truth, Elinor, I'd as lief not have her for *my* daughter-in-law, because I don't think she would make Charley comfortable, and besides his being still very young, he has no need to marry a fortune, although-
. . . where was I? Oh yes – I *was* a little afraid she might

80

throw out lures for Charley, but I don't think he feels for her in that way, do you?"

"Not in the least," Elinor was very ready to agree, since it was obvious that young Mr Hargrave and his cousin were still upon the cheerful terms of childhood. "I think they regard one another quite as brother and sister. And when Charley can be induced to attend an assembly or ball with us, I have noticed that he will make himself useful to Persephone in a kind but *not* an amorous way. Taking her into supper, or dancing with her when she doesn't wish to show favour to some other young man, I mean. It is an admirable arrangement: sensible of her, and very good-natured of him."

"Yes. I don't believe she feels any partiality for anyone as yet – though of course, the Wintringham connection would be most eligible, and one cannot but be gratified by Conington's attentions to her. Not that there is the least necessity for Persephone to be rushing into an engagement at the beginning of her first Season. Especially now I have you to take all the troublesome part of her come-out off my hands!" added Isabella, with engagingly frank self-interest. "Still, it would be a very good marriage. You know, for the first time I begin to understand how mothers of growing daughters must feel, which is something I have never known in just that way before, on acccount of all the boys coming before Maria."

And resting her cheek on her hand in a pretty pose, she fell to musing, well in advance, upon those scions of the aristocracy now bowling their hoops in the Park or throwing tantrums in the nursery, who might one day make eligible husbands for her treasured only daughter.

"I dare say," she observed idly after a while, "that I should know more about little girls if only Catherine's baby had lived, because she would be ten by now, and of course I should have seen a great deal of *her*."

"Catherine?" asked Elinor, quite at sea.

"Edmund's wife, my dear – didn't you know he had been

81

married once?"

"No, indeed."

"Poor Catherine! She was quite lovely, and died in childbed of a baby girl who died too."

"Oh, I am so sorry," exclaimed Elinor, with ready sympathy. "How sad for you all!"

"Yes, for Catherine was the sweetest creature, just like a sister to me, and it's my belief that Edmund has never truly recovered from her loss. He has not shown the least sign of wishing to marry again, as you might think he would, knowing that the baronetcy must come to him some day, and unless he has a son, of course, the line dies out with him. However, he does not seem to care for that, for I have never, in all this time, seen him pay serious attentions to any lady of the first respectability, although naturally he has had – well, *intimate* friends of the female sex!"

"Naturally," echoed Elinor, surprising herself in a rather shocking sense of envy of those intimate friends, if by that term the delicately spoken Isabella meant what Elinor thought she did. Really, this will never do, she told herself, I may not *be* a lady of the first respectability, but I ought at least to make a push to *behave* like one!

"But there!" said Isabella, recalling her thoughts to the present. "I should dearly have liked to have a niece, but it is Persephone I must be thinking of now, and I will say this: I shall be very well pleased if, in the end, she does make a match of it with Conington."

"He is certainly a most agreeable young man," Elinor agreed. "But to be honest, I do *not* think she likes him above the rest."

"Perhaps it is just that she does not seem to?" suggested Lady Yoxford optimistically. "Which is a very good thing, for nothing gives a gentleman such a disgust of a girl as for her to be seen dangling after him. Yes, I have hopes that something may come of it."

Indeed, all things considered, the advent of Persephone had turned out much better than Lady Yoxford had

82

expected, and if there were anything at all disquieting in Miss Grafton's lack of interest in the gentlemen who surrounded her, it troubled no one but Elinor. *She* did wonder uneasily, from time to time, if the memory of the young man who had gone walking in Wales were really dying the natural death she had anticipated and hoped for.

And her doubts were strengthened when Charley brought a Cambridge friend of his to Yoxford House. Lord Conington was already there in the Grey Saloon, calling upon the ladies of the family. Elinor was coming to like him a great deal; he was a tall, well set up young man with easy and engaging manners, and if he could win Persephone's heart she felt, with Isabella, that he would make her an excellent husband. He was talking to her now in one of the window embrasures, while Mr Hargrave introduced his friend to his mother and Miss Radley. The friend's surname was Smith, but his parents had plainly thought to compensate their son for its commonplace nature by christening him Zachary. "Call him Zack – everybody does so!" Charley counselled his mother. "Said he wanted to come here. Don't know why."

Mr Smith seemed so painfully shy as to be incapable of speaking for himself, apart from muttering a confused but civil greeting to Lady Yoxford, but his reason for wishing to come to Upper Brook Street was plain for anyone to see. Elinor recollected meeting him at a rout two nights before. He had been conspicuous there both for his inarticulacy and his negligently romantic attire, had spent most of the evening staring spellbound at Miss Grafton and seemed ready to resume this occupation now. Elinor charitably beckoned Persephone over to meet Mr Smith, but as he was still unable to bring out a word, Conington was soon able to reclaim her attention without incivility.

"Zack's a poet," offered Charley. Elinor supposed that accounted for the young man's careless dress and the drooping lock of hair over his brow. It was to be hoped that he had more facility of expression on paper than in person!

"Mind, I don't understand a word of his stuff myself – but Ellingham does: he's up at Trinity with us and as clever as can be, and *he* says it's not a patch on Byron's verses!"

Goaded into speech at last by this slighting comparison with the late, famous poet, Mr Smith glowered at his friend and said loftily, though with a pronounced stammer, that he did not *as yet* aspire to genius of that high order. Having found his tongue, and discovering that Miss Radley was both friendly and unalarming, he allowed her to draw him into conversation, and disclosed that he was engaged upon a major work on a very new subject, which would be quite out of the common way.

"It's – it's an Ode on the W-wonders of Steam," he confided, and went on to impart to Elinor a number of interesting facts concerning such modern marvels as Trevithick's steam engines, and the very recently opened Stockton and Darlington mineral railway, engineered by Mr George Stephenson, which Mr Smith fancied had never yet featured in literature. Such was his enthusiasm for his subject matter that Miss Radley ventured to wonder whether he might not do well to direct it towards the Wonders of Steam themselves, rather than celebrating them in verse (for the few lines of his poem which he recited to her were not especially felicitous). But it appeared that although such mechanisms did interest him a great deal, steam power was not the kind of thing one could study at Cambridge. "H-however, m-my Ode will show the world a thing or t-two, Miss Radley!" said the poet earnestly. "B-believe me, it w-will astonish you!"

"Never fear, old chap, we'll believe you." Charley assured him, not very kindly. He could not have looked very closely at his friend earlier that day, for he now scrutinized Mr Smith's neckcloth and said, with some irritation, "Dash it all, Zack, you ask me to make you known to my people, and you ain't even wearing a proper cravat!"

Mr Smith, who favoured a loosely knotted neckerchief

instead, retorted with spirit, "W-wouldn't be seen d-dead in a confection like that th-thing you're wearing, Charley! W-what is it?"

"Variation of my own on the Mathematical Tie," said Charley grandly. "I'll teach it to you, if you like. Mind, I don't guarantee you could ever master the trick of it."

"I've g-got b-better things to do," returned the poet.

"Of course he has!" said Persephone, taking up the cudgels on Mr Smith's behalf, to his intense gratification. "As if anyone in his senses would *want* to prop his chin on a great starched edifice like that, Charley! Or wear such a waistcoat either!" she added, gratuitously.

The waistcoat Mr Hargrave was sporting was the gem of his extensive collection, being made of black velvet with little stars sewn all over it, and he was excessively proud of it. He therefore replied, in kind, "Well, and *I* never saw anything half as ridiculous as those sleeves you have on!"

They were certainly striking: made of fine muslin and extremely full from shoulder to wrist, where they were gathered in and tied. "Let me tell you," Persephone informed her cousin, "that they are the very latest thing! What was it Mademoiselle Hortense said the style is called?" she appealed to Elinor. "Oh, I remember – the Imbecile Sleeve."

At this Charley laughed immoderately, and said, "Imbecile, eh? That's a good 'un, ain't it, Zack?"

However, Mr Smith was not disposed to agree with him, and nor was Lord Conington, who put an end to this juvenile altercation by telling Persephone that on her at least they looked charmingly. She smiled very kindly at his lordship, and Mr Smith, jealousy overcoming his awed shyness of her, plucked up courage to say that he had several lyrics, besides his work on Steam, which he would like, with Miss Grafton's permission, to dedicate to her. "One of them I b-began to compose only t-two days ago," he offered, blushing slightly. "It isn't quite f-finished yet, b-but I shall address *you* in it, M-Miss Grafton! It opens: *As fair*

85

D-Diana, b-breaking through the c-clouds . . . "

"My cousin's name ain't Diana," objected Mr Hargrave.

"Mr Smith means the moon, and I shall be *happy* for him to dedicate it to me," said Persephone warmly.

The poet, overcome with delight, plunged on somewhat incoherently into an account of a passage from the Ode in which he also wished, so far as anyone could make out, to address Miss Grafton as *Presiding Goddess of that mighty power, Whose amiable beaming eyes have shone, Upon the wonders of th'hydraulic wheels*, whereupon Charley, listening with growing incredulity, begged him not to make more of a fool of himself than he could help.

"Time you were off, anyway!" he added, glancing at the clock.

It was true that Mr Smith had now overstepped the half-hour which was the correct length of time to be spent on a formal call, but as formality was not a feature of the household in Upper Brook Street, and Lord Conington, who had arrived before him, showed no sign of being about to take *his* leave or even of feeling that it was expected of him, this was rather hard on the poet. However, Charley's reminder evidently cut off his conversational powers as effectively as if it had been a valve in one of his steam engines, and he stammeringly made his farewells to Lady Yoxford and Elinor. He then turned to Persephone, and uttered, in one last burst of painful eloquence, "W-when f-first I saw you, M-Miss Grafton, I th-thought of . . . of *that f-fair field of Enna, where Proserpin g-gathering f-flowers, herself a f-fairer flower* . . . b-but I must go!"

"I should just about think so, too!" said the bewildered Charley, as his friend left the room without deigning to spare him a glance. "Told you his poetry was sad stuff! Did you ever hear such fustian?"

Surprisingly, Persephone rounded on her cousin quite fiercely. "*I* think it was a very pretty compliment!"

"I fancy that was not Mr Smith's own verse, but was written by the poet Milton," remarked Elinor.

"Yes, and what's more, it was very well thought of, because Proserpina *is* my name," Persephone added.

Mr Hargrave sighed. "No, it ain't! Females! Don't you even know your own name? First there's Zack calling you Diana, now you say you're called P – Proser – what the deuce was it?"

"Proserpina," put in Lord Conington, amused. "The Latin version of the Greek name Persephone – am I right, Miss Grafton? To the ancients, the goddess of the underworld."

"Oh, well, the *ancients*!" said Mr Hargrave, with the profound scorn of one who, while supposed to be devoting himself to the study of those worthies at the university, would never, as the son of a viscount and thus eligible to be termed a Nobleman while at Cambridge, be called upon to take the examination which conferred a degree, but would gain that distinction regardless of merit. Not for him the spirit of emulation which had led Lord Palmerston in his youth to petition (unsuccessfully) that he should be subject to the Tripos examinations, though Elinor suspected that Lord Conington, a young man of parts, might well have shared Palmerston's sentiments.

"Yes, that's it," said Persephone, with a warmer smile than she usually bestowed upon Conington. "And it is not really a very *cheerful* name, is it? But I can't help that!"

"I dare say the recipient of a given name is never quite satisfied with it," said Elinor, steering the conversation into less poetic channels, and deploring her own commonplace name which, she said, she had always been used to wish were romantically spelt *Elena*, in the Italian fashion. Lord Conington contributed some humorous remarks on the trials of bearing a family name which was passed on from generation to generation, he himself being burdened with the name of Hadstock, like his father and grandfather before him. "It has always suggested fish to my mind; I must be thinking of haddock, or stockfish, or both! And I suppose any firstborn son of mine will be saddled with it too, since it

87

takes determination to break with such a tradition."

"But surely *you* have determination, Lord Conington?" asked Elinor absently, with a sudden concerned glance at Persephone, whose cheerfulness all seemed to have melted away. She had gone back to the window and was looking out, her back turned to them, with an uncharacteristic droop to her shoulders.

"Yes, I believe I have," he said seriously, following the direction of her gaze. "At least, I do not lack steadfastness of purpose, Miss Radley."

Later, as Elinor retired with Persephone to dress for dinner, she ventured to ask gently, "My dear, are you feeling quite well? You have been so very quiet since Mr Smith and Lord Conington called. I wondered if something was troubling you?"

"Oh, it's nothing," Persephone said, almost crossly. And then, suddenly, her lip quivered and she burst out, "It – it was only when Mr Smith said *that*! About *Proserpin gathering flowers*, I mean. I – I remembered how R – how a friend of mine said the same thing, and explained to me what it was about, so that is how I knew. That – that's all," she finished bravely. And, Elinor felt sure, quite untruly. For if she were not still brooding over the loss of her Bath admirer, then why should such a little thing as the repetition of a pretty compliment have brought the tears to Persephone's lovely eyes?

7

"So I fancy," said Elinor, "that this *friend* has a name beginning with the letter R."

Calling for the first time at Yoxford House on his return from Westmorland, Sir Edmund had found her alone in the drawing room while Signor Pascali gave Persephone her singing lesson, and sat down beside her, asking, "Well, and how do you go on in London?"

Elinor had determined not to burden Sir Edmund with too many of her own misgivings over Persephone's failure to respond as her family would have wished to the pleasures of London life; after all, had she not been engaged specifically to relieve the minds of Persephone's relations of undue concern? None the less, she found herself confiding to him her suspicion that Miss Grafton still believed she had left her heart in Bath (or perambulating about the mountainous scenery of Wales).

"Of course, the mere initial tells one nothing," said Sir Edmund. "It could be Richard, Robert – er, Reuben . . . "

"Roderick, Roland, Rudolph . . . "

"Yes, well, there must be scores of names!"

"Very true, but it does tell one she is still thinking of him, and one might have expected her to have forgotten him by now."

"I dare say she doesn't wish to appear fickle in her own eyes," said Sir Edmund, smiling. "Allow her a little self-respect! No doubt the young man in question has quite forgotten *her* by now, and in time she will let him become a mere romantic memory."

"You think I am making too much of it? I do hope so! In a way, I should be easier in my mind if I thought this man were so entirely ineligible it must strike Persephone herself before long that the connection would not do – but if he quoted Milton in her praise, he must at least be a man of some education," said Elinor thoughtfully.

"No doubt the unhappy young tutor who once aspired to her hand was a man of some education too. It didn't make *him* any the more eligible!"

"True," Elinor agreed, and added, brightening, "And of course she has forgotten all about *him*, and very likely half a dozen others besides. I fancy she couldn't even tell us his name now! You know, it does appear to me that as Persephone is always happiest when she can give most time to her music, it is *that* which will best distract her mind from the young man in Bath. At her age, after all, one does not commonly form a lasting passion."

"No – though you will hardly get a girl of her age to admit as much! So you see music not as the food of love, but the cure for it?"

"Not precisely that – but it means so much to her, you know, that she can forget everything else in her playing and singing. And in hearing music too. We have now been to three concerts at the Argyll Rooms, and I never saw anyone's attention so rapt!"

"And has she ruffled the feathers of all the proud mamas anxious to show off the musical accomplishments of their own progeny?"

Elinor smiled. "Yes, a little! But she cannot help it if her performance is so superior – one would not *wish* it less so! And most of the time she behaves very prettily, always giving up the piano stool to some other young lady at the end of her piece, and very seldom choosing to play or sing anything that is – well, especially long and *brilliant*! She knows she may do that in the Yellow Parlour here. But one thing that has me in a worry," she added, frowning slightly, "is that much as Lord Conington admires her talent, I do not believe he is himself particularly fond of music."

"Conington? Ah, yes, you told me: the suitor of whom Isabella approves."

"Yes, but then, if you don't mind my saying so, Cousin Isabella is not much addicted to music either."

"No, and nor, I fancy, is George. Which reminds me: have you been to the Opera yet?"

"No, and I own I should like to go – for Persephone's sake."

"Not for your own? Have *you* no wishes in the matter?"

She thought he must be quizzing her, and it was a moment before she saw that he was perfectly serious. "Good gracious, it doesn't signify what *my* wishes are, though I should certainly enjoy it!" she said. "But it would be just the thing to draw Persephone out of herself. As I was telling you, she has been a little melancholy lately."

"Now I come to think of it, George doesn't rent a box at the Opera, does he?" said Sir Edmund. "No: I recollect his saying that as he and Bella had no great taste for it, he saw no reason to take a box just to keep up with the fashionable world. But I see I must do something about that, or Persephone will have good reason to think we've failed in our promises to her. In fact, I believe I know of something which will take the child's fancy, so leave it to me! Well – I have heard quite enough about Persephone for the time being, so let us talk of something else until she and Signor Pascali have finished. You have been telling me all about my ward, but what I asked was: how do *you* go on in London?"

Elinor could hardly suppose that her experiences would interest him, but she gave him her impressions of the hallowed precincts of Almack's, and made him laugh by reciting all she could remember of Mr Smith's extracts from his Ode on the Wonders of Steam. In return, he talked of his journey to Westmorland, and they found that they shared a taste for the works of the Lake poets, though agreeing that Mr Wordsworth could sometimes become rather prosy. When Persephone joined them, Elinor could scarcely believe her lesson had lasted so short a time, but when she looked at the clock on the Adam mantelpiece, she saw that Signor Pascali had indeed stayed his full hour.

Sir Edmund was as good as his word. Walking into the Grey Saloon next day to find his sister and brother-in-law there as well as Miss Radley, Persephone and Charley, he produced a playbill and handed it to Isabella.

"Here, Bella – do you care to see this? Any of the rest of you are very welcome to come, of course. I've taken a box for the first performance; they tell me it's expected to be very fine."

"An opera?" said Lady Yoxford, dubiously.

"Yes, though it is not to be performed at the Opera House, but at Covent Garden theatre. I understand Charles Kemble thinks himself very lucky to have secured it."

"Oh, what is it?" cried Persephone eagerly.

George Yoxford chuckled. "No need to ask *this* little puss if she wants to make one of your party, Edmund!"

"No, so I rather expected! It's a new piece by the German composer Herr Weber, Persephone. I gather he has come over from Germany himself on purpose for the first production of this work, despite his very indifferent health."

But Persephone was not listening; she was already hanging over Lady Yoxford's shoulder to study the bill, which announced the performance in three acts, for the first time, of a Grand Romantic and Fairy Opera entitled *Oberon*: or, *The Elf-king's Oath*, with entirely new Music, Scenery, Machinery, Dresses and Decorations. Having enumerated these important items, it went on to inform the public that the Overture and the whole of the Music were composed by Carl Maria von Weber, who would preside in the Orchestra.

Isabella, warily scanning the list of promised delights, said, "Oh, I do not know! A new opera? And three acts – should I not find it taxing to sit through such a piece? Can you be sure I should like it, Edmund?"

Sir Edmund was about to say mildly that no one could be

92

sure of that, but Persephone, generously anxious that no one should miss this high treat, forestalled him, exclaiming, "Oh yes, Cousin Isabella, I am persuaded that you would!"

She received unexpected support from Charley, who was looking over his mother's other shoulder, and said, "Yes, Mama, do come! It sounds good fun." Evidently he had glanced lower down the bill, for he added, "What's more, there will be a farce afterwards, called *The Scapegoat*."

"Pooh! Who cares for farces?" said Persephone scornfully.

"I do!" Charley stoutly maintained. "And as far as I remember, *you* used to like them as well as anyone when last you were in London, miss."

Paying no heed to this provocative remark, Persephone returned to her perusal of the playbill. "Do look, Cousin Isabella! Mr Braham is to sing the part of Sir Huon of Bordeaux, and Madame Vestris that of somebody called Fatima, who is listed among the Arabian characters – and Miss Paton is to be the Daughter of the Caliph. That must be the singer Mary Anne Paton. Oh, I should so much like to hear her – and Mr Braham, as well!"

"By Jove, just look at the Order of the Scenery, too!" pursued Charley, whose surprising enthusiasm for the opera, it now transpired, sprang from anticipation of the spectacle it offered. "Go on, Mama, read it!"

Lady Yoxford complied, and found that the setting ranged from Oberon's Bower (where the audience was promised a Vision), to a Distant View of Bagdad and the adjacent Country on the Banks of the Tigris by Sunset, and the Grand Banqueting Chamber of Haroun-Al-Raschid, subsequently transporting the spectators to the Gardens of the Palace, the Port of Ascalon, and a Ravine amongst the Rocks of a Desolate Island, the Haunt of the Spirits of the Storm. The audience was further promised a Perforated Cavern on the Beach, with the Ocean in a Storm, a Calm, by Sunset, Twilight, Starlight and Moonlight. The scene would then change to a humbler spot, namely the Exterior of the Gardener's House in the Pleasure Grounds of the Emir of Tunis, before rising again to the probable glories of a Hall and Gallery in Almansor's Palace, a Myrtle Grove in the Gardens of the Emir, the Golden Saloon in the Kiosk of Roshana, the Palace and Gardens by Moonlight, and the Court of the Harem. The whole was to end, in what would surely be a veritable blaze of splendour, in the Hall of Arms in the Palace of Charlemagne.

Lady Yoxford allowed that it certainly sounded pretty and entertaining.

"I should just think so!" exclaimed her son. "By Jupiter, I wonder how they contrive to change the scenery so often, don't you, Uncle Edmund? And I dare say the costumes will be something like, too – what with the Franks, Arabians and Tunisians, with Officers, Slaves and Soldiers of the different courts, Fairies, Sprites, etc!"

"I shouldn't be at all surprised," said his uncle. "Indeed, I can hardly wait to see what characters are left to come under the heading of *etcetera*!"

Persephone had passed on from these frivolous considerations to more serious matters. "Books of the Songs to be had in the Theatre, price 10d." she read out aloud. "I shall purchase one."

"You astonish me, Persephone," said Sir Edmund, good-humouredly. "I hope *you* will come, Cousin Elinor? And you, George – shall you accompany us?"

"Well, well, I dare say it will be agreeable enough," said Yoxford amiably, "and just what little puss here will like." Now that Persephone was, as he put it, a grown-up young lady, and he was assured that she would not be a source of anxiety to his cherished Isabella, he had taken a great liking to her. "Tell me, my dear, what's so great about this Weber fellow?" he asked her now.

"Oh, don't you know his *Freischütz*?" exclaimed Persephone. "Why, I believe there were four or five versions performed in London two years ago – but of course

94

I was in Bath, so I never saw any of them," she said with regret.

No one was tactless enough to point out that but for the Unfortunate Business she might have stayed longer in London, and have had the chance of seeing one of these productions. Sir Edmund, however, was able to set her right on one point. "In fact, there were no less than *six* versions done in English that year, or so I was told when taking the box for this present piece – but they went under a number of different titles. One was called *The Black Huntsman of Bohemia*, and another, if I remember correctly, *The Demon of the Wolf's Glen and the Seven Charmed Bullets*, and another – no, I'm afraid I forget the rest."

"And there was *The Fatal Marksman, or, The Demon of the Black Forest*," offered Persephone, rather surprisingly. "I know that," she explained, "because a fr – someone I met in Bath had seen it, at the Royal Coburg Theatre. It is hardly to be wondered at, you know," she added with the engaging air of gravity she assumed when pronouncing on musical matters, "that nobody could fix on a good title in English, because it is not easy to translate *Freischütz!*"

"Fry-what?" inquired Charley, lost.

"Yes, well, you see what I mean!" she told him. "The word signifies a person who has made a pact with the Devil, and in exchange for his soul gets magical bullets which never miss their mark, so he is a man who shoots *freely* – without aiming, that is to say – and that is the meaning of the title, because the young man called Max in the opera has struck just such a bargain. Or no, wait! Another huntsman does so on his behalf, and obtains the bullets, and there is a tremendous scene when the spirit is conjured up, very wild and romantic indeed. I wish so much that I could have attended a performance," she repeated wistfully, regarding her relatives with amazement as she reflected that none of them had gone out to see the work when it was practically upon their doorsteps, and in six versions at that! Except, she concluded, Sir Edmund. "Which one did *you* see, sir?" she

95

asked, turning to him.

"I didn't see any of the English versions, but I have seen the opera in Berlin, where it was first performed," he said.

"Oh, how I envy you!" cried Persephone, and Elinor, watching, saw with some amusement that Sir Edmund had evidently risen suddenly in his ward's esteem, as a man who seized his chance to attend performances of such works as Weber's.

"And I suppose this fellow – what's his name, Max? – gets carried off by the Devil, eh?" Lord Yoxford asked.

"No, because he is betrothed to a very virtuous girl called Agatha," Persephone told him. "Hers is a very affecting part, and her love saves Max in the end. She has some beautiful music . . . I wonder if I can recollect any of it?" And stepping swiftly towards the pianoforte in the corner, she lifted its lid and began tracing out a few notes, feeling her way into a simple, improvised accompaniment. "No, that's not it," she said half to herself, as she struck a false note. "Wait . . . ah, yes, I have it!" And she began, quietly at first, to sing. *"Leise, leise, fromme Weise –"*

"Eh? What?" said Charley, baffled.

"Oh, it is in German, you see," she stopped to inform him, absently. "It signifies *Softly, my pious song* – or something of that nature." And, more confident in her accompaniment now, she allowed The Voice full rein.

Not even Charley would have dreamt of interrupting the song as it rose, strong and steady, soaring to heights of pure and lyrical sound. Since she was singing in German, none of her hearers but Sir Edmund, whose diplomatic career had made him fully conversant with that language, was able to understand the words, but the music held them all spellbound. The Viscount and Viscountess had never before been exposed to the full power of Persephone's singing voice, for in obedience to Miss Radley's gentle hints, and herself instinctively aware that it was not a suitable instrument to be brought into play in a polite drawing room, she

96

had hitherto reserved it for the privacy of the Yellow Parlour. They might not be used to finding themselves moved by music, but they were much impressed. Not in general a very imaginative woman, Lady Yoxford found herself fancying that the spirit of song itself had invaded her saloon. After the last notes had died away, there was a moment's complete silence in the room.

"Upon my word!" uttered Lord Yoxford, at last.

"Good gracious me!" said Isabella. "How very pretty that was, my dear!"

"Pretty? *Beautiful!*" Elinor could not help exclaiming.

"Beautiful indeed," Sir Edmund agreed, and even Charley contributed a hearty, "I *say!*"

Flushed and a little confused, as if she had but just come down to earth from some heavenly region of harmony, Persephone closed the lid of the instrument, and said shyly, "Th-thank you. Well – now you can see why I fancy you would like Herr Weber's new opera! You *must* come too, Cousin Isabella, indeed you must!"

"I didn't know you had learnt German," said Sir Edmund, interested.

"Oh!" Persephone seemed to catch her breath. "Well, I haven't – that is to say, I know hardly any, only the words of a few songs."

"There must be an English version of that aria?"

"Yes, I dare say. Several, I suppose, if there were so many productions of the piece here. But – but I learned the German words when I was in Bath." She seemed to think for a moment. "At the house of Mr Ford, who taught music to the girls from the Seminary."

Later, when Sir Edmund contrived to be alone with Miss Radley, he discovered that she, too, had gained the impression that Persephone was picking her words with care, as if to skirt round a subject while avoiding an outright lie.

"So what do you think of the music master himself as candidate for the part of lovelorn swain?" he asked her directly.

97

"Oh, nothing at all, I'm afraid!" she said, with the delightful laugh he realized he had been hoping to hear ever since he entered the house that afternoon. "For one thing, there had been – had been a little difficulty over a previous music master, or so I collect from Persephone's animadversions on Miss Madden and the *bee she had in her bonnet* about even the most unexceptionable persons, if they happened to be young men! For another, Persephone herself tells me that Mr Ford is old and has a great many children."

"Yes, that hardly sounds the epitome of romance! And I take it – if your other deductions are correct – that he has scarcely abandoned his wife and all the children to go walking in Wales. All the same, there was – how shall I put it? – a kind of glow in the child's eyes when she spoke of learning the piece at his house."

"There was, wasn't there?" Elinor agreed. After a moment's thought, she began, "Perhaps – "

Simultaneously, Sir Edmund said, "It may be –"

Finding themselves speaking together, they both stopped, laughing, and he then continued, "It may be that she learned it from someone else in Bath."

"Precisely," said Elinor, "for you observe she didn't say she learned it *from* Mr Ford, only *at his house*. Oh dear!" she added in dismay. "If the young man is musical too, that makes it so much worse!"

"Does it?"

"Yes! For as you know, I was persuaded that music would take her mind off this unsuitable love affair."

"I suppose we can be certain," said Sir Edmund thoughtfully, "that it *is* unsuitable?" And when she made no immediate reply, he answered himself. "Yes, no doubt we can; otherwise Romeo would have come pelting up from Bath, petitioning me for Juliet's hand!"

"Yes," Elinor agreed. "But if he is musical, you see, the case is different from what I had supposed. For I can't help thinking that a shared interest is – well, a great attraction.

98

Oh dear, what is to be done? I do not like to pry into Persephone's affairs, but if only we knew more about this young man – and at present we know next to nothing of him – it would be so much easier to help her, poor child! However, it would certainly be fatal to ask her outright."

"I'll tell you what," offered Sir Edmund, after a moment's thought. "The estimable Mr Stanfield, in Cheltenham, should have various documents ready for me to sign pretty soon now; I might just as well visit him and deal with the business in person as have him send them to London, and then I could continue to Bath, and pay a call upon this Mr Ford. For all we know," he added meditatively, "among the many children, there could be a grown son of Persephone's own age, who is musical too."

"That might well be it," she agreed. "I own it *would* set my mind at rest to know whether Mr Ford can say anything to the purpose – but you would not go all the way *just* to set my mind at rest, I hope!"

"No, though I will admit that that must ever be an object with me," he said gravely.

She could not be at all sure how serious he was, but laughed. "What a poor creature you must think me! When the very reason that you engaged me was to relieve you and Cousin Isabella of such problems."

"I had no idea, then, that they would persist. For you really do fear we have underestimated the strength of Persephone's attachment, don't you?"

She nodded. "Yes, I do. I am sure she has written to Bath, you know, and had no answer. You should see how she watches for the letters to come every day. Oh, if only she could meet some eligible young man like Lord Conington – "

"Do you favour Conington too? But forgive me, I interrupted you."

"Well, I certainly would favour him, as your sister does, if Persephone showed any real feeling for him beyond mere liking. But she doesn't! I was going to say, if she could only meet and marry someone who was eligible in every way *and* shared her passion for music, then . . . " She saw that Sir Edmund had idly picked up her book from the side table where she had recently laid it down, and was looking at the title, very much as if Persephone's affairs had ceased to interest him. It was Voltaire's *Candide*. "Well, *then*," she finished, smiling, "I should hold, like the good Dr Pangloss in that tale, that all was for the best in the best of possible worlds!"

"But you imply that such a happy outcome is unlikely." He put the book down, and suddenly, disconcertingly, bent his very blue gaze on her. "Cousin Elinor, I do begin to feel I've asked you to undertake a more onerous task than I knew. You don't regret agreeing to it?"

"Dear me, no!" she said, laughing, though a little breathlessly as her eyes met that steady gaze. "How can you ask, Cousin Edmund? So far as *I* am concerned, I am very sure that all *is* for the best in the best of possible worlds!"

8

Elinor was to regret those words. Had anyone, she wondered, ever tempted Providence so rashly? For it was only the next day that the meeting took place which overset her peace of mind entirely.

She had gone, with Persephone, to the weekly Assembly at Almack's. They were not accompanied by Lady Yoxford, who professed herself exhausted by the tiring manner in which they had been racketing about town, but Lord Yoxford's coachman had driven them to the Assembly Rooms, and Sir Edmund, who was dining with Canning the Foreign Secretary and several other prominent members of the Government, was to join them later and escort them home. By now Elinor felt quite at ease in the company where she and her charge found themselves. Lady Cowper came over to them, and endeared herself very much to Miss Radley by the warmth with which she spoke of Sir Edmund, mentioning several tributes paid to his gifts and diplomatic competence by the Honourable Frederick Lamb, perhaps Emily Cowper's favourite among her brothers. Persephone had no shortage of dancing partners, since several other ardent young gentlemen besides Lord Conington were in constant attendance on her. As the country dance into which Conington had been privileged to lead her came to an end, and the music of the band playing in the gallery above the dance floor died away, she rejoined her chaperon, protesting that she was quite breathless, and must sit down for a moment.

"I declare, if dancing in April is such warm work as this, I don't know what it must be like in May and June!" said Miss Grafton, fanning herself with the pretty little tortoiseshell fan she had found in the Pantheon Bazaar, and which went so well with her primrose gauze dress and amber beads. "I tell you what it is, Elinor: I should never have allowed Bates to lace me so tight!" She looked down, with dissatisfaction, at her tiny waist. It was small enough, in all conscience, without any lacing, but Isabella had insisted. Isabella might (and did) occasionally think, wistfully, that it was a pity the high-waisted fashions which had so long held sway were now outmoded. They had been so extremely comfortable! What was more, she had once remarked to Elinor, it was really too bad that when she herself had a waist every bit as small as Persephone's, it was modishly concealed beneath ethereally flowing draperies, whereas now that she had borne six children and in the course of Nature the measure-ments of her figure could not be *quite* what they once were, the waist of a fashionable dress had descended to its proper place on the wearer. But Lady Yoxford was not one to be defeated by the perversities of fashion, and like the rest of her female acquaintance in Society had resolutely adopted tightlacing.

Anxious as she was, moreover, that Persephone should appear to her very best advantage at Almack's, she had prevailed upon her to accept the expert ministrations of her own lady's maid for this evening, and Persephone was now regretting it. "I never *would* have allowed her to lace me up, either, if I had been going to sing tonight," she added. "Not on any account! Elinor, let us see if someone will find us some lemonade. Oh, look! Do you know those people? They certainly seem to know *you!*"

But Elinor hardly seemed to have heard her. Persephone saw that she was already staring, as if transfixed, at the couple on the other side of the room. After a long, penetrating stare at Miss Radley, the gentleman had bent to say something into his companion's ear, and she instantly glanced up and then quickly crossed the floor towards Elinor and Persephone.

She was a tall, fair girl of about Persephone's own age, her features pretty without being anything out of the common way, but she had an endearingly ready, open smile which lent charm to her face. The smile was much in evidence now, as she approached Elinor with both hands outstretched, saying, "It is – it surely must be you, Miss Radley! I cannot be mistaken! Grenville said he was sure he recognized you, and the moment he pointed you out to me I was very sure that *I* did!"

Gathering her scattered wits, Elinor said, a little faintly, "Good gracious, can it really be you, Charlotte? But I fancy I ought to call you Miss Royden now. Why, how you have grown!"

Even to her own ears this last comment sounded inept, but she had to say something, and was finding it difficult to speak at all. However, her words drew a charming laugh from Miss Royden, who said, "Yes, I have, haven't I? When I came to live with Mary – she is married now, you know, and I have been residing with her since Mama died last year – well, Grenville said he thought I should tower above all my dancing partners, and while it isn't quite as bad as that, you can see for yourself that it's bad enough!"

"How delightful to see you again!" Elinor managed to utter. She did not sound at all convinced of the truth of what she said, which seemed to Persephone odd, since nothing could have been more taking than the young lady's frank amiability, or her evident pleasure in seeing Miss Radley. "But I am wool-gathering! Persephone, let me make Miss Charlotte Royden known to you. Eight years ago, she and her sister were my pupils when I was a governess. Miss Royden – Miss Persephone Grafton!"

"Oh, do pray call me Charlotte still," begged Miss Royden, smiling. "How odd it would be if we were to stand on ceremony now."

"Odd indeed!" a man's voice drawled behind her. And what in the world was there in that, Persephone wondered, to make Elinor stiffen? The movement was almost imperceptible, but Miss Grafton thought she had not been mistaken.

"Miss Grafton, this is my brother Grenville," Charlotte Royden introduced her escort. "You will certainly remember *him*, Miss Radley, for he can't have changed as much as I have done."

"Of course I remember him," said Elinor, civilly.

"Of course," the gentleman echoed her. He had crossed the room in his sister's wake, but at a more leisurely pace, and now stood with his gaze travelling lazily from Elinor to Persephone and back again. "How charming to encounter you once more, Miss Radley! Or have you, I wonder, now changed your state, and are you married to somebody?"

"No, Mr Royden. Persephone, let me introduce Mr Grenville Royden to you."

"Ah – the Nightingale of Upper Brook Street!" said Mr Royden, gallantly. "For so I have heard you called, Miss Grafton."

"Have you indeed? How nosensical!" laughed Persephone.

"No, no, I assure you; your fame has gone abroad. What a pity we can have no chance to hear you play or sing tonight! But I must hope for that pleasure on some other occasion."

"You are fond of music, Mr Royden?" There was an instant warmth in Persephone's eyes. Elinor, watching, had perforce to hide her vexation at seeing that Grenville Royden had plainly lost none of his ability to please.

But he was changed, she saw, since their last meeting eight years ago – changed more than she had at first supposed. Of course he looked older; he must now be thirty years of age or more. He was still remarkably handsome – yet scrutinizing the face and figure that had dazzled her when she was Persephone's age, Elinor found their charms decidedly tarnished. One did not at first perceive it, because of the excellent cut of his evening dress, but he had filled out and become less lean and athletic. Self-indulgence? It was not at all unlikely. Though who was *she*, thought Elinor, to hold self-indulgence against anybody else, living as she did a life of ease at Yoxford House under what, she had a dismal feeling, were dreadfully false pretences? Mr Royden's fashionably cropped hair was not quite as thick as it had been, and his complexion had coarsened; in repose, his full mouth drooped, taking on a certain expression of petulance. It was the mouth of one who had always been accustomed to getting what he wanted. But there was still a challenging brightness in his eyes, and a challenge in his smile too as he turned from Persephone back to Miss Radley.

"And so *you* are the cousin who is chaperoning Miss Grafton about? Well, well! I had heard of the musical heiress, to be sure, but I had no notion that you were any connection!"

"The connection," said Elinor, maintaining her tone of civil coolnesss, "is very remote, and is on different sides of the family of Persephone's guardian, Sir Edmund Grafton."

"You must know, Miss Grafton," Charlotte was meanwhile informing Persephone, with easy friendliness, "that Miss Radley was *quite* the kindest governess my sister and I ever had! Miss Radley, you must tell us all your news! I think I have already told you mine, except that Papa died five years ago." Elinor murmured formal condolences. "And so now we are all fixed in London, except that Grenville comes and goes between town and Royden Manor, but the house there is more or less shut up, because he doesn't wish to be at the expense of maintaining a full establishment in the country. How happy Mary will be to know that I have met you! She has a little boy now, and a dear little baby, and because she is expecting another child very soon she does not go out much at present, but you must call upon her. We were both very sorry when you left the Manor so suddenly."

"I was obliged," said Elinor, carefully, "to leave in order to take up the post of companion to Lady Emberley, an elderly relative of mine." For some reason that Persephone could not fathom, she looked straight at Mr Royden rather than at Charlotte as she spoke. And now something occurred which Elinor had been fearing for the last few minutes, but which she saw no reasonable means of averting: she was going to be left alone with Mr Grenville Royden. Lord Conington was approaching with a friend; introductions were made, and very soon Persephone and Charlotte had both been borne off into a quadrille. Looking round rather desperately for a familiar face, Elinor saw a lady whom she had recently met, and, grasping at any straw, was moving away to greet this acquaintance when Mr Royden said gently, "Oh, don't go! I should so much like to talk over old times with you."

His tone might be gentle, but Elinor realized with some indignation that he had actually taken her firmly by the elbow, and she could not pull away without creating a most unseemly little fracas. He released her only when she turned to face him. "Well!" he continued. "To think of you being here, and in the part of a chaperon! Within the sacred halls of Almack's, too! Who would ever have thought it?"

Her head came up. "I think we need not discuss the matter, Mr Royden."

"Mr Royden? Oh, so formal!" He laughed at the fiery glance she shot him. "Oh, don't agitate yourself – you'll allow that I could hardly resist that! So here you are, in the company of Grafton's ward. Did you know he and I are neighbours in the country? No, perhaps not, but so it is."

Now that she thought of it, Elinor did recollect that during her brief period at Royden Manor, the name of Waterleys, which she now knew to be Sir Edmund's place in Hertfordshire, had been mentioned as that of a neighbouring estate, but the circumstance had been of no interest to her at the time. How strange to think that, long ago, she had been so close to Sir Edmund without ever meeting him . . . or no, more likely she had not, she reminded herself prosaically, since he would have been abroad at that time.

She was brought out of her thoughts by Mr Royden's voice, that very irritating hint of amusement still in it. One

106

might suppose, reflected Elinor, summoning all her dignity to her aid, that he would at least be abashed to meet her again, but evidently it was no such thing! For he was continuing, in the same tone, "Grafton, and the Yoxfords – you have certainly done pretty well for yourself, Elinor! You move in elevated circles indeed! But you haven't asked me what *I* am doing in London."

"Escorting Charlotte to parties, I suppose."

"Well, yes, but I'll be frank with you, Elinor. After all, were we not once upon very close terms? I feel sure frankness cannot offend you! I'm here to get Charlotte a husband."

"I should imagine," said Elinor, quite tartly, "that Charlotte will be well able to do that for herself, for she has the most engaging manners, and is sure to take."

"Ah, but you don't quite understand me, my dear. Just *any* sort of husband will not do! Mary married well enough, but not *very* well – and he's a prosy fellow, her husband, and doesn't seem to care for me, I can't think why! No, it's a rich husband I need for Charlotte – rich, and well-disposed towards her only brother, if you understand me."

"I suppose you mean that you have been running through your inheritance." She could well believe it; improvidence had been one of Mr Royden's more notable characteristics as a young man, though as she ruefully recalled, she had been so blind to any faults of his that such mundane matters had not seemed to signify at the time.

"Let's say, the estate was pretty much encumbered already, and I've no fancy for entrenchment, *or* much liking for the life of a country squire. A wife with a handsome dowry might do the trick, but then, matrimony's not in my line, my dear Elinor – never was." Miss Radley suppressed the gasp of indignation that nearly escaped her; Grenville might be baiting her, but she would not give him the satisfaction of seeing her rise to his bait! "No, a rich and obliging husband for Charlotte is the thing, and would pull me out of the suds nicely!" He glanced at his sister, talking

107

to Lord Conington with unselfconscious ease during an interval in the dance, and remarked, "Not such a connection as *that*, of course; I can tell I'd be setting my sights too high there, and besides, the talk is that Conington's infatuated with your pretty Miss Grafton. However, this is a very fortunate meeting, Elinor, for it occurs to me forcibly that you and I might be very useful to one another."

"How so?" she inquired glacially, not troubling to hide her dislike of this style of conversation.

"Why, you may introduce Charlotte into the Yoxfords' circle. She won't put you to the blush; she's pretty enough, though not so beautiful you need fear her outshining Miss Grafton! But Mary and her prosy husband don't move in the *first* circles, let alone the fact that Mary seems to be forever in an interesting condition, and – well, let's say the matter of a – er – suitable husband for Charlotte is becoming tolerably pressing!"

"Poor Charlotte! I collect that she is ignorant of these delightful plans for her welfare! Well, I am sure she will be very welcome in Upper Brook Street, for she is grown into a charming girl," said Elinor, decidedly relieved to find that an introduction was all that was required of her. More, however, she could not do – and would not if she could, as she told Mr Royden, matching his own frankness. "You seem to care more for money than for her happiness in marriage!"

"Ah, but then money *is* important in matchmaking, is it not!" inquired Mr Royden blandly. "As I'm persuaded you must know." She was far too much mortified to make any reply to this, and in a moment he added, "But you haven't asked me what *I* can do for *you*!"

"Nor do I mean to!"

"I'll tell you, all the same," said Mr Royden, close to her ear. The whole distasteful conversation had been conducted in a tone of such confidentiality that no bystander could have caught their words, which made it, somehow, even more nightmarish. "I can keep my mouth shut, can't I? Or

108

not," he added reflectively, his gaze turning towards the door.

Following the direction of his eyes, it was with extraordinary relief that Elinor saw Sir Edmund enter the room and look about him. He was impeccably clad in a blue dress-coat with gilt buttons, a waistcoat of a lighter shade of blue, and pale-coloured pantaloons strapped under the feet. On locating her among the onlookers at the side of the floor, he came towards her with a smile that made her heart lift. It immediately plummeted again as Mr Royden repeated, very softly, "Or *not*, as the case may be."

From the circumstance of their estates marching together on the borders of Essex and Hertfordshire, the two gentlemen were slightly acquainted, so she had no need to perform introductions, for which she was thankful; just then she felt she could not have uttered another word. To her immense relief, Mr Royden soon took his leave and walked away, and Sir Edmund, noting her pallor, caused her to sit down and procured her a glass of orgeat. She sipped it thankfully.

"There, is that better?" he asked, looking at her with concern. "What was the matter?"

"Oh, nothing!" she said quickly. "The – the heat of the room! As Persephone noticed too, it is a very warm evening for the time of year!"

Sir Edmund, who knew a civil falsehood when he heard one, let this pass, but regarded her with no lessening of his concern. She was very glad when he suggested an early return to Upper Brook Street, and when Persephone concurred. Miss Grafton was still regretting the tightlacing to which she had succumbed, and Elinor was thankful indeed to attain the solitude of her own bedchamber after an evening which had quite cut up her peace. And for that, she acknowledged despairingly, she had no one but herself to blame!

But even exhausted as she was by the mingled emotions that

had beset her that evening, it was a long time before Elinor could fall asleep. She lay tossing and turning in her bed, hearing the tall clock upon the landing strike the hours, staring unseeingly at the faint squares of light that the moon, scudding through clouds beyond the oblong panes of the big sash window, cast on the ceiling of her room, as her mind went over not just the day's events, but also those of a summer eight years ago.

Who could ever have thought of her meeting Grenville Royden again? She caught herself up: ridiculous to think in such a way! *She* could have thought of it, and so she should have done! What was more natural than that Mr Royden should come up to London from Essex, to squire an unmarried sister about town? The fact was, she had never stopped to think that by now her former charges must be grown up. She still imagined them as little girls of thirteen and ten, just as they were when she last set eyes on them. To think of Mary's being married! Her conscience smote her, amidst her own turmoil of feelings, for having failed to ask Mary's married name and her direction, but she would make up for that when Charlotte called in Upper Brook Street.

She supposed, however, that the main reason why she had failed to anticipate such a meeting was sheer reluctance to bring that summer at Royden Manor back to mind. She made up for the omission now, deliberately tormenting herself with the memory of her own folly. Eight years ago, listening to sermon after shocked sermon, lecture after lecture from her aunts, both severally and together, some obstinate streak of individuality deep within her had stoutly if silently maintained that it *was* only folly, not utter wickedness, to have fallen so helplessly, hopelessly in love with her employers' eldest child and only son. Sent down in disgrace from Oxford three years earlier, for some misdemeanour which his parents carefully avoided mentioning, although a parlourmaid had hinted to Elinor that it was a very shocking affair to do with the most disreputable class of female, he had never settled to anything since. By chance,

110

young Elinor had overheard one angry scene between Grenville and his father, with old Mr Royden raking down his son for his idleness and lack of interest in the estate. The agricultural troubles following the end of the French wars had hit Royden Manor hard, and the older Elinor could now sympathize heartily with Mr Royden's vain attempts to make his land pay its way.

But at the time she had been wholeheartedly on Grenville's side when he complained to her, bitterly, of his father's unreasonable behaviour in expecting a young gentleman of fashion to apply himself to so dreary a matter as estate management. No, the thing was to employ a steward to take care of all that! He supposed his father thought to *force* him to stay at home by making him such a wretched allowance! His having spent the whole of it for the current quarter, when that period still had six weeks to run, was the circumstance which had brought him to Royden Manor just when the new young governess arrived to take up her post. So he had some reason, he assured Elinor, to be grateful to his father after all! That, naturally, was music to her ears. How could she believe, for an instant, what Meg the parlourmaid had hinted about a woman of the town and a baby – when Grenville so plainly adored *her*, just as she adored him? Mere servants' gossip! She was very glad she had given Meg a setdown, and refused to listen to any more improper remarks!

What easy game she must have been, she thought ruefully. She could still remember, only too clearly, every moment of those brief weeks of bliss: the first time he put his arm round her waist, out in the orchard where she and the little girls were picking cherries, and he had playfully demanded *his* share, with a significant glance at her lips. She had been so afraid that Mary and Charlotte would notice how the mere, fleeting touch of his hand made her tremble! And there was the day when she slipped out of the schoolroom and he kissed her for the first time, in the succession house at the end of the garden. Her cheeks

111

burned as she remembered, all too clearly, the ardour with which she had returned his kiss. Good God, she would not have denied him if he had wanted to take her there and then, among the forced melons and pineapples. (Such luxuries, beloved of Mrs Royden, from whom her son inherited expensive tastes, were one of the reasons why Grenville's father found retrenchment so difficult.)

She *had* felt a good deal of distress – not that she could now allow that to be much to her credit. She was betraying her employers' trust, she was no fit example to her pupils – but how could she help it, she had asked herself? She was sure that love conquered all, and *he* thought so too, positively urged her to think so, said he could not live without her, either. She wondered if he had ever really meant, however fleetingly, to marry her. He had certainly assured her that once the knot was tied, his parents would soon come round to the idea of the match. And the notion of being actually married to him, the prospect of such amazing, incredible, life-long bliss, had so dazzled her as to make her blind not only to virtue but to common sense as well!

Once again, in her mind, she went over that stealthy flight in the post-chaise brought to the Manor gates at dusk; she could still remember how she had trembled as she stepped up into it and into his arms. And then came the bedchamber upstairs in the inn on the Great North Road. She had been a little surprised, at first, that Grenville had not bespoken two rooms – but when it became clear what his intentions were, had she resisted? No, she had not. What Grenville wanted, Grenville should have, and she would give it gladly! How ungenerous to insist on waiting for a mere formal ceremony, when he desired her so much! She knew, in some separate part of her mind, that she was doing wrong, but if it didn't feel wrong, how could she care? And here her memories became such as to cause the blood to rise to her cheeks yet again. In point of fact, she had not particularly enjoyed the experience. Quite apart from her own innocent ignorance, Grenville Royden was not the most skilful and certainly not the most considerate of lovers. But she could hardly have known that, and was only pleased to have made him happy; the idea of their future life together made up for any momentary disappointment. What was that phrase of Shakespeare's? *The heyday in the blood . . .* well, she had let it govern her to the exclusion of all else, which she now supposed *was* wickedness, just as they had all said. Very certainly it was foolish beyond permission!

She had also occasionally, and sadly, wondered how long Grenville would have kept her with him if they had not been discovered next morning. Perhaps he had even *meant* his father to discover them? Certainly the elder Mr Royden had no difficulty in following their trail, and in catching up with them before they so much as left the inn. The most dreadful thing of all, still clear to her mind in every mortifying detail, had been Grenville's ready acquiescence when his father pointed out where his duty lay; his turning on her when she protested, and asking whether she really thought he could marry a penniless girl who would let herself be tumbled so easily? He hoped he had a better notion of what he owed his family! The absolute brutality of this had made her feel quite faint, and had been a little too much even for old Mr Royden, happy as he was to find that he was going to have no trouble with his son and heir over this peccadillo. The old man had given her five guineas to see her on her way to her aunts' house. She would dearly have liked to fling them in his face, but knew she could not, without being left alone and perfectly destitute.

The shock of rejection had, at least, the advantage of numbing her to some extent during the hours, days and weeks of disgrace and constant scolding that followed. It must be hushed up, the aunts all agreed, it *would* be hushed up . . . but that did not mean they had the least intention of holding their own tongues in private. Aunt Elizabeth arrived from London, to add her voice to those of Aunts Jane and Matilda. She was not surprised, she stated with gloomy triumph, to find that a girl who refused such a very

respectable offer of marriage as Elinor had done was capable
of this, too – but neither did her lack of surprise prevent her
from expressing her sense of horror and outrage at interminable length. An atmosphere almost worse than one of
mourning pervaded the house: there were whispered con-
sultations, a letter too urgent to be entrusted to the mails was
sent by special messenger, and a portentous solemnity
settled upon Elinor's aunts as they awaited the answer. It
was almost a relief when that answer came, and Elinor was
dispatched to Lady Emberley, to undergo yet more hours of
strictures.

But even Sophronia Emberley could not continue in that
vein for ever, and there was only one of her, whereas there
had been three of the aunts to take turns in scolding. And
there were small, practical things for Elinor to do about the
Cheltenham house: that helped. She had grown up that
summer, but too painfully. It had taken her a long time to
teach herself how to raise her spirits and make the best of
things. But she did find, at last, that by an effort of the will
she could inure herself to the references Lady Emberley was
in the habit of making to the shocking past – though it was
certainly rather hard, when the Reverend Mr Spalding
became so intimate a friend of the old lady, to discover that
he too had been regaled with the entire story, and to have to
endure solemn reproofs from him, mingled with his ponder-
ous attempts at courtship. With another effort of will,
however, she contrived to persuade herself that she found
that very diverting. Over the years, she had discovered an
inner strength in herself, on which she could rely.

Yet perhaps even that lesson in self-reliance, learnt with
such difficulty, had been a mistake too, and she was justly
served. Or so it certainly seemed in the dead middle of the
night. She did not know how she could face Persephone any
more, or the kind Yoxfords or most of all Sir Edmund! She
turned over once again and wept quietly into her pillow.

At last, common sense reasserted itself, and she recollected that she not only *had* faced Sir Edmund that evening,

he had been all kindness and concern for her. This was a cheering reflection. It was some small comfort, too, to realize that she felt not the least pang of regret for her lost love when she set eyes on Mr Royden again. She had sometimes wondered whether her old feeling for him was completely dead – but now, she could not imagine how she had ever been in love with him! What she certainly did feel for Sir Edmund Grafton, which she now acknowledged to herself, was a very different matter, but *that* would perforce remain for ever locked in her own breast. However, she had been right in telling Sir Edmund, when they were speaking of Persephone, that the passions formed at eighteen did not last.

Another cheering fact was the realization that all Grenville seemed to want was a welcome for Charlotte in Upper Brook Street, in return for the silence by which he evidently supposed she set great store. Now that she thought of it (and she reproached herself for giving way with too much abandon to her own distress), Charlotte and Persephone had plainly taken a fancy to each other, so there was no difficulty there! And hugging these happier thoughts to herself, Elinor at last fell asleep.

9

But the incident marred Miss Radley's pleasure in the first night of *Oberon*, if it could not entirely destroy it. All twelve performances of the work that were to be conducted by its composer had been sold out in advance, and the scene at Covent Garden was a dazzling one. The theatre itself had been rebuilt only some ten years earlier, after being ravaged by a disastrous fire. Tonight, every box was full, and the spectators seemed to be vying with the splendidly costumed performers in the magnificence of their dress and jewels. Looking about her, Lady Yoxford was satisfied that she had done right to come, and when the performance began, the opera itself came as a pleasant surprise to her. It was not at all wearisome! The scenery bore out the lavish promises of the playbill and won applause in its own right, particular enthusiasm being reserved for the effect of a sunset reflected on water in the second act, while the manner in which the Spirits of the Storm materialized out of the rocks was very striking, and the picturesque background of the sea shore made a charming setting for the Mermaid's song.

The small part of the Mermaid herself was taken very well by a young singer, Mary Anne Goward by name, and at the end of her ravishing little aria Persephone leaned back and breathed, so softly that Elinor only just caught the words, "Oh, *how* I envy her!" Next moment, Miss Grafton was sitting forward on the edge of her little gilt chair again, quite transported to the fairy world of the opera. Certainly, thought Elinor, the absurdities of its tangled plot seemed of no account when such a flood of melody poured forth from the singers and the orchestra.

116

She had been a good deal shocked, herself, by the appearance of the man who had written this wealth of tuneful, romantic music, for Herr Weber looked very ill indeed. His face, with its high cheekbones and large dark eyes, was sallow and cadaverous, and Elinor wondered how, in so frail a state of health, he found the energy to direct the music with such spirit. For her part, Persephone gazed at him with rapt interest as he made his entrance. Previously, Elinor had observed, she had also seemed remarkably interested in the members of the orchestra, leaning forward to scrutinize them keenly as they brought in their instruments and began to tune up.

The actual performances of the singers were varied. Mr Braham, though a fine figure of a man and possessed of an excellent tenor voice, made Sir Huon of Bordeaux seem a rather lifeless character, but the vivacious Madame Vestris was all that could have been desired in the soubrette-like part of Fatima, and Miss Paton, as the Caliph's daughter, sang her tremendous aria in the second act very finely. Applause at the end was enthusiastic, and the composer's name was shouted out repeatedly by some sections of the audience, until finally Herr Weber himself went up on the stage to acknowledge their plaudits.

Persephone clapped as hard as anyone, and as the musicians were at last leaving the auditorium she again leaned forward, almost craning over the side of the box and seeming to peer at each individual player. It was almost as if she hoped to recognize someone there, Elinor thought, for as the very last man disappeared from view she heaved a tiny sigh.

But her face was glowing as she turned to the rest of the party, and said to Sir Edmund, "Thank you – oh, *thank* you for bringing us! It was truly *wonderful!*"

So Elinor might have thought, too, but for the fact that before the opera even began, she had caught sight of Grenville and Charlotte Royden seated with a party of people in a box opposite. This was not calculated to promote her enjoyment of the piece, and indeed, just as she anticipated, they had come to visit Sir Edmund's box during the interval. Introduced to the Yoxfords, Charlotte behaved very prettily; there was nothing in *that* to trouble Elinor. What she did not much like was the way that Mr Royden almost instantly drew Persephone into conversation, monopolizing her attention for the greater part of the interval. So earnestly did she seem to be talking to him, in return, that Lord Conington, who had come round to the box too, found himself unable to get near his inamorata. Elinor wished very much she knew what the pair were saying, but she was not near enough to catch their words.

"I see I am quite cut out!" said Conington, ruefully.

"Dear me, I am afraid so!" she agreed in a light-hearted tone. "How do you like the opera, Charlotte? I dare say you will recollect meeting Lord Conington at Almack's."

Charlotte did, and Conington, with his usual impeccable courtesy, turned his attention to her directly, apparently forgetting his chagrin at being unable to talk to Persephone. Perhaps it was not all merely a civil pretence, thought Elinor, for Charlotte's natural friendliness and ease of manner were really very taking. Far less engaging was the sly, knowing look, with what was almost the suggestion of a wink, that Mr Royden gave her as he left the box when the orchestra began to tune up again.

"Why, what a charming child your charge is, Elinor!" he said softly as he passed, for her ears alone. "More so than I had any idea of!"

Since Persephone's charm was undeniable, she could not have said just what there was in that harmless comment to make her uneasy. But uneasy she was. "What had you and Mr Royden to say to each other?" she inquired gently of Persephone later. "You were talking so long! Poor Lord Conington could not get near you!"

"Oh, we talked about all kinds of things!" said Persephone, with enthusiasm. "Mr Royden feels *just* as I do about Weber's music, and quite agreed with what I said

118

about the excellence of the scoring, especially for the woodwind!"

"Did he, indeed?" said Elinor a little drily. She fancied that Mr Royden had not the least notion in the world about scoring for woodwind, but had simply encouraged Persephone to talk of what interested her.

"Yes, and he entered entirely into my feelings about – oh, a great many things! I wonder," added Persephone, apparently losing interest in Mr Royden, "where and how the players in the orchestra live?"

Unfortunately, Miss Radley was quite unable to enlighten her.

"How agreeable it would be to meet such people!" Miss Grafton sighed. "People who can – can *do* something, and something so splendid, instead of simply going about to balls and parties like the company we receive at Yoxford House!"

Elinor was opening her mouth to point out that going about to parties formed a very small part indeed in the life of, say, so busily employed a man as Sir Edmund, but Persephone was continuing.

"Oh, well! I suppose you and Cousin Edmund and Cousin Isabella would say it was *not the thing* to be acquainted with such people."

And for a few moments, though she did not explain why these thoughts should have sprung to her mind just now, she looked quite downcast. However, the power of the music she had been hearing would not allow her to remain cross-tempered for long, and she soon said an affectionate goodnight to Miss Radley and went off to bed, happily humming to herself.

Elinor felt, very strongly, that if anyone with whom Persephone was acquainted was *not the thing*, Grenville Royden best met that description. The trouble was, only she knew it. Lady Yoxford had warmly invited him and his sister to call in Upper Brook Street, and this they did the very day after the opera. Yet again, Mr Royden sought Persephone's company, and Elinor was left talking to Charlotte and wondering just what was in his mind. Her anxiety on this score increased as she found that they kept meeting the Roydens, walking or driving in the Park, visiting concerts or the play, at routs and assemblies. And the calls in Upper Brook Street became frequent. In short, scarcely a day seemed to go by without some encounter between the Yoxford family and the Roydens, brother and sister.

It was very agreeable to call and see Mary again, of course, admire her pretty children and meet her husband, John Stead, who, far from being the prosy fellow of Grenville's description, turned out to be a very pleasant man of modest but respectable means, with a small estate in Buckingham-shire, where, as Mary proudly informed Miss Radley, he was a Justice of the Peace in spite of his comparative youth. "It is such a pity Grenville does not like John," Charlotte told her former governess, in a moment of confidence, "but the fact is, I believe he once applied to him to lend him some money when he – Grenville, that is – was in a little passing difficulty, and John could not see his way to obliging him, so I fancy that is why he doesn't care for John above half. Yes, it is a great shame," she added, wrinkling her candid brow, "because *I* like John a great deal, and anyone can see that he is devoted to Mary and she to him, and the babies are so sweet – but there! You cannot expect a bachelor like Grenville to take much interest in babies, can you?"

Elinor gravely agreed with this wise pronouncement; Grenville had certainly taken little enough interest in his own, if the hints of Meg the parlourmaid eight years ago were to be believed. She reserved to herself the observation that, whether or not Mr Royden liked his brother-in-law above half, he did not let his inclinations prevent him from accepting free board and lodging from him whenever he was in London.

The friendship that had instantly sprung up between

120

Persephone and Charlotte prospered, and Charlotte's whole-hearted admiration of the other girl also won her the liking of Lord Conington. His manners, Charlotte naively informed Elinor, were such as must please, and it was so easy and agreeable to talk to him! Elinor agreed, privately hoping Charlotte would have enough good sense not to lose her heart to him, but she did not dwell too much on the matter; she had enough worries of her own. These worries were rather vague in their nature, but all centred upon the marked attentions which Mr Royden was paying to Persephone, and which she did not seem to find unwelcome. Elinor herself knew only too well how charming he could be when he wished. But surely he could not be trying to win Persephone's heart? He had told her it was Charlotte, not himself, he wished to marry well! Elinor did very much want to know what his real intentions were, but gathered only a strong impression, from the barbed little innuendoes which he dropped into her ear now and then, and the mocking smile with which he was wont to glance at her across a room, that he was bent on teasing and tormenting her with references to the past. He had been inclined, she remembered, to tease his little sisters when they were children, in rather a cruel way, although, deeply in love with him as she had been, she had chosen to shut her eyes to this unamiable characteristic. Well, *she* was the object of his small cruelties now, and if all he wanted to do was provoke her, she could bear that with fortitude!

From what little Persephone said, it seemed she was convinced that Mr Royden shared her own consuming passion for music. Elinor thought that was not the case, but found herself sounding waspish and ungenerous if she hinted as much, and after she once saw a puzzled look appear on Persephone's pretty face, she kept her own counsel. Without making a clean breast of her whole story to the child – and at the moment, she saw no need for anything so drastic – she could offer no compelling reason why a young lady should be wary of Grenville Royden, and really, the idea that he intended a serious courtship of Persephone, so much younger and surely destined to make a far more brilliant alliance, seemed too far-fetched to be long entertained.

As for Persephone's own enthusiasm for the musical life of London, it showed no signs of abating. It was, after all, the circumstance which had induced her in the first place to accept her own removal to the capital with equanimity, and the lengths to which it would take her were borne in on her family a few days after they had been to Covent Garden to hear *Oberon*. Elinor had supposed her to be in the Yellow Parlour, practising the piano, when Beale came to Isabella and herself as they were discussing plans for Persephone's ball and told them Miss Grafton was gone out. He had ventured, he informed Lady Yoxford with an air of lofty disapproval, to drop a hint to Miss that a young lady of rank ought not to be jauntering about on her own, and in a hackney carriage too, which he had observed her to hail out in the street, but she had paid him no heed, saying only that if anyone asked for her, she had gone to Covent Garden to buy a book of songs. It was not *his* place to stop Miss, but he thought my lady ought to know.

"Oh, the naughty child!" exclaimed Isabella. "Yes, Beale, you did quite right. Thank you; you may go. Dear me, Elinor, what should we do?" She was looking quite flustered. "Suppose some harm were to come to her?"

"Dear ma'am, what harm can come to her between here and the theatre, in a hackney carriage?" said Elinor soothingly. "Of course she shouldn't have gone out quite alone, but it is sometimes hard to remember that etiquette in such matters is stricter in London than for a girl in the country. She forgot to purchase the songs from the opera the other night, you know, because she was so caught up in the piece that she could think of nothing but what she had just seen. And now I suppose she has remembered them, and feels she must have them immediately – you know how impulsive she is! Depend upon it, she will be back before long."

122

But time went by, and Persephone was not back. Lady Yoxford began to fret, and Elinor herself became uneasy, working out the greatest length of time it could possibly take for a hackney carriage to go between Upper Brook Street and Covent Garden, and back again. When Charley popped his head into the drawing room, to inform his mama that he was driving out in his tilbury and might not be back till after dinner time, Lady Yoxford seized eagerly upon him. "Oh, Charley, if you have your tilbury there, do pray go and look for Persephone first!"

"Why, where the deuce is she?" inquired Mr Hargrave.

"If I knew *that*," said his mama, quite pettishly, "I should not be asking you to go and find her!"

The matter being more fully explained to him, Mr Hargrave grumbled a little, saying that Persephone was nothing but a confounded nuisance, with her piano-playing and caterwauling and other mad starts, and now this! But he agreed, without too much demur, to do his mother's bidding, and Elinor offered to go with him.

It did not take them long to reach Covent Garden, and Elinor kept an anxious eye open as the tilbury rattled over the cobblestones, afraid of coming upon signs of a recent accident, but no overturned hackney carriage was to be seen.

"Shouldn't wonder at it if there ain't anyone about at all, at this time of day," observed Charley as they drew up outside the theatre.

The same thing had occurred to Miss Radley, but after Charley had given an urchin sixpence to hold his horse's head, and they had knocked on various very firmly closed doors, a morose and elderly man at last appeared and wanted to know their business, asking if Charley didn't know as how no theatre folks was to be looked for afore noon, barring rehearsals, which there weren't none today, and wondering whether all the nobs hadn't gone daft this morning, coming a-plaguing of him! Females, too!

Concluding from these remarks that Persephone had at

123

least arrived at her destination, Elinor explained their errand. A coin tactfully slipped to the old man by Charley elicited the information that yes, a young lady *had* been here, a-wanting to buy songs and asking questions about the players. "Them wot scrapes their fiddles and such, in the horchestray," the old man elucidated. "Couldn't be no manner of use to 'er meself, could I, now? Miss, says I, 'tain't me you want, it's Mr Kemble! *Hif* 'e 'as the time for you, which I wouldn't of supposed, meself! 'Owsomever, 'er insisting on seeing the guvnor, I give 'er 'is direction, didn't I?"

Another coin prised the theatre manager's address from the old man for a second time, and soon Charley and Miss Radley were back in the tilbury, bound for Gerrard Street in Soho.

"Dear me!" exclaimed Elinor, between amusement and mild annoyance, "I hope she is not making a nuisance of herself! It evidently quite slipped her mind that any of us might wonder where she is and become anxious!"

She also had some misgivings, which she kept to herself, about the propriety of Persephone's visiting the lodgings of an actor-manager, even one bearing a name as famous as that of Kemble; she feared Isabella might not be altogether pleased. But that doubt was soon set at rest. Gerrard Street proved to be a very respectable neighbourhood, and as she and Charley were admitted to the rooms where Mr Charles Kemble lived when in London (for his family's main residence was in Weybridge) she heard the murmur of pleasingly modulated feminine voices, the notes of a piano, and – inevitably – a now very familiar soprano briefly raised in song. Persephone was discovered in animated conversation with two middle-aged ladies and a very pretty girl of about sixteen. Her hand flew to her mouth as she set eyes on Miss Radley.

"Oh, good gracious, I quite forgot the time!" she exclaimed.

Mrs Kemble, a lively, dark-haired woman whose voice

held a pretty trace of French accent, made Elinor welcome, saying with a little severity that while she, her sister and her daughter Fanny had been very glad to make Miss Grafton's acquaintance, it was not the thing for her to have been calling on strangers alone! Elinor agreeing whole-heartedly with this, Mrs Kemble softened, and said with a smile, "But there! Girls will be girls, and *now* we are not strangers to one another! How delightfully she sings! Even my husband said as much, before he was obliged to go out, and *he* must be held to know! I am only sorry we could not help Miss Grafton further."

Since the tilbury would not easily carry three of them home, Charley went to procure another hackney for Elinor and Persephone, and when, after an exchange of civilities with the Kemble ladies, they left Gerrard Street, Elinor sensibly forbore to reprove her charge for putting them all in a worry, saying only, "What very agreeable people!"

The slightly apprehensive look on Persephone's face disappeared. She said fervently, "Oh yes! And do you know, Elinor, Fanny was at school in Bath too – only that was when she was quite small, and afterwards she went to continue her education in France. She is the most delightful girl, and excessively well-read, and she means to write plays as well as act in them – is not that clever? We got on famously, though I think her mama did not quite approve of me at first! But Fanny told me that Mrs Kemble and her sister – that is Fanny's Aunt Adelaide, who lives with them – are both very musical, and once I had played a sonatina, and sung, we all went on very well."

"Well, it sounds to me as if Mrs Kemble may have given you a little scold, so I won't add another!" said Elinor, smiling. "But, my dear, what did she mean by saying they were sorry they could not *help you further?*"

"Oh, that . . . Well, I merely wanted to – to make some inquiries, about concerts, and operas, and . . . "

"And performers?" said Elinor shrewdly, recollecting the remarks of the old man at the theatre, as well as

Persephone's intent interest in the members of the orchestra on the night they had heard *Oberon*.

"Yes, and the performers one might hear in London," said Persephone in a rush, and hastened to change the subject. "Oh, and I must tell you that Fanny has the greatest admiration for Herr Weber – he dined with them, you know, when he first came to London, and if he did not have a wife and little children in Germany, Fanny says she would be in a fair way to falling in love with him, and she wears his picture in a locket round her neck!"

She chattered on in this manner until they had reached Upper Brook Street, and Elinor did not inquire any more closely into the nature of the *inquiries* she had wished to make, sensing that she would get no satisfactory answer, and fearing to lose Persephone's confidence.

Lady Yoxford had no such scruples. On hearing that Persephone had gone, all alone, to call on a theatrical family, she seemed about to fall into that long-deferred fit of the vapours which she had expected Persephone to induce in her all along, and had to be swiftly reassured by Elinor as to the great propriety and superior education of the ladies they had just visited. But she could not understand why Persephone had gone there in the first place, and said so, repeatedly.

Somewhat to Elinor's dismay, Grenville and Charlotte Royden called at this juncture. She might have expected it, their visits having become an almost daily event, but she would rather it had not been just now, since their arrival meant that Isabella went over the whole story again, exclaiming frequently that she did not know what inquiries Persephone might have to make that could not be more readily answered by application to – well, to wherever it was that plays and concerts were advertised. "I cannot help wondering *why* you felt you must go to Covent Garden yourself, Persephone!" she said yet again, plaintively.

Mr Royden cocked a quizzical eyebrow at Miss Grafton. "Yes, why indeed?"

126

"I wished to obtain information," said Persephone, distantly.

He was quick to note the reserve in her tone, and for once Elinor felt quite grateful to him, as he applied himself to the task of distracting Isabella's mind by conversing with her on other subjects. But her gratitude quickly enough evaporated when, rather later, she saw that he had manoeuvred himself and Miss Grafton into the comparative privacy of one of the window embrasures, where they were talking in what looked like a playfully conspiratorial manner. As he and Charlotte took their leave, he said to Persephone, within Elinor's hearing, "Well, count on me, Miss Grafton! If I hear of anything I will let you know – but mum's the word!" And he made a comical grimace as he looked Miss Radley's way.

As if I were some old dragon, she thought indignantly. But dragon or no, she knew it her duty to ask Persephone, when they were alone, "My dear, what was it Mr Royden promised to let you know?"

"Only something about concerts," said Persephone, a little sullenly.

Elinor could see no reason why such harmless information should be discussed in such confidential tones, but she forebore to say so. However, her doubts must have shown on her face, for as they climbed the last of the shallow stairs leading up to the landing and bedchambers on the second floor, Persephone said, acutely, "I thought you were great friends with all the Roydens – but you don't like *Mr* Royden, do you?"

"I don't care for him as much as his sisters, certainly," said Elinor cautiously. "Or as much as, say, Lord Conington, whose manners are so very pleasing!"

"So are Mr Royden's!"

Not to me, thought Elinor, remembering those little pinpricks Grenville seemed to enjoy inflicting on her when they met, but she could hardly say it out aloud. She slightly compressed her lips, and after a moment Persephone

127

continued, with a little hesitation, "You – you see, there are things which he understands so well! He is so kind and friendly! I – I cannot go into detail, but he enters into so *many* of my feelings!"

"Very likely." Elinor could not keep the dryness from her voice.

Suddenly, Persephone gave her pretty trill of laughter. "Good gracious, Elinor dear, I do believe you are thinking I may fall in love with him, and because you don't like him yourself, you don't care for the thought of it! Oh, no, Elinor, it is no such thing – there is no danger of *that*, I do assure you, because while he is very agreeable company, my – "

But here she broke off, closing her mouth firmly upon whatever else she had been about to say, and leaving Elinor to complete the sentence to her own satisfaction – or otherwise, for what satisfaction was there in guessing that Persephone had been about to say, *My heart is given to another*, or, *My affections are already engaged*?

10

It was ironic, Miss Radley thought, that Lady Yoxford plainly considered an invitation to Persephone's ball for the Roydens to be a particularly thoughtful attention to herself, Elinor, as Charlotte's erstwhile governess and Grenville's old acquaintance. The actual dispatch of invitations, together with the rest of the organization of the event, fell to Elinor's own lot, and she very much wished she could quietly suppress the cards sent to Mr and Miss Royden. Of course she could not; quite apart from the fact that her conscience would reproach her with depriving Charlotte of a treat, she was sure that Grenville would make some pointed, teasing inquiry into their absence from the list of guests as the day approached. By now, moreover, they were on terms of such intimacy with the family at Yoxford House that it would indeed have been a surprising omission.

For the ball was to be a large one. Elinor knew, from a chance remark of Isabella's, that Sir Edmund was footing the bill. Pressure of business at the Foreign Office had obliged him to postpone his proposed visit to Bath and Cheltenham until after the occasion, which promised to be a magnificent one. Certainly, no expense was being spared! Gilt chairs were emerging from their holland covers in the ballroom, a seldom used but very magnificient apartment on the first floor of Yoxford House; chandeliers were washed and polished until they sparkled; the walls of the ballroom were to be decked with flowers. All white, Elinor and Isabella had decided: quite the most suitable form of decoration to celebrate a young lady's début. Orders for sufficiently lavish quantities of white hothouse flowers

129

must go out in good time, there were extra servants to be hired for the night of the ball and supper and refreshments to be arranged. The Yoxfords' own cook, a very superior Frenchman who was paid the vast salary of a hundred and twenty guineas a year, was on no account to be offended, lest he give notice (for George Yoxford set store by the good table he kept). Monsieur Marcel, therefore, must not be put upon by being asked to do too much, or slighted by being required to do too little. Thus, another of Elinor's tasks was to decide, in consultation with the cook himself and Beale the butler, what should be prepared in the kitchens of Yoxford House in the way of chicken and lobster patties, jellies and creams and confections of marchpane and spun sugar, and what should be ordered from an exclusive catering establishment outside. Ices would be from Gunter's, of course, but how many? And what quantity of champagne and other wines ought to be provided, not forgetting lemonade and other innocuously thirst-quenching beverages for the younger or more abstemious guests? Beale assured Miss Radley that she might safely leave that to him, and she thankfully turned her attention to the rest of the arrangements.

This bustle of activity did to some extent take her mind off her anxiety about Persephone, and in the ordinary way she would have enjoyed it all very much. She had had a thorough grounding in the art of household economy during her years in Cheltenham, and to be able – indeed, encouraged – to turn her skill to the organization of a party where economy itself was apparently not to be regarded in the least was a delightful treat! But it did not blind her to the fact that, for some unknown reason, Persephone had ceased to enjoy her first London Season, and had lapsed into a kind of melancholy. Since an air of decided languor was all the rage just now, no one else seemed to notice. But Elinor did, and another source of concern was that, whereas she had previously enjoyed the child's confidence, she now seemed to have lost it. She thought – and this troubled her – that

130

it had been at least partly transferred to Mr Royden, whose company was one of the few things that had power to raise Miss Grafton's spirits. What *was* it they talked about, Elinor wondered, seeing Persephone discoursing with animation to an attentively sympathetic Grenville Royden? And why would Persephone no longer confide in her, too?

She did think, one day, that their former happy relationship was about to be resumed. Finding Persephone in the Yellow Parlour moping over an open book which she was not reading, Elinor ventured to put an arm around her shoulders and ask, very gently, what the matter was. Persephone leaned against her for a moment, and said in a very small voice, "It is only that – that the friends I made in Bath don't answer my letters, or *anything*, and – and I *miss* them!" These last words came out as a little wail, and she shed a few tears before mastering her feelings and saying bravely, "Oh, dear me, I didn't mean to cry, Elinor! Now I have stupidly crumpled that pretty fichu of yours! I'm tired after last night's rout, and I dare say that puts me out of humour. It's of no consequence!"

Elinor thought it *was* of consequence, but the moment had passed and did not return. She wondered if she were refining too much on Persephone's apathetic moods. Could it be that she herself was actually jealous of Grenville Royden for winning the girl's friendship away from her? After a little thought, she was able to absolve herself of any such base emotion. She would have been only too glad for Persephone to find another sympathetic confidant had it been someone trustworthy– but she could not find it in her to trust the motives of Mr Royden.

At least no one could have suspected any ulterior motive in the guileless Charlotte's friendship from Miss Grafton. As she and Royden drove from the Steads' house on the evening of the ball, she was chattering happily of the pleasures she anticipated. "What fun it will be!" she artlessly exclaimed. "How I long to see Persephone's gown! Elinor says it is the loveliest thing! I am sure, Grenville, nothing could have been more fortunate than meeting Elinor again, and making the acquaintance of all the family at Yoxford House, who are so very kind to me!"

Mr Royden, less inclined to value the kindness of their new acquaintances than their potential usefulness, soon tired of these raptures, and snapped irritably, "So you have said above a dozen times before!" And when Charlotte fell silent, hurt but determined not to show it, he pressed home his point with a piece of brotherly advice. "I wish you would *not* repeat yourself so much – nothing makes a girl more of a bore! And do for God's sake, Charlotte, make an effort not to be forever gushing on about some other chit's perfections! Try for a little wit and sophistication of your own, so that *you* may interest some eligible gentleman! It cannot be *wholly* beyond you!"

Charlotte caught her breath with a little gasp and turned her head away, staring resolutely out of the window. They were both well aware that wit was not her strong point – and it was just a little hard, she thought ruefully, to have sophistication demanded of her in her very first Season. But of course it *was* her duty to find a husband as soon as she could; Grenville had made that very clear to her. It was a pity that no one else could quite measure up to Lord Conington, who was so kind and attentive, but who of course liked to talk to her only because she was a friend of Persephone's. Still, she must endeavour to like some other gentleman – she was sure, she valiantly told herself, that Grenville had only her best interests at heart, and had not meant to wound her.

He *had* meant to do so, and now had the satisfaction of seeing that he had succeeded, though just why it gave him satisfaction he could hardly have said. The fact was that he expected a boring evening. He found Persephone tiresome, and the confidences he was gradually eliciting from her tedious in themselves, however useful they might prove some day. And the teasing and provocation of Miss Radley, from which he had maliciously expected to derive a certain

132

pleasure, was not having exactly the effect he had hoped. There was something about the composure with which Elinor contrived to receive his remarks which put him out a good deal. After all, he thought, the past that lay between them was to *her* discredit, not his! In the circles in which he moved, a young man was rather to be admired for taking anything of that nature that offered, and a young woman censured for giving it. So she might at least appear a little more discomposed by the recollection of that episode! It was also annoying to sense that even had he renewed passionate court to her he would have met with a rebuff, and for no good reason! His conceit of himself was injured.

One way and another, therefore, Grenville Royden was out of humour, and not disposed to accept Charlotte's well-meant peace offering when, recovering herself, she said in placatory tones, "Well, I am sorry, Grenville, and I will try to do as you say. I suppose I talk of Persephone a great deal because it *is* so pleasant to have made such a friend. Elinor says, you know, that Persephone chose the musicians who are to play tonight, and they are the best that can be found in London. And Elinor says – "

"Elinor says this, Elinor says that!" interrupted her brother, quite savagely. "Oh, the *devil* with Elinor!"

Perhaps it was as well for the startled Charlotte's peace of mind that they were just drawing up outside Yoxford House, and she instantly forgot her brother's peevishness in her pleasurable excitement. They ascended to the ballroom, where the Yoxfords and Persephone stood at the head of the stairs to receive their guests to the strains of music, just as Elinor had promised. Whatever Miss Grafton's other preoccupations, music still had power to charm her – Elinor was sure *that* recourse would never fail her – and the one part of the preparations for her ball in which she had taken a real and animated interest was the musical side of it. There was to be a band to play for the dancing, and a string ensemble to entertain the guests as they arrived and again during supper. Persephone had formed a very good notion

133

of the comparative merits of the various fashionable bands and orchestras which she had heard at other parties, and readily gave her advice. Isabella and Elinor, acknowledging the superiority of her ear for music, were equally ready to take it, and Elinor knew her choice had been a good one as soon as the stringed instruments softly began playing.

The wished-for sparkle was back in Persephone's eyes tonight after all, whether brought there by the music, the excitement of the occasion, a consciousness of her own delightful appearance in her ball dress, or perhaps all three. The dress itself was charming, made of pure white silk embroidered with little forget-me-nots that becomingly echoed the blue of her eyes, and were prettily misted by an overdress of gauzy white aerophane. Blue satin ribbons ornamented waist and hem. Beside her, Isabella Yoxford was very fine in a gown of gros de Naples in her favourite deep rose-pink, with a heavy ornamentation of puckered rose crape, and she wore an evening beret of the same deep pink on her fair curls, tilted at a becoming angle and decked with a profusion of artificial flowers.

It soon became plain that the ball was destined to be a great success. By the time most of the guests had arrived, and Lord and Lady Yoxford were able to leave their post, Persephone had already taken the floor in the ballroom with a number of the most eligible young gentlemen of the *ton*.

"Everything is going on as well as ever I could have hoped! I am *so* glad you are here, my dear!" observed Isabella with satisfaction, making her way to Elinor's side, and patting her hand in the friendliest way. "For what we should have done without you, I can't think! Oh, how much I hope that when it is Maria's turn to come out you will still be with us, and able to arrange things just as admirably for *her*!"

Elinor was a little startled by the vision that this wish conjured up of herself remaining with the Yoxfords, a kind of honorary maiden aunt, until little Maria was ready to leave the schoolroom for the ballroom some fifteen years hence. Swept away from Cheltenham in such haste, and with so much happening ever since, she had hardly given a thought to her own future at such time as Persephone had made the brilliant marriage for which she was surely destined – whether it were to Lord Conington, as Isabella hoped, or to some other desirable marital prize. The notion that Isabella would like to see her a fixture in the family ought, she told herself, to be most gratifying, especially when she compared her life here with the bleak years in Cheltenham. She really could not imagine why it made her feel so low, and upbraided herself for rank ingratitude.

Isabella now moved on, leaving Elinor standing in one of the little alcoves which lined the ballroom. From this vantage point she could see Persephone surrounded by a number of young people, including Conington, while Charlotte stood shyly by just outside the group, for she was not very well acquainted with many of them. And yet, thought Elinor with a small pang of anxiety on Charlotte's behalf, she seemed quite happy merely to be standing there looking at his lordship. She was not the only one to have noticed this circumstance, but was not close enough to hear the remark hissed into his sister's ear by Mr Royden, as he passed her in search of the nearest source of champagne, "My dear Charlotte, I certainly told you to make a push to attract some eligible gentleman, but do aim for one within your reach! It is of no use your standing there making sheep's eyes at Conington, who is hardly likely to have any eyes for *you*; you are wasting your time!" With which kindly observation, he went on his way.

Charlotte gasped as if he had struck her in the face, turned very red, and fled to one of the alcoves on the far side of the room. Elinor, watching, and wondering what Grenville had said to distress her, was about to cross the floor and offer comfort, when she saw that Conington too had noticed Charlotte's sudden departure, and was detaching himself from the group with a word of apology in order to follow her. Elinor therefore desisted.

135

Mr Roydon could have said nothing better calculated to destroy his sister's innocent pleasure in her evening. She had not *meant* to stand and stare with her heart in her eyes, and was miserably aware of her foolishness. She knew very well that Conington was not for her – indeed, she had been telling herself so already this evening! But she did wish Grenville had not seen her feelings so easily, and had not been quite so cross! She was struggling to repress tears of mortification when a voice behind her said tentatively, "Miss Royden, I have not yet had a chance to speak to you, and can only hope you still have a dance for me – but Charlotte, what is wrong?" exclaimed Conington, seeing her woebegone face as she turned towards him.

"Oh! Oh – it's nothing," said Charlotte, unsteadily. "I – so stupid of me – only something Grenville said, and I'm sure he did not mean it unkindly!" She turned away again, putting her bravest efforts into blinking back her tears.

Conington let her be for a moment, and then said gently, "I can see you are upset, Miss Royden – sit down for a moment on this sofa!, *I* am sure he did not mean it unkindly too, whatever it was! I dare say your brother still thinks of you as a child at times, and forgets you are now a grown woman."

"Yes, just so!" said Charlotte thankfully.

"We elder brothers, you know," he added easily, settling himself beside her, "are notoriously unable to appreciate our sisters at their truth worth – or so I am reliably informed by mine!"

"You have three sisters, have you not, sir?" inquired Charlotte, remembering an earlier conversation, and glad to have this casual subject raised.

"Yes, three, the eldest of whom, Eliza, is soon to emerge from the schoolroom, and I have it on her own authority that she is destined to take London by storm! She *is* tolerably good-looking, I suppose. I hope you may meet her some day soon, for I know she would like you, and I believe *you* would like *her*. She only says such things jokingly, you understand!"

"I am sure of that!" exclaimed the warm-hearted Charlotte. "How much I should like to know her, to be sure!"

His lordship, whose interest in Miss Royden of late had been more for herself and less for her sympathetic ear than either she or her brother could guess, looked at her with what he was glad was not a fraternal eye, and thought what an attractive picture she made, gowned in pale blue, with the flush of tears now fading from her face. She could not, of course, hold a candle to the lovely Persephone, but despite that Conington was rapidly coming to a decision which might startle some – though not his own family, he knew, when once they were better acquainted with Charlotte! (It was to cause the lady's brother great surprise and gratification, but Mr Royden's feelings entered very little into Lord Conington's mind.) The question he had almost made up his mind to ask her was not, however, one to be put when she had so recently been in a state of distress, so he now merely requested the supper dance.

A much prettier flush tinged Charlotte's cheeks; however, she could not help saying a little dubiously, "Oh . . . but, Persephone?"

"Persephone is going in to supper with her cousin Charles," said Conington, not at all as if he minded. (Charley, summoned by his parents from Cambridge expressly to make himself useful in such ways, had accepted this cousinly duty with a fairly good grace.) He gently insisted that it was Charlotte's company he wished for at supper, where they might share a table with Persephone and Charley, engaged her for two more dances as well, and encouragingly swept her off to be introduced to a friend of his who, he said, desired to make her acquaintance. Charlotte was transported to the seventh heaven, and she would have been more than human if a small feeling of triumph had not crept into her mind, to the effect that *that* would show Grenville!

Unable to hear any of what was said, Elinor had yet

watched this little scene with some pleasure from her own alcove on the other side of the room. She had noticed that for the last few weeks, while Lord Conington was still attentive to Persephone, her obvious indifference to his suit was causing him to press it less ardently than before; indeed, she had thought she saw signs that his fancy was turning towards the sympathetic Charlotte. Suppose he really *did* transfer his affections to her? She would make him an excellent wife, kind and cheerful, with a good deal of common sense, and while of course she was not an heiress like Persephone, there was nothing to blush for in her birth or breeding. The one drawback *there*, thought Elinor, was in the character of her brother, and no one but herself seemed aware of that!

As if summoned pat by her thinking of him, Mr Royden himself spoke close to her, causing her to start. "How charmingly Miss Grafton looks tonight! At this rate she will be married and off your hands before you know it!"

"I certainly expect her to receive many eligible offers," said Elinor evenly, "but I see no signs as yet that she is thinking of marriage, Mr Royden."

"Still *Mr Royden*, Elinor? Ah, your punctilious formality!" sighed that gentleman. His voice, just a little slurred, bore witness to the success of his expedition in search of a copious supply of wine. "Must I remind you again that we were used to be on more intimate terms? Believe me, young Miss Persephone there doesn't insist on treating me so coldly!"

"So I have observed."

"And you don't like it, eh? Perhaps you remember the days when *you* were not so cold? I wonder . . . if I put myself out to be *very* agreeable to the young lady, don't you think I might succeed in – er – breaching *those* virginal defences?"

Elinor turned to stare at him in horror. "You would never dare!"

"No, for marriage would serve my turn a good deal

better!" Mr Royden agreed. This remark had but just come into his head, as a means of alarming Elinor, and he was delighted to see that at last he *had* alarmed and discomfited her. Her shocked reaction was all he could have hoped for.

"Marriage?" she exclaimed, her mind in a perfect whirl. "I thought – you said – I thought you were determined upon a carefree bachelor existence, and it was poor Charlotte who must marry for money to suit you!"

"Who knows, might one not lead an equally carefree matrimonial existence?" inquired Mr Royden, quite surprised, himself, by the good sense of what he was saying. Why, there might be something in the notion after all – he must put his mind to it more seriously some time! "And perhaps, on further acquaintance with the charming Persephone, my ideas have changed. Yes," said Mr Royden, his eyes following Miss Grafton about the dance floor, "upon mature consideration, I do believe that, all circumstances such as fortune, face and figure being agreeable to me, I might bring myself to contemplate matrimony after all!"

"She wouldn't have you!"

"No? Admittedly, her heart is elsewhere at the moment." (Oh, thought Elinor, he is indeed deep in her confidence.) "But it's a silly, girlish little heart; you must know as well as I do that it will change."

"I am not so sure," said Elinor, and found, rather to her own surprise, that she meant what she said. The unexpected strength of Persephone's attachment to the mysterious young man in Bath surely contributed to her present discontent. Not that that was much in evidence at the moment; she was behaving very prettily, smiling at one couple after another as she and Conington moved through the figures of a country dance. "In any case," she added, thankfully grasping at an indubitable fact, "Sir Edmund would never consent."

"You mean I am not a brilliant enough match? Perhaps so . . . but then, if he were presented with a good enough reason to compel him to countenance such a marriage . . ."

139

He was smiling at Elinor in the most unpleasant manner – she was tolerably certain that Persephone had never yet been allowed to see *that* expression on his face – and she stared back at him, absolutely transfixed. She supposed he could only mean that a successful seduction of Persephone would force Sir Edmund's hand, which might be true! Especially if he could so worm himself into the heiress's confidence in the role of friend (as he seemed to be in a fair way to doing) that in the end she would not be entirely unwilling to see him as something more. Did not Elinor herself know how very persuasive and charming Mr Royden could be when he liked?

"And why should I utterly despair," he continued, ironically echoing her thoughts, "of being loved for myself alone? Look at Conington there – the poor fellow has no notion how to handle her! A great willingness to listen to chatter about music is the thing, and a sympathetic ear for her troubles, surrounded as she is by domestic tyrants – I am sorry to have had to present you in that light, my dear, but I saw nothing else for it."

So that accounted for the withdrawal of Persephone's confidence! But he had not quite finished.

"You had much better let me join the hunt, you know," he added, "for if Persephone herself should observe you doing your utmost to ward me off – as you *have* been doing – then your efforts are likely to have just the opposite effect of that which you intend, don't you think?"

At least she saw her way clear now! "Mr Royden," said Elinor, in the low voice enjoined upon her by their circumstances of semi-privacy, "you seem to believe that because of the past, I shall be prevented from telling Persephone what I know of you. I am afraid it is no such thing! If I saw you threatening her peace of mind, I should not hesitate for an instant."

He looked at her consideringly. "Perhaps you wouldn't. But if you did tell her *what you know of me*, as you so delicately put it, wouldn't it seem plain that you were

140

impelled to do so by jealousy?"

"*Jealousy?*" Anger flared in Miss Radley's eyes. "You can't possibly suppose I have the least feeling left for you, Grenville!"

"Very likely not," he agreed. "But would Persephone believe that, in the face of my – my frank and manly regrets for an impulsive, youthful episode now long past?"

"Try it if you dare!" she flashed at him.

"You know, you *have* changed, Elinor!" he remarked. "You were used to be such a spiritless, romantical creature, but I fancy a little temper suits you! You really are in great good looks tonight! How interesting it would be to try if your vaunted indifference to me is as complete as you say . . . but alas, I can't spare the time now. I see this dance is coming to an end, and as I believe my own name is down on Miss Grafton's *carnet de bal* for the next, I must make haste to claim my prize. The waltz is so exhilarating a dance, is it not?" And with this parting shot he left, very well pleased with the conversation and the effect it had plainly had upon Miss Radley.

There was a small couch at the back of the little alcove, and Elinor sank on to it thankfully, feeling her legs too weak to support her. She knew she must return to the main part of the ballroom and mingle with the guests before long, since so much responsibility for the smooth running of this evening's arrangements rested upon her, and she had already stood apart for some time. But if she was to regain her composure at all, she needed a few moments to herself. It would not do to refine too much on what Mr Royden had said. Not now, not this evening; she would put her mind to it later. She had carefully taken a number of deep breaths, and was rising to her feet, when Sir Edmund appeared in the opening of the alcove.

"Away from the dancing, Cousin Elinor?" he inquired pleasantly. "Can I persuade you on to the floor with me? You need not tell me that chaperons don't dance, for Isabella is here to take that part for a change, and in any case we are in your own home. I've had no chance to find you in this crush until now, but here you are at last. How charmingly you are looking tonight!"

In strict point of fact, this was true. Elinor was very becomingly gowned in pale apricot silk with a slightly darker stripe in it, and heavy trimmings of apricot satin rouleaux at the hem. Unlike most of the ladies present, who sported a remarkable collection of evening headgear decked out with quantities of ribbons and laces, feathers and flowers, she wore nothing in her hair but two pretty Glauvina pins and a delicate spray of artificial flowers, apricot-coloured like her dress. However, her cousin's mild compliment echoed Mr Royden's words too nearly for her comfort, and somewhat to Sir Edmund's surprise she said with involuntary forcefulness, "Oh, pray *don't!*" and buried her face in her hands as she sat down again.

"Why, what is the matter?" he asked gently. "Are you feeling unwell? It is certainly becoming hot in here – let me find you a glass of wine."

"No, no. I am quite all right," said Elinor, quickly recovering herself, but Sir Edmund had already procured two glasses of champagne from a passing waiter, and pressed one firmly into her hand. He seated himself beside her and watched the dancers moving through the waltz, as he waited until she should be more composed.

"Ah, there's Persephone, with Royden," he remarked. "Was it not Royden you were talking to just now, when I at last caught sight of you here?"

"Yes," said Elinor, sipping her wine. She had thought her tone perfectly neutral, but Sir Edmund said at once, "Don't you like him? I thought you knew the family so well – and Miss Royden seems a most pleasant, unaffected sort of girl."

"Oh, she is!" Elinor agreed warmly.

"But you don't like *him*," persisted Sir Edmund, thoughtfully. She wished he were not so acute. "He is certainly becoming rather particular in his attentions to Persephone, isn't he?"

142

"Yes, and I – I don't think he would do for her."

"From what little I know of him and his circumstances, I agree with you. I should expect her to make a far better match than that. However, surely you are going too fast? Didn't you believe she was still wearing the willow for this unknown young fellow in Bath?"

"Yes, although I think that if he tried, Mr Royden could make himself very agreeable," said Elinor guardedly.

"Agreeable enough to oust her old flame from her memory? But I thought that you positively *wished* someone else to take her fancy!"

Elinor smiled faintly. "Well, yes, but not – oh, I dare say nothing will come of it," she said, forcing a light tone. And indeed, she realized, she did feel a certain lightening of her spirits. It must be the pleasent, equable company of Sir Edmund that made her recent conversation with Mr Royden seem so improbable. Could they really have been saying such things to each other? Did she really think he intended to attempt the seduction of her charge? No, ridiculously melodramatic! She gave a little chuckle.

"That sounds better!" said the uncomfortably perceptive Sir Edmund. "Are you *sure* you are feeling quite the thing? You've been looking tired, you know, these last few days."

"Have I?" She was both touched and alarmed by his quickness of observation. It would never do, she thought, sternly upbraiding herself in very much the same manner as Charlotte Royden earlier that evening, to let her heart show so easily in her face: certainly not her *whole* heart, which she feared might be all to plainly visible when she looked at him. She therefore glanced away.

"Yes, you have. I fancy Isabella persuaded you to undertake all the work of this evening's arrangements. You mustn't let her impose on you, you know – she's the kindest creature in the world, but bone idle."

"Oh no! I mean, that's not it!" said Elinor quickly, realizing too late that she was confessing, with these words, to the existence of another and unacknowledged trouble.

143

"Then that child is plaguing you," he said, looking none too fondly at his ward whirling past them.

She could not help smiling. "Cousin Edmund, as I have told you before, you brought me here especially so that she might have somebody to plague!"

"Did I?"

She found his direct glance rather disconcerting, and said hastily, to gloss it over, "Anyway, I have enjoyed myself planning this ball. I do assure you that I am glad to be of use."

"I wish," said Sir Edmund, surprisingly, "that I knew how *I* might be of use to *you*. I don't like to leave London when I can see you are in some kind of worry. Doubtless to be laid at Persephone's door! Whoever her husband may eventually be, he is going to have his hands full with that girl – and her music! However, now that I have arranged to see the lawyer in Cheltenham, I suppose I must be off tomorrow morning. By the by, is there anything in that house you would care for, as a keepsake? I swept you away in such haste that I fancy you brought very little with you, except that splendid box of treasures for the children."

She was touched again by his thoughtfulness, and said, "Well, there *was* a picture – a pretty little landscape which hung at the top of the stairs, and I used to be very fond of it. It is a sunlit scene, with water and a bridge, and seemed so different from . . . yes, I own I *should* like to have that. If it is not of any great value, that is," she added hastily.

"Of course you shall have it, whatever its value," said Sir Edmund briskly. "The main thing is that it is of value to *you*! And after I have finished my business in Cheltenham, I'll continue to Bath, as we agreed, and call on the good ladies who keep that seminary, to find out the direction of Persephone's music master. The more I think of it, the more likely it seems to me that he may be able to throw some light on this love affair of hers that troubles you – so pluck up your spirits, Cousin Elinor, and don't let the wretched girl fret you! Come along! I am now going to persuade you on to the floor, and I shall hope to be allowed to take you in to supper later."

In happier circumstances, this would have crowned her pleasure in what, as everyone agreed, was proving a highly successful evening's entertainment. About midnight, Isabella Yoxford remarked with satisfaction to her brother and her cousin that it would be wonderful if Persephone's ball did not quite shine down the coming-out parties for any other of the Season's débutantes! But Elinor's evening was marred by the fact that Grenville Royden was spending quite as much time in Persephone's company as was proper, and perhaps a little more. She would have told herself firmly that this merely showed Persephone regarded him no more seriously than her cousin Charley, but for his murmured remark as he passed her late in the evening: "Wondering what progress I am making with your charge, my dear? Try if you can get her to confide in you!"

This almost overset her again, but she was a little comforted by the firm pressure of Sir Edmund's hand when he said good night, assuring her that he would spend no longer than necessary away from London, and adjuring her not to worry too much about Persephone, or take her duties too seriously. As the last of the guests departed in the pale light of dawn, and the family, yawning, retired to their beds, Elinor thought hopefully, *All may be well*. Who was it who had said that? A character in one of Shakespeare's plays, she fancied, and now she came to think of it, she had a lurking feeling that the personage who had expressed this opinion came to a particularly nasty end very shortly afterwards. But she must not – she *would* not – fall into the dismals. And with that brave determination to cheer her, as well as the memory of the extraordinarily flattering attention that Sir Edmund had paid her throughout the evening (only of course she must not think too much of that), Elinor fell into a deep, exhausted sleep, though still with a lingering worry as to just what might be Grenville Royden's intentions.

No such troubles clouded the daydreams of his sister

Charlotte, who was far too excited to be able to sleep but lay comfortably in bed in the Steads' house, going over the kind things Lord Conington had said to her again and again, and able to dismiss her brother's cutting remarks entirely from her very well contented mind.

11

Unimpeded on this occasion by the necessity of providing transport for a young lady and a quantity of baggage, Sir Edmund was able to travel down to Cheltenham and Bath in an easier and more agreeable manner than on his last visit, driving himself in his own phaeton, and accompanied only by John Digby. "A tamer landscape than some we've seen, John," he observed, as they emerged from the environs of London and took the road westward. "D'you regret the Alps and Pyrenees and the Rhine? Or come to that, the girls of Paris and the gaieties of Berlin?"

"Not I, sir!" replied John Digby, with a broad grin. "Time I settled down, I reckon, and yesterday – why, sir, I got Peg to name the day at last!"

"You did? Excellent! I wish you both very happy, and I'm sure you will be." For Sir Edmund had, over quite a long period, been the recipient of John's confidences concerning his courtship of Peggy, the under-nursemaid at Yoxford House. Peggy was ready enough to marry him but not, as she stoutly averred, to go jauntering off to them nasty foreign parts. From the start, Sir Edmund had assured John Digby that *he* would not stand in the couple's way, and if John left his own service, there would certainly be a good position waiting for him at Yoxford House, but since his man would not hear of that, the courtship had been a protracted one. As might have been expected, however, Sir Edmund's decision to come home to England for good had brought it to a happy conclusion. His congratulations to John Digby now were cordial and sincerely felt.

As they trotted briskly along in the smart black and

primrose phaeton, driving between lush green banks, beneath branches laden with foliage and heavy white hawthorn blossom, and past the tall grasses waving by the roadside, Sir Edmund wondered for a moment why he felt a certain envy of his servant. For a moment, but no longer. He was tolerably well aware of what had been happening to him over the last few weeks, although it was only last night that he had consciously realized it. No doubt about it, he had fallen in love, a thing he had never thought to do again! There was something missing on this journey, compared with the last time he had travelled the road between Cheltenham and London. It was certainly not young Persephone's sulks, nor even the bright chatter with which he had heard her enlivening the way once she regained her temper, but the quieter presence of Elinor Radley. Her shining chestnut hair and grey eyes, he found, had taken the place in his mind of dead Catherine's lovely image, which, instead of evoking that keen sense of loss he had known so long, was faded to a smiling memory – just as he acknowledged Catherine herself would have wished.

There had been women in his life after his wife's death, but these affairs had been of fleeting duration, and the kind of liaison likely to occur in diplomatic circles in the capitals of Europe, where a man might find himself suddenly posted hundreds of miles from his inamorata. It did not do to engage one's affections too deeply. Nor had any of Sir Edmund's mistresses, when separated from him, been witty and intelligent enough to sustain a relationship over a distance and a long period of time by means of interesting letters, as Princess Lieven had done with her correspondence to her lover Metternich. He would certainly never, on finding himself fifty miles from one of these ladies, have felt an urge to turn his horses and drive straight back to her, in order to propose that he and she emulated John Digby and his Peggy!

The notion of marriage to Miss Radley presented itself in ever more attractive colours as he drove along. He wished, however, that he could think she felt for him in the same way. She had given no indication of regarding him as anything but a friend and a cousin. The mildest of personal compliments last night, he remembered, had caused her to shrink with apparent distaste. But then, she was certainly anxious about something just now. *That's not it*, she had said, of the trouble the ball had given her. Was she really just concerned for Persephone's whims and fancies? Perhaps so: Miss Radley certainly took her duties very seriously. As for himself, he realized that he cared very little about his ward's presumed amorous problems – it was his own, as he ruefully told himself, that were in the forefront of his mind. What he *did* care for was to see that expression of haunted, wary anxiety banished from Elinor's fine eyes. Well, let him but get his business at Cheltenham over, discover (he hoped) tidings in Bath to make her easy in her mind, and then, like John Digby, he meant to apply himself seriously to the pleasant task of courtship!

Cousin Sophronia's gloomily righteous shade seemed to him to be still brooding over the house in Royal Crescent, and though there was no need for a fire in the drawing room this fine May day, Sir Edmund missed the warmth he had felt about the place on his previous visit, and which he had fancied even at the time emanated from Elinor herself. Mrs Howell, discursive as ever, and her amiably silent husband, were on the point of moving out to their own little cottage. Sir Edmund easily found the small landscape painting Elinor had mentioned, still hanging on the landing, and saw at once why she liked it. It was from the brush of John Crome, and showed a wide, clear sky and a graceful bridge spanning a stream; it must, he imagined, have seemed a vista of freedom to a girl cooped up in the suffocating atmosphere of Lady Emberley's household.

He was putting up at the Plough again, and having left John Digby there with the phaeton, he next called upon Mr Stanfield, to read and sign the various documents the attorney set before him. Their business completed, Mr

Stanfield produced a decanter of excellent sherry, and begged Sir Edmund to do him the honour of taking a glass with him. He then inquired after Miss Radley. "I have been very glad, I will confess," said he, perceptibly relaxing his punctiliously legal manner, "to know that she is with those who, given a broad interpretation of the term, may be called her family! I will not conceal from you, for indeed I know we agree upon that subject, that I consider Lady Emberley did very ill in omitting the name of Miss Radley from her will! That is a good girl, Sir Edmund, a very good girl!" he added, with unwonted warmth. "Several times Lady Emberley assured me that she would be making adequate provision for her companion, and it is a thousand pities that she never did!"

Sir Edmund was not going to enlighten the lawyer as to the manner in which Lady Emberley considered she *had* made adequate provision, but allowed himself to say, "If she was not going to do so, it was certainly improper in her to single out any *other* person for a bequest. We do indeed agree on the subject of Miss Radley, and I've tried to set matters right, but I couldn't prevail upon her to accept anything but the salary of companion to my young ward."

"I suspected, of course, that that would be the case – and you could hardly *compel* Miss Radley to accept what she would regard as charity! You will allow, sir, that her sentiments do her credit."

Sir Edmund was very ready indeed to allow this, and found, somewhat to his surprise, that he would be happy, in the manner of the most callow young lover, to sit and talk of his beloved at length to Mr Stanfield, for the mere pleasure of pronouncing her name. But the lawyer had turned to that other bequest.

"As for Mr Spalding, sir, you need not be *surprised*, precisely, at the legacy to him. The fact is, Lady Emberley much deplored the laxity of tone prevalent in the society of this town, and, Mr Spalding entering fully into her own sentiments on the matter, she regarded him as – er – an

150

instrument for good." The attorney's tone was perfectly neutral, but he gave a small, dry cough.

"Good God!" exclaimed Sir Edmund, amused. "Is Cheltenham such a shocking haunt of vice?"

"Hm! Well, so Lady Emberley held, for there are persons residing here of whom, she found, she could not at all approve."

"And the good Mr Spalding is supposed to rid the place of them? I wonder just how!"

"I have," said Mr Stanfield, with a wintry smile, "occasionally permitted myself to wonder the same thing! I fancy that he would, for instance, encounter some difficulty in dislodging Colonel Fitzhardinge from Berkeley Castle!" For as Mr Stanfield remembered only too clearly, for the circumstance of being obliged to listen to his late client's lengthy diatribes, that gentlemen had been prominent amoung those of whom Lady Emberley found she could not at all approve. The Colonel and other members of his family had always supposed that he would succeed to his father's title, but on the death of the fifth Earl Berkeley it transpired that his parents had not in fact been legally married at the time of his birth, and the House of Lords ruled that his youngest brother Thomas was the Earl's heir. Thomas, however, refusing to accept his rights, left his elder brother to reside in the Castle and vowed that he himself would never marry, thus avoiding the possibility of any bar to the Colonel's enjoyment of his inheritance. There were those who considered this a touching instance of fraternal affection, but such were not Lady Emberley's sentiments. She thought it very wrong of the altruistic Thomas, and still less did she approve of the Colonel himself: not only stigmatized as illegitimate, but bold-faced enough to continue living at the Castle and cutting a notable figure in Cheltenham society, just as he had done before the shocking revelations about his birth! He had led the Berkeley Hunt through the streets of the town one day, had appeared in amateur theatricals on the stage of the Theatre Royal, had encour-

151

aged the sport of horse-racing, with all its attendant evils, and was no enemy to the holding of the fair! It was all very depraved, to Lady Emberley's way of thinking, and showed only too well the spirit now abroad in Cheltenham. Things had been very different when she first came to live in Royal Crescent as a widow, twenty years before! Mr Spalding was very sure she was right, and she rejoiced to find him of the same mind with her.

But notwithstanding Lady Emberley's disapproval, and whatever reforming powers her legacy and its beneficiary might prove to wield, Cheltenham was still a tolerably lively place, and a pleasant one on a warm May evening. After partaking of an excellent dinner at the Plough, Sir Edmund went for a stroll, viewing (from outside) the Assembly Rooms opened by the Duke of Wellington some eight years earlier, and the Montpellier and Sherbourne Pump Rooms. He was not yet tired, so he next betook himself to the handsome Promenade, and was walking along it, lost in thoughts of what he would say to Miss Radley once back in London, when he was brought down to earth by a gentleman who was hailing him in a loud voice.

"Sir Edmund! Sir Edmund! I am very happy to see you! It *is* Sir Edmund, is it not?"

Sir Edmund admitted that it was. It took him a moment to identify the stout, imposing personage who had greeted him with such cordiality, but he soon placed the man: he was face to face with the recipient of the legacy which he still deplored, as he rather fancied Mr Stanfield did too.

"Mr Spalding," said he, politely. "How do you do?"

"Well, very well, sir, thank you! Thank you, I am very well!" the clergyman assured him. "Allow me to invite you to enter one of the Pump Rooms with me, and try a glass of our excellent Cheltenham water!"

This Sir Edmund declined, having drunk more glasses of unpalatable spa water upon the Continent than he cared to remember, but as he had enjoyed a very tolerable claret with his dinner, he instead courteously begged Mr Spalding to

152

repair to the Plough with him and crack another bottle of it. Mr Spalding fell in with this proposal, though regaling his companion on the way with a convoluted excuse for doing so, to the effect that while he did not in general partake of spirituous liquors – a practice which had, moreover, been abhorrent to that late, generous patroness of St Mary's, Sir Edmund's much lamented cousin Lady Emberley – he supposed that on the Continent, where everyone knew the water was not fit to drink, Sir Edmund must, like many another English gentleman, have fallen into the habit of taking wine freely.

Sir Edmund listened patiently to all this, and noticed that once the claret was set on the table in his private parlour, Mr Spalding seemed far from unwilling to take it pretty freely himself. Smiling inwardly, he stored up this circumstance in his memory to be related to Miss Radley in due course. He then bore for some time with his companion's prosy and highly repetitive conversation, privately wishing that automatic politeness had not compelled him to offer hospitality; a little of Mr Spalding went a long way. After a while, the clergyman asked, "And how, pray, is Miss Radley? I hope she goes on well in London?"

Sir Edmund hoped so, too. The anxiety in her face last night at Persephone's ball had been near the forefront of his mind all day, and the farther he went from London, the more impatient he had become to return to her. He was not a vain man, but he could not see Mr Spalding as a serious rival for Miss Radley's affections, and in any case he had heard her turn down that gentleman's offer of marriage very comprehensively. However, the memory of the infelicitous terms in which Mr Spalding had couched that offer (or rather, supposition) did not endear him to Sir Edmund, who contented himself with saying, "Yes, I think so."

"To be sure! So good of Lady Yoxford to take her in! Elinor must feel obliged in her indeed! Such graciousness – such condescension!"

He was about to expand further on the virtues he assumed

(without ever having met her) in the amiable but indolent
Isabella, but this was a little too much for Sir Edmund, who
interrupted him, saying, "No, no, it is quite the other way
round. My sister is the person who is obliged to Miss
Radley! She is a great favourite with the children, and made
all the arrangements for my ward's coming-out ball, which
took place last night, incidentally, and was most successful"

"I am glad to hear it." Mr Spalding nodded his approval.
"It cannot be denied that Elinor has a gift for managing a
household. I do not despair, you know, of her managing
mine some day. Oh, no, I by no means despair! Indeed, I
quite look forward to it!" The meaning smile which he
bestowed upon Sir Edmund struck that gentleman as
remarkably fatuous, but Mr Spalding was inexorably proceeding. "I am sure she has not forgotten her old friends in
Cheltenham. Miss Dunn, an excellent woman and one of
my parishioners, was asking me only the other day whether
I thought Miss Radley would be returning. A consumma-
tion, in the words of the poet, devoutly to be wished! Of
course, she cannot have much acquaintance in London."

"There you are mistaken," said Sir Edmund, with
satisfaction. "As I am sure you will agree, Miss Radley must
make friends wherever she goes. Another pleasing circumstance is that she has met with some old acquaintances in
town."

"Old acquaintances?" said Mr Spalding, startled. "Why,
she has not been in London since she was a young girl, and
that was only for a month or so! No, no, how could she meet
with any old acquaintances there?" He sounded peevish as
well as proprietorial, thought Sir Edmund, his irritation
with the man giving way to amusement, for all the world as
if Elinor had no right to any friends outside Cheltenham!

"This is a family where she was governess before coming
to live with Lady Emberley," he explained. "A brother and
two sisters by the name of Royden, though the elder sister is
now married."

This innocuous information, much to Sir Edmund's

154

surprise, appeared to have a powerful effect on Mr Spalding. "Royden? Royden?" he uttered – yet not as if the name were strange to him. "Oh, dear me, dear me! Tut, tut! This will not do! Dear, dear, dear!" His face, working busily, was a good deal flushed. "Good gracious, this will never, never do!"

Sir Edmund raised his brows. "Why not?"

"But I thought you were aware . . . I supposed . . . perhaps you are not! Dear me, believe me, it will not do! The association is most improper!"

Assuming an unaccustomed air of hauteur, and liking his companion less and less, Sir Edmund said coldly, "My dear sir, I am at a loss to understand you. I scarcely believe that the company my sister chooses to receive in her house can be described as *improper*."

This overset Mr Spalding even more, and he uttered several disjointed protests as to his perfect confidence in the propriety of Lady Yoxford's household, interspersing these avowals with exclamations of distress over this most unfortunate situation.

"But have no fear!" he weightily assured Sir Edmund, when he had at last regained his composure and his powers of coherent speech. "I have made up my mind! I shall not fail! You may count on me – I shall do what I consider to be my duty!"

"I'm sure you will," said Sir Edmund, patiently, "though what I may count upon you *for*, I really have no notion."

"Ah, so you do not know all! I was beginning to fear it might be so. The matter," pronounced Mr Spalding, "concerns Miss Radley. If I were to tell you – indeed, I *will* tell you!" he finished, righteously.

"Please don't," said Sir Edmund, coldly, for Mr Spalding was someone with whom he decidedly did *not* wish to discuss his beloved. "I really should infinitely prefer you not to, Mr Spalding." His distaste rapidly increasing, he rose to his feet in a manner which unmistakably conveyed the impression that it was time for his guest to finish his wine and depart. This the clergyman did; he was briefly abashed, however, and said with a chuckle, as he took his leave, "Ay, well, mum's the word, Sir Edmund! But I shall not fail you – no, indeed! How unfortunate it is that I am unable to leave Cheltenham just at present. The rector, you understand, is away, so that all the duties of the parish – and they, I may say, are onerous – devolve upon me! But you may expect to see me in town before very long. Pray, at what number in Upper Brook Street do Lord and Lady Yoxford reside?"

Sir Edmund saw no way out of giving him the desired information, but hoped very much, as he saw his guest off, that he would *not* soon be turning up to plague them all at Yoxford House. Especially Elinor. By now pretty well accustomed to Mr Spalding's rhetorical manner, he concluded, correctly enough, that he had been referring to whatever youthful peccadillo it was Elinor had wished to confess to him on their first meeting, before taking the post of chaperon to Persephone. Seeing her distress, he had dissuaded her from doing so at the time, and he certainly did not wish to hear about it now from Mr Spalding. Whatever it was, it was Elinor's private business, upon which he declined even to speculate; he therefore put the matter out of his mind, and proceeded next day to Bath.

After going to his hotel, seeing the phaeton and John Digby well bestowed, and changing into the correct attire for paying a morning call, he went to see the Miss Maddens. He was immediately shown into their parlour. Neither the unmixed pleasure on Miss Mary's good-natured face, nor the expression of alarm that flitted over her sister's countenance before she schooled it to impassivity, escaped him. He hastened to assure the ladies that Miss Grafton was very well, and without precisely saying so made them aware that this was a mere call of courtesy. From the relief he sensed in Miss Madden, he fancied that she had thought he might have come with a tale of some dreadful deed perpetrated by

156

Persephone, for which her former mentors would be held to blame!

"Yes, ma'am, she is surrounded by suitors, and has quite a little court of her own!" he told Miss Mary, smiling, in answer to her supposition that dear Persephone did not lack for beaux. (Selina had frowned a little at her sister's ungenteel choice of noun, but Miss Mary was not deterred by that.)

"Oh, I knew it!" she cried, eyes shining. "I am so glad. I was sure she would – would *take*, is not that the expression?"

"Hmph!" remarked Miss Selina.

"And does she prefer any *one* of them above the rest?" breathed Miss Mary, head coyly tilted to one side.

"Not yet – and we are quite glad of that, as she is still so young. There can be no haste for her to become established." Miss Selina, he saw, looked as if she did not quite agree with this, and might have been about to make some remark, but then thought better of it. "And I was fortunate enough to persuade a cousin of mine, a Miss Radley, to come to London as her chaperon." With a slight effort, he prevented himself from talking any more about Miss Radley who, as a total stranger to these good ladies, could be of little interest to them, and brought himself back to the purpose of his visit. He *had* wondered, though not very optimistically, whether the Miss Maddens themselves would, after all, be able to throw any light on the identity of Persephone's supposed "friends", and so continued, "Besides charging me with her love to you – " Miss Mary, he saw, looked gratified, and Miss Madden decidedly sceptical – "Persephone gave me messages for some acquaintances of hers. Very stupidly, I have forgotten their direction. Perhaps you can help me?"

"Acquaintances?" said Miss Madden. "Oh, you must mean her friends in the school!"

"No, I believe these people reside in the town; does that sound probable?"

"Oh, no, not at all! We *never* allow our girls to mix with the town people!" said Miss Madden firmly, a good deal shocked. "You must be mistaken, Sir Edmund."

Well, he thought, he had not been mistaken in supposing it would most likely be unprofitable to question Persephone's schoolmistresses; whatever she had been up to, she had contrived to pull the wool over their eyes!

"The name, as I remember, was Ford: Mr and Mrs Ford," he said, proceeding to his next and more hopeful line of inquiry.

Miss Madden's brow at once cleared. "Oh, you mean the music master! That explains it! On occasion we *do* let the girls visit his house, where he has a very superior pianoforte, and the space to hold little concerts. I know that Persephone went, several times."

"I'm sure she did. Her musical gifts are remarkable," said Sir Edmund.

"They are, are they not?" Miss Madden sounded relieved again – as if she had feared that the excellence of Persephone's talent might also be held against her personally, thought Sir Edmund. That would amuse Elinor, too; he must remember to tell her! "Mr Ford," Miss Madden was going on to assure him, "is a most accomplished teacher! The parents of all our girls have been very well satisfied with his instruction of our pupils on the pianoforte. Mrs Ford herself plays the harp, and has taught some of the girls as well. When you said *acquaintances in the town*, I did not know it was only the Fords you meant. But let me write down their direction for you."

12

The address to which Sir Edmund made his way was on the outskirts of Bath, and not in one of the town's more fashionable streets. Indeed, it soon became plain that the Ford family would have had some difficulty in squeezing themselves into one of the elegantly narrow dwellings in the modern crescents and terraces. Theirs was a rambling house of mellow stone, set at the end of a long alley which had obviously been a country lane not so long ago, and looking out over an orchard of old fruit trees and a garden, with fields just beyond. Sir Edmund wielded the ornate but tarnished brass knocker, and was admitted by a little maidservant. He found that he had to raise his voice a good deal to make her understand his business, such was the volume of noise, all of it more or less musical in nature, that drifted into the hallway from the other side of several closed doors. One of these doors opened as he handed the maid his hat and gloves, and a very small girl appeared, carrying a violin half her own size. She looked at him with wide-eyed interest, and ran back into the room, where she could be heard shrilly informing Mama and Papa that there was a gentleman come to call.

The melodious notes of pianoforte and harp floated down from the floor above; someone was blowing heartily into a French horn; and when Sir Edmund entered the room into which the tiny violinist had run he had a view, through the long windows at its far end, of a boy of about ten sitting among long grass and cowslips in the orchard beyond, earnestly fingering a flute, for all the world like a faun incongruously attired in nankeen breeches and frilled shirt. Even the smallest infants, it seemed, did not go without

159

musical instruments here, for a child toddling along in leading strings came round a corner of the low garden wall, beating a toy drum, while its slightly older sister pursued it with an air of anxious maternity. A lady whom Sir Edmund took to be Mrs Ford hurried to the window and called, leaning out, "Oh, Eliza, whatever you do, mind he doesn't fall into the lily pond – remember, William has taken a part of the fence down to mend it!"

The maidservant, not surprisingly, had failed to catch Sir Edmund's name in all this cheerful hubbub, so that he was obliged to introduce himself to the master of the house. Mr Ford, described by Persephone as *old*, was not so very aged after all, but a hale and hearty man in his mid-forties, with a shock of thick, greying hair, and an amiably distracted expression on his face. The room where Sir Edmund found himself was a large one, littered with music paper and instruments; there was a bird in a cage, and a great bowl of cowslips on an old oak chest which bore the marks of small, sticky fingers and could have done with a dusting. But that did nothing to detract from the haphazard charm of the place.

"Persephone's guardian! Well, well!" said Mr Ford cordially. "Happy to make your acquaintance, Sir Edmund! Pray let me introduce my wife."

Mrs Ford, having watched her two small offspring safely negotiate the garden wall and disappear among some currant bushes which closed above their heads, turned to greet Sir Edmund. She was a plump, rosy-faced woman with a sweet and slightly harrassed smile, and she adjured her husband to offer Sir Edmund the Madeira – "Yes, John, we *do* have some Madeira! Oh, Susan, pray fetch the cake," she told the little maidservant. "My dear John, look in the corner cupboard – there, beside the bookcase!"

Mr Ford, who had been muttering vaguely, "Madeira . . . is there any Madeira? . . . well, I wonder where I can have put it?" did as she suggested, and with a pleased if surprised smile produced a decanter. "Good

160

heavens, Amelia, you were right! How in the world did you know it would be there?"

"Because that is where we always keep it, my dear! Now, some glasses . . . "

"Glasses, yes. Well, well! Where shall I find *them*, I wonder?" But Mrs Ford had already located the glasses, which were made of handsome cut crystal and were a trifle dusty, like most of the other objects in the room apart from the musical instruments. However, Sir Edmund had cheerfully drunk much worse wine from far more dubious receptacles in the course of his Continental travels, and sipped the wine appreciatively. The maidservant reappeared with a platter on which a handsome slab of cake reposed, whereupon quantities of children materialized as if by magic – how in the world, Sir Edmund wondered, *had* they known? – and went away again with slices of cake in their hands. "Only one piece each, mind!" their mother told them, as one tried to take his place in the line a second time. "No, Georgie, that is very naughty and greedy! Eliza, please don't let Tommy try to stuff any of his into Baby's mouth again, for you know that though he means it kindly, Baby is far too young to eat cake! Oh dear, you must forgive us, Sir Edmund," she added cheerfully. "The thing is that the children have a holiday from school today, and Cook is busy with the dinner, and Susan and I have had no chance to tidy up, so that is why you find us all at sixes and sevens! But I dare say you won't mind! Now, pray sit down and tell us how Miss Grafton is."

Sir Edmund, who had taken an instant liking to the Ford family, was happy to comply with this request. As he gave his news of Persephone, he could see the children through the windows and the open door, coming indoors and going out, wandering up and down the stairs, romping and picking flowers in the garden, and (as the evidence of his ears told him) constantly taking up and laying down a wide variety of musical instruments. None seemed older than sixteen, so he thought that any notion of Persephone's swain

161

being among them might be discounted. "Do *all* your children play an instrument, Mr Ford?" Sir Edmund inquired.

"Why, yes, sir, they all play something! It is only to be expected, you know, when both parents are musical," said the music master, beaming amiably at his guest. "We sing, too; we can make up quite a little family choir. But alas, none of my children has a voice to equal Persephone's!"

"No, indeed," agreed their mother. "But then, *hers* is outstanding!" She suddenly became a little grave, almost intense. "Sir Edmund, I don't know if you are musical yourself, but perhaps I should inform you that with that voice, Miss Grafton might well rival any professional singer of the day!"

"Precisely what my cousin Elinor has said to me – that is Miss Radley, of whom I was telling you. She was very much struck when she first heard Persephone sing."

"The thing is, I have been afraid she may not be able to continue with her singing – I have wondered if she will be able to get the voice properly trained, in London?"

"My dear," interrupted her husband, "I don't suppose that Sir Edmund is much concerned with such matters!"

"Then he ought to be!" said Mrs Ford, quite fiercely. "For it would be worse than a shame, it would be a *sin* to let that voice go unheard! And such a loss – to everyone, not least Persephone herself!"

"I feel sure you are right, ma'am," Sir Edmund hastened to assure her. "Even *I* can tell that her performance on the pianoforte is most superior, and her singing is much admired wherever she goes, though I own that I am not competent to judge how she would compare with a professional singer."

Mrs Ford did not look quite satisfied, but here her husband, who seemed to have been mulling over her remarks, spoke up. "You are quite correct, my dear Amelia, although," he added wistfully, "I suppose that it is immaterial, in Persephone's station in life. But *I* am competent to

162

judge of her ability, Sir Edmund, and I can tell you it is a long time since I heard a singer to equal her. What is more, Amelia, you remember, I am sure, how young Robert praised her voice? And *he* had been in London quite recently, of course, and heard Sontag, and Vestris, and Miss Stephens and Miss Paton, and a great many more. Franz and Josef and Johann agreed with him too, did they not? The very first time they ever heard her!"

Young Robert, indeed, thought Sir Edmund, not to mention Franz and Josef and Johann! He felt pretty sure he was now coming much closer to Persephone's deeply regretted *friends*. And had not Elinor been sure, from an unguarded remark of Miss Grafton's, that R was the initial of her lost love?

"I collect that Persephone visited you quite frequently?" he asked.

"Yes, indeed, the dear child!" said Mrs Ford, her momentary fierceness gone. "I believe it did her good, you know – not that the Miss Maddens are not very excellent women, to be sure, but I can well understand that at times she felt – shall I say, *constricted* in their seminary? There were not very many girls there with any real liking for music, and certainly *none* with a talent approaching hers – sometimes it does seem a shame," she said reflectively, "that young ladies should be made to play the pianoforte or harp just because it is an *accomplishment*, for if they have no taste for it, what good, pray, will it ever do them or anybody else?"

"None at all, I imagine, ma'am," agreed Sir Edmund.

"Although perhaps we should not complain too much, Amelia," suggested her husband, with a twinkle, "since we earn our bread by teaching such accomplishments to such young ladies!"

She laughed. "You are right, John! Dear me, Sir Edmund, I become *so* provoked by girls who will not take the trouble to practise that I get quite carried away. With Persephone, of course, the case was very different. Yes, she got into the

163

way of coming here – not just for her lessons, you know, but whenever there was a half-holiday, or we had a little evening concert in the big music room upstairs, which will hold quite a number of persons. I own, I miss her! The children were all so fond of her, and I do believe she loved them too."

No wonder she had seemed rather disappointed in his unmusical twin nephews, thought Sir Edmund, recollecting Persephone's arrival in London. They must have appeared sadly commonplace by comparison with this charming family of Ford infants who wandered in and out at will, playing on their pipes and fiddles!

"And no doubt she met other young people of her own age here, from time to time?" he gently suggested.

"Oh, yes, but there was not the least impropriety, if that is what you were thinking," Mrs Ford assured him – though a little defensively, he fancied. "She always had permission from Miss Madden, of course, and naturally, when we held a little Musical Evening of our own and invited Persephone to play and sing, I was there as chaperon."

"It all sounds delightful, ma'am, and I wish I could attend one of your Musical Evenings myself," said Sir Edmund, with his warmest smile. "But about the *other* people who were there?" he quietly persisted. "Tell me, were they always persons who live in Bath? The fact is, my cousin has been in rather a worry, because Persephone seemed distressed to have left friends behind her when she came to London, although she will say very little about these friends. Of course, Miss Radley has suggested that she might write to them, and thinks she did so but got no answer – and that too seems to have cast her into the dismals. It's as much to set my cousin's mind at rest as anything that I wondered – "

But here he was interrupted by a dismayed exclamation of "Oh *dear!*" from Mrs Ford. Her rosy face crumpled slightly, and large tears began to roll down her cheeks.

"Amelia!" said her husband, alarmed. "What can be the matter?" Looking around for some means of succour, he took his own glass of Madeira in one hand and the plate of cake in the other, and urged both upon her, begging her distractedly, "Take a little wine, Amelia – take a slice of cake, my dear, and you will feel better directly!"

"No, no!" uttered Mrs Ford, through her tears.

Sir Edmund, who had certainly not meant to provoke such a reaction, was quite alarmed by the effect of his own words. "Please, my dear ma'am, don't let anything I have said distress you. I had no intention of – "

"Oh, I might have *known* how it would be!" wept Mrs Ford, firmly thrusting aside the cake, but taking a sip from her husband's glass. She mastered her sobs. "Of *course* I told her they must not think of such a thing – I told them *both*! I even represented it to them strongly, John, that you and I would be held to blame! And he perfectly understood – and even *she* promised me – but I *have* wondered if they did continue to meet after all!"

Ah, thought Sir Edmund, now we are getting somewhere! "My dear Mrs Ford, no one blames you for anything," he said soothingly. "It is only that my cousin and I did suspect some affair of the heart lay behind Persephone's unhappiness, and I wished to discover the facts of the matter. Do you think you could manage to tell me?"

"And you say she has had no letter? Oh – I can't *wish* her unhappy, but I am glad of it too, since it means he has done just as he ought," said Mrs Ford obscurely, stemming the last of her tears.

"Quite so, Amelia, quite so," her husband calmed her. "*Who* has done just as he ought?" he added, and then, apparently searching his memory, "Can you mean young Robert? Dear me, how very shocking! Not that he has done as he ought, I mean, but that – that the necessity for it should arise. Do I understand, Amelia, that you mean to tell us an attachment of some sort existed between young Robert and Persephone? Well, I am astonished! Who would ever have thought of it?"

"*I* ought to have thought of it! From the very outset!"

said Mrs Ford remorsefully. "But I swear, Sir Edmund, I saw no harm in it, not at the start. You see, he is a most gifted musician, and while he is only five and twenty or so, nonetheless that is some years older than Persephone, and I would never have supposed that a Bath miss still at school . . . but there! It was the voice that first caught his fancy, of course."

"Of course," agreed Sir Edmund.

"And then they came to know each other better, and – and yes, they did become attached. Most sincerely attached, as it seemed."

"Young Robert!" Mr Ford continued to marvel. "Well, well, well! Young Robert!"

"Go on," said Sir Edmund encouragingly. "Tell me about young Robert!"

"Oh, most promising, highly talented, just as Amelia says," replied Mr Ford enthusiastically. "An excellent violinist, you know, and a fine pianist too, but his real interest is in his *own* compositions, and I am pretty sure he will make his name one of these days – oh yes, he will make his name, but meanwhile, of course, one must keep body and soul together, and he has not as yet realized his hopes of obtaining a congenial post providing a regular salary in his native Germany."

"So the young man is German?"

"German or Austrian, I am not perfectly sure which – but having spent long periods of time in this country, he speaks excellent English. The same cannot be said of his young friends, but then the language of music, you know, is universal!"

"Let's hear about the young friends too," suggested Sir Edmund.

"Ah, well, Franz and Josef and Johann are in the way of making up a quartet with Robert from time to time. Robert Walter – that is his full name. They lodge in London, you understand, living, I suppose, on what musical engagements they can get – I believe that Robert does not in fact share the lodgings of the others, but when they come together they call themselves the Lark Quartet. Nothing to do with *larking about*, or anything of that nature," Mr Ford hastily added, lest his guest be led astray by the slang term, "but on account of that bird's tuneful song, and I think also with reference to Haydn's Lark Quartet, a work they frequently perform, as indeed they did when they first came here to entertain our friends at a Musical Evening."

Having offered this punctilious explanation, he paused for breath, and his wife took up the tale, reminding him that she fancied Sir Edmund would rather know about Robert and Persephone than the repertoire of the Lark Quartet.

"You see, the young men have sometimes given recitals here in Bath, and so we have all become good friends, because they come to stay with us – if some of the children sleep two to a bed, we can put them up without too much difficulty."

"Yes, indeed! Most agreeable to have such talented young fellows about the place!" said her husband cheerfully, his mind straying again from the matter under discussion.

"All the same," said Mrs Ford, resolutely, "I *do* hold myself to blame! When he – Robert, that is – was so amazed by Persephone's voice on first hearing it – oh, I ought to have been on my guard! No use now crying over spilt milk, but I should have seen it sooner!"

"You are really telling us, Amelia," the still faintly bewildered music master inquired, "that Robert has taken a – a warm liking to Persephone herself? Not *only* her voice?"

"Well, why not?" asked his wife, reasonably. "You know very well she is a most engaging girl, John! And *he* is a remarkably handsome young man."

"He would be," observed Sir Edmund, resigned.

"So that while I did not anticipate it because of her youth, I suppose it was not so very wonderful, once they had first become attracted. But of course, it will never do!"

"Yes, that *is* the point, I fancy," said Sir Edmund. "You mustn't think I am angry, my dear ma'am, but if I know more of this it may well be helpful to all of us, not least Persephone."

"And of course," put in Mr Ford, still working it all out in his own head, "when they had such an interest as music in common, too – no, you are right, Amelia, it is *not* very wonderful!"

"Well, never mind that now, my dear: it is the outcome Sir Edmund wants to know about – and I am glad to say, sir, there *was* no outcome." She paused, and added, doubtfully, "At least, I had thought not. You see, when first I discovered that they had been meeting privately, out there in the garden, or sometimes all alone together in the music room upstairs, though I am perfectly sure nothing *wrong* took place, Sir Edmund – well, then I represented all the impropriety of it to them both. And Robert perfectly understood, and said he would postpone approaching Persephone's guardian – meaning yourself, of course, Sir Edmund – until he could do so as a man of – of sufficient means to ask for her hand. Oh, such a castle in Spain, poor boy! What chance could he look for to bring *that* about? But then, you see, I think he did not quite realize Persephone's own station in the world."

"How long have they known each other?" interrupted Sir Edmund.

"Oh, it must be since last summer. And then, at about Christmas time – for the Lark Quartet gave us a recital in December, and Robert lingered here, so to speak, after his friends went away again – yes, it was then that I saw what was happening, and spoke to them. And I was sure it was all over! But from what you say – and yes, I own I *had* wondered, later – I suppose she cajoled him into further private meetings."

"You're sure," asked Persephone's guardian, "that it was she who did the cajoling? No, I beg your pardon. I should not ask you that, since I see the young man is a favourite of yours." He saw, too, that poor Mrs Ford was looking distressed again, and added, "She can certainly cajole well enough when she wants to, so I dare say you are right. I take it, from what you and my cousin Elinor have told me, that she wrote to him from London."

"Oh!" wailed Mrs Ford. "Oh yes, she did, for the letter came here, addressed to him care of myself! You see, he had gone off on a tour of Wales when she left for London – "

"Ah, yes: Miss Radley had that much from Persephone herself."

"And it was a settled thing that he would return here, when he had got the inspiration he sought in the wild scenery of the mountains."

"What kind of inspiration was he looking for?" inquired Sir Edmund, mildly interested.

"For his opera, which promises to be very fine," put in Mr Ford, with suddenly revived enthusiasm. "It is to have an Ancient British setting, and while I own I think the story quite absurd, what Robert has so far written of the score is remarkable, truly remarkable!"

"Yes, yes, my dear," said Mrs Ford. "But the thing is, Sir Edmund, that he came back here as we had agreed, so as to have a quiet place – " *Quiet?* marvelled Sir Edmund " – where he could write more of the music. And when I saw the letter, in Persephone's hand – well, I supposed it was a kind of sentimental farewell, that would do her good to write, and you may think it was very wrong of me, Sir Edmund," said Mrs Ford, bravely meeting his gaze, "but I could not bring myself to suppress it entirely, and so I did give it to Robert. But you may be very sure I charged him not to answer it, and he swore most solemnly he would not! And then she wrote to *me*, asking for his direction in London. It was *then* that I began to fear they had been meeting in secret after all, since Christmas time. But of course I would not tell her where to find him – believe me, I knew that would be fatal, since it would serve only to keep both their affections alive." Mrs Ford's kind heart evidently still bled for the young lovers, thought Sir Edmund, a good deal less affected, himself, by the pathos of this sad story. "I told

169

her," finished Mrs Ford, "that I did not know where he was to be found, and very likely he was gone home to Germany. Which was not true, I am afraid, because I did know it, and he had not gone back, but I really could not *connive* any further, could I?" And she began to weep once again, but more quietly this time, while her husband endeavoured to console her. "I was so sorry for them, though I knew it would never have done," she repeated.

Sir Edmund felt considerably more sympathy for Mrs Ford than for the objects of her pity; it sounded to him as if the pair of them had found the poor woman so much wax in their hands, and if, as appeared likely, Persephone's musical suitor had as much engaging charm as she, it was not to be wondered at. He also acknowledged that, despite Mrs Ford's soft heart, she had done her best to nip the affair in the bud, and so he applied himself to the task of soothing her distress. To that end, he allowed the Fords to persuade him to stay for dinner – an excellent notion, for Mrs Ford, a hospitable soul, brightened perceptibly as she hurried away to see what Cook was about in the kitchen, and to supervise the laying of another place at table.

He was glad he had stayed, too. The dinner was excellent; Mr Ford produced a bottle of surprisingly good claret to grace it; and the meal was enlivened by the company of most of the children. Sir Edmund was at last able to count them and establish that the full tally came to eight, including Baby and the toddler who had not, after all, been preserved from the lily pond, but emerging from the currant bushes had tumbled straight in, to be fished out directly, apparently none the worse for it, by his attendant sister and a passing brother. The two youngest did not come in to dinner, but were brought in later by a nursemaid, to be rocked in their mother's arms and fussed over by their brothers and sisters. The presence of so many children might not have been thought conducive to the peace of the dinner table, but in fact the six who shared the meal were very prettily behaved, and Sir Edmund greatly enjoyed the informality of it all. No wonder, he reflected again, that Persephone – and no doubt the impecunious young musicians from Germany too – had liked the easy-going spirit of this house, so different from the starchy atmosphere of the seminary! It was with much mutual goodwill that he eventually parted from the Fords, charged with loving messages to Persephone, and the information that little Eliza was coming along nicely on the pianoforte and often sang the songs Persephone had taught her.

13

Sir Edmund set off very early the next morning, being anxious to reach London before it would be too late in the day to call at Yoxford House for a word with Miss Radley. A private word, he hoped. He looked forward to telling her what he had discovered: it was news which he hoped and trusted would effectively quieten her fears. From all he had heard in Bath, there seemed little likelihood that Persephone's musician would re-enter her life: he appeared to have accepted his dismissal at Mrs Ford's hands. Sir Edmund felt some sympathy for his ward, whose own musical gifts had obviously contributed to her attachment – apparently a stronger one than he and Elinor had at first supposed – but time would certainly heal the wounds. *That* he knew from his own experience of a deeper hurt.

In the event, having washed off the dust of the road and changed into evening dress, he arrived in Upper Brook Street only to find that the family had dined and gone out for the evening. Beale informed him that, except for his lordship, who had gone to his club, they were at Lady Mercer's Brindisi.

"Where?" inquired Sir Edmund.

"I believe, sir, that the term denotes a Musical Evening of a convivial nature. From the circumstance of a drinking song's being known by the name of the Italian city of Brindisi, sir," explained Beale. "I am not perfectly sure that such a derivation is correct," he added scrupulously, "but of course, one might ascertain that by reference to Miss Grafton's singing master, Signor Pascali, when next he – "

However, he had lost his hearer's attention as soon as the words *Musical Evening* were out of his mouth.

172

"You mean they're all round in Grosvenor Square?" interrupted Sir Edmund, taking back his hat and gloves. "Then I'll follow them there! Don't trouble to call a hack; it's only a step to walk."

There was obviously a considerable attendance at the so-called Brindisi. Sir Edmund was well acquainted with the host and hostess of the evening, and although he had received no formal invitation, the lady of the house was delighted to welcome him. "Dear Isabella was saying, just now, she fancied you might join us if you were back in town in time."

"A large gathering!" said Sir Edmund, surveying the scene from the top of the shallow flight of stairs where he and Lady Mercer stood. "And just to my ward's liking – as soon as I heard the occasion was a musical one, I knew how eager *she* must have been to attend." He was looking about him for the Yoxford party – which, as Charley had returned to Cambridge, would consist of the ladies only – but had so far failed to see any of them.

"Dear Miss Grafton! I hope she will play and sing for us all a little later," said Lady Mercer graciously. Since her own two daughters were very eligibly married, she was able to see Persephone shine in company with more equanimity than some of the other middle-aged ladies present. "I hear that people have taken to calling her the Nightingale of Upper Brook Street! Charming! But you must not think we are to depend solely on ourselves for entertainment – dear me, no! I have engaged musicians to play for us, one of whom, I am told, is quite a prodigy! But do go in. I think you will find Isabella and her party in the Blue Saloon." And she turned to greet the next guests ascending the staircase.

Sir Edmund was not surprised to hear that professional musicians had been engaged; it was some time since he had spent a full Season in London, but he knew the Mercers had a great taste for music, and frequently obtained the services of such people to grace their parties. A friend of his had mentioned hearing Henriette Sontag at this house last year,

173

as well as a boy of fourteen then on a visit to England, called Franz Liszt, who played the piano very brilliantly. If such was to be the evening's entertainment, Sir Edmund was not surprised to hear that Yoxford had preferred his club, and poor Isabella would probably find it a bore; he gave her full credit for coming, for he had dropped a tactful word into her ear on the night of the ball, after seeing how tired and anxious Elinor looked, to the effect that she must not delegate *all* her duties to Miss Radley.

He stood on the broad landing, taking his bearings. Through a half-open door, he caught a glimpse of a large music-room where he supposed the professional musicians were to perform, since it contained a good many chairs arranged in short rows and informal groups, a grand pianoforte, and a number of music stands. Just at the moment it was more or less empty. In passing, Sir Edmund briefly noted a few people in sober-hued coats; someone was tuning a cello, while a young man with a great deal of waving dark hair, who was holding a violin, gave him a note on the piano now and then, and meanwhile conversed volubly with a small group of guests whom Sir Edmund did not know. He went on, in search of the Yoxford party.

There were refreshments laid out in a supper room; there was a card room for those whose taste ran to entertainments less elevated than music; and the Blue Saloon, to which Sir Edmund's hostess had directed him, was evidently given over to such of the guests as wished or could be persuaded to perform themselves. It was no surprise to Sir Edmund to find Persephone in occupation of the piano stool in this room. Indeed, he heard her before he saw her: an introductory passage of music, faultlessly executed, caught his ear, and next moment Persephone's voice was raised in a pretty Italian cavatina.

She made a charming picture, sitting at the instrument in a gown of deep blue gauze which matched not only her azure eyes but the decoration of the room itself (Sir Edmund fancied his sister would have remembered its colour, and advised Persephone accordingly as to her toilette for the evening). A number of other young people stood or sat around her, the gentlemen openly admiring, many of the young ladies trying to suppress a certain envy. But Sir Edmund's eyes did not linger on her long; he was looking for Elinor, and had just located her, seated on a sofa beside Isabella, when someone came striding rapidly out of the large music-room he had just passed, and almost elbowed him out of the doorway.

He saw that it was the dark-haired man who had been helping the cellist to tune his instrument. The newcomer paused in the doorway and stood there perfectly still, staring at the singer. Persephone seemed to sense it, for she suddenly broke off short in her song, and looked up. Her hands fell to the keyboard with a small discordant clash, inadvertently knocking the sheets of music off the rack before her. There was a moment's breathless silence, and then, incredulously, happily, Persephone gasped, "*Robert!*"

"Seffi!" cried the young man, in the same instant.

Seated where she was, Elinor had an excellent view of both pianoforte and doorway, and thought that the couple would have flown instantly to one another's arms, but for the fortunate circumstance that each felt impelled not simply to cast aside what he or she was holding, but to dispose of it with some care. The young man was still encumbered with his violin, which he now tenderly set down on top of the pianoforte, and as for Persephone, before she could rise to her feet she had to gather up the pile of sheet music which she had swept into her lap.

Coming fresh from Bath and Mrs Ford's revelations, it took Sir Edmund a split second to grasp the significance of this encounter. Elinor, less well informed than himself, and momentarily confused in any case by the involuntary lurch her own heart gave at the sight of him there in the doorway, just behind the young man who was devouring Persephone with his eyes, was still quick to draw the conclusion that here was that mysterious *friend* whose loss had so distressed Miss Grafton. And unless something was done at once, Persephone was only too likely to betray herself in a manner which would do her reputation no good; rich and beautiful as she might be, even she could not, at eighteen, afford to be considered *fast*. Elinor therefore rose to her feet and walked quickly towards the doorway, saying, "Why, here is Sir Edmund, Persephone! I hope you had a good journey, sir?"

Persephone did glance at her guardian, but very briefly. However, as he himself had moved forward towards Elinor, the prosaic greeting served to break the fascinated silence of the rest of the company; people began to talk again, Elinor urged another young lady to take Persephone's place at the instrument, and then returned to the corner of the Blue Saloon nearest the doorway, where Sir Edmund was still standing.

"And I had thought to surprise you with my news," he said quietly, amusement in his eyes as they met hers.

He had been joined by the puzzled Isabella, and the three of them, forming a small family group, effectively shielded Persephone and Robert Walter – for it could surely be none other – from the eyes of any curious onlookers. This was just as well, since the young couple's own eyes were still locked in an intense and burning gaze, and Persephone at least seemed quite unaware of the presence of anyone else.

"I knew it must be you!" uttered the young man. "As soon as I heard that voice, I knew!" His English, Sir Edmund noticed, was indeed excellent, with only the slightest trace of an accent.

"But Robert, where *were* you?" cried Persephone. "Oh, such an age as it has been – and when I wrote to you in Bath, and had no reply . . ."

Here, Sir Edmund observed, the young man made an impulsive movement towards her, but instantly, and considerably to his credit, checked it. "When I returned from Wales and found you gone – ah, imagine my distress!" he said in a low voice. "I *had* your letter, Seffi, indeed I did –

176

but when she gave it to me, Mrs Ford, good soul, made it a condition I should not reply."

"Oh no! Oh, how angry I am with her! For when I wrote to her asking your direction, she said she did not know it, and she must have known! I *knew* it could not be that you would never go back there! But why would she not at least tell me where to find you in London? I have been hoping – expecting, even – to see you at any moment, and now at last I do! Oh, Robert, only think, we were at the very first performance of Herr Weber's *Oberon*, and you know, I wondered if you might have been playing in the orchestra, but though I looked and looked of course you were not! And I went to see the Kembles in search of you – oh, and such a kind friend has been making inquiries for me, but nothing came of them either. However, never mind that now! You are here! Oh, Robert, tell me – how does your own opera come along?"

At this, although the young man had obviously been feeling a little awkward, and rather more conscious of his very public surroundings than Persephone was, he forgot them entirely; his eyes lit up, and he exclaimed, "*Ach*, Seffi, I am making such progress! Wales! Everything that is sublime! The mountains! The mists, the torrents and cascades, the wild Welshmen! Such inspiration as I found there! Influenced by those grand scenes, I have completed the Druids' Chorus, and *your* song too nears completion – Angelina's last aria. It cannot fail, Seffi, it will surely take all Europe by storm, and then – *then*, whatever the good Mrs Ford may say, then I approach this formidable guardian of yours, of whom you wrote to me. I shall make myself known to him. I shall let nothing stand in my way!"

Realizing that Mr Walter was becoming decidedly carried away, and that Persephone, clasping her hands ecstatically, was about to break into further raptures at any moment, Sir Edmund judged it time to intervene. "Pray *don't* let anything stand in your way, Herr Walter," said he, mildly. "I am happy to make your acquaintance."

Brought abruptly back to earth and an awareness of her family's presence, Persephone darted him a glance of the utmost suspicion, but he continued urbanely, to the young man, "I am only just back from Bath, where I have been hearing a great deal about you from Mr and Mrs Ford."

A stricken gasp from Miss Grafton was lost in Robert Walter's enthusiastic response. "Ah, the good Fords! So delightful, so amiable a family!'

"Just so," said Sir Edmund. "And providing something of a home from home, I collect, for otherwise friendless young people of musical talent on their travels. Not, of course, that Persephone is to be included in that category," he added, the slightest hint of steel in his voice, "since she is far from friendless."

The young man flushed a little, and said rather stiffly, "Sir, I think you perhaps misapprehend! You *are* Sir Edmund Grafton? Delighted to make your acquaintance. Miss Grafton and I, you understand, are old friends."

After what had just passed, Sir Edmund could not but be amused by this masterpiece of understatement, but he said only, "Yes, so I had concluded. Isabella, Elinor, let me make Mr Robert Walter known to you. Mr Walter: my sister, Lady Yoxford, and my cousin, Miss Radley. And is it you whom we are to have the pleasure of hearing perform this evening?"

"Ah, yes, indeed!" he was assured. "Seffi, only think – Franz and Josef and Johann, they are all here; the Quartet is to play. How glad they will be to see you! Lady Yoxford, Miss Radley, your servant!" he added punctiliously, if a little late in the day. "Come, Seffi: let us go and find them." And grasping Persephone's hand, he drew her towards the doorway.

"I believe," said Isabella ominously, "I am going to faint!"

"Not now, Bella," said Sir Edmund into her ear. "Don't do it! If you have any sense in your pretty head, you'll seem to countenance this."

He was about to follow the young couple, with Elinor close on his heels, but there was no need. Franz, Josef and Johann had been on their own way to see what was keeping the fourth member of the Lark Quartet, and an ecstatic reunion now took place just outside the Blue Saloon. Exclamations of surprise and delight gave way to a perfect torrent of conversation in a mixture of English and German – for, as Mr Ford had indicated, the other three young men were not so proficient in the former language as their friend, and Persephone had very little German, so the whole was necessarily held together by Mr Walter's fluency in both tongues.

"I'll enlighten you about all this when I can," Sir Edmund remarked quietly to Elinor, and joined the young people's conversation in his own easy German, whereupon Persephone gave him another look of the liveliest apprehension. But whatever it was he was saying seemed to be quite unalarming. Indeed, though Elinor knew no German herself, she rather fancied that he was uttering the merest polite commonplaces, which were seized upon eagerly by Franz, Josef and Johann in their pleasure at being able to converse with someone outside their own small circle.

All, in fact, was a picture of the utmost propriety when Lady Mercer advanced upon the group, all smiles. "Ah, so you are already acquainted with our musicians, Sir Edmund!"

But he disclaimed previous acquaintance, explaining truthfully, "It is Miss Grafton who has met Mr Walter and his friends before, at musical gatherings in Bath which she and her school friends attended."

"Ah, yes!" Lady Mercer smiled graciously at Persephone. "You must know, Mr Walter, that Miss Grafton herself is an excellent performer on the pianoforte, and the possessor of a remarkable singing voice."

"I do know, Lady Mercer, I do! It is indeed remarkable!" agreed Mr Walter, just a trifle too fervently, but her ladyship had moved on and was speaking to other guests, tactfully suggesting that they might now repair to the music-room, so that first a few persons, and then more, began to drift slowly in that direction. "But I believe it is nearly time for us to play, Seffi," he told Miss Grafton. "You will like it! It is to be Haydn: the Sunrise. I had thought to play the new Beethoven – you recollect, the E flat, the one I brought back from Germany last year. But then I looked around me, I saw these people, all this fashionable crowd; no, said I to myself, I think *not* the Beethoven, is is beyond them – but no matter, since we also play the Haydn very well indeed," he finished, with a positively engaging lack of modesty. And with these words he seemed to gather up his three colleagues and sweep them off into the big music-room in one vigorous move- ment, Persephone eagerly following in their wake. In their turn, Elinor, Sir Edmund and the still bewildered Isabella closed ranks, and followed too.

Mr Walter's confidence in the abilities of the Lark Quartet was not misplaced: they did indeed give an excellent account of the Haydn work. In other circumstances Elinor would have enjoyed it a great deal; the young men played with the greatest feeling and delicacy, and the applause at the end, considerably more than merely polite, was well deserved. However, a large part of her attention was taken up by Persephone, who had installed herself in a chair as close as she could get to the performers, and was listening and watching with an expression of perfect ecstasy on her face, never taking her eyes off the handsome and vital figure of Mr Walter as he took the first violin part.

There was an encore: a lively scherzo for violin and piano, with Mr Walter playing the former instrument while Johann (Elinor thought it was) moved to the pianoforte. "It is of Robert's own composition!" Persephone whispered to Miss Radley, watching her beloved, who was playing with the utmost verve. At the end of the fiery little piece he flung back the lock of dark hair that tumbled over his forehead and smiled round at the whole audience. But it was on Persephone's face that his eyes came to rest.

180

Elinor resolved, if need be, to stick close as any limpet to Miss Grafton, lest she devote herself too exclusively to the young man for the rest of the evening, but as it turned out, she need not have feared. With the greatest ease of manner, Sir Edmund again took charge, joining in the conversation of the Lark Quartet in German, breaking into English now and then so as to draw Isabella and Elinor into it, and making it seem there could have been no more happy coincidence than this encounter. As Persephone certainly thought! Elinor saw how her delight brought a kind of incandescent glow to the delicate rose of her cheeks, and made her a very different creature from the languid girl who had taken to moping disconsolately about Yoxford House these last two weeks. Lovely as Persephone always was, Elinor thought she had never seen her appear to better advantage, and the members of her little court of admirers plainly thought so too. Sir Edmund casually hailed those of them he knew, first one and then another, so that soon there was quite a crowd around the Yoxford party, all desiring an introduction to the gifted Mr Walter.

Nothing could have been better; the embarrassment of that first moment of reunion was quite smoothed over. Conversation became general once more, Persephone was persuaded back to the piano in the Blue Saloon, and although Mr Walter went with her and indeed insisted on accompanying her in some songs by Schubert, by now it seemed quite unexceptionable. He nodded approval of her singing several times, but also criticized now and then, something no one else present would have dared to do. Nor, indeed, would Persephone have accepted criticism so meekly from anyone else! One dowager did inquire, in tones of slightly malicious curiosity, "One might almost suppose you had performed with Mr Walter before, Miss Grafton?" To which Persephone, turning guileless eyes on the lady, immediately replied, "Oh yes, I have! I took singing lessons from him at my school in Bath."

This caused Sir Edmund to choke slightly, and Elinor's

eyes were full of amusement as her gaze met his, for he had
seized an opportune moment while Persephone was at the
piano to give her a rapid account of his visit to Bath, and she
correctly imagined that the notion of the Miss Maddens
countenancing any such singing lessons from a good-
looking young man was ludicrously inapposite.

She feared there might be some difficulty in inducing Miss
Grafton to leave the party at all, but that obstacle was
surmounted when Mr Walter told her, in a brisk and almost
business-like tone, "And now that we have met again by this
lucky chance, Seffi, and I find your guardian not so terrible
after all, I must hear your voice in Angelina's aria before I
can be sure whether the conclusion I had in mind will do.
Where may we see one another?"

Had Elinor thought there was anything but music in the
young man's head just then, she would have gasped at the
audacity of this. But it was Sir Edmund who answered the
question, in as matter-of-fact a voice as that in which Mr
Walter himself had put it.

"You had better call at Yoxford House – hadn't he,
Isabella?"

"Y-yes!" said Lady Yoxford, faintly. "Yes, to be sure!
Pray do call, Mr Walter. How delightful it is for Persephone
to meet old friends!" She was still pretty much at a loss,
but earned a smile of approval from her brother for this
effort.

The prospect of a further meeting next day allowed
Persephone to take leave of Robert Walter with equanimity,
favouring his friends as well as himself with radiant smiles.
She almost danced the short way home from Grosvenor
Square to Upper Brook Street, impulsively kissed Isabella
and Elinor goodnight, and positively ran upstairs with a
buoyant spring in her step.

"I think that between us all, we managed to brush
through *that* tolerably well," remarked Sir Edmund, left
downstairs with the two older ladies.

"Yes, tolerably well," said Elinor, smiling, and then

looked grave. "Only – only it won't *do*, Cousin Edmund, will it?"

"It certainly will not do," he agreed. "But you know, I think we need not fear that that young man will act improperly."

"No, indeed! I should hope not!" said Isabella, a good deal shocked.

"He seems to be a young fellow of reasonable good sense, under the excitability," continued her brother, "and I fancy that when he sees the kind of circles in which Persephone moves, he will recognize for himself that it really is as Mrs Ford told him, and any alliance would be out of the question. For I don't think him a fortune-hunter."

"*Alliance*?" gasped Isabella, who had not yet heard the full tale as revealed by Amelia Ford. Controlling her feelings with a strong effort, she said, "Edmund, do you mean to tell me that – that there has been an attachment – an attachment of a *serious* nature between that young man and Persephone?"

"Why not? Nothing more likely, once they had met – and what's more, found a strong community of interests. You must own they are a good-looking couple. He reminds me of somebody, too, though I can't think who it is," he added thoughtfully.

Not to be side-tracked by such considerations, Lady Yoxford said tragically, "I might have known it, after that Unfortunate Business of the tutor! And I had thought her to be beyond the age of such escapades now. But after all, it is just as I feared before you ever brought her here, Edmund. I confess, when I saw the warmth with which they met, the glances they exchanged, I did wonder – but you sat there talking all the time, and in that horridly difficult language too, as if there were nothing at all the matter, so that I was soon sure there was nothing in it."

"What do you think I should rather have done – played the part of outraged tyrant?" inquired Sir Edmund, smiling. "I fancy that's what Persephone expected."

"You must own, Cousin Isabella, he did bring the thing off splendidly if he could even take *you* in." added Elinor.

"But Edmund, I *still* do not perfectly understand," Isabella complained. "You positively invited him to call here!"

"Exactly so!" said Sir Edmund, unperturbed. "I feel none of us wishes to see Persephone revelling in the part of star-crossed lover, don't you agree? I'm persuaded, Isabella, you can't want to have her mooning about in the sulks, bearing us all a hearty grudge."

"No, very true," admitted his sister, much struck by this piece of sagacity. "Only – will it *answer*?"

"Well, forbidding her to see him certainly won't. As has already been proved! And if absence makes the heart grow fonder, we may as well try whether presence won't have the opposite effect."

14

There could be no doubting the fact that Miss Grafton was a girl transformed. She had been in the seventh heaven that evening, waiting to waylay Elinor when she came upstairs to bed, and it was plain that her reunion with Robert Walter engendered in her such goodwill to the whole world as to dispel that coolness and withdrawal Elinor had recently sensed in her. She impulsively embraced Elinor, crying, "Oh, how happy I am! I couldn't tell you all before, you see, because I felt you would disapprove, like Mrs Ford, but now that you have met him I *know* you must understand! Even Cousin Edmund did, didn't he?"

Dismayed to find that Sir Edmund seemed to have played his part a little too well, Elinor said hesitantly, "Well, I *do* understand, my dear, and Mr Walter is certainly a very agreeable young man, and most gifted. But you cannot be thinking that your meeting again by chance will – will lead to anything!"

Persephone took no notice whatever of this, but continued blithely, "You see, I was afraid, just a little, that he had forgotten me, or did not love me any more – but I might have known he could not forget me, any more than I could forget him, and now everything will be all right!"

"Persephone," said Elinor, more firmly, "you cannot be thinking of marriage!"

"Well, of course we are! Not *directly*, of course, because Robert says Mrs Ford is right, and it would be wrong in him to offer for me yet, and *I* think it was very stuffy of her to put such a notion into his head, but there! I do not like having to wait, but if I must, I will! You see, Robert will very soon obtain a post in one of the German courts where they are sure to require a person of his genius to – to conduct in the theatre, and arrange all the concerts, and everything of that nature. And his own opera will make his name, and he will be rich and famous, and we can get married, because then no one will care a button for my fortune, and there will be no objection in the world!"

Contemplating this hopeful programme, Elinor reflected that even if the events so confidently predicted by Persephone came to pass, there would be every objection from Persephone's family. She scarcely saw them countenancing the heiress's marriage to a professional musician in the employ of some German princeling. It seemed hard to cast a damper on Persephone's high spirits, but she hoped she was being cruel only to be kind when she suggested, "Perhaps, Persephone, Mr Walter sees the difficulties of such a course of action a little more clearly." For she believed, from what Sir Edmund had said and she herself had observed, that such was probably (and very fortunately) the case.

She need not have feared to dash Persephone's spirits; at the moment nothing had power to do that. "Oh, yes!" said Persephone cheerfully. "I fancy he *may* have some silly scruples, but nothing to signify! I promise you, I shall soon overcome them."

This was hardly reassuring to Elinor, who thought Persephone capable of doing exactly as she said, unless Mr Walter could sustain an attitude of proper resolution. But *one* good thing, she thought as she prepared for bed, was that Grenville Royden's nose would be thoroughly put out of joint!

Neither he nor Charlotte had been at Lady Mercer's party, and before the more startling events of the evening began to unfold, Persephone had expressed mild surprise to Elinor, saying she knew they had received cards. Elinor, only too thankful for Mr Royden's absence, did not stop to wonder much at it, and pretty soon, in any case, Persephone's reunion with Robert Walter drove all else

186

from her mind. However, the reason for the Roydens' failure to attend the Brindisi became clear the next morning. The three ladies of the Yoxford household had come down to breakfast at much the same time— Persephone, though Elinor suspected her of having slept very little that night, appearing none the less with the previous evening's radiance quite undimmed. It was otherwise with Lady Yoxford, whose face clearly showed her own lack of sleep and was marked with unwonted lines of anxiety. She was listlessly scanning the *Morning Post* as she sipped tea, and suddenly put her cup down, exclaiming in a tragic manner, "Oh *no*! Oh, this is above everything! And to happen *now*! I declare, it is too bad of them!"

"Too bad of whom, Cousin Isabella?" asked Elinor, and even Persephone emerged from her dream of bliss for long enough to inquire, "Why, what is the matter?"

For answer, Isabella merely pointed to the page before her, where her companions, bending over the newspaper to look at the lines indicated by the quivering finger, read the announcement of the forthcoming marriage between Hadstock James Morrell, Viscount Conington, elder son of the Earl and Countess of Wintringham (here followed a rather imposing list of residences), and Miss Charlotte Jane Royden, second daughter of the late Mr and Mrs John Royden, of Royden Manor in Essex.

"Oh!" exclaimed Persephone. "I am *so* glad! I thought that might come about, didn't you, Elinor? Dear Charlotte!"

"Dear Charlotte, indeed!" said Isabella, crossly. "Sly, scheming Charlotte, if you want *my* opinion! She has snatched Conington up from under your very nose, Persephone, that's what she has done, and you could easily have prevented it, if only you had made the slightest push to do so!"

"But good gracious, why in the world should I wish to? Especially now!" said Persephone, in transparent amazement. Elinor, afraid that she was about to start singing the praises of Mr Robert Walter and pointing out that neither

187

Conington nor any other young man of her acquaintance could hold a candle to him, quickly put in, "But this is excellent, Cousin Isabella! You may certainly acquit Charlotte of scheming! She is in love with Conington, I am sure, and I have seen him paying her a great deal of attention recently. Her fortune may not be great, but the Wintringhams cannot object to her birth or breeding, and are sure to like her. She will make Conington a very conformable wife, which Persephone would never have done, you know."

"No, I would not!" agreed Miss Grafton, decidedly.

Her spurt of bad temper subsiding, Isabella smiled a little at this, and was able to greet the blushing Charlotte graciously when Conington brought her to call in Upper Brook Street later that day. Inevitably (as it seemed to Miss Radley) they were accompanied by her brother, who watched with evident satisfaction as Charlotte and her betrothed received congratulations.

They had dined with Conington's parents last night, so Charlotte confided to Persephone and Elinor, while Conington and Grenville Royden were engaged in conversation by Lord Yoxford and Sir Edmund, who had just come in: Yoxford from his man of business, Sir Edmund from the Foreign Office. The Earl and Countess had been so welcoming, so very kind! Everything that was amiable! Her eyes kept straying to Conington as she spoke, an adoring expression in them, and Elinor saw that his sought her face and rested on it with almost equal warmth. That augured well, she thought. Charlotte expressed herself amazingly happy, and only hoped Persephone too might find such a husband!

"Oh yes!" cried Persephone. "Oh, Charlotte, I have so much to tell you – you will never guess what happened last night! If you were to come up to my room, where we may be private . . ."

But Charlotte demurred, evidently not wishing to go anywhere that took her from the sight of her beloved, and in any case, Persephone's own desire to be private with her was instantly dissipated by the entry of Beale to announce Mr Robert Walter (whose name he firmly pronounced in the English manner).

Mr Walter, as remarkably handsome in his sober but well cut morning dress as he had appeared in Grosvenor Square last night, behaved, Elinor had to admit, with great propriety, accepting introductions, modestly receiving compliments on the performance of the Lark Quartet by those who had been at the Brindisi, proffering his own polite congratulations to the engaged couple when their recent betrothal was mentioned to him, shaking hands with Mr Royden, and bearing with fortitude Lord Yoxford's remarks to the effect that he, for one, thought it very strange for a fellow to spend all his time scraping the fiddle, but he would be the first to admit he hardly knew one note of music from another, and there was no accounting for tastes! Mr Walter then exerted himself to be agreeable to Lady Yoxford, whose initially chilly manner towards him soon thawed. Persephone had nothing to blush for in her musician's social manners, thought Miss Radley; indeed, she seemed a little put out by the fact that he was wisely not paying *her* very much attention.

But her moment was to come. A civil query from Sir Edmund concerning the progress of the opera mentioned to him by Mr Ford caused Robert Walter to produce a small sheaf of music paper, with a modest flourish, from an inner pocket of his coat, and turn to Persephone.

"Here it is, Miss Grafton," he announced. (Thank goodness, thought Elinor, he has realized that it is most improper for him to address her as *Seffi* the whole time, and in public too!) "Angelina's second song! I added the ending after parting from you last night, and now we shall see if it will do. You may sing it in English, because by a most fortunate chance, I fell in with a very amiable clergyman walking in Wales, who undertook to put the words of the opera into your own tongue for me, and he did part of the work while we were staying at an inn, and it rained. Where

189

may we try out the song?"

"Oh, in the Yellow Parlour!" cried Persephone eagerly, her eyes lighting up as she leapt to her feet.

Elinor made an impulsive movement, and was on the point of exclaiming, "No, Persephone!" But she was forestalled. Miss Grafton was prevented from the impropriety of bearing Mr Walter off to the seclusion of her own apartments by Sir Edmund, who at once said amiably, "Do let us *all* have the pleasure of hearing it, Mr Walter!"

Nothing loth, Robert Walter seated himself at the pianoforte in the corner of the saloon and embarked upon a few trial passages, meanwhile informing his hearers that the opera in question, a grand romantic work set at the time of the Roman conquest, was to be entitled *Boadicea Queen of Britain*, and took as its subject the resistance of that Ancient British lady to the Romans, a circumstance which he intended as a compliment to the country that had shown him such hospitality. The main part of the action, he added, took place in the mountains of Wales.

"Wales?" inquired Lord Conington, of the well-informed mind. "Did not Queen Boadicea rule the Iceni? Forgive me, Mr Walter, but I fancy they inhabited quite a different part of these islands – the eastern counties, I believe!"

"Yes, but you have no mountains there," said Mr Walter, simply. "It does not signify – the music is all! Though the story, written for me by a friend of mine in Germany, is also very affecting. Besides the dramatic conflict of Boadicea and the Roman governor Paulinus, there is a love story between Sempronius, a captain in the Roman army, and Angelina!"

"Angelina?" ventured Elinor, who had been wondering for some time who this character might be.

"Yes, she is Boadicea's daughter, and torn between love and her duty! Do you not think the name good, Miss Radley?" he asked, suddenly anxious. "I confess I had my doubts, but my friend was sure that was the name for my younger heroine. Of course, he has never been to England,

and may not be quite conversant with British nomenclature of the time . . . however," continued the composer, dismissing so minor a point from his mind, "the couple first meet in the forest, while Sempronius is out hunting. Here we have the Hunting Chorus – so!" And he played a snatch of a very rousing tune, the words of which the helpful clergyman in Wales had evidently not yet tackled, although they were simple enough, being in the main cheerful cries of "*Juchheisa! Juchhei!*" He then continued with his tale. "Overcoming all obstacles, the couple confess their love to an aged Druid, a small but fine part for bass voice, who consents to wed them, and the Druids sing a chorus of blessing. Failing to free the Queen, they are obliged to flee, and Boadicea, after uttering a noble defiance to the might of Rome, takes her own life. But here is Angelina's aria, in which she declares her readiness to fly with Sempronius to the ends of the earth!"

Persephone had been rapidly casting her eye over the music as he spoke. Preposterous the plot of the opera might be, but there was no denying the power of the wild, sweet music which presently issued from her throat. Mr Walter accompanied; the words, as rendered into English by his chance-met acquaintance, were certainly not very distinguished, consisting as they did largely of Angelina's declaration, "*Over the ocean, over the sea, over the waves I will fly with thee*," repeated a great many times over. But the music was quite another matter. At the end, when Robert Walter nodded to Miss Grafton in a matter-of-fact way and said simply, "Good!" Elinor could not prevent herself exclaiming, "Good? Mr Walter, it is remarkable!"

"You like it? I am glad. A little less vibrato on the high C, I think," he said to Persephone.

"Yes," said she with perfect docility, to her family's amazement. "I will remember."

"Well, well – and so what becomes of this Angelina and – what's his name – Sempronius?" asked Lord Yoxford.

"Ah, here my friend who wrote the words had a very

happy thought!" said Mr Walter with enthusiasm, turning to his host. "At first I had Angelina and Sempronius thrown to the lions in the Circus of Rome! But then it struck me that it might not be possible for the management of *every* theatre to present such a scene, which must be very magnificent or it is nothing! Nowadays gladiators, wild beasts, all must be shown, or I fear the audience will not like it. So we thought of your legend of King Arthur and the island of Avilion, whither the lovers are to flee, and there is a grand processional scene with the Knights of the Round Table. They rejoice at the couple's escape, and offer thanks to Hymen – thus!" And he turned back to the keyboard, breaking into a song which declared, presumably through the agency of the Knights of the Round Table, "*All hail to the Patron of marriage and mirth! Was ever such merriment know upon earth?*"

Conington appeared about to open his mouth – perhaps, thought Elinor, watching appreciatively, to suggest that a considerable period of time separated Boadicea from King Arthur, even supposing the existence of that legendary hero to have any basis in fact. But much to his credit he refrained, and exchanged a glance of amusement with Charlotte instead. "And so," concluded Mr Walter, as the last chord died away, "all ends well!"

"Except for Boadicea! But I suppose you could not go against history there," suggested Sir Edmund.

"No, just so. Moreover," said Mr Walter, engagingly, "I was by then writing the part of Angelina for Sef – for Miss Grafton, and how could I endure to make her dead? So, a happy ending for the lovers!"

"You were writing it for Persephone?" said Isabella, rather faintly. "But, Mr Walter, you surely did not envisage her *performing* it? Upon a *public stage?*"

Robert Walter looked as if he would say something, but thought better of it. Persephone was plainly not going to show any such restraint, but Sir Edmund, coming to the rescue yet again, said, "Not on the public stage, I'm sure,

Bella – but perhaps in private theatricals, some day."

Neither composer nor singer looked as if this suggestion found much favour with them, but Elinor was quick to back Sir Edmund up, declaring, "How pleasant that would be! Of course, Mr Walter, you did not so much imagine Persephone herself in the part as take her voice for your inspiration!"

"To be sure," he said, but a little brusquely, and though Miss Grafton looked as if she violently disagreed, she held her tongue.

"What a very pretty story!" commented Mr Royden, who had kept remarkably silent until now. "Exceedingly affecting!"

He was looking directly at Elinor as he spoke, and she was unable to tell whether he referred solely to the subject matter of *Boadicea Queen of Britain*, or meant anything else besides.

"And how we must rejoice," he added, " at such a happy outcome!"

Now what, thought Elinor crossly, as she remembered his remarks from time to time during the next few days, what was there in that to destroy her new-found peace of mind?

For peace of mind, oddly enough, was what the advent of Mr Robert Walter had brought her. It should not have done so: it prolonged, if it did not perpetuate, a relationship that could never come to anything. And yet she felt instinctively that Mr Walter could be trusted to behave as he ought, and that much as he plainly felt for Persephone, he would not overstep the line. She knew she could never have placed any such reliance on Grenville Royden, by his own confession! But then, perhaps that was only because she knew him all too well, and he had felt free to be devastatingly frank with her. Perhaps *all* men were really like Grenville at heart? If so, it behoved her to guard Persephone all the more carefully.

But no, she answered herself, all men were *not* like that. She sensed that Mr Walter was not; she *knew* Sir Edmund was not. It was a source of chagrin to her (and had she known it, even more to him) that only a couple of days after his return to London, duty, in the authoritative form of Mr Canning, had summoned Sir Edmund to meet a very influential Austrian minister at Dover, accompany him to London, and on account of his own knowledge of the matters of policy on which this personage was visiting the country, remain close to him during the whole of his stay. This meant that he was very seldom seen in Upper Brook Street, and much as Elinor would have liked to talk to him about Persephone, she was unable to do so. Well, she told herself, she must just rely on her own judgment.

Unfortunately, this faculty told her not only that she might trust Robert Walter, but that the mutual infatuation between himself and Persephone showed no signs of abating. Mr Walters's calls were frequent, and countenanced by Isabella because Sir Edmund himself had first invited him. He gave the Yoxford family seats for a concert at the Argyll Rooms in which the Lark Quartet was performing; by means of influence with the management he procured a box at the Opera for a performance of *Medea*, with Giuditta Pasta in the name part, which Persephone had wished to see but which was sold out by the time she heard of it; he wrote a couple of little songs for the children, so catchy in their rhythm that even the twins found the tunes caught their fancy. Elinor saw with dismay that what Sir Edmund had described as the community of interest between Robert Walter and Persephone showed every sign of actually strengthening their attachment.

And if it were so, Elinor caught herself thinking, could she really find it in her to blame them? Did the difference in rank and fortune truly matter so much, with a lifetime's happiness at stake? Good God, she told herself, shocked, I am becoming as bad as Persephone! Anybody would suppose, only because *I* am in love too – not that anyone else will ever know of *that* – I am as foolish as a girl of eighteen following the dictates of her fancy! Well, I *did* follow them once, did I not, when I was eighteen myself? And look what came of that!

However (and her thoughts kept coming full circle) Robert Walter was a very different creature from Grenville Royden. She was half resolved to suggest to Sir Edmund very tentatively, when next they had leisure to talk, that if Persephone's affection really did stand the test of time – say another three years? – the alliance might at least be considered, though she did not honestly see how that could be. There would be less difficulty if the child were not such an heiress! But since she was, how could Sir Edmund, as a conscientious guardian, ever agree?

She was careful not to relax her vigilance: clandestine meetings between the lovers, such as had certainly occurred in Bath, would never do, least of all in the middle of the London Season. But the sympathy she felt for the younger girl had brought them closer together again, and their old, affectionate relationship had revived. The temporary coolness between them, as Elinor knew, had been largely of Mr Royden's contriving, and she was still at a loss to know what he made of the appearance of Mr Walter upon the scene. It had undoubtedly thrust a spoke into the wheel of any hopes he himself had of matrimony – or had he only been teasing her, after all, when he told her of them? Now that Charlotte had made such a fine match, he ought to be content!

She got a little insight into the former relationship between Grenville and Persephone when, walking home with her from a visit to a silk warehouse one day, the latter pointed out an alley. "*That* is one of the streets where Mr Royden thought he had heard of some young musicians from the Continent lodging, but of course it was not Robert, or even the others. Poor Mr Royden!"

"Why do you say *poor* Mr Royden?"

"Oh, because he was in love with me himself! He told me so!" explained Persephone, sunnily. "But of course I let him

195

know directly how things were, and he immediately said he *fully* partook of my sentiments, much as he must regret them for his own part, and he honoured me for them."

"Did he, indeed?" said Elinor, a little drily.

"Yes, and he tried to be so helpful to me. Naturally, nothing came of it, because Robert did not arrive in London until a couple of days before the Brindisi, just long enough to rehearse with Franz and Josef and Johann."

"Do they all live together when they are in London?"

"No, for the others are here most of the time, lodging somewhere in Soho, while Robert goes about the country more, and he has taken rooms of his own in West Brompton, wherever that may be – I am not perfectly sure," Persephone chattered on. At least, Elinor reflected, that meant there had not (awful thought!) been any secret visits to Mr Walter's lodgings. Not that she supposed there could have been; she had been so dutifully close in attending on her charge that she must surely have known of such a thing.

"And do you know," continued Persephone, "only the other day, too, poor Mr Royden told me how, having met Robert, he now saw only too clearly the vanity of his own aspirations to my hand! Those were his own words – don't you think it was prettily said? And he told me how he felt for both of us, and would do anything in his power to assist us! It was most affecting, and I felt quite sorry for him."

Elinor forebore to make any reply to this, although it troubled her a little for a while. Then she put it out of her mind. After all, she thought, they did seem to be weathering quite remarkably well the potentially disastrous irruption of Mr Robert Walter into their lives.

15

Such a happy state of affairs could not last; Elinor supposed that this would have been too much to hope for. All too soon, the family's peace was disturbed by Persephone's discovery that the Yoxfords intended to go down to their house in Hampshire at the end of July, as usual, to spend at least two months there.

Her reaction was one of sheer dismay. "*I* can't go! I *won't* go!" she declared.

"But my dear, *everybody* leaves London at the end of the Season," protested Isabella.

"No, they do not! You cannot tell me there is nobody left at all to – to run the businesses, and sell things in the shops, and so forth!"

"I mean everybody of our sort," said Isabella rather helplessly, at which Persephone curled her lip with unutterable scorn. "Besides, in August, you know, it is not at all healthy in town. One would very likely catch the most horrid fever if one remained here."

"*I* wouldn't," stated Persephone, with sublime confidence. "I can very well stay here on my own with Elinor, and just a couple of the servants, of course."

"Suppose Elinor wants to go to the country?" remarked Lord Yoxford. "What about that, eh, puss?"

"Persephone, it would not answer," said Elinor quietly. "I am afraid that it would not be at all the thing. You will like it in the country when we get there. I have never been in Hampshire myself, but I believe it is very pretty, isn't it, Cousin Isabella?"

"Who cares for that?" said Persephone fretfully. "I shan't see any of my friends!"

"Oh, well, as to that, you certainly wouldn't see them if you stayed in town, since they'll all be gone out of London too," said Yoxford cheerfully, in the fond belief that he had now cleared up the difficulty.

Persephone's mouth was ominously mutinous, and it cost her an obvious effort not to state what was perfectly clear to everyone but his lordship: namely, that the person she most desired to be near would not be taking part in the general exodus of polite society from London at the end of the Season. Later, Elinor tried to console her by pointing out that the removal to Hampshire was still some weeks ahead, but Miss Grafton was not to be comforted. "The time will go so fast, I know it will! And then perhaps I shall never see him again!" she wailed.

She became her vivacious self once more as soon as Mr Walter came near her, but Elinor was very sure that there were night-time fits of weeping, for the traces of tears were often visible on Persephone's face in the morning. It was hardly surprising, thought Elinor, when she came down to breakfast one day pale, with swollen eyelids and a generally listless demeanour, that she subsequently complained of a sick headache and declined to accompany Isabella and Elinor to walk in the Park, saying she would go and lie down instead.

The two ladies had not been walking very long when they encountered Lord Conington, with Charlotte and Grenville Royden, and the two parties fell in together. Isabella, who was not without some native common sense, had soon realized that nothing would ever have come of Connington's original admiration of Miss Grafton, and by now acquitted Charlotte of snapping him up from under Persephone's nose – indeed, no one acquainted with Charlotte's warm, forthright nature could seriously have considered her capable of such intriguing, and Lady Yoxford, a warm-hearted woman, was quite in charity with her again. She was therefore willing enough to stroll on ahead with the engaged couple when Mr Royden showed that he would like to walk with Elinor, saying easily that it seemed a long time since he and she had a comfortable cose.

A *comfortable cose* was precisely what Elinor did not expect from Mr Royden, and her thoughts must have shown in her face, for ascertaining that the others were out of earshot, he laughed and said, "Don't look so wary! Do you not anticipate my grateful thanks to you, which I believe I have so far neglected to offer, for bringing *that* about?" He nodded towards Conington and Charlotte. "Just the kind of thing I required of you!"

"It was none of my doing, and I certainly do not set up as matchmaker," said Elinor tartly.

"Come, don't snap my head off! But perhaps it is only because you are tired – you do look a little tired. I fancy the task of watchdog to Miss Grafton isn't always an easy one, with our musical friend for ever in the offing."

"That is nothing to do with you, Mr Royden," said she, wearily, for she was indeed tired and had no desire to prolong this *tête à tête*.

"No? But perhaps I am distressed at being cut out."

"Nonsense!" she said roundly. "You know very well that while you wormed your way into the child's confidence as a *friend*, and though you may now have spun her an affecting tale of noble renunciation – "

"Told you that, did she?" he said thoughtfully.

"Yes, and I don't know or wish to know your reason. The point is that you don't care a scrap for her, and you must be aware that, very luckily, she never had any tender feeling for *you*. You had better be content with Charlotte's marriage, as you told me you would."

"Ah, but who knows if Conington there will prove quite as open-handed as I would like? I must say, the idea of matrimony has taken quite a hold upon me," he said lightly. "And to think of that fortune of Miss Grafton's being thrown away on a feckless, romantical musician wrings one's heart."

"Don't let that trouble you! They will not marry."

"Suppose they were to elope, though? For they might, might they not?"

But this seemed to Elinor so wide of the mark that she even smiled. "Hardly! Mr Walter may not be an eligible husband for Persephone, but I have a considerable esteem for him; he would never do anything so shocking!"

"She might persuade him, though . . . I fancy she could be very persuasive. Of course, she doesn't gain possession of her fortune for some while yet – particularly if she marries against her family's wishes, I suppose – but love has been known to find a way, as *you* must be aware." She bit her lip, trying not to show her vexation. "How would it be," he continued meditatively, "if I were to play Cupid to our lovers? Or is it Pandarus I mean?"

"Good God, what possible good could that do you?" she said, startled.

"Ah!" said he, that maddeningly teasing note in his voice. "Wouldn't you like to know what I have in mind? To tell you the truth, I'm not quite sure of it yet myself, but when I am I think that this time, my dear Elinor, I won't tell you! Look, I fancy it will not be long before these roses are in bloom" he added innocuously, as the other three paused for himself and Elinor to come up with them at the end of the pathway.

Although this conversation had been distressing, Elinor was pretty sure that its sole aim was to torment her yet again, and resolved not to let it prey upon her mind. By the time she and Isabella reached home, she was tolerably composed. It was all the more dismaying, therefore, to walk straight into the midst of a stormy discussion (if so it could be called) of the very thing she had assured Mr Royden could never occur.

Looking in at the door of Persephone's bedroom, she found it empty, and the sound of agitated voices led her to the Yellow Parlour, where she discovered Miss Grafton attired in a gauzy déshabille of jonquil silk – not at all the kind of garment in which to receive callers – and Robert Walter, to see whom she had presumably risen straight from

200

her sickbed, headache or no. Persephone was flushed and tearful; Mr Walter, leaning against the pianoforte, very pale. "You don't love me at all, then! You *can't* love me!" Persephone was dramatically protesting.

"Seffi, I do ; you know I do! But even to think of such a thing – no, we could not!"

Here they both became suddenly aware of Miss Radley in the doorway, and Persephone, turning to her, uttered a gasp of dismay, her hand flying to her throat. Mr Walter, Elinor thought, seemed rather relieved than otherwise, and no wonder! For he instantly appealed to her. "Miss Radley, I believe *you* are our friend – tell her, tell Persephone I cannot run away with her!"

"Oh!" wailed Persephone, fresh tears overtaking her.

"Run away? I should think not, indeed! Goodness, what a fuss there would be," said Elinor mildly, hastening to deprive the scene of some of its drama. "And how hurt the Yoxfords would feel! You can't have thought of that, Persephone, I am sure."

"Who cares *how* they feel?" cried Persephone.

"Well, I think *you* might, for they have been excessively kind to you."

"Kind! When they are going to drag me away to Hampshire, and it will be months before I see Robert again, if ever!" she sobbed.

"*Liebchen*, do not cry!" he begged. "The time will pass! We have only to wait – "

"Wait!" repeated Persephone, in tones of utter despair.

" – and when I obtain a good post, when my opera is performed – "

"Robert, no! Even then, do you think my guardian will ever consent? No, he will still insist I must make what is called a good marriage! There is nothing for it: like Angelina and Sempronius, we must fly, we *must*!" she exclaimed urgently, and buried her face in her hands.

Mr Walter spread his own hands helplessly. "In her innocence," he said quietly to Elinor, "she wished me to

201

elope with her, taking her jewels." These, comprising a fine string of pearls and several other valuable trinkets, Elinor now saw lying on the table in front of Persephone. "As if a man of honour could do such a thing – but she does not understand; she is too young, her nature too sweet!" he added fondly.

Elinor fancied that Persephone perfectly understood the impropriety of what she had suggested; after all, it had been very fully pointed out to her at the time of the Unfortunate Business. Upon finding her lover and her friend both ranged against her, however, she once again succumbed to helpless weeping, and it was not the moment to be too bracing. Gently putting an arm round her, Elinor said, "Mr Walter, I am so sorry for this – and for your own distress, but I really think you had better go now and leave her to me, don't you? You may rest assured that I *am* your friend, and I shan't tell anyone about this notion of Persephone's."

"Thank you, ma'am; you are very good," said he, distractedly. At the door he hesitated, glancing back with speaking eyes at the bent head of his lachrymose beloved, but then he turned and went quietly away.

Well, thought Elinor soberly, what an excellent young man he is, after all!

It took Persephone a good deal of time to quieten down, and Elinor, holding her comfortingly and murmuring a soothing word now and then, had leisure for reflection. One thing is certain, she thought, mechanically stroking the girl's hair with her free hand, we must not have any more of this! Who knows but that her tears might wear him down in the end? By the time Miss Grafton had drenched her own handkerchief, and Elinor's, and another, large one which Mr Walter had presumably been obliged to produce at some point, and had then run out of tears to shed and become calm enough for rational conversation, Elinor had come to a decision.

"I *do* feel for you, you know," she said gently.

"Do you?" Persephone's voice was pathetically small and

unhappy. "Oh, Elinor, I *cannot* live without him!" Even her reddened eyes could not quite dim her sorrowful beauty as she sat there, clutching Mr Walter's wet handkerchief like a treasure. "Do you really understand?"

Elinor's heart was decidedly wrung. "Yes," she said, assuming a mater-of-fact tone, "and what is more, Persephone, I have come to believe that if all other circumstances were equal, you and Mr Walter might well be happy together."

"Only other circumstances *aren't* equal!" said Persephone mournfully. "I only wish I had no fortune, and so does Robert too, for I suppose it is only because of that Cousin Edmund will never agree."

"Well, you know, Cousin Edmund is far from being an ogre. *I* think," said Elinor warmly, "he is the kindest person I ever met. But the thing is, he is very much aware of his duty, because he was so much attached to your papa. Well, he would be neglecting that duty sadly if he let you marry, at eighteen, quite out of the sort of circles where your family is used to move. It is only natural that he should be wary of persons desirous of getting their hands on your fortune."

"As if *Robert* – " Persephone began, But Miss Radley firmly interrupted her.

"Now, my dear, will you listen to me for a few moments? Of course I cannot promise you anything, but I'll tell you what I *will* do: I'll speak to Sir Edmund – "

"Oh, yes!" cried Persephone, a watery radiance returning to her face. "He will listen to *you*, because he thinks the world of you!"

"Does he?" Elinor was a good deal startled, but it was not the time to enquire further into this surprising item of information. "Well, when I find a convenient moment, I will speak to him, and – represent to him what I think is the strength of your mutual affection. He has remarked, himself, on your shared interest in music, which *I* think does make it more likely that your attachment would endure."

"Of course it will!" said Persephone, fast recovering her spirits.

"Only naturally, you would have to be patient, Persephone. Even if Sir Edmund were to say that eventually you might be married, you would have to wait quite a long time, I am sure, to prove your constancy."

This was not quite so pleasing, and Persephone said, "I don't need to prove it. Nor does Robert. We *know*!"

"Then why," asked Elinor reasonably, "are you so dreadfully upset by the notion of spending a couple of months away from him in the country?" A reproachful glance from Persephone told her that to any young girl, the prospect of going so much as twenty-four hours without a sight of her beloved seemed an age; it had been so with herself, and she had to own that even now she felt very low when she could not see Sir Edmund for some days on end. But she must not go too easily with Persephone. "For I suppose *that* is what put the idea of an elopement into your mind. I may say, it does Mr Walter great credit that he would not entertain such a notion – but I shall not tell Sir Edmund about any of that part of it."

"No. I suppose I should be in the most dreadful disgrace again," agreed Persephone, sadly. "But two months! If not more! It is too long – how can anyone bear it? If only," she continued fretfully, as her grievances took a new direction, "if only one were a man instead of a young lady, nobody would make one go about with one's tiresome family, and one might travel alone, or in what company one pleased, and never mind stuffy notions of propriety." Propping her chin on her hands, she gazed gloomily at the pretty gold and white striped paper on the wall. "Though all things considered," she added after a while, "I had as lief not be a young man, for who is to know but that I might then have had quite an ordinary voice, nothing out of the common run at all?"

Since Persephone so patently regarded her singing voice as an entity separate from herself, this speech was disarmingly free from self-conceit. She was a resilient creature, thought Elinor, although easily swayed by the overpowering emotion of the moment, and sure enough, in a little while she added, far more cheerful now, "Well, thank you for saying you will take our part and try what you can do with Cousin Edmund. And perhaps," she continued, brightening yet further, "it is not so very bad after all, for if you can't help us, I dare say other people will."

Elinor's mind leaped back, most disagreeably, to her recent conversation with Grenville Royden. Could he possibly – but to what conceivable end? – have offered already to connive at an elopement? Oh, surely not! And yet she could not put it past him, after what he had said. Drawing a deep breath, she said carefully, "Persephone, please understand this: you *must* not think of running away with Mr Walter, even if you could persuade him to do it, or do *anything* of that kind which you know you ought not to. You would only regret it bitterly! Believe me, I know what I am talking about, for I was once in a situation a little like yours myself."

She had been thinking rapidly but carefully, and decided just what part of her own story she should now tell Persephone. Charlotte had become a close friend of them both: while she would dearly have liked to set Persephone on her guard against any suggestions that might come specifically from Grenville Royden, she did not want to mention him by name, for fear of the story's going farther and even, perhaps, damaging Charlotte's brilliant marriage prospects. She did not think Conington would care what her brother had done, years ago, but his parents might have very strict notions of propriety, and in any case she did not wish Charlotte, who had nothing whatever to do with *her* misconduct, to run the least risk of suffering. Besides, naming names seemed too much like tale-bearing, and was distasteful to her. She therefore omitted them entirely from her tale, making it appear, without actually saying so, that her seducer had not been any part of the household at

Royden Manor, but had lived in a large country house a little way off.

She did not, however, spare *herself* anything in the telling, but resolutely described the whole wretched little episode in a level voice which shook only when, at the end, she said: "And naturally I have regretted it ever since. So you can see what comes of giving way to one's impulses in such a matter. I ought, of course, to have told Sir Edmund the whole of this when he asked me to come and bear you company, and I did try, but – well, he is so kind that he would not let me, and I was so glad to come here, too. However, you know, the world would say I was not a fit person to look after you. And the world would probably be right," she said firmly.

The recital of Elinor's story had certainly taken Persephone's mind off her own troubles; she had been sitting there open-mouthed with amazement, but at this she exclaimed, "Oh, nonsense!"

"What?" said Elinor, startled.

"I said *nonsense!*" repeated Persephone, adding indignantly, "I never heard of anything so shabby in my life as that man's behaviour! How *could* he leave you so? *That* is what I think is shocking! Very shocking! I can't think how you ever came to fall in love with such a person."

"To tell you the truth, nor can I!" said Elinor, a good deal moved by such staunch partisanship from Persephone.

"Well, I call it the most shameful way for him to have gone on – and his papa too! Robert, of course, would never act in such a manner, but," she said thoughtfully, "I can quite see that that is beside the point, because if I were to run off with anyone at all, even Robert, people might say that you had not instilled proper principles into me, which would be monstrously unfair!"

"I – I suppose so!" said Elinor, not quite knowing whether to laugh or cry. "Though I – I hadn't looked at it exactly like that."

"Oh, Elinor – pray don't cry! I won't do anything to

distress you, truly I won't. I won't run away, even if Robert would let me!"

But, to Mis Radley's considerable surprise, she discovered that her tears *would* come, and it was her turn to find herself clinging to the younger girl and weeping her heart out.

It was fortunate that the evening was to be that rarity, a quiet one spent at home, for both young women were pretty well exhausted by the emotional upheavals of the afternoon, and very ready to retire to bed as early as seemed proper. Touched by the embrace that Persephone gave her as they said good night, Elinor could at least reflect that her confession had probably served its deterrent purpose, if not exactly in the way she had intended.

Thanks to Miss Grafton's kind offices, a yet more nerve-racking interview was in store for her, but luckily she was not to know that, and so she slept long and deeply, and was surprised, when at last she woke, to see the sun streaming into her bedroom at an unwonted angle as the maid drew back the curtains and poured hot water into the basin. "Good gracious, what can the time be?" she exclaimed.

"Past ten o'clock, miss, but Miss Grafton said you had the headache and wasn't to be disturbed."

Well, she had certainly been glad to have her sleep out, and was glad too, on passing the door of the Yellow Parlour as she went down stairs, to hear Persephone carolling happily as she sat at her instrument, obviously much recovered. Walking into the breakfast parlour, however, Elinor was brought up short by the unexpected sight of Sir Edmund sitting in an easy chair by the window, reading the newspaper.

It was far too early an hour for anyone but a member of the family to call, but the informality of Yoxford House made it easy for Sir Edmund to stroll in and out as he liked, and having seen his Austrian minister safely dispatched to

Dover the previous evening, he had repaired to Upper Brook Street as soon as he felt he decently could. The interview he had promised himself with Miss Radley was, he thought, very long overdue, and he was impatient to see her. However, he had been met instead by Miss Grafton, up and dressed, lying in wait for him, and eager to unburden herself of a tangled confession in which she profusely and penitently begged pardon for the trouble she had given, adjuring him frequently not to blame Elinor for *anything*. By the time he had got from her a reasonably coherent account of what it was for which Elinor should not be blamed, he was quite as indignant on her behalf as Persephone, but since he was a good deal better at controlling his feelings, he suppressed the forcible expressions which rose to his lips, contrived to soothe and reassure his ward, and sat down to await Miss Radley, aware that the task before him might be more difficult than he had hoped.

He rose as soon as she entered the room, saying in answer to her look of surprise, "Yes, I know: a shockingly early hour to call, but I have been so busy, and have missed seeing you so much, that I had to come at the first opportunity. Have you slept well?"

"Oh, yes!" she said, feeling slightly breathless. *Missed seeing you*, he had said. But of course it would be the family he had meant, not her!

"You still look tired," he said with quick concern, studying her face. "Which is hardly to be wondered at, from what Persephone tells me."

She went absolutely white as paper, and had to sit down. "What Persephone tells you?" she repeated, voice faltering. "What – how much did she say?"

"Well, that child does nothing by halves, does she?" said he, with some amusement. "After a period of total absorption in her own romantic affairs, she is now overwhelmed by remorse for the trouble she has caused you, and in a most salutorily penitent spirit, nothing would do for her but to make a clean breast of the whole." Keenly aware of the distress in Miss Radley's face, he kept his tone very light, on purpose to reassure her.

"The *whole*?"

"Or so I suppose. Of course, she had no business to be telling me anything of what you had said to her in confidence, but – "

"Oh, dear heaven! What must you think?" she said, almost in a whisper. "Oh, I *did* want to tell you, and I have known all along I should have done, only – "

"Only I prevented you! My dear girl, I almost wish I hadn't, for then I could have assured you earlier that you were exaggerating the thing out of all proportion. As for what I think – well, let me merely say I would happily murder the fellow, if you would tell me his name and I could but lay hands on him!" he said rather grimly, but then resumed his light tone. "Though I suppose that would hardly do, which is a pity! Here – you had better have a cup of tea."

He gave her one, with so encouraging a smile that, to her own surprise, she managed a faint smile in return, and said weakly as she sipped the hot liquid, "You – you seem to take it very calmly!"

"Why not?" said Sir Edmund, briskly. "Unlike Persephone, you know, I am not much given to falling into strong hysterics – and *you*, my dear cousin, while not in general a hysterical female, are certainly refining far too much upon an unhappy incident of the past."

"Refining too much upon it?" She attempted another smile, and said, "I don't seem able to do anything but repeat what you say! But – well, you don't mean you still think me a – a fit person to have the care of Persephone?"

He was glad to see that the tea appeared to be doing her good; a little colour had returned to her cheeks. "Of course I do," he said, matter-of-fact. "Indeed, a particularly fit person, in that you have a great deal of sympathy for her, and some experience of what her own present feelings must be like – now, what in the world have I said to overset you?"

he demanded, as she put down her cup and quietly began to weep, for this was all rather too much for her. She was provided with his own large, clean handkerchief – what a great lending and borrowing of handkerchiefs we are all indulging in, she thought irrelevantly – and soon managed to control herself.

"Dear me," she said then, voice rather stronger, "how very mortifying it would be to discuss such a matter with anyone who was not such – such a very kind friend as you have been to me!" And she turned to look out of the window, feeling the treacherous prickle of tears behind her eyelids again.

Irrationally, Sir Edmund found that he did not at all care to be described as a kind friend. He had hoped to be something more, and had come to Upper Brook Street with the fixed intention of declaring his feelings, only to find Persephone intent on making a great song and dance about hers. It was many years since he had even thought of making an offer of marriage, and practised diplomat as he was, he found himself now, ridiculously, at a loss for words. He decided to turn the course of this conversation into another direction, until Elinor should be feeling better, and said, with that end in view, "Another thing: I'm persuaded you have been unnecessarily anxious about young Persephone. She won't come to any *harm*, precisely, with her young musician, you know."

"Oh, I do know!" agreed Elinor fervently, turning to look at him again. She could not say it was because of Grenville Royden she had been concerned, but seeing her chance to make a first attempt to intercede on behalf of the young couple, as she had promised Persephone to do, she said earnestly, "I know you said it would not do – and I thought so too – but they *are* most sincerely attached, and I don't believe he cares a bit for her fortune."

"No," agreed Sir Edmund, smiling, "but he does for her voice! Angelina, indeed! I wonder if they would ever have become so attached without it?"

210

"You see," pursued Elinor, "it did seem like a passing fancy at first, but I now believe it is not. And if not, what is to be done? I – well, you are right, I *do* understand what it is to love someone in *that* way. A lasting passion, once formed, is very hard to shake off."

For some reason, he had become remarkably still where he stood at the window. "You mean, you believe from your own experience that one may never recover from it?"

She thought, briefly; she had recovered from her silly, girlish infatuation with Grenville Royden, but saw little hope of her present feelings for Sir Edmund changing. He was so – well, she was not going to let herself dwell upon his virtues. That would be fatal to her peace of mind. She was only sure that the case, now, was very different with her. "Yes, I know what it is like not to recover from such a thing," she said quietly, her whole heart in her eyes if he would but have looked that way.

But he did not. So his hopes, he was thinking, were well and truly dashed before he even embarked on his declaration. She was still attached to the memory of that fellow, scoundrel as he was! He might have known, he thought ruefully, that constancy would be among her qualities. Just as well, perhaps, that he had not begun to tell her of his feelings; they were both saved from embarrassment. He said only, looking out of the window, "*I* know it, too."

His voice gave nothing away, but remembering what Isabella had told her of his wife, Elinor thought: he is still mourning for his Catherine. She wished she could find words of sympathy, but nothing seemed appropriate. And so they remained in silence for a little while, until at last he roused himself to say, without great enthusiasm, "Yes, well, Persephone! I must think what is best to be done. One thing I do beg you, though: don't let her plague you!"

And with that he turned, rather abruptly, and was gone from the room, leaving Elinor gazing after him, a prey to her conflicting feelings.

211

16

I t had really been a most agitating interview: one from which Elinor could not quickly recover. Kind and considerate as Sir Edmund was, she found it quite impossible to compose her spirits when she thought of all Persephone had seen fit to tell him. Him, of all people! She wished most heartily that the heiress's indignantly partisan friendship had not carried her to such lengths. But there, it was done now, and *she* was in no position to reproach Persephone! Her old aunts, and Lady Emberley, and Samuel Spalding would all have said she had only herself to blame, and she was much inclined to think they would have been right.

And while Sir Edmund might seem to make light of the matter, she could not help but notice a subsequent coolness in his manner towards her. That was hardly surprising, and it was surely most unreasonable in her to feel regret. Things could not be otherwise! When he went out of town again she told herself that she was glad of it, for the sake of her own peace of mind. She wished she were not so illogical as to miss him, all the same.

She would have been amazed to learn that it was his own chagrin at the dashing of his hopes concerning herself that took him away, although a visit to his property of Waterleys on the borders of Hertfordshire and Essex was certainly overdue. He had had no leisure to go there since his return to England, with so much business over the Grafton estate and Lady Emberley's property to be settled, and he hoped that in his childhood home he could, to some extent, put Elinor out of his mind – though he was far from sure of it, for he was as little confident as Miss Radley herself that time would heal this particular wound.

212

Quite soon, however, Elinor found she had not much time left for brooding over her own troubles. She would have been quite glad, but for the fact that the cause was something which once again cast Persephone into great affliction. Suddenly, and without a word, Robert Walter had ceased to call in Upper Brook Street. Persephone bore it cheerfully on the first day; on the second, she took to wandering to the window whenever she heard the slightest sound in the street below, and would stand there a long time tapping her foot impatiently; on the third day she became openly fretful, wondering aloud and at frequent intervals what could be keeping him; on the fourth, when the dressing bell rang in the evening, and there could be no hope of anyone else's paying a social call that day, she flung herself on Elinor's breast and wept as though her heart would break.

"Oh, my dear, don't cry so!" Miss Radley begged her.

"I can't *help* it!" sobbed Persephone. "He – he hasn't even sent a note, or *anything*! Oh, where can he be?"

"In his lodging, I expect, quite absorbed in the process of composition!" said Elinor. "I believe that when persons of an artistic turn of mind become visited by inspiration, they are quite oblivious of all else."

"He would never be oblivious of *me*!"

"Depend upon it, he has no idea how time is passing! I dare swear that, once he has finished this piece of music and realized how long it is since he saw you, he will be amazingly contrite." Oh dear, thought Elinor, I am positively encouraging her, when I ought instead to be glad of Mr Walter's absence. Yet she herself could not believe that he had suddenly tired of the adoring Persephone and walked away from her without a word. Indeed, she would have sworn that his affections were almost as deeply engaged as Miss Grafton's, and she sincerely felt for Persephone's distress. Did she not feel much the same herself over the absence of Sir Edmund – although she was denied the luxury of relief in such copious tears as Persephone could shed, and of course it was ridiculous for her to be downcast. She should be very grateful for Sir Edmund's equable reception of the tale of her youthful follies; she might well now have been searching hopelessly, because without references, for some other post as governess or companion, and then her situation would have been a desperate one indeed. Instead, she was to spend the summer months in what sounded like the most delightful country residence, she knew that Isabella hoped she would remain permanently with the family – what could there be in any of that to destroy her comfort? Well, she knew very well what, even if it was ungrateful of her, and so her sympathy went out wholeheartedly to Persephone.

Miss Grafton eventually consulted her as to the propriety of approaching the other members of the Lark Quartet for news of Mr Walter, and Elinor thought there could be nothing wrong in a friendly inquiry. A note, duly dispatched to their lodgings, brought Franz to call at Yoxford House. He seemed at first to think he must have been summoned for musical purposes; all of the Lark Quartet were ready and able to play upon more than one instrument, and producing the parts of a clarinet from his pocket, Franz began to fit them together in a businesslike manner. But once the ladies had managed to convey to him their real reason for asking him to call, he bent his mind to the problem. Their conversation was rather laborious, although his command of English was a little better than that of Josef and Johann, and ended disappointingly in the discovery that Robert Walter's friends had no more notion than Persephone of his whereabouts. As they had no immediate professional engagements together, Franz indicated, they were not particularly surprised at his having gone out of town without letting them know.

"He is, perhaps, into the country gone?" Franz suggested.

"Yes, to compose further passages of his opera, do you think?" said Elinor.

"*Ja, ja!*" Franz thought this a happy notion, and beamed cheerfully at both ladies. "*So ist es, ganz sicherlich!*"

Aware at least that this signified assent, Persephone said, miserably, "But without a word to me? Without even writing, Franz?"

He could only shake his head helplessly, and offered, "Shall I to his rooms go?"

"Oh, yes!" said Elinor. "And we will come with you; why not?" So the party set forth to take the air, and a silent little party it was, for as well as the language difficulty, there were thoughts of their own to keep both Elinor and Persephone busy. Nor did anything much come of the expedition: Mr Walter's landlady in West Brompton, an amiable, motherly soul, could only say that yes, the young gentleman *had* left, in a great hurry (though paying his shot first), and no, she didn't remember him saying when or even whether he would be back. But there, she added indulgently, that was Mr Walter's way!

"Did he take his things with him? I mean, did it *look* as if he were coming back?" Elinor asked.

As to that, Mrs Jenkins could not say either, seeing as Mr Walter preferred to travel light, so to speak, barring that precious fiddle as he seemed to carry everywhere with him, and he hadn't brought much baggage to her house in the first place. However, she said kindly, she wouldn't be letting Mr Walter's rooms to any other gentleman yet awhile, in case he should be back.

Persephone did not look as if there were much in this to console her. And yet perhaps, on reflection, she had found a modicum of comfort in the good lady's words after all, for on the evening of the day after their visit to West Brompton, she suddenly cheered up considerably. Elinor was glad of it, though a little afraid that Persephone might be clinging to too tenuous a hope.

Had she known of the incident which really raised Miss Grafton's spirits, she would have been seriously alarmed, but she remained in happy ignorance of this event. Miss

Merriwether the governess was indisposed, so that Elinor had been in the schoolroom amusing the younger children while Persephone had her singing lesson. At the end of the lesson, Signor Pascali had recollected something, and said vaguely, as he left, that he fancied there was a gentleman wishing to see her: a gentleman who had spoken to him in the street, asking that she would remain in the Yellow Parlour after her lesson, when he – this gentleman who had accosted Signor Pascali – would come up to her. Having carefully discharged this message, he was gone, leaving Persephone full of sudden, delighted anticipation, for who could it be but Robert?

She did not stop to reflect that it was unlike him to make such a secretive rigmarole about calling, as if on purpose to find her alone, or indeed that it was she who had contrived their occasional *tête à têtes*, such as the one into which Elinor had walked just in time to take Robert's side. Her face therefore fell quite ludicrously when there came a tap on the door, and an interested parlourmaid ushered in not Robert Walter, but Grenville Royden.

"You!" she exclaimed, in undisguised disappointment. "Oh, I'm sorry to sound uncivil, Mr Royden, but – "

"But you were expecting, or hoping, to see someone else? Well, set your mind at rest, Miss Grafton!" said Mr Royden. "For *I* am that person's emissary!" he dramatically announced. And he closed the door carefully after him.

When he left thirty minutes later, Persephone's demeanour was quite remarkably changed. It was with an effort that she suppressed her elation before Elinor, who must not know of the news her caller had brought. But suppress it she did, for had she not been bound to complete secrecy by Robert himself, through the agency of Mr Royden? Recollecting all Elinor's kindness, she did not like to keep such good news from her – but an awareness that her friend might not necessarily think the news as good as she did helped her to keep her promise of silence, and Miss Radley remained unaware of anything in particular that

216

could have occasioned the obvious improvement in her spirits. No doubt, thought Elinor a little ruefully, the young were simply more resilient.

Poor Miss Merriwether continued indisposed. The weather was at present rather hot, even for early June, and the governess, who had taken to her bed with a feverish cold, was further debilitated by the course of Blue Pills and quinine draughts prescribed for her, and found that the oppressive heat delayed her recovery. Isabella felt the heat too, and sympathized. She did not mind bearing her part in the care of her younger children while the governess was ill, but confessed that she was glad to have Elinor there, ready to take much of the burden from herself and Nurse. How delightful, in such weather, that her old school friend Jane, now Lady Darsham and widowed young, but with a comfortable jointure, should have invited them to spend the day! For Lady Darsham lived in Richmond, quite close to the Park. "So the twins may romp about there, and work off some of those high spirits. And Edward can play with Jane's little boy Richard, who is just his age, and it will be so pleasant for the rest of us. Dear Jane's house is a very pretty *cottage orné*, Elinor; you will like to see it, and so will Persephone."

Elinor was not so sure of the last part of this proposition, but to her relief Persephone assented to the expedition willingly enough, and did not seem inclined to remain in Upper Brook Street instead, in the secret hope of receiving some word of Mr Walter, from whom nothing had been heard for nearly two weeks now. The party consisted of the ladies of the household and the schoolroom contingent, along with Peggy the under-nursemaid. The Yoxford family carriage was required to transport so many people, even if some of them were not very big, and it transported them at a sedate pace to Richmond, where Lady Darsham, a pleasant woman of Isabella's age, made them welcome with an elegant cold collation. The house was certainly a pretty one, and the children all seemed ready to enjoy themselves. In the afternoon, they repaired to the Park, where the little boys all played, and Persephone and Elinor helped Maria's chubby fingers to create a daisy chain, while the two mamas rested comfortably in the shade at the end of Lady Darsham's garden.

But perhaps the sun was rather too strong for Maria, or perhaps it was that her bonnet had slipped to one side a little: at all events, after a while she became fretful, and began to sneeze and complain that her head hurt her. "Oh, poor darling!" exclaimed Isabella, when Maria was brought back to her and clambered into her lap, where she sat contentedly enough, though still sneezing every now and then. "Can she have caught poor Miss Merriwether's cold, I wonder? No, I think not, for *that* is a feverish cold, and Maria's forehead is quite cool – but what can be making her sneeze so?"

"I think it may be the pollen from the grasses," suggested Elinor. "It does take some people in that way."

"Yes, you are very right; so it does. Oh, dear me, Elinor, what should we do? Ought we to leave now? What a shame, when I can hear the boys enjoying themselves excessively, and Edward is so pleased to see his friend! But perhaps, Jane, we *should* go . . . I really do not know!"

After a little further consultation it was decided that, as the two mothers were reluctant to cut short the visit and spoil the pleasure of the four little boys, and Maria, though a little sleepy, seemed better now she was removed from the long grasses of the Park, Lady Darsham's own chaise should be brought round, to take the child home with one companion. Elinor offered to go, and as she was a favourite with Maria, and Peggy was still in the Park keeping an eye on the twins, the offer was thankfully accepted. Maria dozed in her arms most of the way home to Upper Brook Street, where she was delivered over to the loving care of Nurse, and Elinor herself, with time on her hands, went to the Yellow Parlour to occupy herself by playing Persephone's pianoforte.

No one with any understanding of music could have

218

mistaken her strumming for Persephone's very superior performance, but the parlourmaid – the same girl who had shown Mr Royden into the Yellow Parlour a couple of days earlier – was not musical, and almost at once put her head round the door with a conspiratorial, "Oh, Miss Grafton!" Seeing her mistake, she broke off, covered with confusion, a circumstance which mildly puzzled Elinor.

"Yes, Molly; what is it?" she asked.

"Well . . ." said the parlourmaid, doubtfully, and then, seeing nothing for it, held out a sealed letter. "It's for Miss Grafton, miss, and I *was* to be most particular to bring it up the back stairs and give it her as soon as ever she came in. But I s'pose I can give it to you just as well, miss?"

"Yes, to be sure," said Elinor, and the girl's brow cleared, as if she were glad to get the errand safely discharged. "Just put it down on the table there, Molly, will you?" And she went on playing until it suddenly occurred to her – as surely it had to Molly? – that there was something odd about a letter's being delivered to Persephone in such a manner: up the back stairs and straight to her own private rooms, instead of being left in the hall to be brought up by the butler in the normal way. Word from Robert Walter at last? But the back stairs, Elinor thought, were not much in Mr Walter's style.

She rose from the piano, and idly scanned the direction on the letter; almost at once she stiffened, and stood there staring at it. She knew that hand. It was some years since she had last seen it, but she knew it only too well. Grenville Royden had not been a man who composed lengthy love-letters – though *she*, she remembered wryly, had been much given to heartfelt effusions on paper, such as she now blushed to recollect! But there had been occasional notes of assignation. Oh yes, she knew that hand!

What should she do? Wait, she decided: wait until Persephone came home, and then gently ask the reason for this clandestine correspondence. She could not like it, and something told her that it was not, as she would have preferred to think, a harmless and insignificant matter.

As she stood there, a flurry of light footsteps came running up the stairs. Persephone, she thought; were they back already, then? Perhaps one of the other children had fallen a-sneezing too. But no. Next moment the door burst open, and in came Charlotte Royden, in a state of great agitation.

"Oh!" she cried, as much taken aback as Molly had been. "I thought Persephone would be here – but oh, Elinor, I am glad to find *you*, for I think it might be *better* to tell you, and I must – I *must* tell someone!" With which words she became incapable of telling anyone anything, and cast herself on Elinor's breast in a flood of tears.

Perfectly bewildered, and thinking absently with one part of her mind that it would be very pleasant if *she*, for a change, were able to throw herself into somebody's arms (preferably Sir Edmund's) and sob her own heart out, Elinor patted Charlotte gently on the back, stroked her hair, uttered soothing remarks, and generally did her best to calm the half-hysterical girl. She at last succeeded in this endeavour, and said, guiding Miss Royden to a couch by the window, "There, Charlotte dear! Now, tell me, what has happened to upset you?"

"Oh *dear*!" hiccuped poor Charlotte. "I am so sorry – I am not commonly so silly, only – only the thing is, I don't know what to do! I thought at first I would go straight to Conington, but then I could see that it concerned Persephone, and so – "

"That *what* concerned Persephone?" asked Elinor patiently.

Still sniffing, Charlotte opened her reticule and handed Elinor a somewhat crumpled piece of paper.

"This," she said.

It was in a hand that Elinor thought at first she did not know. A spiky, sloping, foreign hand. Then she recollected seeing certain songs written out by Robert Walter for Persephone; this note, too, was addressed to Miss Grafton.

Plainly set down in a hurry, it nevertheless assured the recipient that all was well, that the writer, alas, had no time to call now if he were to catch the packet from Dover, but she was to rejoice! He had heard from Germany: the wished-for position at Heldenburg was his! He must make haste to present himself to the Prince and accept the offer, to see his father and tell him of his intended marriage – "and then, *Liebchen*, I return to England to claim you, within these two weeks, God willing. I adore you! In great haste," wrote Mr Walter, though not in too much haste to rule out the stave and add a couple of lines of music, which Elinor, sight-reading them, identified after a moment as the happy conclusion of that notable work *Boadicea Queen of Britain*, wherein the Knights of the Round Table offered suitable praises to Hymen.

The note, she saw, was dated the very day that Mr Walter had first failed to call in Upper Brook Street, occasioning Persephone such distress. "But Charlotte, how came you by this?" she asked, puzzled. "Yes, it is certainly for Persephone, but I would swear she has never had it!"

"I was afraid you would say that," said Charlotte unhappily. "I – I didn't precisely come by it. That is to say, I think *Grenville* did."

"*What?*" Elinor's eyes flew to that other, sealed letter addressed in Mr Royden's hand.

"I had better tell you the whole," said Charlotte, resolutely gulping back the tears that threatened her again. "You see, Conington gave me a little silver pencil, with a most ingenious mechanism, for writing in my *carnet de bal* and so forth – and of course I treasured it. Well, last night at the Winters' rout, I let Grenville have it when he wished to write something down, and looking for it about an hour ago I remembered lending it to him. So as he was not in, I went to look in the pockets of his coat – the one he was wearing at the rout. I did find my pencil, but – well, I found that too. And I know, for she has told me, how unhappy Persephone has been, believing Mr Walter did not write her even a word of farewell – but he *did*, after all, didn't he? And there it is!"

"Indeed he did," said Elinor, thinking hard, and rapidly.

"And I cannot – well, I cannot think what Grenville should be doing with it, unless . . . " Her voice faltered.

"Unless he intercepted it," said Elinor quietly. "Picked it up in passing through our hall, perhaps?" She was casting her mind back to the events of the day whose date stood at the head of Mr Walter's letter. "Was the coat in which you found it, I wonder, the one Grenville wore when you and he and Conington dined here, before we all went on to the play together?"

Charlotte too thought, and nodded.

"Then that is what he did! And he kept it from Persephone."

"But *why*?" cried Charlotte, baffled and unhappy.

"That," said Elinor, "I think we may now discover." With no further hesitation, she picked up the letter Molly had left on the side table, and opened it.

Like Mr Walter nearly two weeks earlier, the writer was in haste, or purported to be. "I have now heard from Robert," he informed Persephone, "and alas, he is in sad straits! Those jackals, his creditors, are hard on his heels! But as I told you, he swears he will not leave this country without taking you with him as his bride. We have contrived to arrange a passage for you both from Dover, but you must leave this very night, for I fear they will not be long in discovering his hiding place! Once in France, your minds may be easy. I shall have a post-chaise and pair ready at any hour from five o'clock today, to take you up as soon as you can slip away and convey you to Robert in Dover. It will be standing round the corner from Upper Brook Street, in Park Lane. Believe me, dear Miss Grafton, when I say how happy I am that it has at least fallen to my lot to be of use to you in this sad tangle, and that I remain for ever your most devoted servant, G.R."

"Good God!" said Elinor, staring at this remarkable

222

epistle. "What a farrago of nonsense!"

"What?" inquired Charlotte anxiously.

Elinor hesitated, and then passed her the letter. "Don't let it distress you too much, my dear Charlotte, but I think perhaps you *had* better see it," she said gently.

It was a little while before Miss Royden could take in the sense of her brother's note, and then she sat shaking her head in bewilderment, and saying, "But I don't understand! What does Grenville mean? These letters – they cannot *both* be true!"

"They are not both true," said Elinor, who was beginning to feel extremely angry, "and I am sorry to have to tell you, Charlotte, that I place a great deal more faith in Mr Walter's veracity than your brother's. Naturally you are fond of Grenville, and he would not show his worse side to you, but – oh, I cannot go into detail now, but pray remember that I have known him for a good many years, and – well, he has not always behaved as he ought. However, never mind that now! So far as I can tell from all this, he has spun Persephone a tissue of lies about Mr Walter, with the object of luring her away from this house with him, under the impression that she is to elope with her lover – something which I know very well Mr Walter himself would not countenance! No, I don't believe it for a moment," she continued, taking back Mr Royden's note from Charlotte, and speaking half to herself. "Why, that landlady of his said that even in his haste, he stopped to pay what he owed her! How could Persephone credit such a ridiculous tale? If she had only thought how unlikely it was that he would not write to her himself – though I dare say Grenville told her it would place him in danger of discovery by these supposed creditors, or some such nonsense, and she believed him, for after all, one does *not* think very clearly when one is in love. Well! How very fortunate, Charlotte, that Mr Walter's own note has come into our hands, even if belatedly!"

"But why should Grenville do such a thing?" cried Charlotte.

"To be blunt with you," said Elinor, her mind ranging back over her various mortifying conversations with Mr Royden, "I fear he intended to compromise Persephone in such a way that her family would be glad to see her married to him! He — he has hinted at something of the kind . . . Charlotte, I am truly sorry that you should learn of your brother's character in such a way, but no blame attaches to *you*, none at all! To me, if anyone, for I *did* have some idea of it! But now, what should we do? Five o'oclock, did he say? It is just on five o'clock now!"

Her anger was increasing as she thought of what, it now seemed plain to her, Mr Royden had planned for Persephone. It would explain, only too well, the advantage he had seen for himself in *playing Cupid*, as he had called it. Well, she, Elinor Radley, was going to have the last word! How very surprised he would be to see her coming towards his post-chaise instead of Persephone - indeed, she rather thought she would *not* let him see who it was until the last moment, lest he perceive the failure of his plan and drive off before she had a chance to say that highly satisfying last word! Snatching up the light pelisse which had covered her gown during the drive home from Richmond, she put it on, and pulled the hood up over her head.

"Wait here, Charlotte, and try not to fret!" she said kindly. "I am only going to be a minute! If – if Persephone should come in while I am out, though, you had better not let her come out into the street, where I am going to speak to your brother. Just give her both those letters! And if she seems displeased with what I have done, tell her that – that the person whom I told her I had known in Essex was Mr Royden. *That* will make her stop and think – and then she will not believe his lying letter, either. I am sorry to ask you to do this, Charlotte. I suppose you have left word with Mary, or with Mr Stead, where you are gone? In any event, I shall be back soon!"

17

But she was not back soon. Poor Charlotte, sitting in the Yellow Parlour and expecting her return at any moment, became increasingly distressed as she puzzled over the significance of those two letters. Though never especially close to her brother, she found it shocking to believe him capable of the subterfuge Elinor read into his own note. And yet Elinor had sounded so certain, and as if she knew far more than she would say! What did that last remark of hers mean, about knowing Grenville in Essex? Of course she had known him in Essex! Charlotte could not understand; it was all a puzzle, and a wretched one at that. She only wished Conington might come and comfort her.

Her wish was to be granted. When half an hour had passed, and Elinor was not yet back, the house, which had stood empty all day but for the servants and the indisposed Miss Merriwether, rapidly began to fill with people. The party from Richmond came home, the little boys all happily tired from exercise in the fresh air. Isabella went to the nursery, and after ascertaining that little Maria was perfectly stout again, though rather sleepy, said that she was tired too, and would rest on her bed until it was time to dress for dinner.

The last member of the party, Persephone, was about to go up to the Yellow Parlour to find Elinor when she met Lord Conington, whom Beale had that moment shown in. Conington, going to call on his betrothed, had learnt from her sister Mary that she was visiting Persephone at Yoxford House, and had decided to follow her there and take her to drive in the Park before escorting her home. He and Persephone agreed that Charlotte and Miss Radley were likely to be found together, and they therefore both went on to the Yellow Parlour.

Here, however, they found only the woebegone Charlotte, who rose with a gasp of relief at the sight of Conington and cast herself thankfully into his arms, before remembering the message she had undertaken to deliver to Persephone. She did her best to carry out her instructions, but was not very coherent about it, so that all Persephone could at first gather was that Elinor had gone to meet Mr Royden in her stead. This intelligence caused her to stand perfectly still, her lovely brow rapidly becoming perfectly thunderous in appearance, while she uttered, "Oh, how *could* she? I suppose she meant well, but *why* must I be out today, of all days? How unlucky! When your brother said he could arrange everything, I did not think it would be so soon! But where is he now – where is the carriage? I must go!" And suddenly galvanized into motion, she made for the door again.

"No, no, Persephone, you don't understand!" cried Charlotte, tearing herself from Conington's arms and snatching up the two letters from the table "That is, *I* don't perfectly understand either, but it is to do with Grenville's behaving ill in some way – I thought, oh, I *feared* so when I read *this*, which I found in his pocket – but here, you must read it! You had better read them both!"

It was Conington who took the two sheets of paper from her, spread them out on top of the pianoforte, and then, with one agitated damsel on either side of him, studied them earnestly. Persephone, naturally enough, first turned her attention to her own much-delayed letter from Mr Walter, and read it with dawning comprehension and delight. Her mind, both quicker than Charlotte's and less understandably reluctant to attribute duplicity to Mr Royden, leaped, almost as soon as Elinor's, half-way to Elinor's own conclusion.

"Then it was all a hoax!" she exclaimed. "Oh no! Do you know, Charlotte, your brother told me, and he said it was in the *strictest* confidence, that he – Robert, that is – had been obliged to flee London in the greatest haste for pressing financial reasons, so that it was not safe for him to communicate with me directly, but knowing him to be a friend to us, he said Robert had turned to him for help. And he had this letter in his possession all the time! Oh, how could I be so taken in?"

Poor Charlotte, ready to sink, was comforted only by the reassuring pressure of Conington's hand on her shoulder. "I didn't know!" she said faintly. "Oh, Persephone, I am so sorry, but how could I believe it at first, even when I found the letter? Though I could tell there was something wrong, and so I brought it straight here, indeed I did!"

"My dearest, don't distress yourself!" Conington told her. "You did very right." Since he was in possession of fewer of the facts of the case than the two girls, he was still frowning over the letters. "Sit down, my love, and let Persephone tell us just what passed between your brother and herself."

Charlotte readily obeyed, and Persephone was composing her thoughts to try to answer Conington's question as best she might, when another person walked into the room, unannounced and quite unexpected. Pausing in the doorway, Sir Edmund said affably, "Good afternoon, Miss Royden, Persephone – how d'you do, Conington? I'm just back in town, and Beale told me most of the family now at home might be found upstairs. Where is Elinor, Persephone? Good God," he said, surprised, as he took in the nature of the expressions on the startled faces turned towards him, "is something the matter? What has happened?"

At this three mouths opened to pour forth a torrent of disjointed information, but it was Persephone's voice that eventually rose above the rest as she recollected the message from Elinor which Charlotte had delivered, and which it now seemed to her a matter of considerable urgency to impart to her guardian.

"And so you see," she finished, "it was *Mr Royden*, of all people, who behaved so shabbily to Elinor eight years ago – *that* must be what she meant, Cousin Edmund, and of course if only I had known, I would never have believed a word he said about anything! But she had not mentioned his name, which I suppose was to spare you, Charlotte, for though I'm sorry to speak ill of your brother, and *you* could not help it, all the same – "

"Just a moment," interrupted Sir Edmund grimly. Persephone's revelation made him feel as blazingly angry as Miss Radley herself had been, not so long before, but the fact showed only in a certain tautness about his mouth. "Let us try to get this staight, shall we?"

And by dint of some patient questioning, he and Conington eventually more or less achieved this end. "So," Sir Edmund summed up, "as far as one can tell, Mr Walter went to Germany on perfectly respectable business connected with his career, first writing you a note, Persephone, in which – but we won't stop to discuss its contents now."

"I should think not, indeed!" said Persephone, with spirit. "It is *private!*" She had taken belated possession of the document in question, and was regarding it fondly.

"Yes, well: this note, however, never reached you till now, but was intercepted by Royden. Or so we assume from the circumstances in which Charlotte discovered it. I wonder, though, why he kept it so long before approaching you with his kind offers of help, Persephone?"

"I have been wondering the same thing myself," Conington put in, "and I believe I have the answer. I fancy that this note having fallen into his hands, he may merely have toyed for a while with the thought of what he might do with it – after all, he is not entirely a villain," he remarked to Charlotte, evidently meaning to comfort her. "But the fact is, he suffered some – er – severe losses at the gaming tables a few nights ago. No, my love, he did not tell you – " this to Charlotte's gasp of surprise" – but he told *me*, for he applied to me for money. Which, Sir Edmund, having had a word

228

with my future brother-in-law Stead about Royden's proclivities, I declined to lend him, thinking it best to begin as I meant to go on."

"Wise of you," agreed Sir Edmund. "But yes, I see your point: it was *his* pressing financial difficulties – *not* Robert Walter's, Persephone – which may well have precipitated his decision to try making reality of something that had, perhaps, been only a fancy before: getting himself a rich wife by hook or by crook! A charming fellow, I must say!"

"If only I had known sooner!" sobbed Charlotte, in her lover's arms.

"Try not to distress her," Conington begged.

"I *am* trying not to distress her, but by God, I should dearly like to distress her brother!" said Sir Edmund. "Well – meanwhile Miss Radley, better acquainted than any of us with Mr Royden's true character and quite rightly distrusting him, was unaware that he had approached *you*, was she not, Persephone?"

"You see, he told me not to mention it to anyone – and I *knew* Elinor did not like him," Persephone said in a small voice.

"So he managed to hoodwink you into believing that Mr Walter had been obliged to flee his creditors – not, you know, something I would have thought a likely circumstance in connection with that young man," said Sir Edmund thoughtfully, fixing Persephone with his very blue gaze.

She hung her head. "I don't know what Robert will say to me!" she murmured.

"Well, *I* have a very good notion," said her guardian, "but that's hardly to the purpose now. This communication – " he indicated Mr Royden's letter with fastidious distaste, "arose from a previous conversation with you?"

"Yes," she agreed. "He – he said he had only to make the final arrangements, and then he would transport me to Dover."

"Which Elinor, with her superior knowledge of him, took to mean – or so Charlotte says – that he had the intention of abducting you and thus obliging you to marry him, with your family's approbation! Good God, Persephone, you do seem to be adept at creating an aura of melodrama about yourself!"

"It's not *my* fault," she protested.

"No: you merely infect others with your own liking for such heroics," said Sir Edmund, more cuttingly than he had meant, for he could see she was upset, and had not intended to let his inclination to blame her distract him from the point at which he was driving. "Very well: so Elinor went out in your place to meet Mr Royden, and tell him his amiable plan was frustrated. No doubt she had some very well chosen words to say to him! We learn from *this* – " he again indicated the letter – "that there was to have been a post-chaise waiting on the corner of Upper Brook Street and Park Lane at five, which is when you, Charlotte, say she went out. *I* saw no such equipage when I came that way twenty minutes ago. It is now nearer six than five o'clock. *Where*, then, is Elinor?"

There was a moment's stricken silence as the implications of what he had said sank in, and Sir Edmund looked grimly from one to another of his companions.

"Good God!" said Conington, at last. "Why did we not think of that before? You don't mean, sir – can you think it possible that Royden has – well, carried off Miss Radley instead of Persephone?"

"Oh *no*!" moaned poor Charlotte.

"It does look rather like it, doesn't it?" said Sir Edmund.

He was making for the doorway as he spoke, but there he was brought up short by an excited threesome chattering to one another in German: Franz, Josef and Johann, all remarkably cheerful, and followed by a rather flustered Beale, who exclaimed, catching sight of Sir Edmund, "Oh, sir, these foreign gentlemen – they *would* come up to see Miss Grafton, sir, and really, there was no stopping them!"

It was plain that the three young musicians were delighted to see Sir Edmund, that fluent speaker of German; they shook him heartily by the hand, and embarked upon much excited verbiage in their own tongue. Equally plain, to the others present, was the fact that Sir Edmund was barely able to force himself to stay and listen to them for civility's sake. Or perhaps it was also for Persephone's sake, since after a while he cut them short, to communicate to her the drift of what they had been saying

"Well, you may put all Royden's fustian about creditors, and so forth, out of your head," he told her. "It seems that your friends here have just met with some fellow from the Continent – a Flemish flautist, I understand?" A vigorous nod from Franz confirmed this. "Yes, well: a Flemish flautist who is himself acquainted with Mr Walter, and indeed met and conversed with him on his way to Germany last week. He was then bound for the state of Heldenburg, just as he says in his note, where he intended to transact his business with all possible speed – again, just as he says there. By your friends' reckoning, and given a good passage, he should be back in London at any time now. That is, if he hasn't changed his mind about you, Persephone – damned if *I* wouldn't change my mind over a girl as ready as you to believe such stuff," he added, unchivalrously.

Persephone took surprisingly little offence at this. "Yes, I *should* have known it was all a hoax," she agreed. "And I am sure Elinor will say so too. But, Cousin Edmund, where are you going?"

"To find her, of course – where do you suppose?" And he was thrusting his way past the three young musicians when Conington, who had been doing some thinking of his own during these last exchanges, said, "Just a moment, Sir Edmund!"

"Yes?"

"Another thing has occurred to me: suppose, after all, Royden did not mean to be in the post-chaise himself, but commissioned his servants to carry Persephone off? They might not have known Miss Radley was *not* Persephone!"

"The same thought struck me, too," said Sir Edmund,

"since I can tell you, from my own experience, that no one who had any alternative would choose to go a long journey cooped up with Persephone in a closed carriage! No, I am assuming that Miss Radley has been bundled into this damned chaise, and borne off to be delivered to Royden instead of my ward, when she thought only to confront him here in the street. Unwise of her, perhaps, but in all the circumstances very understandable."

"And when he finds out the mistake," said Conington carefully, picking his words with one eye on his betrothed, "do you think she is likely to come to any harm?"

But Sir Edmund's temper was visibly wearing thin. "Any possibility of that," he said, "is just what I am anxious to avert."

With which he turned on his heel and was gone from the room, not stopping to shut the door, so that the others could hear him as he made his way downstairs, urgently commanding Beale to have his phaeton brought round again instantly from Lord Yoxford's stables, with four fresh horses put to it.

"He does seem *concerned* about Elinor, doesn't he?" inquired Persephone pensively, of nobody in particular.

At the front door, however, Sir Edmund seemed to suffer some further delay, for his voice could be heard mingled with that of another man, and with occasional interpolations from Beale. The conversation, whatever it was, was brief enough, and was concluded by Sir Edmund, his voice rising in barely controlled impatience, saying, "For God's sake, man, I've no time to discuss that! Not now! Oh, go on up, you'll find 'em all in the Yellow Parlour, but I can't stay for anything whatever just at present!" And the door slammed behind him as the other man's rather lighter tread was heard on its way up the stairs.

No more than Sir Edmund himself did the newcomer appear to feel that he required to be formally announced by the butler. A moment later, to the inexpressible joy of Persephone, Mr Robert Walter entered the room, crying,

"Seffi! You are here!"

The fact that *he* was there was perhaps the more surprising, as Persephone, from the depths of his embrace, incoherently tried to make him understand. She was not very successful.

"But no, no! A good, swift crossing, a chaise and four, and I am back," he assured her fondly. "What is all this about a note? Two notes? *Liebchen*, this I do not understand, but it can be of no moment now. Listen: though my father does not quite like me to marry an Englishwoman, all else is well, and he will soon come round to it, so do not distress yourself." And he kissed her again.

No one present was disposed to censure the manner of their ecstatic reunion. Conington and Charlotte were pretty closely entwined themselves, to the great easing of Charlotte's mind, and the remaining members of the Lark Quartet were beaming expansively upon the two couples and uttering exclamations which were evidently expressive of surprise, delight and congratulation. It was left to Beale, standing in the doorway, to utter a reproving cough.

"Ahem! The Reverend Mr Spalding!" announced the butler, before beating a rapid retreat from what was now a distinctly overcrowded room.

Since the large clerical gentleman who had advanced into the Yellow Parlour in Beale's wake was a perfect stranger to all its occupants – who, besides, had their minds on matters quite other than the ordinary forms of social etiquette – they could none of them think of a word to say, but simply stared at him. Mr Spalding, for his part, was peering round in search of a familiar face.

"Miss Radley?" he inquired. "Miss Radley? Dear me, I do not see Miss Radley here! I passed Sir Edmund Grafton in the street, or should I say, I was passed *by* Sir Edmund Grafton in the street, but he would not stay to give me the information I sought. Indeed, he did not appear to recognize me, but no doubt that was because he was not expecting to see me here so soon. Where, pray, is Miss Radley? I do not," he added, as if aggrieved, "know anyone *else* here!"

At this Lord Conington, a well-bred young man who was normally punctilious in observing social forms, withdrew his arm from Charlotte's waist and said civilly, "Pray let me introduce you Mr – Spalding? Miss Persephone Grafton, who is Sir Edmund's ward; Miss Charlotte Royden, who is engaged to marry me – I am Conington, by the by; Mr Robert Walter – er, Franz, Josef and Johann, whose surnames I am afraid I have not yet learnt myself in the course of our acquaintance, but no doubt Mr Walter, their compatriot, can supply them. I don't believe, as you say, that we have had the pleasure of meeting before, but you must be a friend of Lord Yoxford's."

Franz, Josef and Johann, their amiability unimpaired, continued to beam upon the company at large, while Robert and Persephone showed not the smallest inclination to move apart from one another, and thus drew the clergyman's stern glance to themselves. He did not try to claim intimacy with Lord Yoxford, but turned to the matter immediately before him. "The latitude that young people will allow themselves these days is, I believe, remarkable!" he pronounced. "Is this, I ask in some surprise, Miss Grafton, *is* this behaviour suited to a young lady of your years, not to mention your birth and upbringing?"

These reproaches caused Mr Walter to glower at the latest arrival and to ask his loved one, "Seffi, who is this person?"

"I haven't the remotest idea!" said Persephone, regarding Mr Spalding with mild surprise, and remaining as close to her Robert as before. "I've never met him in my life!"

"Ah, perhaps not, Miss Grafton, but *I*, I fancy, have had the pleasure not precisely of *meeting* you, but of *hearing* you!" said Mr Spalding, becoming playful and wagging a finger at her. "In Cheltenham, at the house of the late Lady Emberley, whose devotion to the maintenance of the highest moral standards still makes her sadly missed from our congregation – however, yes, it was while I was calling upon Miss Radley that I chanced to hear you executing a

234

piece upon the pianoforte, and singing, and if I may say so, a very superior performance it was!"

"Yes, very likely," said Persephone, never one to waste time on unnecessary displays of modesty, "but what in the world can that signify now?"

"I am come, as soon as my parish duties would permit," Mr Spalding told her, "in search of Miss Radley herself – of Miss Radley whom, as I have previously remarked, I do not at the moment see present." He looked accusingly round at the company, as if supposing that one of them might be concealing Elinor from him.

"No, indeed you don't," remarked Conington, recalled to a sense of Elinor's present supposed plight. "The fact is, Mr Spalding, that Sir Edmund has gone off after her! That, you understand, accounts for his not having leisure to stop and talk to you, for we think it probable that she has been abducted by Mr Grenville Royden, Miss Royden's brother – or some agent of his – in error for Persephone."

"*What?*" exclaimed Robert Walter and Samuel Spalding, as one man, and Mr Spalding would have said a great deal more too had not Conington added swiftly, "And I think I had better at least *try* to explain the whole to you, Walter."

This he manfully proceeded to do, aided by occasional contributions from Persephone and nods of confirmation from the afflicted Charlotte. Mr Spalding, although the explanation was not directed at him, had sat down and was listening open-mouthed, now and then exclaiming, "Scandalous!" or "Shocking!" while Mr Walter himself made certain interruptions, turning at one point to stare indignantly at his beloved and demand, "You thought this of *me*, Seffi? That I – *I* should run up debts and then fail to satisfy my creditors?"

He was so obviously outraged at the notion that Persephone, wilting under his fierce gaze, said meekly, "A – a great many gentlemen of the *beau monde* think nothing of it, you see, Robert, but truly I am sorry. If I had only

235

stopped to think, of course I should have known you would do such a thing.

At the end of Conington's careful recital, Mr Spalding, in whom a considerable head of steam had been building up as he listened (though it turned out that he had not been quite able to follow the whole story), was at last able to get his word in. "Disgraceful! Elinor – ah, poor unhappy creature! I had thought, a brand saved from the burning! But I suppose one might have feared the worst. Well! I was never so shocked in my life! Perhaps, however, she may yet be saved from herself. Frailty, thy name is woman!"

"Are you talking about my cousin Elinor?" asked Persephone, a dangerous gleam in her eye, while Conington said patiently, "Sir, I am afraid you have mistaken my meaning."

"No, no. For I must inform you," said Mr Spalding, weightily, "that I am acquainted with Miss Radley's history."

"Then I beg you will keep it to yourself," said Conington, quite sharply for so amiably behaved a young man, and Mr Spalding, a little daunted, fell silent long enough for Mr Walter to put in, "Yes, what is to be done for Miss Radley? Can we be sure Sir Edmund will find her? Should we call in the officers of the law?"

At this, Charlotte uttered a small distressful cry, and Conington said quickly, "Not, I think, unless there's nothing else for it. I hope we may be able to hush this up without going to such lengths."

"Oh yes!" said Persephone. "Poor Charlotte – and poor Elinor too, and it is not *their* fault, not in the least, that Mr Royden is so horrid after all. And when my cousin Edmund catches up, I dare say it will turn out well enough."

"Not Dover, Lord Conington!" said Robert Walter suddenly. "I have been thinking. *Not* Dover! I mean, I do not suppose he intended to convey Persephone there. For though he could not know the day I should return to London, it was always possible we might have met on the

236

road. Indeed, with the good crossing I had, we almost certainly *would* have met – and though *I* might not have spared a second glance for a hired post-chaise, suppose Persephone had caught sight of *me*, baiting at an inn, for instance? That would have ruined all. No, since I suppose he did not really mean to take her out of the country, there could be no advantage in his going to Dover."

"You are right," said Conington, impressed by this reasoning. "We should have thought of that before. Where, then, would he take her?"

Charlotte, summoning up her courage, said diffidently, "I should suppose to Royden Manor, dearest. You see, the house is almost shut up now, with only our old housekeeper living there, and it is quite isolated, so I can think of nowhere more suitable for – for what we think Grenville had in mind!"

This earned her an approving glance and another comforting embrace from Conington. "Well though of, Charlotte! Depend upon it, Walter, she's right," he said. "And there is Sir Edmund, more likely than not gone off on a wild goose chase! Well," he added briskly, "I see nothing for it but to go after them ourselves, do you, sir?"

"Just what I was about to suggest, my lord!" said Mr Walter promptly, and the two young men regarded one another with considerable approbation for a moment, before Robert Walter turned to his musical colleagues and spoke to them in German. "There, that is settled," he told Conington. "They will also come. I supose you know the way to this place, my lord?"

Conington looked a little doubtful at the addition of so many persons to the party, and even more so when Persephone said very firmly, "And I will come too."

"My dear Miss Grafton, you cannot!"

"Oh yes, I can! In fact you will *need* me!" she said triumphantly. "For suppose you cannot drive out to Essex and back to London tonight? Then you will require another female to – to lend Elinor countenance."

"You know, you may be right," said Conington thoughtfully. "To avoid the least breath of scandal . . . yes, that *is* a consideration."

"Perhaps I ought to come as well?" Charlotte heroically offered.

"No, no, there can be no occasion for that," he assured her.

"No," agreed Persephone, who was obviously, if rather reprehensibly, beginning to enjoy this adventure now that she was reunited with her Robert. "It would only distress you, Charlotte. But I'll tell you what: you must stay and try to make my cousin Isabella understand what has happened, for I think we should be off at once, and not lose any more time."

"A carriage," said Mr Walter. "We must procure a carriage."

"The best thing," continued Persephone, falling into a practical, not to say a managing mood, "will be to take Cousin George's britzka. That is quite a large carriage, and he will not mind, in fact I dare say he won't even know it is gone from the coachhouse, but the grooms will not object, Lord Conington, if you and I both say we have his permission. Now, let me see – the britzka will easily take four inside and two up behind in the dickey – oh, but there are six of us already, and then there will be Elinor on the way home . . . "

"We'll take my curricle as well," said Conington. "I have it outside; I'll send my groom home, and someone else may come up beside me. Then, if either carriage should lose a wheel or suffer some other accident, we shall not be quite at a standstill."

"Yes, very good!" Robert approved.

"I, too, am coming!" unexpectedly announced Mr Spalding, who had been sitting silent for a remarkably long time. "*I* shall come to lend countenance to this extraordinary venture – for extraordinary I may say it is! But I perceive it would be useless to attempt to turn you from your

238

purpose."

"I should just say so!" remarked Persephone indignantly. "Don't you *care* what happens to Elinor? I thought you said you were a friend of hers."

"I do not know when I have seen the like of it!" pursued Mr Spalding, taking no notice of this. "I do not know when *anyone* has seen the like! Peers of the realm conspiring to circumvent the due processes of the law! Females engaging in very shocking activities, and *not*, as they ought to be, censured, but positively countenanced by other females! Persons conversing in foreign tongues, so that one does not know what they may be saying!" This with a suspicious glance at Franz, Josef and Johann. "Well, I see that, so far as Miss Radley's good name is concerned, I have come just in the very nick of time, as one might say!"

"No, one might not!" snapped Persephone, who had taken Mr Spalding in great dislike. "And anyway, you haven't! My cousin *Edmund* came in the very nick of time—at least, I dare say he thought so, although we hadn't worked it all out properly then. *Robert* came in the very nick of time! But as for you, I still do not know what you are doing here. Oh, Robert – Lord Conington – let us go and see about getting horses put to the britzka *immediately*! Good, here is Cousin Isabella!" she exclaimed, as that lady, utterly bemused, appeared in the doorway of the Yellow Parlour handsomely dressed for dinner and looked around her. "Cousin Isabella, we *may* take the britzka, may we not, and you will tell Cousin George that we have borrowed it, and we are taking Lord Conington's curricle too, for we have to rescue poor Elinor, and it is *urgent*, and here is Charlotte, who will tell you all about it!'

And with that she, Conington, and the four musicians were gone from the room, Mr Spalding lumbering in their wake.

"Good gracious me!" said Isabellan, faintly. "Charlotte, who was that clergyman? I am sure *I* do not know him! And what is Persephone taking about? Rescue Elinor? Where *is*

239

Elinor? But, my dear child, you look worn to a thread! What in the world is going on?'

With a truly noble effort, Charlotte set herself to attempt the explanation.

18

For about the first mile in the post-chaise, Miss Radley's overpowering sensation was one of sheer anti-climax. On turning the corner of the street, she had immediately seen the vehicle with its two postilions. One of the men was standing by the head of a saddle-horse, no doubt to travel as an outrider, and did not wear the usual livery of a post-boy, but had a caped frieze coat on. Seeing her advance purposefully towards him, this fellow had stepped forward with the words, "For Dover, ma'am?" and in answer to her nod, had held open the carriage door and then closed it behind her, whereupon the chaise instantly set off at a spanking trot. She had not even been forced in, but had stepped up into the carriage of her own free will! All the cutting things she had been rehearsing in her mind to say to Grenville Royden froze on her lips, as she perceived that she was the only occupant of the vehicle. She felt remarkably foolish, to say the least of it, but was soon almost ready to laugh at herself.

After a while, however, indignation took over. Mr Royden, so far as she recollected, had written that he would have a post-chaise ready; he had not said in so many words that he would be in it himself. The object of his absence, she presumed, was to avoid the necessity of answering awkward questions from Persephone. For it soon became clear to Elinor that they were not taking any road that could possibly lead in the direction of Dover, and while Persephone might have been rather longer in realizing this, it was bound to have occurred to her sooner or later. Puzzling it all out, Elinor eventually came to the same conclusions as did the company gathered in the Yellow

Parlour at Yoxford House, a little later: since there could be no advantage to Grenville in actually conveying Persephone to the coast, she fancied that the chaise's most likely destination was Royden Manor.

She had not the faintest desire to revisit that house, and thought she had better make haste to apprise the post-boys of their mistake, inform them that there would be no passenger with them after all, and induce them to return her to Upper Brook Street before they drove away with the empty chaise.

But this proved rather difficult. She knocked upon the sides and roof of the vehicle, to no avail. The windows appeared to be jammed, perhaps purposely, so that the glass could not be let down. She fancied that the doors might also be secured, and in any event she had no wish to risk life and limb by jumping from a fast-moving carriage. Very likely the postilions had been told to pay no heed to any sounds from within the chaise! It was very vexatious, but she would have to wait until they stopped to change horses.

They did this some ten miles from the beginning of their journey. By now they were well out of London. Elinor had been right: neither door would open from the inside, but when she began knocking on the glass again to attract notice, the frieze-coated man appeared at the window as if he had been expecting some such thing, undid the door just a crack, and said hoarsely, "Best cut that out, miss! You keep mum, and no 'arm'll come to ye!"

He then closed the door again, and leaned against it the whole time that the ostlers at the posting-house were changing the horses. A new post-boy came with the new team, but the frieze-coated man, no doubt one of Grenville's servants, was evidently going to accompany the chaise all the way.

She had no alternative but to settle back on the lumpy squabs of the carriage, which was not a hired yellow bounder but certainly no more comfortable than one of those notorious boneshakers, and wait until she reached the journey's end. For the Manor, as she recollected, was less than thirty miles from London, and while the Green Dragon inn in the nearby village was also a posting-house, they would hardly be stopping there within a mile or so of the Manor – if she was correct in supposing that to be their destination.

Sure enough, as they proceeded on the next stage of their journey, the road began to look familiar to her. She *had* been correct: they had now left the main turnpike, and were wending their way past cornfields and pastures, along the narrower and rutted roads of the countryside. How it brought back memories! Memories of her first arrival at the Manor eight years ago, so eager to take up her post – such a change, she was sure it would be, from the monotonous life she had lived with her aunts. She was more than willing to like her employers and her little charges, and remembered wondering, with happy anticipation, what she would find at her journey's end. Well, *this* time she had a very good notion! And at least, she reflected, she would have a chance to say those cutting things to Mr Royden after all. Or would it be wise to do so? Presumably he would be much put out to find that the wrong lady had been carried off. For the first time, remembering that she had been told the house was now shut up, with only the deaf and aged Mrs Beasley in residence, Elinor began to feel a little trepidation.

They were coming to the village now, passing the first row of thatched cottages, where she had been used to bring Mary and Charlotte to visit their old nurse. She saw the comfortable, well-maintained buildings of the inn, the Green Dragon breathing its emerald and vermilion fire on the newly painted sign that swung in the gentle breeze this fine evening. And there was the village green, with the duckpond. It was not long before she recognized the urns crowning the Manor gateposts as the chaise turned in between them, driving into the strong rays of the declining sun.

Here, she saw, there was alteration indeed! Despite his

financial troubles, old Mr Royden had at least made some effort to keep the place up: now, however, the signs of neglect were plain. Unpruned shrubs straggled beside the drive; the tall grass ought to have been mown from the lawns long ago. Here and there a fallen branch which no one had troubled to remove lay on the ground. The air of neglect was even more marked when the house itself came into sight. It had once been a very handsome building, but now it badly needed a coat of paint, most of the windows were shuttered, and some of the shutters hung askew on their hinges. The carriage sweep in front of the house was sprouting a fine crop of weeds. The only signs that there was anyone in the place at all were the unshuttered sash windows of the ground floor drawing room, the lower half of one of them pulled up to admit the evening air.

As the chaise drew up at the front door, Elinor felt a distinct qualm. The frieze-coated man opened the carriage door, jerked his head towards the porch of the house, and said unceremoniously, "In there, miss!" There was no help for it; the moment had come to step out of this stuffy and uncomfortable vehicle, although she found she rather shrank, now, from meeting Mr Royden, and instinctively pulled up the hood of her pelisse again as if to delay the moment of confrontation. Which was perfectly ridiculous, she told herself, for after all, she was entirely in the right and had outwitted him: a pleasing thought, although somehow it did not make her feel any better.

The hall of the Manor was rather dark, so that Mr Royden, standing just within the doorway, did not recognize her instantly. He had dismissed the post-boy and outrider, and sent the chaise wheeling off across the overgrown gravel towards the stables, before he turned to her, closing the door and guiding her into the drawing room as he said, "Well, now I must explain matters, my dear. I dare say you are feeling a little surprised."

"Not much," said Elinor, putting back her hood and looking very steadily at him. "Well, not at all, in fact! As

244

soon as we began to come out of London, I had a strong notion that this was where we were bound!"

He had recoiled at the sight of her with an exclamation of surprise and (she thought) dismay. "*You!*" he said furiously. "I might have known you would meddle if you could!"

"Indeed you might," she agreed.

"What the devil brings you here?"

"Your post-chaise, of course, and very uncomfortable it was! I did try to make them turn back – after all, I had only stepped out of the house to let you know your trouble was wasted – but I'm afraid there was no making them pay any heed, so you will be at the expense of sending me back."

She hoped she sounded more assured than she felt, for she found she did not at all like being alone with him behind that firmly closed door. And he had been drinking; she could smell it on his breath. Perhaps to give himself Dutch courage for the thing he had determined to do! When he put a hand on her arm in a positively savage grip, she uttered a small gasp as she tried, vainly, to shake it off again.

"You scheming, double-dealing . . . " Words seemed to fail him.

"*Scheming* is pretty good, coming from you, Grenville!" she said. "In fact, thanks are due to Charlotte for discovering Mr Walter's letter to Persephone and bringing it to me – Charlotte is very much distressed, poor girl." She tried pulling away once more.

"*Damn* Charlotte!" he said, but he let go of her. She forced herself not to give him the pleasure of seeing her rub her arm where he had hurt it. He began pacing up and down. "Hell and the devil, *now* what's to be done? If I post directly back to London – see the girl, persuade her to Dover with me in good earnest – yes, perhaps it may still serve."

"Good heavens, Grenville," said Elinor, astonished, "you can't think that now Persephone has Mr Walter's letter, as she *will* have by this time, she would believe any more of your ridiculous tales for an instant?"

He stopped pacing, and stood leaning on the table in the

245

middle of the room, thinking aloud. "Such a piece of luck that it came in my way – and to have you spoil all! Ah, but wait! Suppose I had had word from Walter *after* he wrote to her, and had thought it kinder to keep his letter from her? Or say his hopes had come to nothing, and he was in far worse case than he had ever told her of, and he now confided in me . . . "

"Grenville, I truly think you must be a little out of your mind," said Elinor honestly. "You have let this scheme of yours obsess you until you can't see facts when they are staring you in the face! I suppose you must have been brooding upon it for days before you plucked up the courage, if so it can be called, to put it into action," she added, contempt in her voice.

He glowered at her. "I need money, urgently."

"So I take it your intention was to compromise the poor child by forcing her to spend the night here with you – but do you really think that, knowing her unwilling, Sir Edmund would meekly have handed her over to you, along with her fortune? No, whatever had happened, I am sure he could have got around it somehow." She meant what she said, her own confidence in Persephone's guardian being unbounded.

He uttered an angry expletive, expressive of his opinion of Sir Edmund. "And what makes you so sure she'd have been unwilling?" he added, an ugly look in his eyes. "*You* were not so unwilling, once!"

"The more fool me, then!"

And that had been unwise; she knew it as soon as the words were out of her mouth. He was more drunk than she had realized at first, and his fury and frustration showed in his face. "Oh, so that's what you think, Miss Milk-and-Water? Well, one thing's certain, *you* must remain here tonight, safely locked in, while I go back to London – but suppose I were to change your mind for you first? Yes, I do believe, dear Elinor, that I *will* do so!"

Really alarmed now, she ran towards that half-opened

246

sash window, but he was between her and it in a moment. She tried the door, but it was locked, and as she tugged frantically at the handle she heard someone come into the hall with a gruff inquiry. She thought it was the voice of the frieze-coated outrider who had escorted her from London. In answer, Mr Royden called through the door a command for the man to stay there and not budge, addressing him as Joe. So there would be no escaping that way! And she had to move away from the door in any case, for Grenville Royden was advancing upon her, saying in a quieter but more unpleasant voice than any she had yet heard from him, "Why, my dear, don't say you are piqued because I prefer pretty Persephone to you? Perhaps you are! She has the fortune, to be sure, but you must have pleasant memories of the past – wouldn't you care to revive them? I believe you would! Wasn't *this*, perhaps, what you came for after all?"

"No!" she cried, revolted. Until this moment, she had not truly believed that her involuntary masquerade placed her in any physical danger, but now there could be no doubt of it! "Grenville, no!"

But the glint in his eyes, whether occasioned by drink or lust, was brighter, and she saw, to her alarm, that her resistance seemed to excite him. His next words confirmed it. "And if you are *not* willing, why, that will add spice," he said softly.

She was unable to get away in any direction, backed into a corner, and he was smiling almost in her face. She uttered one more frightened, "Please, Grenville, *don't!*" His eyes were so close to hers that she was half mesmerized by the look in them, and it was a second or so before she could grasp the fact that suddenly they were *not* so close any more. Nor was this due to the force of her own plea, or to any sudden access of remorse on Mr Royden's part, but to a firm hand which had plucked him back, none too gently, by the collar of his coat.

"Good evening, Mr Royden," said Sir Edmund, his voice dangerously mild.

He came through the window, Elinor thought thankfully – he came in through the window while Grenville and I were staring at one another!

"Oh, thank goodness!" she gasped, and finding suddenly that her legs would no longer support her, she sank into a heap on the floor.

Sir Edmund thrust Mr Royden away from him so hard that that gentleman staggered against the table, struck it involuntarily with his stomach, and remained lying half-winded across it. He was then beside Elinor in an instant.

"Are you hurt?" he demanded, helping her up. "Are you all right, Elinor?"

"No – I mean yes, I shall be quite all right – oh, I was never so glad to see anyone! But how *came* you here? I thought you were not in town – and Charlotte found a letter from Robert Walter to Persephone, and . . . and . . . "

"Hush," said Sir Edmund gently, settling her in a chair. "I know all about that." His eyes travelled to the form of Mr Royden, spread-eagled over the table. "Didn't it occur to you, Royden, that even if you had carried out your amiable plan with regard to my ward, you'd have had me to deal with?"

Mr Royden, gasping for breath, was able only to say, sullenly, "She'd have been obliged to marry me – and I *would* have married her!"

"Would you, indeed? Very good of you, I am sure," said Sir Edmund, who had had much to occupy his mind as he made his way from London to Essex (having come to precisely the same conclusions about the chaise's destination as were worked out a little later by Lord Conington and Mr Walter). His phaeton and four could go a good deal faster than a post-chaise, and at the speed with which he was travelling it took some skill to manage the horses along narrow lanes, but Sir Edmund was an excellent whip, and was not so busy with his team that he had no time for some extremely agitating reflections, mostly revolving around that brief verbal message left by Elinor for Charlotte to deliver to Persephone.

He therefore now said grimly to Mr Royden, who had managed to get up, and stood glaring at him, "Let's have no more absurd bluster about anyone's being *obliged* to marry you! Indeed, let me inform you instead that if there's any woman to whom *you* are in honour bound to make an offer of marriage, it is Miss Radley." Here Elinor sat up suddenly in the chair where Sir Edmund had placed her, but he was still speaking. "And if, as it appears, she wishes it – God knows why, but I'm damned if she shan't have whatever she wants – then *one* thing I mean to do here is ensure that you make her that offer!"

"Oh, indeed?" said Mr Royden, very unpleasantly. "A woman I've had already, and could have again, I dare say, if she weren't so coy that – "

But he got no further. Elinor's indignant gasp coincided with the satisfying sound of Sir Edmund's fist planting a very nicely timed blow on Mr Royden's chin. It knocked the recipient back against the drawing room door, where he clung to the handle in order to remain on his feet.

Meanwhile Elinor, leaping up, was running forward to catch Sir Edmund's arm, crying out, "No, no, you quite mistake the matter! It is the very last thing on earth that I want! What could make you think so?"

He had been watching the other man and rubbing his knuckles, but at this he turned to face her. "You *don't* wish it?" he said, puzzled. "But, good God, Elinor, you told me – you said you knew that a *lasting* passion, once formed – "

And he, in his turn, was cut short. It had been a mistake, Elinor realized, for him to turn his back on the door. Mr Royden must have had the key about him, and had seized his chance to turn it and summon Joe and another man into the room from the hall, where they had evidently been waiting. They were both armed with stout cudgels. Elinor's cry to Sir Edmund to take care was just too late. Her acquaintance of the caped frieze coat had come up behind him, and Sir Edmund, taken completely by surprise, was felled to the ground, where he collapsed unconscious.

19

He came back to his senses, head aching vilely, to hear a soft but distraught voice close to his ear, saying repeatedly, "Wake up, Edmund, oh, do, do wake up!" A hand was stroking his face, apparently in an attempt to rouse him, for the voice continued, rather desperately, "Oh, *dearest* Edmund, you *must* be all right, or I can't bear it!"

Pleasant listening, he thought hazily, placing the source of these remarks. But when, in Miss Radley's agitation, the stroking changed to a rhythmical slapping, Sir Edmund decided it would be best to apprise her that she had succeeded in her purpose of bringing him round. Struggling unsuccessfully to sit up, he got his eyes open and said, with an effort, "I shall do! Only a crack on the head. Damn the fellow – I never even saw him coming!"

Gingerly, he felt his head, winced, and closed his eyes again, at which Elinor uttered a soft cry, and he re-opened them to find her face solicitously close to his. "Rather more important," he added, in a stronger voice, "what was that you were saying?"

Miss Radley was instantly covered with confusion. "Oh, please – it doesn't signify! I didn't mean – that is, I didn't know you had come round. At all events," she finished, none too coherently, "it's of no consequence!"

Pulling his scattered thoughts together with commendable rapidity, and finding that the throbbing in his temples was mercifully receding, Sir Edmund at last managed to haul himself into a sitting position, saying, "There you are very much mistaken!" He gathered both her hands in his and looked hard into her grey eyes, which were still bright with unshed tears; this, though a gratifying circumstance, was not a state of affairs he wished to see prolonged. "It is of the greatest consequence! At least, it is to *me*! I love you, you see," he added, very careful, this time, to make himself clear beyond possibility of misapprehension. "And I thought, when you spoke to me so feelingly about the enduring strength of a *lasting passion*, it was Royden you meant – not that I then knew his identity – and I stood no chance."

"Oh, no, no, no!" she cried. "How could you think so? But I couldn't *tell* you it was you for whom I had formed a lasting passion!"

"I wish you had!"

"And how could I suppose that *you* entertained any such sentiments for me? I mean, you have been positively avoiding me, and you went away from London, and oh, I have missed you so much!" said Miss Radley foolishly, shedding tears of pure happiness.

"I went away because I thought that if I couldn't have you, it would be better not to come near you at all," said Sir Edmund, taking her into his arms. "Only the thing was too strong for me, damn it, so back I came – and just at the right moment, one might say, except that I do *not* appear to have acquitted myself very creditably in the business! Where are we, by the by?"

"Oh, along the corridor from the hall, in a little room which they used as a store chamber when I was governess here," Elinor told him. "The men Grenville has with him – it was one of them who hit you, you know – well, they put us both in here and locked the door, and I rather fancy, from what I heard them and Grenville say, he has driven off to London. I suppose he either has fresh horses here, or will get them in the village, and I only hope," she said, quite vindictively, "that he may drive them into the village pond, which would not be at all surprising, for he is decidedly drunk, and seems to have some mad notion that if you and I are kept out of the way he may still wheedle himself somehow into Persephone's good graces and run off with

252

her, under pretence of standing friend to her and Robert Walter. But that he will *not* do! I fancy we may rely upon Charlotte to put a stop to any such thing – Charlotte has behaved very well indeed, poor girl."

"No need to rely on Charlotte," said Sir Edmund. "By the time I left Upper Brook Street, she had the support not only of Conington, but of young Mr Walter himself. Not to speak of Franz, Josef and Johann!"

"You mean Robert Walter is back already? Oh, I am so glad!"

"Back, and extremely eager for serious conversation with me! But once I had discovered what must have happened to *you*, I had no time or inclination to stop and listen to him!"

"Then his errand in Germany must have prospered!" exclaimed Elinor. "And so I suppose he feels he can approach you, as Persephone's guardian. For he is very correct and punctilious in such matters, you know. Oh, Edmund, *do* you think – supposing his family should be at least respectable, and after all, we know that *he* is a person of education – do you think such a marriage might after all be possible?" she ventured to suggest.

"Just at the moment," said Sir Edmund, re-possessing himself of her hands, "I am not half as much interested in Persephone's marriage as my own! Elinor, I can't aspire to the interminable eloquence of your suitor Mr Spalding, but now that we have cleared up our misunderstanding, and we find we are *not* indifferent to one another, *will* you marry me?"

"Need you ask?" was all she could say before being enveloped in a crushing and very satisfactory embrace, and kissed so hard that for some moments she would have been unable to utter another word anyway, even had she wished to.

"Delightful as all this is," said Sir Edmund presently, "I can't but think we might be more comfortable elsewhere. Put it down to decrepitude and advanced old age if you will, but I fancy that if I'm obliged to spend the night here, only for the sake of Royden's disordered fancies, I shall awake with rheumatics as well as a sore head! I believe we should put our minds to the question of making our way out of this room. It strikes me as a damnably chilly, uncomfortable sort of place."

This was true: the room was small and bare, and in spite of the warmth of the summer evening, the flags of the stone floor seemed dank. But an inspection showed nothing that seemed to offer a likely way of escape; the door was locked, of course, and the one window too small and high up to allow egress.

"Do you know how many people Royden has here?" asked Sir Edmund.

"Yes, fortunately I do!" said Elinor. "Because while he was having us put in here, he was – well, *gloating*, in the most stupidly melodramatic way! And he made quite a point of telling me that there were only those two men, and the housekeeper, who is deaf as a post – indeed, she was very hard of hearing even when I knew her eight years ago – so that I could not expect anyone to come to our aid, however hard I shouted."

"Two of them – hm," said Sir Edmund thoughtfully. "And he has left them both here, while he goes haring off to London?" She nodded. "Well, if I could take at least one by surprise . . . do you think, my love, you could make a pretence of strong hysterics?"

"I hardly need to *pretend*!" she said ruefully. "If I had only kept my head better, they would never had had a chance to knock you down! And you are quite right, we *should* get out of here, because I am persuaded you ought to see a doctor."

"Now, that's well thought of – not that I share your opinion, but let us try for a fit of hysterics, in the course of which you make it clear that you are seriously alarmed for my health. Can you manage that?"

"Easily," said Elinor, shuddering at the memory of those dreadful few minutes when she had thought he might be more than momentarily stunned.

"Then let's see what we can do."

It proved simpler than might have been expected. Elinor hammered loudly upon the door, screaming at the top of her voice, "Is there anyone there? You must come *at once*! Oh, is there *nobody* there?" In a little while these tactics brought heavy footsteps treading along the passage, and Joe's hoarse voice adjured her to shut her row. Ignoring Joe, she continued, in frantic tones, "Is Mr Royden there? I must see Mr Royden!"

"Can't," said Joe succinctly. "He's gone to Lunnon, haven't he?"

"Then *you* must fetch a doctor! At once!" she said urgently. "For it was you who hit poor Sir Edmund, wasn't it? And I can tell you, you will very likely hang for it! Oh, I am so afraid! He is dreadfully pale, and – and his breathing has changed most alarmingly!"

Giving her an encouraging smile, Sir Edmund lent colour to this statement by drawing several extremely noisy breaths, intermingled with rattles and snores. The man on the other side of the door was presumably impressed by these stage effects, for he hesitated, apparently in a quandary, and eventually, when urged once again by Elinor to think that Sir Edmund's death would be laid at his door, summoned his companion. "Here, Bob – come and hark at this, will 'ee?"

More footsteps in the passage heralded the arrival of Bob, whom Sir Edmund obliged with an increase in the volume of his noisy breathing, while Elinor, summoning up histrionic powers which she had never suspected in herself, declared plaintively, "*There*! Am I to be left alone in a room with a dying man? I dare say you will *both* hang, for you may be very sure Mr Royden will not put himself out to shield you, so if I were you, I would summon a doctor *instantly*!"

A whispered conference ensued between Bob and Joe, at the end of which Joe said, guardedly, "Reckon we'd best take a look first, miss. Now, don't you try nothing on!"

255

"Don't be absurd; how could I?" snapped Elinor, as one at the end of her tether. "Yes, *do* take a look, and *then* tell me if he does not stand in need of medical attention."

In the event, as Sir Edmund, perhaps influenced by the prospering of his love, had made a remarkably good recovery from the blow which knocked him unconscious, it was his assailant who soon stood in more need of a physician. Joe fell an easy victim to Sir Edmund's swift lunge the moment the door was opened, and while he fell stunned to the floor, Elinor seized her chance to put out a foot to trip up the other man, Bob, whom she sent flying.

"Good girl!" said Sir Edmund approvingly, as he picked up Bob's cudgel and dealt its owner an efficient blow. He surveyed his handiwork, rather pleased with himself. "You might not think it, but I'm a peaceable sort of fellow in general," he remarked. He then turned briskly to the task of tying up the pair with their own belts, and a couple of ropes that Elinor fetched from the drawing room, where they had been holding back the curtains. By the time he had finished the two men were beginning to stir and to utter imprecations, but he took no notice of these, stopping only after he and Elinor had left the little room and locked the door, to toss the key out of the nearest unshuttered window. It fell almost soundlessly among unseen foliage.

"The shrubbery, I think," said Elinor. "Which must be excessively wild and tangled by now."

"Good," said Sir Edmund. "Not that I suppose Mr Royden will have their welfare very much at heart, but anyone else looking for them will probably have to summon aid to break down that door! Now – did you say there was a housekeeper in the place?"

"Yes, but she is very deaf. I don't think she will hear us if we tread cautiously going past the kitchen, and I fancy that will be the best way to go, because the back door is less likely to be locked."

Elinor led the way along the corridors to the servants' quarters. Her memories of the house were accurate; after all, she had spent long enough in going wretchedly over and over in her mind those few months of her brief career as governess here. As they passed the kitchen, whose door stood ajar, they glanced in; sure enough, it was deserted except for the old lady who sat dozing in the chimney corner, cap awry, and quite undisturbed by the shouts now beginning to sound faintly behind them.

In a moment they had carefully pulled back the bolts of the door that led out to the stable yard. They stood here for a moment taking deep breaths of the evening air, pleasantly scented as it blew from the tangled wild flowers that had invaded the now twilit gardens.

"Very well: now for my phaeton," said Sir Edmund briskly. "And if I can obtain fresh horses in this village, we'll go back to London – though I'm half tempted to bear you straight off to Waterleys, which is not so very far! However, you'll see it soon enough, and to do Persephone justice, she is concerned for you, and we ought to set her mind at rest."

At this point, however, they met with a check. Rounding the corner of the out-buildings to find the spot where he had left his horses tied up, Sir Edmund stopped and exclaimed in annoyance.

"Damn the fellow – he must have taken my phaeton to help him on his own mad way!"

"I dare say it looked more convenient than his own wretched post-chaise – and more comfortable too, as well it might!" said Elinor feelingly. "Well – we could take the chaise, perhaps?"

"I doubt if he has any fresh cattle in the stables, or why risk taking mine, which he must have guessed would not be rested? Yes, that's one consolation: I pressed them hard to get here, and he'll have to change them very soon. I imagine the horses that brought you here on the last stage have been dispatched back to their own posting-house by now. No, I think we had better walk to the village and look for some means of transport there – unless you prefer to stay here while I go?"

"Certainly not," said Elinor, "I am coming with you."

"I own," said Sir Edmund, taking her arm as they set out across the carriage sweep, "that I would as soon not let you out of my sight again. I've suffered quite enough anxiety on your behalf for one day."

"Well, and so have I on yours – oh, Edmund! Do you hear that?" She stopped suddenly, holding up a hand.

"Good God," said Sir Edmund, a moment later, his mind ranging back over the vicissitudes of the day. "Are we to suppose that the Ancient Britons too are in hot pursuit of you?"

"Well, I think it *is* the Hunting Chorus!" said Elinor. "Out of *Boadicea*, you know! Though what on earth . . . ?"

Her voice died away as a remarkable little procession came into sight around the bend of the drive. It was led by Lord Conington in his curricle, with one of the Lark Quartet – Josef, as it turned out – in the seat beside him. The main party was in the Yoxfords' britzka, a handsome, spacious vehicle, but less cumbersome than the family travelling carriage. On this fine evening the calash and hood were not in use, and it stood open to the air. It was being driven by Mr Robert Walter, with Persephone seated on the box next to him, both of them tunefully singing the Hunting Chorus, with hearty emphasis on the repeated melodious cries of, "*Juchheisa, juchhei!*" Two of their passengers were Franz and Johann. The former was providing his own version of the accompaniment to the chorus on a small horn, while the latter, facing backwards in his seat but still joining in the singing now and then, maintained a firm hold upon the bedraggled figure of Mr Grenville Royden, who was to be seen uncomfortably crouched in the dickey up behind, dripping water all over it.

20

"*Juchhei!*" observed Mr Walter, with a last flourish of his fine baritone, as the little cavalcade rounded the carriage sweep and drew up in front of the Manor.

"Ah, Sir Edmund! So you too concluded that this was where he planned to bring Miss Grafton," said Lord Conington, alighting from his carriage. "And we were all correct. Miss Radley, I do trust you've come to no harm?"

"Elinor!" cried Persephone, scrambling down headlong from the box of the britzka and running to her friend. "Oh, how glad I am to see you! And I am so sorry, for it was all— well, *nearly* all my fault, and Robert was quite angry with me, but as you can see, we have come to rescue you."

"Thank you, Persephone, but we contrived to rescue ourselves," Sir Edmund pointed out.

"Yes, I suppose you did." Persephone's face fell. "What a pity!"

"Why?" he inquired.

"Because it did seem to me that you and Elinor . . . well, never mind that, but I thought Robert would be the means of saving Elinor, and earn your undying gratitude, and then you would place no more obstacles in our way," she said, disappointed. "Oh, well, I suppose it can't be helped now! I must say, I had imagined there would be *dozens* of desperadoes here, who would quite overpower poor Elinor. However," she added generously, "I am glad for her sake there were not dozens."

"Only two," said Elinor gravely, "and Sir Edmund dealt with those most competently."

"But I rather think that Robert, or somebody, *has* earned

259

my undying gratitude," remarked Sir Edmund, scrutinizing the damp and shivering figure of Mr Royden in the dickey. On closer inspection, his person appeared to be not merely drenched through, but plentifully covered with duckweed and slime, and his face bore the marks of rather more rough treatment than Sir Edmund's one blow could possibly have inflicted. "Er – what precisely did you do with him, Mr Walter?"

"Oh, it was splendid!" said Persephone enthusiastically, answering for her suitor. "You see, we met him at the inn, where he was trying to obtain a change of horses. We had stopped there to ask the way, because none of us had been to this house before, not even Lord Conington. Well, Mr Royden was excessively surprised to see us, and tried to run into the inn and hide in the landlord's snug, but Robert was *much* too quick for him, and he and Franz and Johann and Josef all took him outside, and I am not perfectly sure just what they did next, but in the end they threw him into the duckpond, and it made the most tremendous splash!" finished Persephone, with glee.

The treatment he had received certainly appeared to have sobered Mr Royden up; the bravado had all gone out of him, along with any grandiose notions of seductions and forced marriages. As soon as Johann let go of him, he clambered down from the dickey in a decidedly undignified manner, scuttling off towards the yard and the back door through which Sir Edmund and Elinor had recently come, and trailing slime and pond-water.

"Robert, you are not going to let him get away?" cried Persephone.

"I don't quite see what else we can do, Miss Grafton," remarked Conington, who had been seeing to the secure hitching of the horses. "Since it appears that Miss Radley is not after all harmed, he has done nothing, perhaps, to merit more punishment than he has already suffered. And there is Charlotte to be considered, you know – *she* has not deserved to have any scandal attach to her name."

"No, very true. Charlotte has behaved most admirably," said Elinor warmly, smiling upon him.

"I suppose you are right," said Mr Walter regretfully, watching his rival disappear damply round the corner of the house. "I wish, *now*, that I had – what is it you English say? – had planted him a few more *facers* before we threw him into the duckpond, but no matter! An excellent pond!" he remembered with satisfaction. "So very muddy, so extremely full of weeds!"

"Yes, I can see it was," said Sir Edmund, appreciatively. "By the way, has anyone set eyes on my phaeton?"

"Yes, indeed. It is at the Green Dragon inn, where I have ordered a private parlour, anticipating that we should soon be returning there and might well need refreshment," Conington assured him.

"It was when we saw Mr Royden driving up in it, and I knew it for yours, that we supposed you and Elinor must want rescuing," added Persephone, evidently still unwilling to relinquish her vision of heroics on the part of Mr Walter, for there was a hint of grievance in her tone.

"In that case," said Sir Edmund, "I suggest that we adjourn to the inn, all of us – *all*? Good God, whom *else* have we here?" he inquired, his eyes for the first time falling on the passenger sitting in the far corner of the britzka.

"Yes, that is a puzzle to me, too," Persephone confided. "*I* never met him before. He *would* come with us, and I can't for the life of me tell why."

"It's Mr Spalding!" exclaimed Miss Radley, following the direction of Sir Edmund's gaze.

"Yes, Elinor, it is indeed I!" announced the clergyman. His intention was obviously to expatiate upon this theme, but Persephone ruthlessly interrupted him.

"And he has been prosing on all the way, about coming to save you from yourself, Elinor, and so forth – such stuff! I never heard *anyone* talk so!"

"I believe you!" said Sir Edmund.

But Mr Spalding himself was no longer to be deterred.

261

Rising to his feet in the britzka – a move which caused one of the horses to shift and snort nervously, so that the clergyman's stance became somewhat precarious and he was obliged to hold on to the back of the seat – he began to address the company in general and Miss Radley in particular.

"I should like," said he, "to understand the full meaning of this! I have never in my life known anything to equal it. I have been jolted about in what may only be described as a reckless and headlong manner of proceeding along the public highway. No regard has been paid to my sensibilities -"

"Well, no one asked you to come," Persephone pointed out, but to no avail; he swept on, taking no notice of her interruption.

"I have been thrown into the company of persons speaking a foreign tongue, of persons singing in a riotous fashion, and persons playing on musical instruments whilst driving along the road, something which I should not be astonished to find was against the law of the land! In all, Elinor, I have passed what I can only describe as a very uncomfortable couple of hours, and I believe I am owed an explanation! I had not thought you so lost to all sense of propriety – so much a stranger to right conduct – in short, so deluded as once again to go astray in the company of – well, to name names, of Mr Royden! Not that I condone what *these* persons have done, either. No, I do not condone it. Neither do I understand it at all."

Sotto voce, Persephone supplied her commentary. "And it is of no use whatever trying to explain it to him, because he will not listen."

"I had come to London – at, I may say, considerable personal inconvenience," proceeded the clergyman, "with the express intention of preventing you from adopting such a course of action, but I see I came in vain. I must say directly that, as a man of the cloth, I feel it incumbent upon me, indeed part of my duty to my flock, to think seriously whether I should not reconsider my intention of marrying. I

262

am not sure, after all, that your frivolity may not be so ingrained as to make you unfitted to be the wife of a clergyman, and – "

"That will do, Mr Spalding," said Sir Edmund, losing patience, and feeling himself now justified in expressing indignation on Elinor's behalf, as she drew closer to him in the face of this verbal onslaught. "She isn't going to be the wife of a clergyman, she is going to be the wife of a diplomat now seconded to the Foreign Office in London, and if you continue in your present vein I shall very likely begin to resent it, so kindly guard your tongue!"

"Guard my tongue? Wife of a diplomat?" exclaimed the bewildered Mr Spalding, sitting down rather suddenly as the restive horse shifted once more.

Persephone, however, taking in the fact that her guardian had his arm very firmly and comfortingly round Miss Radley's waist, cried out, "Oh, famous! I was right! Oh, Elinor, how glad I am! You see, when Cousin Edmund was so very agitated to find you had been carried off, I *thought* it might be so. And I *was* right! This is above all things great – isn't it, Robert?"

"Sir Edmund, Miss Radley, I wish you very happy," said the punctilious Mr Walter, bowing correctly. "Allow me to congratulate you."

"By all means!" said Sir Edmund. "Anyone may congratulate us who likes, but *do* let us first leave this derelict spot to its deplorable owner, and locate the superior comforts of the Green Dragon."

Apart from the welcome appearance of Sir Edmund himself at Royden Manor, the Green Dragon was the most pleasing sight to meet Elinor's eyes that evening. It was a cheerful hostelry of fair size, which also handled all the local posting business, and kept quite a large stable for that purpose. On being informed by Sir Edmund, however, of the number of fresh horses that would be required later, the landlord shook his head a little doubtfully. Two teams were already bespoken, and he hadn't expected all this coming and going on a day which was nothing out of the ordinary! No one, Sir Edmund sympathetically agreed, *could* have expected it, and having ascertained that there would at least be a fresh pair for his phaeton and another for Conington's curricle, he ordered wine and supper, and joined the rest of the party in the private parlour set at their disposal, where a small fire was burning to keep off the night-time chill as darkness fell.

The events of the evening already had the staff of the Green Dragon in quite a buzz. Rumour had it that Squire had tried to run off with Miss, though which Miss none could rightly say. Squire had certainly turned up driving a phaeton which was none of his, and was subsequently ducked in the pond by the foreign gentlemen, which in the usual way a person wouldn't hold with, but if Rumour was true, then Squire richly deserved it!

Grenville Royden, whose neglect of his inheritance had thrown a number of people out of work, was not a popular figure locally. But Lord Conington, while not previously known to the landlord and his wife, had introduced himself as Miss Charlotte's future husband, and Miss Charlotte had always been a prime favourite in the village. Her betrothed was instantly recognized as Quality of the Right Sort, the more so as he had bestowed some pretty generous vails earlier in the evening, while providently ordering the private parlour to which the party (now numbering two more) had returned, and also vouching for his foreign friends while they cast Squire into the pond. And certain it was, said the landlord, that my lord had known the phaeton that wasn't Squire's directly. The gentleman as it *did* belong to, the landlord now asserted, glancing at the coin Sir Edmund had slipped into his hand, was another of the Right Sort too! As for the clergyman, what *he* was doing in the party none could tell, unless so be as he had a special licence to marry somebody to somebody else. Though it was a puzzle to know who, Miss Charlotte herself not being present.

Few of the visitors could have offered much enlightenment as to Mr Spalding's business in their company, either. He himself, deprived for once of speech by the rapid course of events, and having in any case met his vocal match in Persephone, had subsided into a comfortable chair in one corner of the pleasant, oak-beamed parlour, and was merely muttering, under his breath, "Dear me! First Mr Royden, now Sir Edmund! I do not know – I really do not know!"

No one but Elinor heard this, and when Sir Edmund, his colloquy with the landlord concluded, entered the room and closed the door behind him (to the disappointment of such of the inn servants as had hoped to learn more about this sudden influx of gentry), the clergyman fell entirely silent.

Not so Mr Walter, who took Sir Edmund's arrival as the signal to rise to his feet. Standing very straight, he announced, "Sir Edmund! I wish to speak with you!"

"Do," said Sir Edmund, amiably. "I thought you *had* been speaking with me for the past thirty minutes or so, but pray continue. Ah, they've brought the claret. Have some, Mr Walter. Are you and the Larks provided for, Conington? Excellent! Elinor, you must drink some too; it will do you good."

"I mean," stated Mr Walter, cutting across all this, "that I have something very particular to say to you." Persephone nodded vigorous assent. "At my father's behest, sir, I have been to Germany, where I was offered and have formally accepted the post of Kapellmeister to the court of His Highness Prince Ernst Ludwig of Heldenburg. The post carries with it a salary which, I believe, may well be considered munificent, for the Prince is a considerable patron of the art of music. I have also been to my home at Adelstein – "

"Adelstein?" said Sir Edmund, his attention suddenly caught. He looked keenly at Robert Walter for a moment, and then leaned back in his chair, sipping his claret. "Go on."

"I went to my home to tell my father and mother of my

intention of marrying, and I now, Sir Edmund, beg to ask *your* leave to pay my addresses, in due form, to your ward, Miss Persephone Grafton." With which he glared rather defiantly at Sir Edmund.

"Very nicely put!" said that gentleman, affably. "Yes. Do have some of this claret; it really is quite tolerable."

"But what do you *say*?" cried Persephone, in tones of anguished impatience.

"Yes. Didn't you hear me?"

Miss Grafton was looking almost aghast at the simplicity of it. "You mean you will *allow* us to marry?"

"Yes," said Sir Edmund patiently, for the third time. "I have for some while been of the opinion that Mr Walter is an admirable and sensible young man, just the person for you, Persephone. Besides, as you rightly surmised he might, he has earned my — what was it? — undying gratitude by throwing Royden into that duckpond for me. Also, and perhaps most important of all, Elinor approves of him as your husband. I suspect," he finished cheerfully, "you may be very happy together."

"*Oh!*" cried Persephone, and flung her arms first around Mr Walter, then Sir Edmund, and finally Elinor, exclaiming through tears of joy, "Oh, thank you, Elinor, thank you! I owe it all to you! My life will not be blighted after all, and I shall not be cut off without a penny!"

"It does not matter if you *are* cut off, Seffi," said Mr Walter, with the air of one who has explained a point many times before, "since I was determined not to offer for you until I knew *I* could respectably support you, without assistance from your own family or mine."

"You know, I couldn't cut her off without a penny even if I wished to; the money is left in trust, but it is her own," Sir Edmund put in mildly, but the lovers were paying him no attention.

"It is my father, dearest Seffi, who is still to be won over," Robert Walter was continuing earnestly. "But when we approach him together, *you*, I know, will be able to do it."

266

Persephone did look a little daunted at this prospect, but nodded hopefully. "He is not, perhaps, so formidable a man as he may seem, my father," Mr Walter went on. "You do not know him Seffi, but – "

"But I rather think *I* do," remarked Sir Edmund.

"What?" said Mr Walter, gazing blankly at him.

"I said: I believe I know your father," repeated Sir Edmund, studying the wine in his glass. "As soon as you mentioned *Adelstein*, I knew who it was of whom you had reminded me now and then, ever since I first met you. Though I didn't know old Sigismund had a son who had taken up music as a profession. Yes, I fancy your father is a very old acquaintance and – er – occasional adversary of mine at the conference table. Would I be right in supposing him to be Count Sigismund Heinrich Walter von und zu Adelstein?"

For once, Mr Walter was taken aback. "Yes, sir," he said, quite meekly, "you would!"

"Why in the world," inquired Sir Edmund with interest, "aren't you using your full name? Nothing to be ashamed of, you know!"

"I wish, sir, to belong to the aristocracy of the Muses, and no other!" said Mr Walter, a little stiffly. "The estate, besides, will go to my elder brother, and – "

"Yes, yes, all very well, but – ah, good, here comes supper!" said Sir Edmund, interrupting himself as two rosy maidservants entered bearing laden platters. "Just the thing! Elinor, my love, you must be famished. Persephone, stop staring so, and have some of this cold fowl, which looks excellent. Now where was I?" as the door closed again after the maids. "Yes – did it never occur to you, Robert, that you might have saved yourself and Persephone a good deal of trouble merely by letting me know that you were your father's son?"

"But you said," pointed out Persephone, "that Robert's father was an *adversary* of yours."

This appeared to amuse Sir Edmund, who said, "My dear

Persephone! In the friendliest and most mutually appreciative of manners! You know, I really do not believe there is any need for you to anticipate a further career in the role of star-crossed lover! By the by, and just as a matter of interest, have you told your father the extent of Persephone's fortune, Robert?"

"I should scorn to do so!" said Mr Walter, stiffening up again. "Besides – "

"Besides, you too rather fancied yourself in the star-crossed line," said Sir Edmund, sighing. "Just like your own Sempronius and – what was the girl's name?"

"Angelina. Anyway, he *couldn't* tell anyone the extent of my fortune," pointed out Persephone. "He doesn't know it. *I* don't know it myself."

"No, I suppose you don't. I foresee," said Sir Edmund, with considerable enjoyment, "an interesting time haggling over marriage settlements with my friend Sigismund. It will certainly make a change!" He caught Elinor's eye, and said with a chuckle, "Wait until you meet the gentleman we are discussing, my dear one. You will then see where Robert here gets his remarkable determination. Prince Ernst Ludwig has a very formidable and wily minister in old Adelstein. But never fear, he will take to Persephone – and he will certainly take to *you* when you become acquainted."

"*Is* Elinor going to become acquainted with Robert's papa?" inquired Persephone, bewildered.

"I don't see why not," said her guardian. "Very pretty place, Heldenburg: you'll like it, Elinor. Castles and torrents and cascades and so forth, just in the true romantic line! How would you like to go there on the second part of our wedding journey?"

"Very much," said Elinor demurely, aware that she would happily have agreed to visit the North Pole on her wedding journey had that been Sir Edmund's suggestion.

"Why not the *first* part of your wedding journey?" demanded Persephone.

"Because I want Elinor to myself for a while, before we

become any further embroiled in your affairs, Persephone. Italy first, I thought – you've never been to Italy, have you, Elinor? You'll like that, too."

"But in any case, you will get married *soon*, won't you?" Persephone urged her guardian.

"As soon as it can possibly be contrived," said he, obligingly.

At this point Mr Spalding, who had been sitting in his corner, two of the Lark Quartet very kindly plying him with claret and cold chicken (which he was relishing despite his inability to keep up with the general course of events), found his tongue again.

"Strange!" he remarked. "Very strange. I fear, Elinor, it argues a remarkable lack of steadiness in you."

"What does?" said Sir Edmund, his good humour evaporating with alarming rapidity.

"It appears that she is betrothed to you! Miss Radley, I mean. But," said Mr Spalding, shaking his head, "quite apart from running away with Mr Royden, not once but twice, she was betrothed to *me*!" He sounded quite plaintive.

"No, I was not!" said Elinor roundly, a good deal put out.

"No, she certainly was not," Sir Edmund agreed. "My dear sir, weeks ago, in Cheltenham, I myself heard her refuse you in the most categorical manner."

"One was not to suppose," complained Mr Spalding, "that that was final! One does not, I may say, expect such conduct in the wife of – "

But seeing that Sir Edmund was obviously preparing to say something very crushing indeed, Miss Radley hastily intervened. "I dare say one doesn't! Pray, Edmund, leave this to me, because it is perfectly clear that he will take no notice of anything one says, so *you* at least may as well save your breath. Samuel, you must see by now that you are very well out of any imaginary contract you may have supposed to exist between us – and purely imaginary it *was*, I do assure you! Well! You have indicated yourself that you are better off out of it, and *I* think you should go home to Cheltenham and – and marry Miss Dunn!"

"Hm," said Mr Spalding.

"Who *is* Miss Dunn?" inquired Sir Edmund, amused.

"She will make you," Elinor pursued, "the most admirable wife."

"Hm," repeated Mr Spalding, and then, after a moment's consideration, said, "There may be something in what you say. Yes, there may indeed be something in it. I believe I will think the matter over. I will sleep on it – yes, that is what I shall do, and in the morning we shall see what counsels prevail. Good night, Elinor. Good night, Sir Edmund." And he withdrew, contenting himself with a stiff bow to the rest of the company.

"Can he sleep on it – here, I mean?" asked Conington. "Has anyone asked if they have a room for him?"

"Yes, I have, and they do," Sir Edmund disclosed. "There will be rooms, as well, for Franz and Josef and Johann, and Robert too if he wishes. The landlord can't provide fresh horses for the britzka till morning – however, *you* will have a pair tonight, Conington, for you must be wishing to return to Charlotte, and I'll be obliged if you will take Persephone with you. Whether you all squeeze up for Robert to make a third in the curricle I must leave it to the three of you to settle! I am taking Elinor back to London now, and no one is going to make a third with *us*!" he said firmly.

Out in the stable yard, as the phaeton, with a pair of fresh horses between its shafts, moved gently away, he said again, "Do tell me more about Miss Dunn. I believe I've heard you extol her merits to Spalding before."

"Well, she *is* a very worthy lady," said Elinor.

"Plain?" he surmised.

"Rather plain, I own, but *that* she cannot help! And she *would* make Samuel Spalding a very good wife – and she would be so glad to marry him!"

"Setting up as matchmaker along with Bella, are you?" said Bella's brother, smiling.

"No," replied Elinor, smiling back at him, "but I am so happy that I suppose I should like everyone else to be getting married and just as happy about it too!" At which he naturally felt obliged to rein in his horses and kiss her once again.

"It must," he observed, "be something in the air."

"Good God – it *is* something in the air!" she exclaimed a moment later, emerging from his embrace. "They are at it again! Listen, Edmund!"

He listened, and found that she was right. The window of the parlour in the Green Dragon stood open, and someone had evidently produced a couple of the musical instruments which the Lark Quartet seemed to carry constantly about their persons. He thought he heard a flute, and the horn again. To the accompanying strains of these instruments, the stirring finale of *Boadicea Queen of Britain*, in all its absurd splendour, came floating out to them through the peaceful dark of the Essex countryside.

"All hail to the Patron of marriage and mirth!
Was ever such merriment known upon earth?"

"The answer to that is no!" said Sir Edmund. "No, decidedly not!" And he let the horses move on.